# MINE

## J.L. BUTLER

HarperCollins*Publishers*

HarperCollins*Publishers* Ltd
1 London Bridge Street,
London SE1 9GF

www.harpercollins.co.uk

First published by HarperCollins*Publishers* 2018

This paperback edition published 2019

2

A catalogue record for this book is available from the British Library

ISBN: 978-0-00-826243-3

Set in Sabon Lt Std by Palimpsest Book Production Limited,
Falkirk, Stirlingshire

Printed and bound in the UK by CPI Group (UK) Ltd, Croydon CR0 4YY

MIX
Paper from
responsible sources
FSC™ C007454

This book is produced from independently certified FSC™ paper
to ensure responsible forest management.

For more information visit: www.harpercollins.co.uk/green

To JP

He wants his wife to disappear. So do you . . .

# Prologue

I don't remember much about the night I was meant to die. It's funny how the mind can block out the memories it no longer wants to store, you must know that. But if I close my eyes, I can still hear the sounds of that night in May. The howl of an unseasonably cold wind, the rattle of the bedroom window, the rasp of the sea against shingle in the distance.

It was also raining. I remember that much, because the thin scratch of water against glass is still vivid in my head. For a minute it was hypnotic. For a minute it disguised the sound of his footsteps outside: tap, tap, tap, soles against flagstone in slow determined steps.

I knew he was coming and I knew what I had to do.

Lying under the duvet on the iron bed, I willed myself to keep calm. A faint glow from the string of bulbs on the coastal path leaked into the room. Usually this spectral darkness soothed me, but tonight it made me feel more alone, as if I were floating in space without a tether.

I balled my fist, hoping, praying that the comforting twilight of the new day would present itself at the window. But even without looking at the clock, I knew that this was at least four or five hours away and I didn't need to tell myself that it would be too late. The footsteps were right outside the house now, and the faint metallic grumble of a key being pushed into the lock echoed up the stairs. It was hard to disguise sounds in the big, old building, it was too tired and weary for that . . .

How had I let myself get into this? I had gone to London for a better life, to improve myself and meet a more interesting set of people. To fall in love. And now here I was: a cautionary tale.

I heard the front door creak open. Chilled air seeped through the cracks in the window pane and pinched my nostrils shut. It was as cold as a mortuary; a macabrely apt simile. I was even lying like a mummy, arms by my sides, trembling fingers tucked under my thighs, as heavy and immobile as if they were dead weights, anchoring me to the bed.

As the footsteps reached the top of the stairs, I pulled my hands out from the warmth and settled them on top of the cool cotton duvet cover. My fingers were clenched, nails pressing against my palms, but at least I was ready to fight. I suppose that was the lawyer in me.

He hesitated outside the bedroom door, and the moment seemed to compress into a cold, suspended silence. Coming here had not been a good idea. Closing my eyes, I willed the single tear not to weep on to my cheek.

A soft push of wood against carpet as the door opened. Every instinct in my body told me to leap out of the bed and run, but I had to wait and see if he would, if he could, do this. My heart was hammering out of my chest, my limbs felt frozen with fear. I kept my eyes shut, but I could feel him looming over me now, my body retreating into a menacing shadow. I could even hear his breathing.

A hand pressed against my mouth, its touch cold and alien against my dry, puckered lips. My eyes opened, and I could see a face only inches from mine. I was desperate to read his expression, desperate to know what he was thinking. I forced my lips apart, ready to scream, and then I waited for things to run their course.

# *Chapter 1*

**Three months earlier**

I had only been back in chambers five minutes when I felt a presence at the door of my office.

'Come on, put your coat back on. We're going out,' said a voice I recognized without even having to look up.

I carried on writing, concentrating on the sound of my fountain pen scratching across the paper, an old-world sound in the digital age, and hoped that he would go away.

'Chop-chop,' he said, demanding my attention.

I glanced at our senior clerk and gave him a grudging smile.

'Paul, I've just got back from court. I have work to do, orders to type up . . .' I said, taking some papers out of my pilot case. I noticed it had a rip in the leather and made a mental note to get it repaired.

'Pen and Wig for lunch,' he said, picking my black coat off the rack by the door and holding it out so I could slip my arms inside.

I hesitated for a moment, then resigned myself to the inevitable. Paul Jones was a force of nature and insubordination was not an option.

'What's the occasion?' I asked, looking at him as if a lunchtime excursion was the most extraordinary suggestion. Most of the time, it was. I don't think I'd had anything other than a sandwich at my desk for the past six months.

'A new partner's started at Mischon's. I thought it was time you met.'

'Anyone I know?'

'She's just moved down from Manchester. You'll get on.'

'Wooing clients with the Northern card,' I smiled, flattening out my regional accent for comic effect.

I grabbed my handbag and we walked out of my office, down the long sweep of stairs into the bowels of chambers. It was like a ghost town, although at this time of the day – a little after one o'clock – that was not unusual. The clerks were on their lunch breaks, phones went quiet and the barristers were still at court or making their way back.

Stepping out on to the street, the crisp, February wind slapped against my cheeks and made me catch my breath. Or perhaps it was the sight of Middle Temple, which after fifteen years of working here, still had the power to dazzle me. Today it had a particularly bleak beauty. Sandwiched between the river and Fleet Street, Middle Temple, one of London's four Inns of Court, is a warren of cloisters and listed buildings, a sliver of London that has remained locked in time, one of the few places in the city still lit at night by gas light, and it suited dank and grey days like today.

I thrust my hands in my pockets as we walked to the pub. 'Good day?'

This was Paul-speak for *Did you win?*

It was important to Paul to know how well we did in all

our cases. I liked our senior clerk a lot, he was supportive – paternal even, although I didn't pretend for a moment his concern was altruistic. Work for all barristers in chambers came in by referrals and personal recommendations, and Paul, who as senior clerk juggled the entire system, got a percentage commission of all the fees that came through the door.

'You've got something interesting this afternoon, haven't you?' he said.

'Pre-First Directions meeting with solicitor and client. Big-money divorce.'

'How big? Do you know yet?'

'Not Paul McCartney big.' I smiled. 'But big enough.'

Our senior clerk shrugged.

'Shame. We could do with a few more headline-making cases. Still, nice work, Miss Day. A divorce that size is usually a job for silk, but the solicitor requested you specifically.'

'It's Dave Gilbert. I send him excellent Scotch at Christmas and he's good to me all year.'

'Perhaps he knows you're the best-value wig in London. I'd come knocking at your door if the missus ran off with a millionaire scrap-metal merchant,' he winked.

The Pen and Wig, a typical Temple pub that had fed and watered barristers since Victorian times, was located a few minutes' walk away from chambers. I was grateful for the warm blast of air as we were sucked inside the cosy, wood-panelled room.

I frowned in puzzlement as I recognized a group of my colleagues huddled in a raised alcove area, at the far end of the bar. It was unusual to see so many of them in one place, unless they were gathered for clients' drinks at chambers.

'What's this?'

'Happy birthday!' Paul grinned as Charles Napier, our head

of chambers, turned and waved over the tops of the heads of our two petite female pupils.

'So we're not meeting a solicitor?' I asked, feeling stitched-up and self-conscious. Although my very line of work demanded that I stand up in court, I hated being the centre of attention. Besides, I had deliberately kept the fact that I was turning thirty-seven that day under wraps, not least because I wanted to forget about my march towards forty.

'Not this lunchtime,' he grinned, leading me through the pub.

'Bloody hell. Decent turnout,' I whispered, knowing how difficult it was to corral so many of my colleagues in one place.

'Don't let it go to your head. Rumour has it old Charlie-boy has made the short-list for High Court judge. I think he was in the mood for celebrating and promised everyone champagne if they came down.'

'And here I was, thinking he actually wanted to raise a glass to me.'

'What are you drinking, birthday girl?' asked Paul.

'Lime and soda,' I called after him as he headed for the bar, leaving me to make my way over to join Vivienne McKenzie, one of the most senior barristers at Burgess Court.

'Happy birthday, Fran,' said Viv, giving me an affectionate hug.

'I think I've hit the age where I want to pretend this·is just another day,' I said, taking off my coat and hanging it over a chair.

'Nonsense,' said Viv briskly. 'I've got two decades on you and I always relish the idea of new starts and fresh resolutions – a bit like New Year without the cliché and pressure of failing by Epiphany.

'So. You know what day it is tomorrow?' she continued, with a hint of complicity.

'The day after my birthday?'

'The Queen's Counsel List is posted. Which means . . .' she prompted.

'The fulfilment of someone's lifetime dream.' I smiled.

'It means that the application round for next year's silk list begins,' she replied in a theatrical whisper.

I knew what was coming next. Hoping to avoid the conversation, I let my eyes drift across the pub.

'Are you thinking of applying?' she pressed.

'No,' I said, with a finality that I had not been wanting to admit even to myself.

'You're not too young, you know that?'

I glanced up cynically.

'Just what every woman wants to hear on their birthday.'

'It was meant to be a compliment.'

Viv was studying me intently. I had seen this look many times before. Nostrils slightly flared, eyebrows raised a fraction, her grey eyes unblinking. She had the best court face in the business and deployed it to great effect. When she was my pupil master, I used to watch her in court and practise at home in front of the mirror.

'You are one of the top juniors in the industry,' she said with feeling. 'Solicitors adore you. I can think of a dozen judges who would give you an excellent reference. You need to start believing in yourself.'

'I'm just not sure it's the right time to apply.'

'Wine and soda for you,' winked Paul, struggling with two goblets, a bottle of Pinot Grigio and a small can of Schweppes.

'How did you know it was my birthday?' I smiled, taking the glasses out of his hands.

'I make it my business to know everything that goes on in Burgess Court.'

He poured the wine and looked up.

'So. Silk. Are you up for it, Fran?'

'Paul, not now,' I said, trying to make light of the interrogation.

'Why not now? Applications open tomorrow,' he said, glancing at Vivienne.

The broad back in front of me twitched and then turned.

'I think it's time to join this conversation,' said a smooth baritone.

'Hello, Tom,' I said, looking up at my contemporary in chambers. He was several inches taller than me, his rower physique toned on the Thames. 'I thought Eton taught you the art of good manners,' I chided.

'It did, but I'm not above eavesdropping. Not when something sounds so interesting,' he grinned, helping himself to a top-up.

'Well?' said Paul. 'What are Burgess Court's brightest juniors thinking? To apply or not to apply for silk . . .'

'Well, I'm under starters orders. Aren't you, Fran?'

'It's not a competition, Tom.'

'Yes it is,' he replied bluntly. 'First day in pupillage, remember? What was it you said? Despite my "so-called superior education and astonishing self-confidence", you wouldn't just beat me to silk, you'd beat our whole year.'

'I must have said it to annoy you,' I said with mock terseness.

'You were entirely serious.'

I looked at him, silently admitting my own surprise that Tom Briscoe was not yet a QC. His reputation was growing as the go-to barrister for trophy wives in unhappy relationships – and what wife wouldn't want him representing them. Handsome, clever, single Tom Briscoe. He didn't just give women legal advice, he gave them hope.

'I think Charles is about to give a little speech,' said Tom, nodding towards our head of chambers, who was tapping a spoon against his wine glass. 'I'm going in for a ringside seat.'

Paul stepped outside to take a call and I was left alone with Viv.

'You know what Tom's problem is?'

'Too much testosterone coursing through his bloodstream?' I smiled, watching him flirt with one of the pupils.

'You should at least think about it,' said Viv more seriously. 'All that time, the effort, the expense of applying for silk . . . And what for? Two thirds of us will get turned down.'

'You've done your homework.' Viv folded her arms in front of her and sipped her wine thoughtfully.

'You know, Francine, I have a theory about the gender pay gap.'

'What is it?'

'Women simply don't ask.'

I snorted.

'I'm not joking. I've seen it time and time again. Men believe in their own brilliance – warranted or not.'

She paused for a few questioning moments.

'What's really putting you off?'

'People like Tom.'

'Don't let him get to you,' she said, rolling her eyes.

'It's not him. It's the system,' I said quietly, voicing the fear, the paranoia I had felt ever since being called to the Bar. 'You can't deny how snobby it is.'

'Things are changing,' said Viv in those crisp Cheltenham Ladies' College vowels that reminded me she didn't really understand.

'How many state-school-educated QCs are there, Viv? How many women, Northerners, ethnic minorities . . . The very top end of our profession is still full of white, upper-middle Oxbridge men like Tom.'

'I thought you'd see that as a challenge,' she said as a more insistent sound of metal against glass rang around the pub. 'You just need a big case, Fran. A game-changer that will get you noticed.'

'A case that will change my life,' I said softly.

'Something like that,' Viv smiled approvingly, and we both turned to listen to Charles.

# Chapter 2

I only stayed for one drink at the Pen and Wig before drifting back to chambers. I decided to go the long way, through the maze of quiet back allies, so that I could have a cigarette. It wasn't even two o'clock and already the day looked as if it was drawing in, the skeletons of the naked trees imprinted against the pewter sky like cave paintings, the dark clouds pressing down on the rooftops, lending the city a wintry gloom.

I got back to Burgess Court a few minutes past the hour, in time for a meeting that was scheduled for a quarter past. Ours is predominantly a family law set, with a little bit of criminal work thrown into the judicial mix. I like the word 'set' to describe the collection of barristers that room together in chambers. It makes me think of badgers, an image that pretty much sums up this division of the law: wise, industrious men with their long black gowns, white horsehair wigs and Caucasian complexions, although there is a little more diversity in our chambers, which is probably why they let me in – a Northerner with the scar of a nose-piercing and a comprehensive school education.

These days I have two areas of speciality. Matrimonial finance and children-related cases. I thought the latter would be satisfying, crusading work, but the reality is difficult and heart-breaking cases. So now I concentrate on high-net-worth divorces, for the entirely shallow reason that the work is generally less distressing and, regardless of how long proceedings go on, you know that they have the money to pay my fee. I don't go home and think I have changed the world, but I know that I am good at what I do and it pays the mortgage on a maisonette with an N1 postcode.

David Gilbert, the instructing solicitor, was already waiting for me in reception. He was dressed for the cold in a heavy navy woollen coat although his head was bald and shiny like a Burford brown egg.

'I just saw Vivienne,' he said, standing up to kiss my cold cheek. 'Apparently, you've had a chambers trip to the pub for someone's birthday and you didn't even tell me.'

'Would you have come bearing gifts?' I chided.

'I'd have come to the office with champagne at the very least. Happy Birthday, anyway. How are you?'

'Older. Wiser.'

'Mr Joy will be with us in a moment.'

'I've just got to pop upstairs. Do you want to go through?' I said pointing towards the conference room. 'Helen can bring Mr Joy in when he arrives.'

I climbed the stairs to my office, a small space beneath the eaves at the very top of the building. It was little more than a broom cupboard, but at least I didn't have to share it with anyone.

I scooped up the case files, grabbed a pen from the pot and ran my tongue around my teeth, wishing that I still had a packet of Tic Tacs on my desk to get rid of the sour tang of alcohol and cigarette smoke on my breath. When I came back

14

downstairs meeting room two had been prepared for clients in the usual way, with a tray of sandwiches and a small plate of Marks and Spencer's biscuits in the middle of the conference table. The pump-action coffee pot I could never work sat ominously on a chest of drawers by the door, alongside miniature bottles of Evian.

David was on his mobile phone. He glanced up and indicated he would just be a minute.

'Water?' I asked, gesturing towards our catering.

'Coffee,' he whispered, and pointed at the biscuits.

I grabbed a cup, faced the coffee pot with determination and pushed the top hard. Nothing happened so I pushed it again, harder, spurting coffee over the back of my hand.

I winced in pain as the liquid seared my skin.

'Are you OK?'

Someone handed me a tissue and I used it to wipe my stinging hand.

'I hate these things,' I muttered. 'We should buy a Nespresso machine and be done with it.'

'Or maybe just a kettle.'

I looked up and a suited man was looking at me intently, momentarily distracting me from the burning sensation on my skin.

David snapped his phone shut and turned to us.

'Do you two know each other?'

'No,' I said quickly.

'Martin Joy – Francine Day. It's her birthday. Maybe we can put a match in one of those fancy biscuits and sing to her.'

'Happy Birthday,' said Martin, his green eyes still fixed on me. 'You should go and run that under the cold water.'

'It's fine,' I said, turning to throw the tissue in the bin.

When I faced the table again, Martin had already poured

two cups of coffee. He went to sit across the table from me, next to David, which gave me the chance to observe him. He was not particularly tall but had a presence that filled the room, something I noticed a lot with very successful people. His suit was sharp, his tie neatly drawn into a Windsor knot. He was around forty, but I could not say a precise age. There was no sign of grey in his dark hair, although a hint of stubble around his jaw glinted tawny in the strong lights of the conference room. His eyebrows were flat and horizontal across mossy green eyes. Two frown lines carved into his forehead gave him an intensity that suggested he would be a very tough negotiator.

I looked down and gathered my thoughts. I felt nervous, but then I always did when I was meeting clients for the first time. I was conscious of my desire to please those who were paying my fee, and there was always a certain awkwardness dealing with people who thought they were tougher, smarter than you were.

'I take it you've read the file,' said David. 'Martin is the respondent. I've recommended you to him as leading counsel.'

'So you're the one who's going to fight for me in court,' said Martin, looking directly at me.

'I'm sure David has explained that no one wants to go to court,' I said, taking a sip of my coffee.

'Except the lawyers,' replied Martin without missing a beat.

I knew how this worked. I had been in this situation enough times not to get offended. Family law clients tended to be angry and frustrated, even – *especially* – with their legal team, so first meetings were often tense and fractious. I wished he wasn't sitting opposite me – a configuration I hated. I preferred to remind people that we were all on the same side.

'Actually, I'm a member of an organization called Resolution. We favour a non-confrontational approach to marital dispute, avoiding courts where possible, encouraging collaborative legal solutions.'

'Collaborative legal solutions,' he repeated slowly. I wasn't sure if he was making fun of me by using the stiff legalese. He was certainly judging me. The woman. The Northerner. The junior.

He leant forward in his chair and looked at me.

'I don't want this to be difficult, Miss Day. I'm not an unreasonable man; I want this process to be as fair as possible, but I can't just sit back and let my wife take everything she wants.'

'I'm afraid the concept of "fair" isn't for you or Mrs Joy to decide,' I said carefully. 'That's why we have courts, judges, case law . . .'

I shifted tack: 'Do we know her starting position?' I knew some detail about the case already having spent two hours of the previous evening digesting it. But it was always better to hear it from the horse's mouth.

'My wife wants half of everything. The houses, the money, the business . . . Plus, a share of future earnings.'

'What is it you do?' I asked briskly.

'I head up a convertible arbitrage fund.'

I nodded as if I knew what that meant.

'We trade off anomalies in the market.'

'So you're a gambler?' I asked.

'It's financial investment.'

'And is it successful?'

'Yes. Very.'

I was reminded of Vivienne McKenzie's words. About men and their buoyant self-confidence that makes them believe they are kings of the world.

'We have only thirty employees, but it's a very profitable business. I set the company up with my partner, Alex Cole. I

17

own sixty per cent of the business, he owns the rest. The bulk of my assets are my shares in the business. My wife wants the valuation of my shareholding to be as high as possible. She'd prefer liquid cash to shares.'

'When did you start the business?' I said, writing it all down.

'Fifteen years ago.'

'Before your marriage,' I muttered. According to the file, they had been married for eleven years.

'We should probably go through the Form E,' said David Gilbert.

I nodded. I had seen the financial disclosure documents for both Martin and his wife. His were remarkably similar to the dozens of other declarations of wealth I had seen over the years. The properties dotted around the world, cars, art, and overseas bank accounts.

I ran my finger down the form that his wife had submitted.

Donna Joy, a thirty-four-year-old with a Chelsea address, had the typically heavy expenditure and low personal income that seemed standard for a woman in her position.

There were pages of it, although my eyes picked out the more remarkable details.

'Annual expenditure on lunches: £24,000,' I muttered out loud.

'That's a lot of sushi,' said Martin.

I looked up and our eyes met. I'd been thinking exactly the same thing.

'She claims she is unemployable. Mental fragility . . .' I noted.

Martin gave a soft, quiet snort.

'Has she ever worked?'

'When we met, she was the manager of a clothes shop, but she handed her notice in once we got married. She said she wanted to educate herself, so I paid for a lot of courses. Art courses, mainly. I set her up in a studio. She works there, but she won't call it work for divorce purposes.'

'Does she sell her stuff?'

'A little. Honestly, it's more of a vanity project, but she enjoys it. Her paintings are quite good.'

His face softened and I found myself wondering what she was like. I could picture her now. Beautiful, a little bohemian . . . high maintenance, definitely. I felt I knew her without having met her.

'And everything that's listed here. That's it?'

'You mean, am I hiding anything?'

'I need to know everything. Pensions, off-shore accounts, shareholdings, trusts. We don't want any surprises. Besides, she's asking for forensic accounting into your affairs.'

'So what do you think?' asked Martin finally. I noticed that his shirt was very white.

'Your wife is young, but she enjoyed a very high standard of living during the marriage. You had what we call a mid-length marriage. Her claim would have been more concrete if you had been together over fifteen years, less so if you were married under six years.'

'So we're in a grey area that the law loves.'

'Provision for the financially weaker spouse is generous in this country. The start point is generally one of equality. But we can argue that she didn't really contribute to the accumulation of wealth, that the business is a non-matrimonial asset.' I scanned the file, checking a detail. 'You haven't got children. That helps.'

I looked up at him, realizing I shouldn't have said that. For all I knew, the relationship might have broken down because of an inability to have a family. It was one of those things I never found out as a divorce lawyer. I knew that people wanted to get divorced, and I advised them how to do it. But I never really knew *why*, beyond the broad strokes of infidelity or unreasonable behaviour. I never truly got to know what made two people who had once genuinely loved one another, in some cases, grow to hate each other.

'We're keen for a clean-break settlement,' said David.

'Absolutely.' I nodded.

'What sort of split do you think I can realistically expect?'

I didn't like to be drawn on a number, but Martin Joy was the sort of client who expected answers.

'We should start at a seventy–thirty split and go from there.'

I put my pen down, feeling exhausted, wrung out. I wished I hadn't touched that wine and soda at lunchtime.

Martin shook his head, staring at the desk. I thought he might have been pleased at the suggestion that we could avoid a fifty–fifty asset split, but he looked absolutely shell-shocked.

'What happens next?'

'The First Directions meeting is in ten days' time.'

'Will any decisions be made then?'

He had seemed composed throughout the meeting, but hints of anxiety were beginning to show.

I shook my head.

'The clue is in the name. All very preliminary stuff, I'm afraid.'

'Fine,' he said uncomfortably.

It was dark outside now. He stood up to leave and pulled his shirt cuffs down from under his jacket sleeves. One and then the other. Then he looked at me.

'I'll see you then, Miss Day. I look forward to it.'

I stretched out my hand and as he closed his fingers around mine, I realized I was looking forward to seeing him again too.

# Chapter 3

I liked getting the bus home from work, not just because I was a little claustrophobic and hated the tube system. The number 19 took me from Bloomsbury all the way home to Islington. It was not the quickest way to get to and from my place of work, but it was my favourite way to commute. I liked the head-clearing walk down Fleet Street and Kingsway to the bus stop, past the red telephone boxes outside the Old Bailey, and the church of St Clement Danes, especially when its mournful bells rang out the tune to the old nursery rhyme, 'Oranges and Lemons'. And once I had boarded the bus, I enjoyed observing the sights and sounds of the city. When I first came to the capital, I used to spend the whole day riding the number 19 route, face pressed to the glass, watching the city drift by: Sadler's Wells, the twinkling lights of the Ritz, the exclusive stores of Sloane Street, then down to Cheyne Walk and Battersea Bridge. It was a distilled version of the best the city had to offer, all for the price of a Travelcard. It was the London of my childhood dreams.

As I sat down and wiped the condensation from the window with my fingertips, I wondered if I should have made more of an effort on my birthday. Even David Gilbert, a workaholic if ever I've met one, thought I was off out for birthday drinks. But I didn't see why I should break my weekly routine just because I was another year older. One of the perils of my job has always been the lack of a social life. There were plenty of pubs around Temple, and people to have a drink with, but I had always taken the view that, if you wanted to get the job done properly, then you had to make sacrifices.

I pulled my mobile out of my bag and phoned my local Chinese takeaway. I couldn't decide between the beef with fresh basil or the yellow bean chicken, so I ordered both, along with a side order of dumplings and chow mein. What the hell. It was my birthday.

Ending the call, I thought back to my conversation with Viv McKenzie about applying for silk, and wondered what becoming Francine Day QC might mean.

There had certainly been little other change in my life in the past five years. I'd lived in the same flat on the sketchy edges of Islington since my late twenties, settled into an ordered routine. I went to the gym the same two evenings every week, took a ten-day holiday to Italy every August. Two short-lived romances punctuated a long stretch of being single. I saw friends less regularly than I should. Even the small detail of my life had a satisfying familiarity. I bought the same Starbucks coffee on my way into work, my copy of the *Big Issue* from the same Romanian man outside Holborn tube. Part of me liked this reassuring familiarity, and saw no need to change the status quo.

Peering through the water droplets on the cold window, I realized we were on St Paul's Road. I nudged the snoring commuter beside me and squeezed off the bus, walking the rest of the way to my flat on the road that descended into Dalston.

As I neared my flat I groaned as I saw the headlight of a delivery scooter pull up and stop. I started to run but the pavement was wet. Almost slipping, I hissed a curse and slowed to a halt, fishing around my bag for my purse, tickets and sweet wrappers falling to the floor like blossom blown from a tree. I bent down to pick up the litter, but already the scooter was setting off again into the dark.

By the time I reached my front door, I was out of breath. There was a figure in the doorway holding a white carrier bag stuffed with cartons.

'You owe me twenty-three quid,' said my neighbour Pete Carroll, a PhD student at Imperial who had been living in the downstairs apartment for the past eighteen months.

'Did you give him a tip?' I winced.

'I'm a student,' he said with mock disapproval.

I debated running after the delivery man. They were my regulars. They gave me free prawn crackers and I didn't want to short-change them or have them think I was tight.

'I only called them fifteen minutes ago. They usually take ages.'

I handed him a twenty-pound note and an extra fiver, and stepped inside our neglected hallway, picking up my post and putting it in my bag.

'Tuesday night is a bit decadent for takeaway,' smiled Pete folding his arms awkwardly.

'It's my birthday,' I replied without even thinking.

'I wondered what the brightly coloured envelopes were doing scattered among the junk mail.'

'So you're not going out?'

'It's mid-week. I've got work to do.'

'Killjoy.'

'I've got to prepare for court tomorrow.'

'You boring sod. I'm going to march you down to the pub.'

'Pete, no. I'm really busy. Work with a pork dumpling chaser,' I said holding up the bag of Chinese. 'I know that might seem an odd way to celebrate your birthday, but that's what happens when you're almost forty.'

'I'm not taking no for an answer,' he said, with a zeal that told me he meant it.

'I suppose I've bought too much Chinese. I'll supply the chow mein if you've got any drinks. But I've got to be at my desk in an hour.'

'I'll be up in a minute,' he grinned.

Pete disappeared into his ground-floor flat and I walked up the stairs to mine.

Leaving the door slightly ajar, I hung my coat on the rack and set my bag down in the hall. I slipped off my shoes, enjoying the soft feel of carpet under my feet, and undid the top button of my blouse.

My flat was my sanctuary. A cool, calm, Farrow-and-Ball-painted haven for one, and I instantly regretted having invited someone in to share it.

Resigning myself to a visitor, I pulled two plates out of the kitchen cupboard, just as Pete appeared in the hall with a four-pack of lager.

'Pass me a glass. I assume you're not a straight-out-of-the-tin girl.'

He poured me a frothy glass of lager, then opened another can for himself as I carried the Chinese into the living room.

'So, you're almost forty,' he said, perching on the sofa next to me. 'You don't look it.'

'I'm thirty-seven,' I said, realizing how little Pete and I knew about each other. We spoke more than most London neighbours: we saw each other at the bus stop, he was a willing fixer of laptops and fuse boxes. On one occasion last summer, I'd been walking past the local pub and he'd been having a beer outside. He invited me to join him, which I did because it was hot and sunny and I was thirsty from the gym, but I did not consider him a friend.

'By the way, I got a letter from my landlord, yesterday,' said Pete, peeling the foil top off the chow mein box. 'He's putting my rent up. The freeholder says the roof needs doing. Reckons both leaseholders have got to put fifteen grand into the sinking fund.'

'Shit, I've not heard about that.'

'But fifteen grand is just a day's work for a distinguished lady of the Bar,' he smiled.

'I wish.'

'Come on, you're loaded.'

'I'm not, I promise,' I replied, shaking my head. 'I am a jobbing barrister, in debt, thanks to thousands of pounds' worth of unpaid invoices.'

'You'll get paid. The banks know you're good for it. And then you'll be rich.'

Rich, I scoffed quietly. My family thought I was rich, but everything was relative, and in London, mixing with lawyers and businessmen like Martin Joy, it was easier to view my financial situation through another prism. Perhaps if I made silk, things would change. I would land big, juicy cases, my hourly rate would double, so that one day I might even be able to afford one of those Georgian houses in Canonbury – the ones that had drawn me to the N1 postcode in the first place, the ones I still liked to walk past and dream about.

I thought about the £15,000 I would need to find from somewhere and took a commiseratory slug of beer, though I knew I shouldn't.

'You know, today, I was dealing with someone who spends £24,000 a year on lunch,' I said, dipping a dumpling into some soy.

Pete shook his head. 'And you're missing a birthday night out on account of these people.'

He laughed and I knew he had a point.

'I'm acting for the husband in that particular divorce. But you'll be glad to know that tomorrow's case, the case I should be preparing for, is a more deserving cause.'

'Another poor rich husband about to get screwed,' he smiled.

'Actually, no. My client's a man who is about to lose access to his kids. Just a regular guy who found his wife in bed with another man.'

'People,' said Pete quietly.

I nodded. 'I bet you're glad you only have to deal with computers all day. Things that don't have feelings.'

'Yet.'

'Yet?'

'If you subscribe to one model of how our brains create consciousness, you'll believe that sentient computers will never exist. Other schools of Artificial Intelligence thought believe that the day is coming when computers will be able to imitate humans.'

'That's a scary idea. They're going to make us all redundant, aren't they.'

'Some jobs are more future-proof than others.'

'Like divorce lawyers?'

'Machines are logical. Love and relationships are anything but. I'd say you'll be all right for the foreseeable future.'

'Glad to hear it, with a new roof to pay for.'

There was a long silence. We had eaten our food and run out of conversation.

'I should get on with some work.'

Scooping up the leftovers, I took the plates into the kitchen. When I turned round, Pete was in the doorway. He took a step towards me and cupped his hand on my jaw. Gasping in surprise, I didn't have time to think whether he had misinterpreted this as a sign of my desire, because his lips were already on mine. I could taste the ginger and yellow bean on his breath. His saliva smeared across my cheek.

'Pete, you're my friend. And you're drunk,' I replied, pulling away.

'Sometimes you need to get drunk,' he said.

I took a step away from him. I couldn't say his approach had been a complete surprise. The way he had loitered outside with the takeaway should have alerted me.

'It's the age difference, isn't it?' I registered the pique in his voice. Men and their self-confidence. 'If I was a thirty-seven-year-old man and you were my age, no one would even bat an eyelid.'

I felt guilty, cruel. I don't suppose he had any reason to think I would turn him down. After all, I had invited him up to my flat, for dinner, on my birthday.

'I'm sorry,' I said quietly. 'I know I'm a miserable old spinster, but I like it this way.'

'Do you?' he said, challenging me.

'I work eleven hours a day, Pete, I come home, and I work some more. There's no room for anything else.'

'Stop blaming your job.'

There was a time when I wouldn't have cared that Pete was not my type, when we'd have ended up in the bedroom, but tonight, I just wanted him to go.

'I should leave,' he said flatly.

I nodded and he exited the flat without another word. And as I closed the door behind him, I leant forward, pressed my head against the door and puffed out my cheeks.

'Happy birthday', I whispered, desperate for the day to be over.

# *Chapter 4*

There was no getting away from the fact that I needed a new bag. Over the past week, the rip in the seam of my trusty Samsonite case had been getting longer and longer. Work had never been busier, with new instructions and cases springing to life after weeks of dormancy, and the numerous files that needed transporting between court, home and chambers, meant that my bag was one vigorous pull of the zip away from fatal damage.

I was brought up to be thrifty and part of me thought that I just needed to fix it. But I had no idea who repaired bags these days – cobblers? Tailors? In our consumerist society it seemed our only option was to buy a new one.

Glancing at my watch, I noted that it was not yet seven o'clock. Burgess Court was well placed for pubs but less convenient for retail therapy. But I calculated that if I took a taxi, I could be on Oxford Street by quarter past, out of there by seven thirty, and home in time for a ScandiCrime drama that was starting that week on cable.

'You off home?'

Paul was standing at the door to my office with a bundle of files.

'In a minute,' I replied, fishing around in my desk drawer.

'I've got something for you tomorrow, if you fancy it.'

I knew I should have turned it down but saying no to work had never been one of my strong points.

'What is it?'

'Freezing application tomorrow. Listed for nine thirty.'

I hesitated; the only reason I had earmarked a night in front of the TV was because my workload for the following day was relatively quiet.

'I can get it biked round to Marie or Tim,' he offered.

'Give it here,' I sighed. 'It'll save you hanging around for the courier.'

Paul looked at me, a smile playing on his lips. 'You know, it's fine to have the night off sometimes.'

'I'll sleep when I'm dead,' I replied. Not finding what I was searching for in my desk drawer, I glanced up at him. 'I don't suppose you've got a spare carrier bag? My case is fit to burst and I'm worried it's not going to make it home.'

'I'm sure we can do better than a carrier bag for a sophisticate like yourself,' he laughed, disappearing downstairs. He returned a couple of minutes later with a cloth tote bag branded with the Burgess Court insignia.

'What's this?'

'Marketing. By the way, I popped the QC application forms in there for you.'

'A master of subtlety, as usual.'

I left the office and hurried across Middle Temple, past our grand Elizabethan hall and the fountain firing a silver flume of water into the night sky. It was eerie after sunset, when the gas lamps had flickered on; the cloisters threw shadows around the square and the sound of your shoes against the cobbles tricked you into thinking you were not alone.

Increasing my pace, I threaded my way down the thin, dark alley of Devereux Court, one of the artery routes on to the Strand, just as the rain began to fall. A cab responded to my outstretched hand and I jumped in before it really began to pour. The driver asked me where I wanted to go and I said the first department store name that came into my head: Selfridges.

I am not a great shopper. That gene escaped me and I don't think it's because I was once on free school dinners. I remember one client, a Russian model, who in one breath told me how she used to pick up rotten fruit from the markets to take home to feed her family, and in the next breath told me that she needed at least a million pounds in maintenance per anum from the property magnate husband she was divorcing. Growing up poor sent you one way or the other.

The taxi dropped me off on Cumberland Street. The rain was pelting down now and the pavements looked black and oily. Cursing the weather, I ran into the store.

I knew within minutes that I was in the wrong place. I hardly ever came to Selfridges and I had forgotten how expensive it was. Boutiques lined the outer perimeter wall: Chanel, Gucci, Dior, each one like a jewellery box, glitzy and polished. I preferred the shops in the City, where everything seemed more ordered and less dazzling for time-pressed people like me. But in the West End, in Knightsbridge, shops were caves of temptation for tourists and trophy wives, retail labyrinths designed to make you get lost and spend, whereas I just wanted to find a bag and go home.

Taking a breath, I told myself that it wouldn't hurt to look, that my bag, my image, was my calling card. I browsed the central handbag area and a beautiful bag displayed on a plinth caught my eye. It was smaller than the pilot bag I had been carrying around the past five years, its black leather soft and buttery to the touch. It was a QC's bag, I realized, as I picked it up and hunted around for the price tag.

'I thought it was you,' said a voice behind me.

I turned round and for a second I didn't recognize him. His hair was damp from the rain, and he was wearing glasses with smart, tortoiseshell frames.

'Mr Joy.'

'Martin,' he smiled.

'Sorry, Martin,' I replied.

'Retail therapy?'

I started to laugh. 'You make it sound pleasurable. I'm actually on a mercy mission to replace my briefcase.'

'A woman who doesn't like shopping,' he said, his eyes playing with mine.

'There are some of us.'

'Nice bag.' He nodded towards my hands and I shrugged.

'Well, I can't find the price tag, which is never a good sign. If you have to ask, you can't afford it and all that,' I said, feeling suddenly self-conscious to be talking about money with a client.

'You've just had a birthday. Treat yourself.'

'Yes, my birthday,' I said, surprised that he had remembered. 'That seems a long time ago now.'

He held my gaze and I could count the spots of rain on his forehead.

'What are you doing here?'

'My office is round the corner. I wanted to pop into the wine shop downstairs on the way home.'

'Sounds good.'

'It had better be.'

There was a brief silence. I didn't know whether to make my excuses and leave, although I didn't want to.

'So I'm seeing you on Friday . . .'

31

I nodded. 'The First Directions hearing. It's all pretty harmless.'

'Harmless? Donna has a lawyer whose nickname is "the Piranha".'

'Well, you don't want to know what they call me . . .'

'Are you going to buy that?' His voice was soft and low, with a rasp that hinted of late nights and cigarettes.

I looked down and saw that I was still clutching the bag. My hands had made two long sweat marks across the leather.

'Sorry, no. They probably think I'm about to steal it,' I said, setting it back on its plinth. 'I should let you go and buy your wine.'

He still hadn't taken his eyes off me.

'Any last-minute tips for Friday? In fact, while you're thinking, come with me. Come and help me choose a good red.'

Before I could even think about refusing him, I was following him down the escalator into the basement, conscious of the thrill heightening as the escalator descended.

'Just over here,' he said as I followed him into the wine room.

I was impressed. It was large, well stocked and came complete with a bar that looked as if it belonged on the set of some glamorous Manhattan-based movie. There were racks of wine glasses hanging from the ceiling. The light was rich and low.

'Drink?' asked Martin. 'Or do you have to rush off?'

'I think I can stay for one,' I replied without even thinking.

We walked towards the bar and he motioned towards a stool. The bartender handed me the menu. I wasn't supposed to drink but I chose the 1909 Smash, a delicious-sounding concoction of gin, peach and mint. After all, that's what you were supposed to do in the movies.

I perched awkwardly on the stool and wished my cocktail would hurry up.

'So . . . Friday's court hearing.'

I glanced over to him and realized that he was probably trying to get free information. There were no time sheets here at Selfridges' wine shop, and suddenly I felt disappointed and duped.

'Tips for Friday?' I said, as coolly as I could. 'Just stay calm.'

'Why, what are you expecting?' he said with a slow, cynical smile.

'It can get quite heated and that generally doesn't solve anything.'

The bartender returned with our cocktails. I took a sip and it was cold, sweet and refreshing on my tongue.

Martin swilled a stirrer around his drink so the ice cubes clinked against the glass.

'David speaks very highly of you.'

I tried to brush off the compliment with a modest shrug.

'David's good. Really good. And I don't just mean because he recommended me as counsel. Why did you choose him?' I asked, always interested in the process.

'I googled "top divorce lawyer" and his name came up.'

'That's how it works, is it? Like picking a plumber.'

'Something like that,' he said, looking at me over the rim of his glass.

'And thank you for instructing me. Most men prefer male lawyers. I suppose they think they'll be more macho in a fight. So hats off for not thinking like an alpha male.'

'Actually, I did have my doubts about you,' he said, putting his glass on the marble counter.

His candour caught me off guard.

'Ouch,' I said into my drink.

'I'm just being honest. I know divorce isn't about winning, but I wanted a QC. And I was worried that you're not.'

'The word "junior" is a bit of a misnomer,' I said, looking back at him. 'There are some barristers I know who were called to the Bar thirty years ago and who aren't silks, not because they're not brilliant but because it wasn't the right decision for them.'

'Is that the case with you?'

'I'm probably going to apply this year.'

'So if my case drags on, I won't be able to afford you.'

'I doubt that.'

'To Francine Day QC,' he said, clinking his glass against mine. 'I'm glad you're representing me. Although you're going to have to explain what's the bloody point of having both a solicitor and a barrister.'

I laughed. It was a question I got asked a lot and I gave the standard answer.

'It used to be the right of audience in court,' I shrugged. 'That's changed now, but I would say barristers are generally more comfortable with the advocacy side of things. Solicitors come to us with the more complex issues too.'

'So you're saying you're cleverer than solicitors.'

'We have different skill sets, that's all.'

'They say that, don't they?' he replied. 'That politicians and barristers are just frustrated actors.'

'Is that so?'

I caught the playful tone in my voice and I was aware that I was flirting with him.

There was a long complicit silence.

Martin observed me carefully, as if he was assessing me. It made me feel interesting.

'I can imagine you treading the boards at Oxford.'

'That's such a long way from the truth it's not even funny.'

'Oh yes. LLB Birmingham. First class.'

I glanced at him in surprise.

'Your CV is on the website.'

'My dad is a bus driver. I went to a comp. I was the first person in my family to go to university.'

'Then we're not so different, you and I.'

I smiled cynically. Every ounce of him had the polish of a public school and Oxbridge. He caught my eye and knew what I was thinking.

'Let's get some food,' he said, signalling the waiter. I have never been particularly good at reading men's signals, but I could tell he was showing off.

We ate and danced around one another, easy conversation between mouthfuls of food, small plates of tapas that we shared. Only occasionally did I feel fleeting moments of panic that I shouldn't be here, with a client, in a low-lit bar three days before the First Directions for his divorce proceedings.

'Another drink?'

I noticed that the bar had emptied out.

'I'd better not.'

He pushed his shirtsleeves up and I noticed what good forearms he had: strong and tanned with a light trail of hair across the top.

'You probably think I'm a wanker.'

'Why would I think that?'

'The husband with money. Out to screw his wife.'

'I'm here to help, not judge.'

'Still, you've probably met a lot of men like me.'

'I like acting for men. I think they get screwed a lot of the time, especially when there are kids involved.'

'Your job – it must put you off marriage.'

'How do you know I'm not married?'

'I don't.'

'I'm not,' I said holding his gaze a moment too long as the mood shifted instantly between us.

'I think we're about to get thrown out,' said Martin, looking around. The place was empty. The waiter looked as if he was tidying up for the night. It couldn't have been later than nine o'clock, but it felt late and intimate like the dregs of the day.

The bartender put our bill on a small silver tray. Martin picked it up and had it settled before I even had a chance to reach for my purse.

'Let's go,' he said, putting his right hand on the small of my back.

We were ushered out of the store by a security guard and exited on to Duke Street. It was raining more fiercely than it had been when I came into the store, so hard that the rain bounced off the flooded pavements. My heels sliced through a puddle, splashing cold, dirty water on to my stockings.

'Where's a taxi when you need one?' I shouted across the West End noise. My canvas Burgess Court tote was already sodden and I feared that the QC application form wouldn't survive the downpour.

'There,' he said, as we lifted our coats over our heads, laughing, and groaning as we splashed through puddles.

'Where do you live?' he asked.

'Islington.'

'Then we can share,' he said as he opened the door, and before I knew it I had jumped in.

# Chapter 5

I expected him to live somewhere different. Notting Hill or Chelsea, I thought, trying to remember the details of his property holdings from the Form E. But he instructed the taxi to go east.

'Spitalfields?' I said, when he had given the driver our two destinations.

'Surprised?'

'I had you down as a West London man.'

'I suspect that's not a compliment,' he said, glancing out of the window.

'No, I suppose not.'

'When I bought it, before my marriage, before the Gassler Partnership, I was working on Finsbury Square at Deutsche Bank, so it was handy. Donna never really liked it. She made us move as soon as she could persuade me. But I kept hold of it and moved back in when we separated. If you're going to live in London, you might as well live in London. For me, that's what this city is all about. You can feel the Dickensian grit, the ghosts of Jack the Ripper and Fagin. The bright lights of the City, the gas lights of the back streets. It's the ultimate melting pot – everyone has lived here – the Huguenots, the Jews, Bangladeshis . . . You can buy the best bagels, the best curry, in London.'

'You're beginning to sound like an estate agent.'

'I just love it. I don't want to leave.'

'Leave?'

'Splitting the assets . . . Sorry, I forgot we weren't supposed to talk about the case.'

As we slipped into Clerkenwell, I tried to imagine Donna living around here. Of course, I knew what she looked like – a Google search after my first meeting with Martin had thrown up a few images. Donna at the Serpentine party, at a photographic exhibition: long dark-blonde hair, wide cat-like eyes, a crisp defiance around the mouth. She did not look like an artist, she looked like a Chelsea wife, she looked as if she did not belong in Spitalfields. But Martin didn't either.

'You like living near Jack the Ripper's stomping ground?' I said, trying to lighten the tone.

'Now you're making me feel weird.'

'Well, you said it.'

'I meant the atmosphere, the Hawksmoor churches, the history.'

'You old romantic,' I teased.

We looked at each other and it was as if we could not tear our gaze away from one another. I felt our fingertips touch on the soft upholstery of the back seat, and the sweet shock of his touch made me stop breathing for a moment. I didn't pull away and Martin leant forward towards the driver, as if he had read my mind.

'Spitalfields first. Is that all right?'

He looked at me for approval but I didn't need to say anything. He took my hand and it seemed the most natural thing in the world, the thing I had wanted, I realized, since that first meeting at Burgess Court. We turned away from each other, our eyes trailing out of opposite windows. The taxi seemed to speed up and the shimmer of danger was palpable.

Spitalfields was London in microcosm, a strange organic meld of the ancient and the space age, jagged silver-and-glass rocket ships pointing to the heavens, next to crumbled, soot-stained tenements, unchanged since the Ripper stalked through the fog. But the grasping crawl of gentrification was everywhere you looked: old wholesalers turned into hip Mexican cafés, neon cacti hammered into their two-hundred-year-old facades, an artisan weavers' loft turned rabbit-hutch studios for jewellers, DJs and web gurus. Even on a cold night, young clubbers were roaming the streets, looking for craft beer and the elusive scene.

Not everywhere was touched by progress, however. Martin's building was located just behind Hawksmoor's glowing white slab of Christ Church, a stone's throw from the iron marquee of Spitalfields Market. Somehow this pocket of old London had survived the Luftwaffe and the developers, a time capsule of narrow cobbled streets lined with black railings and glowing faux-gas lamps. Sandwiched between thin Georgian terraces with walk-up steps and brass knockers, it was an old ware-house conversion that still bore the name of its former occupants – W.H. Miller and Co carved in a sandstone pelmet around the roof. It looked new yet old, like a Dickensian film set; I half-expected Patrick Stewart dressed as Scrooge to come out, or a horde of urchins to appear behind the gaslight singing 'Who Will Buy?'

The taxi stopped and Martin paid the driver. There was no discussion about whether it would continue its journey to Islington. I simply got out of the car.

The street was deserted, but even so, I looked around to

make sure no one could see me. Not on this street, with the dim yellow light and the tall windows covered with shutters. No one here but ghosts.

Martin took my wet tote and pushed a key into the door. The cavernous atrium was dark with the same manicured, industrial feel – exposed brickwork and steel beams – as the exterior of the building.

'Top floor,' he said as he led me towards an old-fashioned lift built for cargo. The noise of my heels, clicking across the concrete floors, echoed around the building. The iron grille clanked shut and the lift stuttered into motion. The light was low in the lift. In a film this would be the part where we would start kissing, fucking. He would press me against the cold steel walls, hold my arms above my head and lift up my skirt. Instead we stood there in restrained silence until the lift stopped six storeys up.

'This way,' he said, but there was only one door for the whole top floor.

He let me enter the apartment first, then closed the door behind him. It was dark inside but light seeped in through a bank of arched floor-to-ceiling windows that looked out on the City. The hall, empty except for an expensive looking racing bike, led to a cavernous and sparse space, like a New York loft, with big sofas and a dining table that seated at least twelve. The pale walls were lined with art but I could see little in the way of personal knick-knacks – no photographs or other clues about who he was or what he liked. It reminded me of a very expensive hotel suite – an idea I found seductive.

'Look at that,' I whispered, dazzled by the torpedo-shaped tip of the Gherkin.

I turned round and watched Martin take off his coat. We stood there motionless for a few moments, our eyes not leaving each other's, and then he moved towards me. My heart was racing. If I was briefly nervous that someone could see us through those big, big windows, then that fleeting unease was forgotten when he was so close I could hear the sound of his breath.

'You're wet.'

'I know,' I whispered.

He took my face between his hands and stroked my damp cheek with his thumb.

His fingers trailed down towards my neck, my shoulders until he gently held the tops of my arms.

'You should take this off.'

He turned me round, slowly, carefully, as if it was happening in slow motion, and helped me take off my coat.

I closed my eyes and shut out the view. He was standing behind me now. I could feel the starchiness of his shirt against the thin silk of my blouse. He pushed my hair over my left shoulder and I could feel his warm breath, then his lips on the soft skin at the back of my neck. I tilted my head to one side and inhaled through my nose so that I made a soft shudder of satisfaction.

Perhaps he took that sound as approval to proceed. I wanted him to. I wanted him to unzip the back of my skirt and let it fall to the ground. I wanted his hands to wander down the curves of my body, over my waist, my hips, until they stopped at the bare expanse of thigh above my stocking tops. I wanted him.

His fingers moved to the waistband of his trousers and I heard him unbutton his belt. The leather sprang back against the small of my back like a short, sharp slap. I started undoing the buttons of my blouse until the fabric fell open and I felt the cool air on my skin. He pushed the blouse off my shoulder and kissed the smooth scoop as if he were tasting me. And when the blouse slipped off with little resistance, I turned around and we had just enough distance between us for him to observe me. Naked, except for my bra, thong, hold-ups and heels. I saw him smile, a small curve of the right-hand side of his mouth, and I felt turned on, not just by the thought of what was to come, but by the way I had made him feel. My power over him.

Part of me knew that we would end up like this from the moment I had first seen him. From the second I had burnt my hand and he had put the napkin over my flesh.

We were on the sofa now, leaving a trail of clothes and underwear behind us. He sat down and took my hand, pulling me towards him until I straddled him. His eyes closed and my fingers trailed the soft hair on his chest, lower and lower until I took his cock and teased it into me. I had not had sex for some time but I knew what I was doing and I could see the pleasure on his face.

For a second I thought about Vivienne McKenzie and David Gilbert, imagined what they would say if they could see us like this. But the heat flooding my cheeks was not a rush of shame but of burning desire, an urgent need to feel him deeper and deeper inside me.

I rotated my hips around him and arched my back. He cupped my breast with his one hand and leant forward to draw it between his lips. He teased my nipple with his tongue, playing with it, biting it softly, sweetly at first, then harder until I screamed out loud. There was not enough space around us for our need, our desire. We fell on to the floor and some-where I registered a soft burn of carpet fibre against my skin, but it was forgotten as his hands were in my hair, his hungry mouth devouring my lips, my cheeks, the lobes of my ears. He was on top of me now. One hand pushed my legs wider apart and I could hardly breathe. I started to gasp as the pressure built. Heat radiated from my core. I cried out, my fingernails digging into his skin, my belly tensing as darts of sweet exquisite climax fired around my body. I wanted to capture that feeling, bottle it, I never wanted it to end. And as I looked up at the ceiling, waiting to hear my breath regulate, feeling him roll over and lie beside me, I wondered how long I would have to wait before we did it all over again.

It was a relatively straightforward hearing the next day in court. The emergency asset-freezing injunction was not a particularly complex application, although I would have aced it even if it was.

In my first week in chambers, Viv McKenzie had told me that life at the Bar was about confidence and I was on fire that morning in court; articulate, nimble, prepared to deflect whatever opposing counsel had in their arsenal. It hadn't mattered that I had only skim-read the file that morning on the Central Line. Hadn't mattered that I was so tired from the night before; a night we had spent more time fucking our way around the loft than sleeping. It hadn't mattered that I had rolled into court, just a few minutes before our 9.30 a.m. appointed start date, in yesterday's clothes and a fresh pair of sixty-denier tights I had bought from Boots at Liverpool Street station. I didn't need my armour, my stockings, my red lipstick, my freshly starched shirts. I had the memories of him.

After a few minutes of small talk with the client's solicitor on the steps of court, I returned to chambers, across Fleet Street and into the sanctum of Middle Temple. It surprised me how fresh and different my familiar surroundings seemed to be. The shady cloisters and alleyways that at times unnerved me, were now places for secret assignations and amorous trysts. I had missed taking my medication last night and this morning, and I knew I would soon feel a comedown, panic or derailment, but for now, my mind was consumed by him and all felt well.

I stopped at the reception of Burgess Court and asked Helen our receptionist if I had any messages.

'I've sent you an email, with the names of everyone you have to call back,' she said, fishing under the desk. 'And this parcel came for you.'

I frowned as I looked at the big black box with grosgrain ribbon tied around its belly.

This was not a brief. Not even one from the most prestigious ranks of solicitors.

I took it upstairs to my office and put it on my desk, hesitating a few moments before I pulled at the ribbon and opened the box. Inside, there was a cloth sack and inside that was another bag. The bag. The butter-soft black leather case I had seen in Selfridges the night before. My mouth felt dry and I bit my lip to stop a smile.

I unzipped it carefully. I never did find out how much it was but it felt luxurious and expensive. I dipped my hand inside, wondering if there was some kind of card or note, even though I knew exactly who it was from. As my hand disappeared further and further into its depths, I felt something else. Not the sharp, smooth lines of paper but something soft yet textured.

Puzzled, I removed it from the bag to inspect it and laughed out loud when I saw it was a delicate black lacy thong.

'All right, Fran,' said Paul's voice behind me. 'Couple of jobs for you here.'

I thrust the thong back into the bag and tried to summon my court-face but as I turned to Paul, I don't know who looked more embarrassed. Me. Or him.

# Chapter 6

I don't know who first came up with the nickname 'the Piranha' for Robert Pascale, but it was wholly appropriate when it came to his legal reputation. A former investment banker turned divorce lawyer, he had created a lucrative niche for himself at the very top end of the market – his speciality being the sort of bank-balance depleting, pip-squeezing court cases that made *Daily Mail* headlines and millionaire businessmen shiver.

But Robert Pascale did not look like a ruthless carnivore. His appearance was that of an old-school dandy, silver hair swept back from his face, impeccable suits with a top pocket in a contrasting shade of silk. Out of court, he was invariably charm itself, and I knew that charm was about to be directed at me when I saw him in the corridors of High Holborn's Central Family Court.

He put his mobile phone back in his pocket as I approached him.

'Francine, How are you? You're looking so radiant I'd have to kiss you if I wasn't afraid the client might see us and think I was fraternizing with the enemy.'

I laughed nervously at the mention of his client. I had come early, without David, without Martin, for two reasons. The thought of being alone with Martin was one that filled me with both terror and excitement. I had not seen him since I had left his Spitalfields loft two days earlier. We had texted like teenagers the afternoon I had received my leather bag and panties, but our correspondence had tailed off to more sober exchanges that involved me reassuring him about the First Directions meeting, and the anxiety that had invariably followed had made me think that my forgotten medication had been more damaging than I thought.

But I also wanted to come early to see her. To see Donna. I did not want my first sight of Martin's wife to be in a windowless courtroom, when I knew that all eyes would be upon me, and I could not be trusted to hide my curiosity and my emotions.

'I'm very well, Robert,' I said, glancing around the corridor. 'So where are your troops? I thought you'd be locked in conference.'

'Jeremy Mann is here. We're just waiting for the client,' he said, starting to send another text before he diverted his full attention back to me. 'So. Tell me about the rumour that you are applying for silk this time around.'

I gave a good-natured snort. I figured it wouldn't do my career any harm if word got out that I was applying.

'Would it mean you might instruct me every now and then?' I asked him pointedly, not needing to remind him that he was one of the few leading family law solicitors who had never done so. I suspected it was because Robert Pascale was a snob and, despite the fact that his stock in trade was representing women, he was also a dyed-in-the-wool misogynist.

He leant in and touched me on the shoulder.

'If you are applying for QC, Francine, go easy on any

headline-grabbing stunts. This is a divorce case, two people's lives, not a professional showcase,' he said with a hint of warning.

'You know I always play fair,' I replied as I glanced up at the big clock and knew that David and Martin would soon be here.

I excused myself and went to find a free interview room, texting David to let him know where he could find me.

I pulled the small bottle of Evian water from my bag and took a sip and glanced around the room. The Central Family Court lacked the grandeur of the Royal Courts of Justice on the Strand, where you could feel the years of history. It had the look and feel of a comprehensive school and the room in which I was sat was cold and bland.

After a few minutes I heard the door open behind me and David and Martin came into the room. I had been willing myself to remain calm, but at the sight of him I felt my heart race and all I could think about were the words of a text he had sent me two days previously.

*I like the taste of your cunt.*

I avoided shaking hands by motioning towards the table. They sat down and I launched into a prepared speech about what we could expect that morning, how I proposed to apply for a high court judge to preside over the Financial Dispute Resolution, how to keep things as straightforward and non-confrontational as possible.

'Jeremy Mann has brought Richard Sisman with him,' I informed David.

'Who's that?' Martin cut in.

I took another sip of water and noticed that my hand was trembling.

'Richard is Jeremy's junior counsel.'

Martin frowned.

'Shouldn't we have someone else?'

His voice had a note of accusation and panic in it.

'You don't need anyone else at a First Appointment.'

'Then why have they got one?'

His hostility unnerved me. I didn't know what I had been expecting. Had I expected him to flirt with me? Comment on the new leather bag I had brought with me?

'The attendance of counsel isn't necessary at these preliminary meetings,' I said, feeling my heart pound faster.

'Then why are you here? And why's Donna got two barristers?'

I glanced at David Gilbert and shifted uncomfortably in my chair.

'Games,' I said with as much authority as I could muster. 'Two barristers at a First Appointment is the legal equivalent of a military show of might. The Russians parading their weapons. But it's pointless, unnecessary and expensive. I'm all for a bit of posturing, but within reason. Robert Pascale, on the other hand, is an expert at spending other people's money.'

'But perhaps that's why he's so successful. Spend to earn.'

'Martin. You have to trust us.'

Our eyes locked and I saw a softening apology in his expression. I knew I had to take everything less personally, but it set my resolve to do whatever I could for him.

'It's almost ten,' I said, scooping up my files. 'We should go.'

We walked in silence to chambers, one of the small courtrooms used for more informal proceedings.

The judge was already in the room at the head of the long conference table. Jeremy Mann and his junior were also sitting down. Robert was standing in the corner of the room checking his messages. I could not see Donna Joy anywhere.

I took a seat opposite Mann and arranged my papers and collected my thoughts. I put my pen horizontally above my file, pointing to the left. A mechanical pencil and a block of Post-it notes were put to the left and right like a knife and fork.

Soft murmurs rippled around the room, otherwise all we could hear was the ticking of the clock on the wall.

It was now a few minutes after ten o'clock and still there was no sign of Mrs Joy. I glanced towards District Judge Barnaby and caught his eye. He was a judge of the old school, on the verge of retirement, irascible but efficient, and I could tell by the arch of his brow that he was anxious to get on with another day at the coal-face of the breakdown of human relationships.

'Are we ready?' asked District Judge Barnaby finally.

Robert Pascale looked unhappy.

'We're just waiting for my client,' he explained.

Barnaby tapped his pen lightly against the table.

'And are we expecting her soon?' he said pointedly.

'Any minute,' Pascale said glancing at his watch. 'I'll just go and wait outside for her. She might have got lost.'

I didn't dare look at Martin, who had started muttering to David in such a low voice that I couldn't hear what he was saying.

Robert left the room for what seemed like a very long time. When I heard the door open again, I couldn't resist turning round, expecting to see her, immaculate and unflustered despite her late arrival, but instead it was Pascale, looking unusually agitated.

'No sign,' he said.

'Have you called her?' asked Jeremy Mann pompously.

'I've tried, but it's going straight to message. I spoke to her yesterday, and she was all set for today.'

'Maybe there's bad traffic.' Martin said it as if he didn't believe it.

'Five more minutes,' said Barnaby witheringly. 'I have a very busy court list.'

'I suggest that we start without Mrs Joy,' said David, looking at me for approval. I knew what he was about to ask without him saying anything.

Robert objected but District Judge Barnaby raised a hand.

'Fine,' he said, looking seriously unimpressed.

'Well, that was embarrassing,' spat Martin as we left chambers forty minutes later.

'Her presence really wasn't necessary,' reassured David.

We watched Robert and his team disappear down the corridor.

Martin was still shaking his head.

'Are you going to speak to her?' I asked.

He gave a light snort. 'I don't think anything I say will have any impact on her behaviour.'

'Behaviour?'

'It's just so bloody typical of her.'

David looked sympathetic. 'It's not the first time a client hasn't turned up to court. Happens more often than you might think. And perhaps Robert had implied that it was just a fairly rudimentary hearing . . .'

I tried to catch Martin's eye, tried to work out what he was thinking but he looked unhappy and distracted.

'What happens now?' He focused his entire attention on David. I felt a heavy thump of disappointment.

'As you saw in there, we set out a timetable for events. Now we need to gather information, liaise with Robert, wait for a date for the FDR.'

'Which should be when?'

'Six to eight weeks, with a bit of luck. If the forensic accounting doesn't hold us up.'

'Let me know. I'm off to Switzerland tomorrow; it's been booked for a while and I don't want to cancel, but it's only for a week.'

I knew this information already. It had been mentioned in passing at the Spitalfields loft and at the time I wondered if he had been gearing up to fob me off.

'Will do,' said David, shaking his hand.

Martin turned to me to repeat the gesture.

He took my palm and held it a moment longer than necessary. As his fingers curled against mine, I thought about them inside me. Where they had been on Tuesday night. Where I wanted them to be right now.

'See you next time,' I said finally.

He nodded, and turned to leave without another word. I watched his form retreat into the distance and I was so transfixed I didn't even stop to wonder if David Gilbert had noticed any spark or awkwardness between me and our client.

'One day people with money will find themselves some manners,' said David when he was out of earshot.

'Martin?' I asked with panic.

'The wife. It's so bloody disrespectful.'

'Maybe she's ill. Or got the wrong day.'

'Maybe,' said David cynically.

'I think we should consider a researcher,' he added after a pause.

'What for?'

'I handled a divorce recently. It was pretty unremarkable from a legal point of view, but it was a soap opera of a story. That wife didn't turn up to her First Appointment either. We thought she was just being cavalier until I found out that she'd moved to LA without telling her husband. Hooked up with some multimillionaire record producer out there, all the while trying to screw my client for fifty per cent of his business.'

'So you don't trust Donna Joy either.' I was aware of the glee in my own voice.

'I just want to know what we are dealing with at her end,' said my instructing solicitor. 'If we can prove she is seeing someone . . . a rich new someone . . . that might help our cause.'

'I know just the person who can help us,' I replied.

There was little left to say to David. His thoughts had already turned to his next meeting, another client. We said our goodbyes and I stood in the lobby wondering how to kill time before a prohibited steps application that was listed for noon. There was no point returning to chambers so I went to Starbucks for a coffee, and read through my notes.

Sitting by the window, I pulled out my iPad and used it to surf the net. Usually I checked the headlines or the weather, but today I found myself typing in *Donna Joy*. The first three pages of search results yielded nothing I hadn't read before, but as I dug deeper, I found the name of the studio from which she worked, a gallery that had exhibited her work, a party she had been to the previous summer. Most revealing of all was her Instagram account – endless stills of exotic locations, glamorous friends and smiling selfies, a window into a gilded world that made my own life seem lonely and colourless.

I stuffed the tablet back in my bag, put some red lipstick on in the loo and returned to court for my prohibited steps. I fed my coat and bag through the scanners and said hello to an acquaintance from law school who had also just arrived. The instructing solicitor for my next case had already texted to say that she was running late, so I hung around the foyer and read the court list.

I first noticed her out of the corner of my eye. It was her coat that grabbed my attention – hot pink and expensive-looking, the sort of item I would not wear myself on account of its colour, but could nonetheless admire.

I looked closer, and knew it was her. She was smaller than I expected, in the same way that the only two celebrities I have ever met were pocket-sized. Her hair was darker, more a rich toffee than a dark blonde. Her bag was large and exotic-looking – a textured skin I did not recognize. Lizard, alligator? I wondered if he had bought it for her.

'Can I help you?' I asked.

She turned to face me and I tried to absorb every detail of her face. Thin lips, strong brows, surprisingly little make-up on her pale, creamy skin, a long swan-like neck, around which hung a delicate gold necklace with the initial 'D'.

She muttered under her breath with undisguised annoyance. 'Not unless you can turn back time.'

I wanted to tell her that she was one hour fifty-two minutes late. That her solicitor would now be back at his office and that the wheels were in motion for her divorce. I wanted to ask her why she was so late. Was it a blow-dry to impress her husband, I wondered, looking at the smooth waves that fell over her shoulders. Or had she simply not bothered to write down the details of that morning's application in her undoubtedly stuffed diary?

I stood motionless for a moment, my heart beating hard, wondering if I should introduce myself. But I knew she would find it strange and coincidental that the barrister she had met at the court lists was her husband's own lawyer.

'I'm afraid I can't help you there,' I replied, gripping my leather bag tighter.

Her face softened as she smiled at me, and I knew exactly what Martin Joy had seen in her. The collar of my shirt felt tight against my neck, and I headed straight for the exit, desperate to get some fresh air.

# Chapter 7

I wasn't the one who suggested meeting in Islington. Martin texted me from Switzerland asking me to dinner and when I said yes, he had a table booked at Ottolenghi within minutes.

I took this as a good sign. Ottolenghi was not in Soho or Chelsea. It was on Upper Street, a stone's throw away from my flat, a short stagger back and I knew I had to – wanted to – prepare for that eventuality. Years of self-imposed singledom don't make for the highest levels of grooming, and slinky underwear had been replaced by over-washed comfort across the board: something had to give. Most Saturday mornings I'd be at the Toynbee Hall free legal advice centre in Stepney, where I've done volunteer work for years, but that week I decided to skip it and instead spend the morning at a little Korean beauty spa on Holloway Road so that I would at least be waxed and smooth. I then went to my favourite deli, La Fromagerie, and bought creamy brie and fragolino grapes to stock the fridge and I put fresh linen on the bed, even spraying them with lavender scent in a bid to make them smell like those starchy sheets you find in expensive hotels. I wanted to make my flat a delicious haven he would never want to leave. Which, I was starting to realize, was exactly what I wanted.

I chose a black dress and hot pink heels and deliberately left five minutes late. I was useless at playing games, always had been, but it was my one concession at 'playing hard to get'.

As I walked along Upper Street, passing the early evening crowds, groups of four or five, loud, laughing, I breathed in hard, wanted to feel some of that energy, some of that abandon, the sense that anything could happen tonight. A smile crept on to my mouth. *Anything.*

I crossed the road, my heels clacking on the tarmac, my coat flying. Would he be there already, waiting for me? Or would I find an empty bar and a message on my phone, some excuse about work or delayed flights? I had never been convinced Martin Joy would contact me again after the First Directions hearing, but once we had arranged a date, I had naively assumed that he would turn up. Now I wasn't so sure. Should I call him to ask if he was on his way? *Think positively,* I told myself. *Good things can happen. Even to you.*

And there he was: my heart skipped as I saw him through the glass. Facing away from the street, lounging against the bar, his broad back moving, his strong hands carving through the air. He was talking to someone. The smile on my face slipped; no, he was *with* someone. A couple. I paused for a step, my hand hovering above the door handle, fighting disappointment. Had I misread the situation? Wasn't this a date-date? But I couldn't stand there wavering: the door was glass and anyway, Martin had turned and seen me.

'Fran,' he said warmly, as I pushed inside. He reached for my hand, guiding me towards him. A crackle of static passed between us as our skin touched, but he didn't flinch, just smiled and whispered one word into my ear, low enough that only I could hear it: 'Sexy.'

'Francine,' he said, turning to the others, 'this is Alex, my business partner, and this is Sophie, his wife.'

'Just his *wife*,' she said with a conspiratorial wink, stepping across to shake my hand. 'No one important.'

But she was impressive: blonde, tall, a little bit horsey, like the captain of a lacrosse team. When she stood up off her stool, she was at least six inches taller than me. Even in my heels I was barely five feet five, but I had never felt smaller than I did right then.

Though Alex laughed along, I sensed more reserve in him. Thin, upright, not a wrinkle in his grey suit. Maybe I wasn't the first woman Martin had introduced to his friends since the divorce, or perhaps Alex was still loyal to Donna – friends did that, didn't they? They took sides.

There was a brief, awkward pause and then Martin filled the space.

'You did get my text?'

'Which text?'

'About Alex and Sophie joining us for dinner.'

I shook my head.

'We won't be staying long and I promise that Alex will be on his best behaviour,' said Sophie, flashing me a conciliatory look.

Martin inspected his phone as his friends went ahead to the table.

'It didn't send. Text failed.'

He touched my fingers, a gesture of apology, and I felt his heat against my skin.

'It's fine. I want to meet your friends,' I said, wondering how convincing that sounded.

We were shown to our table and Martin ordered two bottles of orange wine and a selection of starters. Everything was so well chosen, I knew he had been here many times before.

'So you were skiing?' I said, aware that I should chip in with some small talk from the get-go. I had no idea what Sophie and Alex knew about our relationship, such as it was, but until I had some sort of signal from Martin that this was a date, that Sophie and Alex knew it was a date, I decided to proceed with caution, keeping conversation to the vague and unrevealing.

'Heli-skiing.' Martin nodded.

'Spitalfields' very own Milk Tray Man,' joked Alex.

'It's great. Have you tried it?' asked Sophie, with the confidence of someone who had spent her life on skis.

'I'm happier with a hot chocolate and viennoiserie down at the bottom,' I said, not wanting to admit that the only time I'd spent rushing down snowy slopes was tobogganing in the park as a child. It took a strength of will not to grill him further, desperate to know who he had been in Switzerland with – no one went heli-skiing alone, surely? – but knowing it looked needy to ask.

'So you work alongside Martin?' I asked as we sat down at a table tucked away at the back of the restaurant.

Alex nodded, but Sophie pursed her lips and gave a tight shake of the head. 'Not me. Not any more. I'm sure you know better than most people that working together does not always make for a happy home life. We tried it in the early days, but ended up wanting to strangle each other, so I've stepped aside and taken on a more' – she sucked her teeth – 'advisory role.'

'Meaning she tells us both what to do,' smiled Martin.

'He likes to make it sound like I'm some sort of nag,' said Sophie. 'But without a woman's eye for detail, I dare say the lights would have been turned off years ago.'

Alex took her hand and kissed it.

'There – your reward, darling.'

She tapped his cheek playfully and I felt a pang of jealousy.

They'd probably been married, what? . . . at least a decade, and she obviously still adored her husband.

I slowly began to relax and enjoy myself as the three joked and teased each other the way only old friends can do. Martin held forth about his recent trip, 'coming out of the powder looking like Frosty the Snowman', while Sophie told me about a disastrous skiing holiday she and Alex had been on to Courcheval, where a complete lack of snowfall had turned the resort into 'the seventh ring of hell' where there was nothing to do for the Russian tourists but show off. 'The only place I've seen more fur was in San Diego Zoo!' she laughed.

'So where did you all meet?' I asked, envious of their tight bond.

'University,' said Alex.

'Economics Society.'

'It was that trip to New York, wasn't it? To Wall Street. We were room-mates in that crappy hotel in the East Village.'

'I like to think of myself as a matchmaker,' said Sophie. 'I knew they'd get on, so I fixed it.'

'I thought she became president of Econ Soc to get on, but really she just liked playing Cilla Black.'

'Guilty as charged,' she said, raising a hand.

Conversation flowed on with the wine, some delicious orange-scented white that filled my head, and I began to feel glad that Martin had invited his friends along on our date. The modern, chichi restaurant, Alex's easy intelligence, Sophie's knowing asides: it was a heady mix of the chic and metro-politan, and I ached to be part of this. I could see the admiring glances we were getting from couples at other tables; we were the beautiful people, sophisticated and urbane, and for once I was one of them, right at the beating heart of London.

'So you haven't really told us about you,' said Sophie, when she'd finished telling the waitress what she wanted for dessert. 'In another life, I'd like to have been a divorce lawyer. I got wooed by a few commercial firms on the milk round, but it seemed way too dull. Family law, on the other hand, must be fascinating.'

'Fascinating sometimes,' I said honestly. 'Often difficult and emotional. We tend to find that, when it comes to divorce, feelings take over. People waste huge amounts of billable hours arguing over the smallest things because they don't want the other side to win. I recently had a couple at loggerheads for six months over the ownership of a teapot.'

'A teapot?' said Alex.

I nodded. 'Quite a nice teapot, but probably only worth a hundred pounds, tops. They'd bought it on their honeymoon and they'd each have given up the entire contents of their Kensington house to get it away from the other one.'

They all laughed, but it was an awkward moment, like breaking the spell, reminding everyone who I was and how Martin and I had met.

'Actually, Fran, I wanted to ask you something. A professional query . . .'

'Is there something I should know about, darling?' said Alex, his eyes comically wide, but she ignored him.

'Obviously, Martin's getting divorced, and we've all been wondering . . .'

'Crapping ourselves, more like,' said Alex.

'. . . how it's going to affect the business,' said Sophie. 'Could Donna come after us? I mean, we've always been friends, but as you say, people do funny things when they get in a courtroom.'

I looked around, feeling horribly exposed and duped. I'd thought this was a date, but it was looking as if I had been brought here as part of a fact-finding mission.

'We were worried that Donna might go after Martin for future earnings.'

I glanced at Martin. 'We'd fight that, of course,' I said, gripping the stem of my glass.

'So?' pressed Sophie.

'It's true that divorce can have some corporate ramifications. But the Gassler Partnership doesn't trade on the stock exchange so I expect that any impact will be limited. To be on the safe side, I can recommend a PR who specializes in deflecting negative attention – but, honestly, I don't think it will be necessary.'

I looked at Martin, who smiled back at me reassuringly. I could tell my assessment was largely what Sophie and Alex had wanted to hear.

'Speaking of divorce, did you hear about Mungo Davis?' said Alex. 'Caught his wife in bed with their driver – and do you know what she said?'

I never did hear what Mungo Davis's wife said, because I excused myself and headed for the loos.

When I reached the sanctuary of the bathroom, I put both hands on the side of the basin and inhaled deeply. As I gazed back at my reflection I wondered what I needed to do to be happy. I liked Martin Joy. I'd thought he liked me, but clearly I had misread the situation.

I took my lip gloss out of my handbag and applied it carefully in the mirror. The overhead lights made me look paler than usual and I raised my hand to touch my cheek.

*You can do this,* I told myself as I prepared myself to go back into the restaurant. Keep your dignity.

Martin was paying the bill when I got back and Sophie was slipping on her coat.

'The gatecrashers are going,' she smiled.

'We'll see you out,' said Martin.

I stood awkwardly on the pavement as we said our good-byes. When Sophie and Alex disappeared into a taxi, I pulled my coat further around my body, ready to start walking home.

'That was great,' I said tightly. 'They're really good fun.'

'I'm still sorry,' he said, shuffling from one foot to the other.

I felt my shoulders relax.

'Alex called me in Switzerland. He was feeling jumpy about my divorce and was talking about getting his own legal representation. When I mentioned I was seeing you, he asked if they could come along. I didn't think they'd stay for three courses.'

I shrugged and smiled. I didn't want to make myself vulner-able and suggest what we do next.

'The night's still young,' he said, gazing at me from under his dark lashes.

My heart gave a little leap, although I tried to stay cool.

'What did you have in mind?' I shrugged.

'Don't you live around here?' he said, taking a step closer.

'Just down there, if you want to walk me home,' I said.

As he threaded his arm through mine, my whole body relaxed.

'Was that true?' I said after a moment. 'The story about Sophie fixing you and Alex up.'

'She organized the trip, allocated the rooms, so I guess so. I owe Sophie a lot. She even sorted out a bursary for me to go to New York. I wouldn't have been able to afford it other-wise.'

I looked at him in surprise. He'd hinted that we had similar backgrounds, but I'd assumed it was just talk.

'My parents died when I was five. I was brought up by my grandparents. They valued education, did everything they could to support me through school, university. But there wasn't much money to go round.'

He looked straight ahead as if he didn't want to talk about it any more.

'So tell me about Switzerland,' I said as we walked, enjoying his heat through the sleeve of my coat.

'We were in Verbier.'

I vaguely remembered Tom Briscoe mentioning Verbier once in chambers; it sounded like a Sloaney hotbed of black-runs and après-ski and I couldn't help but think of Martin with a bevy of blonde chalet girls in some outdoor Jacuzzi. After all, I didn't like the use of the word *we*.

'I had some meetings in Geneva first, but I managed a couple of days on the slopes. It was good to get away from all this.'

'Thanks,' I laughed.

Martin stopped and turned me towards him. 'I didn't mean it like that,' he said, with such intensity it made me tingle.

'So tell me, what've you been up to?'

'Working. Writing.' I shrugged.

'A female John Grisham, eh?'

'Not exactly.' I smiled. 'A paper: "External relocation mediation involving non-Hague convention countries".'

'Perfect sun-lounger reading,' he laughed.

'I know, I know.' I held up my hands, 'It's for my silk application. It looks better if you've had something published.'

'I think you can do anything if you put your mind to it. In fact I'm sure you can. Perhaps I can read it later.'

There was heat in his words. I liked the assumption that he would not just be walking me to my door. And yet, the mention of the silk application had slipped in a sliver of doubt, a thin, distant voice reminding me he was a client. So I slowed my pace, tried to keep the conversation on neutral ground.

'I wanted to be a writer,' I said. 'When I was younger, when our house felt too small, I'd take myself off to the local library and lose myself there. I've always loved words, the way they can make you laugh or cry, hurt you, help you – the way they can transport you somewhere entirely different. I've always thought that words held magic.'

I glanced up and he was looking at me as if I was the most interesting person in the world.

'So what made you do law?'

I shrugged. 'I grew up in a terraced house in Accrington, went to a failing comp. No one I knew was particularly successful, let alone someone who could make a living being a writer. Instead I saw crime, and broken marriages and home repossessions and I realized that the only people who seemed to benefit were the lawyers. Win or lose, the lawyers always won.'

'So now you use words to win and make money.'

'I suppose so, yes. Does that sound selfish?'

Martin laughed. 'You're asking the wrong guy. I have "capitalist" tattooed across my chest.'

He looked at me, serious now. 'But making money's easy. I'm in awe of people like you who can find a tiny chink in the other guy's armour to win a battle. I'm not sure I'd be mentally agile enough.'

'I doubt that,' I said.

I didn't want to mention that I'd read almost everything I could get my hands on about Martin Joy. The general consensus in the dry trade papers that I had trawled was that he was a genius, one of the smartest financial minds of his generation. I loved the fact that he was so modest.

As we walked, we traded secrets about our lives. We discussed the box-sets we both wanted to watch but were too busy for, disclosed our favourite corners of the city – Postman's

64

Park in the City, the Roosevelt and Churchill bronze on Bond Street, the Bleeding Heart restaurant in Clerkenwell for its excellent red wine. I liked how easy it was to talk to him. I liked how much we had in common. He had once lived in Islington, just streets away from me in Highbury Fields, and although he had left for Spitalfields before I had even arrived, it gave me a secret thrill that our lives had once shared the same routine and rhythm.

'Come on,' I said, taking his hand and leading him down a side street, 'I'm this way.'

He squeezed my fingers tighter and I lost all sense of everything going on around me, shrink-wrapped in our own little bubble.

For a moment I was reminded of my younger self, on the odd occasions I had met someone new and exciting. I was no different from the other young people looking for sex, love, leaving pubs and clubs with a boy, girl, suggesting dive bars or parties, wanting to stretch the night out longer, not wanting the spell to break.

But tonight I was very much an adult. Tonight we were heading straight home, and we both knew how the night would end.

'Donna wants to meet me,' said Martin suddenly. 'Tuesday.'

My heart sank again, and I realized, right then, how much I liked this man. I didn't want to feel needy, but I did – and it was Martin I needed.

'Does she want to apologize for missing the First Directions?' I said, glancing across.

'I think she just wants to talk.'

'Are you asking my opinion, or have you made up your mind to go?'

'What do you think?'

My heart was beating fast now. I could feel the sword of

Damocles hanging over me in the dark sky, like the black clouds that sometimes descended.

'I think you should go,' I said, knowing there was no other way to respond.

'I thought so too,' he said, gripping my hand tighter. 'You said it's better to try and stay out of the courts, right? It's best to try and settle.'

'Talk, yes, but don't agree to anything.'

'It's only a conversation, Fran. I want to hear what she has to say. Without the lawyers around us. I just want to know what she's thinking . . .'

He said it with a smile, but it felt like a reprimand. *Without the lawyers around us.* Without me.

'How did it end, Martin?' I asked, the words out of my mouth before I could stop them. 'I mean, what actually happened?'

He looked at me, clearly weighing up whether it would be a good idea to tell me.

'I went to Hong Kong,' he said finally. 'Business. I came back two days early and Donna wasn't there. She'd just disappeared. That's why I wasn't surprised when she vanished this time. It's Donna's modus operandi. I finally tracked her down in New York, courtesy of the $47,000 credit-card bill. Hadn't thought to tell me. She never thought about me. I wasn't a person, a partner. I was just the provider,' he said, his tone hard.

'And you resented that?'

He shook his head. 'Not then. By that time, I just didn't miss her. I remember sitting in the house, in the dark, listening to the silence, and thinking how good it felt to be on my own, thinking *this is how I want it to be*.'

'I'm on a date with a hermit,' I laughed nervously.

He stopped, looked at me. 'I'm just someone that wanted

66

to get out of a marriage that had long passed its sell-by date. When she got back from New York, I told her I wanted a divorce.'

'But she filed first,' I noted. I knew the case file backwards. Knew that she had filed the divorce petition first.

'She made sure she did that,' he replied as if he was silently cursing himself for being slow off the mark.

'And here we are,' I said.

'And here we are,' he repeated.

The number 19 bus, my bus, stopped a few feet ahead of us, a flash of red, like a warning sign. A handful of people got off, buttoning their coats against the cold, and it hit me with a jolt that I recognized one of them. Pete.

*Shit.*

Instinctively, I let go of Martin's hand.

'Hello.' Pete looked at Martin and then me.

'Hi, Pete,' I said politely, trying not to think of the last time I had seen him, when his lips had brushed against my neck. 'Been out?'

'Just popped to Ottolenghi.'

'Popped, eh?' he repeated, looking at Martin quizzically.

'Oh, Martin – this is Pete Carroll, my neighbour.'

'Martin Joy,' he said, extending his hand. Pete kept his hand firmly in the warmth of his pocket.

'Pete's at Imperial. Doing a PhD,' I said, trying to break the awkward mood.

'Impressive,' said Martin. 'What in?'

'Machine Intelligence.'

'Oh, I work in fin-tech. We should talk when you finish.'

Martin hesitated for a moment. I thought he was going to produce a business card and was relieved when he didn't. Perhaps Pete would forget his name, although I knew deep down I was fooling myself.

'Well, I need some milk,' said Pete, turning towards our local shop.

'See you in the week,' I said, as casually as I could.

'I think he likes you,' whispered Martin, as Pete disappeared inside.

'Are you jealous?'

'A little. Because I like you too.'

We were at my front door now. I knew this was my chance to tell him how I was feeling about Donna. That I was jealous and upset about them meeting. But we were on my front doorstep, close, so close, and I didn't want to do anything that could jeopardize the evening, and I knew that meant keeping quiet.

'I had a good night,' I said finally.

'It's not over yet,' he smiled, pushing the door as I turned the key.

# Chapter 8

I go way back with Clare Everett. Back to the day when I'd travelled down from Accrington to Birmingham with my lifetime's possessions straining in a fifty-litre rucksack I'd bought from Millets in Manchester.

She had been assigned the room next to me in our hall of residence, and was unlike anyone I had ever met before; a Home Counties beauty who owned a horse and car, and had been to boarding school. Ours should have been a fleeting friendship, one of geography and convenience, that evaporated as soon as we located people in our halls, on our course, with whom we had more in common. She was a bit pony-club in those days, but I like to think I helped to make her cool. By Christmas she had swapped her Next dresses for jeans and Doc Martens. For her part, Clare helped me to fit in with the middle classes. Despite our differences, our unlikeliest of starts, we grew close and remained that way, even after she married her university sweetheart Dominic ten years ago.

Clare settled back into her bar stool in the Ham Yard hotel bar and picked at a tray of wasabi nuts. I didn't usually come to places like this and although I was wearing a new dress that sucked me in in all the right places, I didn't feel as if I belonged here. Clare, on the other hand, hadn't lost her show-pony polish and fitted into this sophisticated scene like a slim hand slipping on an elegant leather glove. In fact, tonight, I thought she looked like a Hitchcock Blonde. Too much like a Hitchcock Blonde, suddenly nervous about where we were going and who we were meeting.

'I'm starving. We should have gone for something to eat. Do you think there's still time?' she said, twisting her mid-length hair over one shoulder.

'Party starts at seven thirty and it's twenty past,' I said, eager to go.

'So tell me more about this party we're going to.'

'Some launch of an exhibition.'

I took the tickets Martin had given me out of my handbag and handed them to her.

'Art,' she said, glancing back at me archly. 'Have you started collecting?'

'As if. I was given some tickets, that's all.'

'Delauney Gallery,' she read down the bridge of her nose as if she were developing short-sightedness. 'Helen North. I haven't heard of her. Although she must be good to have landed a show at the Delauney.'

She glanced over at me playfully.

'At least there ought to be some interesting men there. Collecting art is the new golf, someone was telling me the other day.'

'I thought cycling was the new golf.'

Clare laughed. 'Whatever. I'm just glad you're getting out a bit more. By the way, I hope you're still coming to the opening of Dom's restaurant. I'm rounding up all the single men we know for your benefit.'

I finished my drink and looked at her. Clare was the one

person I could tell anything to. She knew all my stories, my dark corners. Not just because she was my friend, but because it was her job as a psychologist.

'As a matter of fact, that's why I wanted you to come out tonight,' I said tentatively.

'You're not coming?'

'Of course I'm coming to Dom's launch. I meant tonight. I wanted to introduce you to someone.'

Clare stroked her ponytail. 'I'm a happily married woman, darling.'

'Me,' I ventured carefully. 'I've met someone. And he's going to be there later.'

My friend perked up instantly. I knew how it worked with the happily marrieds. They relied on their single friends for gossip and salacious tales of life in the field, if only to remind themselves how grateful they were to be not still searching for 'the one'. I was consistently a disappointment on that score, being the sort to keep my private life to myself, but now I was offering something.

'Fuck,' she said after a moment.

'It's not that shocking,' I smiled as I finished my mocktail.

She fixed me with her most questioning psychotherapist stare.

'So who is he?'

'His name is Martin,' I said vaguely.

'Good solid name. Where did you meet? How long have you been seeing him? What does he do?'

'I hate that,' I winced, waving my hand. 'It's shorthand for "what are his prospects?"'

'Too right. I'm vetting him. He has to be good enough for my best friend. I assume that's why you want me to meet him.'

'I've been seeing him for about six weeks. He works in finance,' I said, ignoring the question of where we met.

71

'Oh, Fran. Not a banker,' she sighed, her shoulders slumping. 'And it was all sounding so promising.'

I couldn't tell if she was joking or not, but I decided that the best way to proceed was with a lightness of touch.

'Banker-bashing is so predictable.'

'It has nothing to do with the amount of money he makes. Bankers share quite a lot of traits with psychopaths,' she said, crossing her legs. 'Lack of empathy, huge ego, often quite charming. You'll find the highest levels of psychopathy in bankers, CEOs and psychiatrists.'

'You're saying my new boyfriend is a psycho,' I said, trying to laugh.

'I'm saying, be careful with the rich alpha male.'

'Anyway, he's more of a businessman, than a banker. He's got some sort of fund that predicts the market.'

She started to laugh. 'So he's the CEO of a finance company. Double Whammy.'

I wasn't going to let her get away with it.

'You say I have a problem, avoiding relationships because of my job, but you're just as bad. You psychoanalyse people and make a judgement before they even have a chance to prove you wrong.'

'Or right.' She smiled. 'Anyway, you've only got yourself to blame.'

'Me?' I frowned as I picked up my bag.

'You were the reason I became a shrink,' said Clare, and we got up and left the bar.

# Chapter 9

The gallery was an intimidating strip of a building in Mayfair. Wide plate-glass windows shone silvery white light on to a line of expensive-looking cars outside. The crowd queuing up to get in looked po-faced. But I was glad to arrive.

Clare had asked far too many questions about Martin on the way there. I didn't want to divulge anything about his circumstances, particularly how we met, and I wanted to keep the good stuff private – the weekends we had spent in bed, watching box-sets and eating takeaways, or our Sunday-afternoon drive to Lulworth Cove, where we sat on the cliffs and watched the colours of the tide shift from emerald to peacock blue. And I didn't want to tell her how upset I had been the night Martin had gone to meet Donna to 'talk' about the divorce. How I'd gone to the gym after work that evening, driven myself to my physical limit, pushing weights, running hard until sweat dripped from every pore of my body, hoping to take my mind off the fact they were meeting up. How it hadn't stopped me calling him – calling him three times, even though each attempt went straight to voicemail, or how I went home and drank two bottles of wine and woke up the

J.L. Butler

next morning to find vomit in the toilet basin. I didn't tell her, because although I knew I was falling in love with Martin Joy, I didn't love the way he sometimes made me feel. Helpless, adrift and out of control with my emotions, the person I used to be, another lifetime ago.

'So is he here?' she whispered, as we each accepted a flute of champagne from the waitress. We'd been waved past the velvet rope and found ourselves in a parallel world where elegant people in towering heels and loafers dropped a year's salary on some remedial daubings they declared 'amusing'. The artist *du jour* was Helen North, a painter who printed huge monochrome photos of naked elderly people, then covered those images with thick slashes of black and white paint. I found them depressing, but then I wasn't here for the art.

Looking past the designer dresses and Savile Row blazers, I didn't recognize anyone, let alone Martin. But I wasn't looking for him, I was looking for Donna, terrified that she would walk in, larger than life and twice as glamorous. The art world, after all, was Donna's territory. Even if she hadn't heard that Martin had been invited – along with a mystery plus one – there was a strong chance that a juicy opening night like this would bring her out from whatever rock she'd crawled under. I cursed myself. I'd promised myself I wouldn't sink to hating Donna, however tempting it was. As a family lawyer, you only got to see one side of a relationship. As a girlfriend, even more so. I wanted to see Donna as uncaring and selfish and malicious, but it was never that simple, was it? However happy Martin made me, he couldn't be entirely blameless: which of us were?

Perhaps reading my mood, Clare touched my arm.

'Are you OK?'

'Yes, fine. Just a little nervous about you meeting Martin, I suppose.'

'You really like him, don't you?'

74

'He's nice,' I said with contrived breeziness.

'Then why do you want me here, playing gooseberry?'

I looked at her.

'Because you're my best friend and it's important to me that you like him too.'

Clare nodded. 'OK, but do tell me when to scarper. I assume you're going home with him.'

'You don't mind, do you?'

'I'm good – provided you have a clean pair of undies and a toothbrush in your handbag.'

'I've got a toothbrush at his place.'

She raised an eyebrow. 'Not quite a ring on your finger, but it's a start.'

'Well, considering he's still technically married, I'd say so.' I forced myself to watch Clare's reaction. Not shocked or disapproving, just confused.

'He's married?'

'Separated. Six months ago.'

'At least he's not a client,' she replied with an arched brow. I smiled nervously.

'Actually . . .' I began, but a blonde whirlwind swept up, arm outstretched.

'Fran! How are you?' Sophie Cole pulled me into a hug, air-kissing both sides, like a long-lost sister. 'I didn't know you'd be here!' she exclaimed. 'I was worried the whole night was going to be deadly dull.'

She looked at Alex, who arrived at her side, for confirmation. He gave only a short nod of assent, but at least he was smiling.

'Oh, this is Clare, my friend,' I said, snapping into formal mode. 'Clare – Sophie and Alex Cole. They're Martin's business partners.'

'More like his agony aunt, in my case,' said Sophie, shaking Clare's hand. 'So what do you think of the art, Clare?'

I waited to hear her response. Clare was much better at judging these things than I was. 'Interesting,' she said. 'I like the way she uses light and shade.'

Sophie paused, then laughed. 'No, I can't stand them either!' She leant in to whisper: 'But Helen's a good friend of Martin's, so don't repeat that in front of him.'

I looked at her in alarm. I didn't like the sound of 'good friend'.

'Are you a lawyer too?' said Sophie, looking at Clare.

'Psychotherapist,' said Clare.

'Sophie's dream friend. All she likes to do is talk about herself,' chided Alex.

She swatted his arm. 'You'll have to excuse my husband, he's an idiot.'

'She's the co-owner of a restaurant as well, aren't you, Clare.'

I couldn't resist getting in a plug for Dom's new restaurant. Sophie and Alex were the sort who ate out every night and, besides, I liked the thought of our friendship groups inter-twining.

'Hardly co-owner. It's my husband's. Launches next month.'

'Darling, you're friends with a divorce lawyer. Speak to her and then tell me you don't want your name above the door, however much of a sleeping partner you might be.'

'Believe me, I don't want to get involved,' laughed Clare. 'If I tell my husband I want more involvement, he'll have me making choux pastry swans before I know it. And I hate cooking. I can't even make fairy cakes.'

'Well, remind me to introduce you to my friend at *The Times*. Food critic. Maybe we can all go down for dinner and he can write something.'

'That would be amazing. Thank you,' said Clare. 'Perhaps you could come to the launch?'

'We should go and say hi to Helen,' said Alex diplomatically.

'So long as I don't have to tell her how much I love her work,' Sophie said, rolling her eyes at me. 'Excuse us, Franny – lovely meeting you, Clare.'

Clare raised her eyebrows when they had gone. '*Franny?*'

'Term of endearment.' I smiled, noting her disapproval.

'Well, it had better not stick.'

'It was good of her to say she'd introduce you to *The Times* critic,' I said. Suddenly it seemed important to get Clare's approval for my new friends.

'If it happens,' said Clare, taking another glass of champagne.

'He's here,' I said, my words trailing off as I looked across the crowd.

As Martin entered the room, my heart juddered with anticipation, excitement and anxiety. He hadn't seen us, he was too busy shaking hands and slapping backs, a handsome charismatic centre of attention in a dark suit, moving like a jungle cat, at ease but powerful. I glanced at Clare, watching her watching him, and it was obvious his magic was already working on her – and I felt smug in the knowledge that I was the one who would be going home with him.

'He's sexy,' she said, not taking her eyes off him. I couldn't help feel disappointment, but what did I expect her to say? *He's fascinating, he's brilliant, he's damn-near perfect?*

Clare didn't know Martin, hadn't met him, how could she see him as I did? And did friends ever really approve of partners? I didn't much like her husband Dom, that was true. Perhaps Clare, with her shrink's hat on, could explain it to me, but for some reason it was deeply important that the two people I was closest to should get along, impossible though that seemed.

Finally Martin saw me and I felt a crackle in the air as our eyes met. Murmuring something to the woman he was talking to, he made a beeline for us.

'Francine, you came,' he said, kissing me on the cheek. 'And you must be Clare. I've heard a great deal about you.'

I thought he would turn the full force of his laser-beam charisma on her, but instead he gave a shy smile. 'Sorry I wasn't here when you arrived. I hope you weren't too bored.'

I noticed Martin kept his eyes on Clare as he said it, paying attention to her, deferring to her. He knew the charm playbook inside out, but then I was sure Clare knew exactly what he was doing: tics, tells, all of those little manipulations people used to deceive were a psychiatrist's bread and butter. It was like watching two grand masters try to out-think each other.

'Martin's one of the sponsors of tonight's event,' I said nervously.

'And a friend of the artist,' added Clare.

'More like client of the artist.' He shrugged. 'I can't lie, it's a business move,' said Martin with the ghost of a smile. 'High-level contacts are vital to the Gassler Partnership, and I don't think you'll find a greater concentration of wealthy individuals than at an art gallery opening. Especially when the artist is as hot as Helen North.'

'I do actually like her stuff,' said Clare.

'You do?'

'Really. I wasn't joking when I said about the light and shade. I'm all about the light and shade.'

Martin laughed. 'Me too,' he said, taking Clare by the arm. 'Come on, I'll introduce you.'

As he led her away, Clare turned and grinned, giving me a discreet thumbs-up. She was a tough nut to crack at the best of times and had always been suspicious of my boyfriends, so to get her approval was everything. I let out a long breath and took a swallow of my champagne: it was already making me fuzzy.

'I think you're good for him.'

I turned. Alex was watching Martin work his way around the room.

'Well, I am a very good barrister,' I said.

He twisted his mouth. 'You know what I mean, Fran. I'm his friend, not the Bar Council,' he said, his expression softening into a smile.

I'd wondered how much Alex had worked out at our dinner at Ottolenghi. Whether he had guessed that I was Martin's lover as well as his lawyer.

'Besides, you're two consenting adults and he's my business partner. We've built something good together. I don't want it destroyed because of that woman.'

'Well, I don't think it will come to that.'

He nodded, but I don't think he was really listening.

'After Donna, before you, he was drinking Jack Daniels for breakfast. Whatever you're doing, keep doing it, because he's in a better place now than he was three months ago, and I think that difference is you.'

I was stunned to silence. On the one hand, it was what I longed to hear – confirmation of Martin's feelings for me. But Alex's words also unsettled me. I had worked long enough as a divorce lawyer to know that toxic relationships brought a lot of emotions to the surface, not all of them positive. Jack Daniels for breakfast suggested a different version of events to the one Martin had given me about the breakdown of his marriage.

I could see him through the crowd and felt an unsettling prickle of envy at how good he looked standing next to Clare. I was about to look away but our eyes met and he smiled, and it was so intimate and reassuring that I felt a little bit lighter.

I almost didn't notice Tom Briscoe. At first he blended in so well with the smart surroundings that I didn't recognize him, but then there he was, helping a Sloaney blonde out of her coat. I felt bound to the spot, until a voice in my head told me to get out of there. This wasn't like bumping into my neighbour Pete by the bus stop near our flat. This was Tom, my colleague. He couldn't see me with Martin; it would take an analytical mind like Tom's half a nanosecond to put two and two together.

'I'm just going to the cloakroom,' I said to Alex as I made my excuses and crossed the gallery.

Clare was deep in conversation with Sophie Cole. Mouthing 'sorry' to Sophie, I pulled Clare to one side.

'I have to go,' I said quickly, glancing at my watch.

'But we've only just got here,' she said with obvious disappointment. 'Sophie was just telling me who else she knows in the food world. She reckons she can get Giles Coren along to the opening of Dom's restaurant.'

'I'll make sure she does, but I really do need to go.'

I pulled out my phone and texted Martin:

Colleague here from chambers. Got to leave.

'Sure you don't want to stay for the dessert canapés?' pressed Clare. 'I just saw some mini éclairs and strawberry tarts doing the rounds.'

She frowned, then followed my gaze towards Martin.

'Ah, I see,' she said, lowering her voice. 'I'm not surprised you want to shoot off for a shag.'

'For an educated woman, you can be very crude,' I said, struggling to sound light-hearted. My mobile phone beeped in my hand. Martin.

I'll come with you. Just let me say my goodbyes.

I glanced around the room but I had lost sight of Tom. Wherever he was, it gave me the opportunity to collect my things from the cloakroom. I handed over my ticket and waited impatiently as the coat-check girl gossiped with her friend, moving at a glacial pace. Come on, come on. My head was beginning to whirl. My throat tightened and I longed for a breath of fresh air.

'Fran?'

Feeling a tap on my shoulder, I closed my eyes in defeat. Of course he'd seen me. *Of course.*

'Tom!' I said, turning and forcing surprise into my voice. 'What are you doing here?'

'Don't sound so surprised – I have an appreciation for the arts,' he smiled. He was wearing a sharp navy suit with one of those stripy old-school ties you're supposed to be able to decipher but I never can. Tom gestured to the girl next to him, the same blonde I'd seen him with earlier.

'Fran, this is Hannah. Francine is my colleague from chambers.'

'Nice to meet you,' I said, extending a hand. 'Unfortunately, I'm just leaving.'

I saw Hannah shoot a look at Tom, the kind that said, I *told* you we'd be late. Any other time I'd be interested in that nugget of information and what it told me about Tom's relationship, but I was far too distracted and focused on escape.

'Sorry to be a bore, shooting off,' I said, looking over Hannah's shoulder, convinced I'd see Martin bearing down on us. 'You must go and speak to the artist, she's fascinating.'

'Surely you can stay for one drink,' said Tom. 'It is Friday night, after all.'

'No rest for the wicked,' I said with a thin smile as I was finally handed my coat and made a bolt for the door.

Clare was standing on the pavement, watching me.

'Are you OK?' she asked.

'Course I am,' I said, inhaling the cold spring air.

Clare didn't seem to buy it. 'Then why the sudden need to leave?'

I couldn't tell her, couldn't let on what had spooked me.

And now I was out of the stifling, crowded gallery, it didn't seem so desperate. Would Tom know Martin was my client? Possibly not. I certainly had no idea who *he* was representing. Would he have asked how I came to be invited? Unlikely, Tom was far too well brought up to ask such a loaded question. But it was possible. And that was far too much of a risk.

'Do you want me to wait with you until Martin comes?' asked Clare, her eyes searching mine.

'No, don't be daft. You go,' I said, pointing to the cab which had just pulled up at the kerb. 'He'll be out in a minute.'

'I'm happy for you, Fran,' said Clare, giving me a kiss on the cheek. 'Now just let yourself be happy, OK? You *do* deserve it.'

For a moment we were both lost in the past. Knowing how much she had done for me, I gave her a grateful nod.

'Thanks,' I said simply. 'I'll try.'

But as her cab pulled away, I looked back towards the gallery, back towards him – and wondered if that would be enough.

# Chapter 10

I loitered in Hanover Square until Martin directed me to a waiting car. We didn't speak much on the journey back to Spitalfields.

'I didn't drag you away too soon, did I?' I said as we rode the lift to his apartment.

'I just had to show my face. It'll be over soon anyway.'

'I need a drink,' I replied, feeling tired and unsettled.

'There's a very nice Friday-night Chardonnay in the fridge that needs opening. We can take it up to the roof,' he said, disappearing into the bedroom and returning with two sweaters.

He threw one over to me.

'There. You might want to put that on.'

I pulled the sweater over my head, slowly, carefully, inhaling it and feeling heady with his smell. The sleeves fell over my hands and I felt as if I had been zipped inside him.

When I looked up, he was holding a bottle of wine, two tumblers and a blanket. We went outside to the small decking area and up a thin spiral staircase that led to the highest point of the building. I spread the throw on the dusty asphalt and sat down. It was quiet up here. Black velvet sky surrounded us like a cloak. I could see chimney pots and distant lights from office blocks. I smiled to myself that there were people out there who worked harder than I did. I wanted to tell them to get a life.

Martin sat cross-legged next to me, poured wine into the two glasses and handed me one.

'I would have stayed longer but I saw someone from chambers,' I said finally.

'I don't see why we have to keep sneaking around the shadows. Alex knows. Worked it out even before we went to Ottolenghi. Said I'd been whispering and giggling like a schoolboy in the office, which made me sound incredibly uncool. I don't want to hide you away,' he said with an intensity that made me shiver.

'I don't want to hide you away either,' I replied. 'That's why I brought Clare – I wanted you to start meeting my friends. But you're still my client and I'm applying for silk. I have to be careful.'

He tipped his head back for a long slug of Chardonnay.

'I just can't wait for all this to be over.'

'Over?'

'The divorce.'

The view was quite spectacular. I felt as if I was on top of the world, empowered, ennobled. Alex's observation that Martin had been a wreck after the breakdown of his marriage suddenly seemed immaterial, replaced by a clear and romantic sense that everything was exactly as it should be.

'Why aren't you married?'

I laughed but he just looked at me, waiting for an answer.

'I've never been good at relationships.'

'I'd say we're doing pretty well so far.'

I felt as if we were both stripped naked, as if I could tell him anything. I took a breath before I spoke again.

'When I was nineteen I was diagnosed with bipolar disorder. Manic depression,' I added, to clarify.

'The scars on your arms . . . I never wanted to ask.'

'Self-harm, not a suicide bid. They're old,' I said, rubbing my hand self-consciously. 'Second year at university. It was a difficult time. I almost dropped out of college but I got through it, thanks to Clare, my tutors and good medication. It's under control, but I find relationships difficult.'

'Why?'

'It's just easier to stay single.'

'Is it?'

I shrugged, fixing my gaze on a distant red neon sign.

'I've always wanted to keep my life as uncomplicated as possible, control things as much as I can. When you've had quite literal ups and downs, you just want things to be predictable.'

'Everyone needs someone, Fran. Deserves someone.'

'But letting people in brings problems. We find it difficult enough to control our own emotions, let alone other people's. I like you, you like me, but what happens when Donna wants to talk again or says she wants to give your marriage another go?' I said, thinking back to the night when he went to meet her, when I called him up, longing to hear his voice and his reassurance, and was met with nothing but a cold and sterile recorded message.

'That's not going to happen,' he said finally.

'It might.'

'Come here,' he murmured, inching towards me on the roof. He pulled me close then shifted his position so that he was facing me. He stroked my hair and held my head between his hands.

'We just have to hang in there and soon, really soon, it's going to be this. Just us. No Donna, no sneaking around, just me and you.'

'Do you promise?' I wanted to stay up here, almost touching the clouds, forever.

'I promise,' he whispered, and I shivered as he kissed me, knowing how completely I had fallen for him and how much that could damage me.

# Chapter 11

'Have a good night on Friday?'

I was filling the kettle in the small chambers kitchen when I turned and saw Tom standing in the doorframe.

'Yes, thanks. It was fun,' I replied, busying myself with lids and plugs so I wouldn't have to look at him. *Please leave,* I said in my head, hoping it would work like a spell, but my magic was weak because Tom leant against the counter. Clearly he was in the mood to chat.

'Hannah wanted to know where your dress was from.'

I froze, wondering if this was his way of saying that I was very dressed up at the gallery. Men didn't usually notice those sorts of things, but then Tom Briscoe was the kind of man who didn't generally miss anything, especially if he could use it to his advantage.

'Hannah seemed nice,' I said, dropping a teabag into my cup. 'I didn't know you had a girlfriend.'

'I don't,' he shrugged.

'Does Hannah know that?' I asked, sliding the box of Twinings English Breakfast Tea towards him.

He stood in silence as we listened to the kettle bubble and finally click off.

'So why were you there on Friday?' he said. 'Was it a date?'

So it wasn't just a casual chat, Tom had smelt something in the air at the gallery.

I shook my head.

'You really can't believe I have anything resembling a glittering social life, can you?'

'I'm sure you do on the quiet,' he said. 'All I meant was, that was a bloody hot ticket. Hugh Grant turned up after you'd gone.'

'Should have stuck around then, shouldn't I? Shame I'm so dedicated to my job.'

'That's why you left?' he said with disbelief. 'To go home and work?'

'If you had my dedication, Tom,' I said, filling my mug with hot water, 'you might get on in your career. Instead, you're hobnobbing with film stars and not having a girlfriend.'

'Hannah? Well, Hannah's . . . she's a friend,' said Tom defensively. I waggled a spoon at him.

'Exactly what every woman wants to hear.'

'It's a complicated relationship.'

I nodded. 'Yeah, well, aren't they all?'

'Ah, so it *was* a date,' he said with a teasing smile.

'Nope. But it's nice you're spending so much time thinking about *my* love life. Hannah will be pleased.'

I took my mug and backed out of the kitchen, waving. He gave me a sarcastic smile, but there was still something in his face. A curiosity, a hint that he knew – or at the very least suspected – something. It scared me more than it should have.

Brooding on what Tom might or might not know put me in a terrible mood. Outside, the sky echoed my mindset: dark clouds that looked like they could burst at any moment. Even so, I decided to go the long way round to get to my next appointment. The route took me past the river and the view of the silvery Thames always soothed me.

It was an unremarkable café. A chalkboard sign outside advertised tea and bacon sandwiches, there was an unappetizing selection of factory-made cakes in the display cabinet, the smell of old cooking fat was so strong it seemed to have soaked into the walls. Few barristers came here – and that was precisely why Phil Robertson liked it.

He was waiting for me at the back of the room when I arrived.

'You're late.'

'So sue me,' I grinned, glad to see him.

I'd known Phil for years. He was smart and funny, a former men's magazine journalist who had been made redundant and used his research skills to reposition his career. These days he called himself an enquiry consultant, but really he was a snoop, a private investigator who did our dirty work. It wasn't something our profession talked about much, especially after the press got into all sorts of trouble for doing it, although they went too far and broke the rules. But the truth was, the law needed people like Phil Robertson. Barristers are wordsmiths and nit-pickers, but to win, we need information, ammunition. We need missiles to throw at the other side. And it's all done in the client's best interest.

I ordered a black coffee and watched Phil tuck into a muffin.

'So what have you got for me?'

'She has a nice life, this one, doesn't she,' he said, wiping brown crumbs from his chin. 'Posh lunches, nights out, shopping sprees . . . Remind me to marry well in my next life,' he said, as I leaned forward, eager to know more about Donna Joy.

The waitress put a mug in front of me and I took a sip of the thick, black liquid.

'It's the nights out we want to know about.'

'You mean, is she seeing anyone?'

I curled my fingers around the mug and looked at him expectantly.

'I think she is,' said Phil finally.

A shot of energy surged through me and I knew it wasn't the coffee.

'Donna's seeing someone?' I asked, feeling the euphoria build.

Phil nodded.

'Who?'

'Not sure.'

'Phil, come on. What am I paying you for?'

He peered down his nose at me. 'Here's the rub. I think it might be the husband.'

Although I was sitting, it was as if I was suddenly falling, down, down through a trapdoor that had opened and sucked me into a dark and bottomless void.

'Look, I know it's not what you want to hear . . .'

The truth of his words almost made me laugh.

I tried to compose myself but I felt weak and dazed.

'Are you sure? Martin Joy left his wife. He's the one who wants a divorce. From my reading of the situation, he has a pretty low opinion of her . . .'

The words were coming out of my mouth as quickly as I could think them.

Phil finished his muffin and rolled the paper case up into a ball.

'Look, I've asked around and tracked her – which, believe me, wasn't easy.'

'Why not?' I asked, as coolly as I could.

'Lots of parties I couldn't get into. Trips overseas – one via Heathrow on March twelfth and a Eurostar journey last weekend. I couldn't get through the gates on both occasions to see where she went. I did text David Gilbert for authorization for overseas expenses but he said not to bother.'

'And you think these were mini-breaks? With her husband.'

'I don't know who she was with. All I can be certain of is that she travelled to the airport and King's Cross on her own. And there were three or four other occasions when she didn't return home. That made me think she was seeing someone. Then I saw her meet a man for dinner and they went back to the house in Chelsea.' He opened a document wallet that was on the table and took out a photo.

'There they are, Donna and Martin Joy.'

I forced myself to look. It was a black-and-white image that reminded me of a Robert Doisneau photograph. Donna was laughing, her long hair whipping around her face in the wind; Martin's profile was handsome and strong. There was no denying that they looked beautiful together.

'When was it?' I could feel my lips in a thin, tight line. My throat was dry, a white-hot hatred for Donna Joy had muted me.

Phil indicated the photo. 'Date's on the back.'

I turned it over and saw that it was the Tuesday night when Martin had told me they had gone to talk.

'This doesn't mean much,' I said, trying to reassure myself.

'I know what you want here,' said Phil, holding up his hands. 'Proof that she's seeing another man, that she's got a new, serious relationship that could affect any maintenance payments your client will have to pay. But this isn't it.' He sighed. 'I'm sorry, but if you ask me, these two look as if they're still in love. I bet they don't even want to get divorced.'

He smiled and put the photograph back in the document wallet. And my tepid, black coffee began to make me feel sick.

# Chapter 12

I was one of the first to leave chambers that night, much to the bemusement of Paul, who caught me on the way out. I took the District line to Sloane Square, and got lost in a sea of commuters as we piled out of the station. It was a grey day, the light poor, the dying sunlight blocked by clouds clotted with rain, and on any other occasion, I would have wanted to hurry home to a glass of wine and the central heating turned up full-blast. But I couldn't go home tonight. Not yet. Not after my conversation with Martin.

He'd called a few hours after my meeting with Phil Robertson. Usually I loved hearing the sound of his voice, but that afternoon I could hardly bear to speak to him, not after the things Phil had told me which had jolted me into a reality I did not want to face. That I had allowed myself to be fobbed off by Martin's casual assertions that he was meeting Donna simply to be polite and keep a dialogue open. That I had dismissed Alex Cole's remarks that Martin had been a mess after his marriage had broken down, even though it contradicted his version of events. But before the call had ended, a masochistic and inquisitive impulse had kicked in and I had suggested dinner. I wanted to look him in the eye, like a defendant in the witness box, and see if he could lie to me. Or perhaps I just wanted him to convince me that I had nothing to worry about.

'Supper, tonight after work,' I'd said, and it had been impossible to miss the hesitation, the guilty, pregnant pause before he told me he couldn't, he was busy. 'Something's cropped up. How about tomorrow?'

I knew where Donna Joy worked. It was one of many things I knew about her by this time. Her studio was in a little mews in the warren of streets behind Peter Jones. An arch led to a cobbled courtyard and I peered into the building. The complex was dark, eerie, deserted, like an old, abandoned school.

Through the window of one of the units I could see a middle-aged redhead turn off the only light in the block and lock up.

I turned to leave but she emerged into the courtyard and asked if she could help me.

'Is Donna around?' I asked, picking at the cuticles of my nails.

The woman smiled as she tied a floral scarf around her neck.

'You've missed her by a minute. She just left.'

Thanking her, I hurried back on to the street and peered into the twilight, cursing myself for not getting there earlier. I took a second to plot my next move. Thoughts raced round my head like dodgem cars: stop, start, collide, reverse. But as my gaze fluttered, I caught a glimpse of pink, a wink of colour in the distance, telling me I was not too late. I set off in pursuit, my stride breaking into a jog as I hurried to catch up with her. Donna turned left and I quickened my pace further, until the roar of the King's Road traffic grew louder and louder and I was back in the throng of shoppers and commuters.

The pink coat guided me like a beacon. She crossed the road, but I kept my distance. Specks of rain started to fall and she stopped to look for a taxi. There were none of course. Not at this time, in this weather. So she carried on walking, while I weaved through the crowded pavements, determined not to lose sight of her. Finally she stopped outside a restaurant and went inside. I pulled my hat out of my pocket and put it on. The rain began to fall hard. Donna had avoided the brunt of it of course, but I was caught in the downpour. Not that I really noticed it.

A sense of dread swelled in my stomach as I crossed the road to the restaurant. I pretended to read the menu in the window while I steeled myself, then opened the door and stepped inside. The maître d' was helping a couple with their coats, which gave me a few seconds to peer into the interior. I saw them immediately, sitting at a table at the rear. She had just said something and Martin was laughing as he ordered a bottle of wine. My heart hammering, I slipped out of the restaurant, back into the dark and thunderous street.

There was a bus stop on the other side of the road. I darted through the traffic, my breath ragged, my ears oblivious to the blast of horns as I weaved perilously between the cars. I blended in with the sombre, damp people in the queue, letting one bus pass, then another and another, all the while watching the door of the restaurant while the rain soaked me to the skin.

I woke up fully clothed on the sofa. There was a blanket over my body and I felt stiff, groggy and nauseous. Pulling myself up, I swung my legs on to the floor and put my head in my hands, my fingers peeling slowly away from my eyes as I tried to focus and make sense of why I was there. I looked down and saw a long ladder in my stocking. Congealed blood was stuck to the nylon but I had no idea how I'd cut myself.

I blinked hard and glanced around. It was dark, but not so dark that I couldn't tell that this room, although familiar, was not mine. I rubbed my temples and exhaled, grateful, at least, that I was on the sofa, alone. My handbag was next to me on the rug and I was tempted to take it and let myself out, but I needed to know what had happened.

I stood up, unsteady on my feet as I searched for memories from the night before.

Pete's place was smaller than mine with a similar layout, although his was not a maisonette. I went straight to the kitchen and ran myself a glass of water. I was dehydrated and my hands trembled as I held the glass. My breath quickened in panic as I realized that my lithium levels were too high.

I located his bedroom and peered inside. There was a faint, sour smell of sweat and running shoes, and I could see the curve of his body under the duvet. I felt guilty about waking him, but he stirred as if he was aware of the presence in the room, and pulled himself up on the pillow.

'I'm going,' I whispered after a moment. 'I'm so sorry about this. I must have had too much to drink. I don't remember what happened, but . . . well, I'm sorry.'

The red digits of his clock glowed in the dark. It wasn't even six o'clock. Pete rubbed his eyes and turned on his bedside lamp.

'How are you feeling?' he asked, his voice rough with sleep.

'Shit. Absolutely shit,' I replied, feeling exposed and self-conscious.

I ventured further into the room, aware that he was watching my every step. The cut on my leg was smarting as I moved.

'Pete, why am I here?' I asked finally.

'You don't remember?' he said, sitting up straight.

I shook my head slowly. I couldn't remember anything. Not from about nine or ten o'clock, anyway. I had followed Martin and Donna from the restaurant to a quiet street behind Cheyne Walk, a street that reeked of success and money, and they had disappeared into one of the white, stucco-fronted terraced houses. There was a pub almost opposite and I'd found a seat by the window where I could see the property. I recalled thinking the house looked peaceful and at rest, except I knew that Mr and Mrs Joy were not sleeping. I recalled ordering a double vodka tonic to try and dull the pain of betrayal. After that, I remembered nothing.

'I had a lot to drink,' I said, looking at him, an invitation for him to fill in the gaps as much as he was able, while I perched awkwardly on the end of his bed.

'There was banging on the front door at around two o'clock in the morning. It was some mini-cab driver – you were passed out in the back seat of the car. Not in a great way. Apparently, you collapsed in Chelsea,' he added apologetically.

'I don't remember,' I whispered, feeling my cheeks pool red with shame.

Pete gave a weak, sympathetic shrug. 'Cabbie said someone found you, got you in a taxi. I don't know how they got your address. I'm guessing you told them or they found it in your bag. Wasn't sure I could manage you up the stairs,' he said awkwardly. 'Besides, I was worried about you. You hear all these stories about people vomiting in their sleep and dying and stuff. I thought you might be safer here. I made sure you were propped up. Just in case.'

'Thank you,' I said, my humiliation almost complete.

'The evils of alcohol.'

Neither of us spoke for a few moments. I could hear the rumble of the night bus outside and a lonely tweet of the dawn chorus getting under way.

'Big night?'

'I got drunk. I just got very, very drunk. Alcohol doesn't agree with me.'

'Is everything OK?'

'It will be if you remind me never, ever to drink again.'

'Where were you last night?'

I closed my eyes, my body yearning for sleep.

I'd been crying for a few moments before I realized it.

'Shit. Are you OK?' he said awkwardly. He swung his legs out of the bed and came to sit next to me. He was wearing just a T-shirt and boxer shorts but I was too dazed to take in the intimacy of our situation.

'I'm fine,' I said wiping my eyes with the back of my hand.

'Man trouble?'

I made a soft sound of disapproval.

'Is it that bloke I saw you with the other week? Martin. Martin Joy.'

Looking back, it was strange that he remembered the most fleeting of introductions, but at the time, it didn't register. I was desperate to talk about Martin and Donna, even if it was with my barely dressed neighbour.

'I shouldn't have been too surprised that he turned out to be unreliable.'

'Rich commitmentphobe?'

I shrugged. 'He has a wife. They're separated, but it looks like she's not exactly out of the picture. I saw them together,' I said, puffing out my cheeks and struggling to compose myself.

'And you got totally wasted,' said Pete sympathetically.

'I can't remember how much I drank.'

'We've all been there.'

I gave a quiet, nervous laugh. My hands were still shaking and it alarmed me.

'Are you sure you're OK?'

'My lithium,' I whispered, dipping my head. 'I shouldn't really drink alcohol. Dehydration affects the levels of my medication.'

'You're bipolar?'

I nodded.

'Should I call a doctor?' His young, eager face looked concerned.

'I don't know. No. Look, I should go. Thank you for everything. How much was the taxi?'

'It's all right,' said Pete, looking at me intently.

I needed to be sick. I had to get out of there.

'He's not worth it, Fran,' he said as I got up to leave. His voice was cool and measured and in the darkness it had a quiet and convincing authority.

# Chapter 13

I went to see my doctor a few hours after waking up at Pete's flat. I didn't want to go, but all the signs of toxicity were there, nausea, diarrhoea, tremors. Dr Katz had been treating me for years, although to date it had been little more than a maintenance job. He took my blood, checked my lithium levels and warned me that binge drinking on my dosage of medication was incredibly foolish. We talked about my condition. I explained that I had not had any manic or depressive episodes in a while. I considered my bipolar to be under control although my blackout hinted that it was still hiding in the shadows. Dr Katz confirmed it always would be.

I didn't go back into the office until Thursday, until I physically felt human again. I used the time to finish my QC application form – the closing date was hours away – and I welcomed the distraction. I even phoned my mother and enjoyed her banal chit-chat about the woman in the post office and the price of potatoes in the Co-op, conversation I once found dull and alien, but which now seemed like a comforting fairy tale about a world I wished I could fall back into. The rest of the time, I slept. I slept and I read and dug out a self-help book that had once been useful. *This too shall pass.*

Burgess Court had a library on the first floor. It was one of the things that almost made me weep with joy when I turned up here on my first day of pupillage. There was a view over Temple Gardens from the leaded bay window. Hansard reports and leather-bound books lined the room. For serious study, I went to the Inner Temple library, but this was a place to think and plot and wonder. Usually it was about case law, but today I was on my laptop, scrolling through various medical websites and bipolar forums. Some of it was stuff I had known for years, some of it was impenetrable – extracts from papers scribed by psychiatrists and academics. Most useful were the threads. Real people and their experiences of blackouts. The drug-takers, the army vets, the depressed and the damaged.

I heard the door open. Paul stood there for a moment and closed it behind him. He paused, then turned the key.

'What's this? A lock-in?' I asked, clicking the browser back to Google.

'There's nowhere to properly talk in this place. You can't get two people in your office, there's not a minute's peace in mine.'

I smiled and put my pen down.

'Preparing for tomorrow? The Joy vs Joy FDR.'

I wasn't sure if he had seen the papers on the desk. The valuations for Martin's business, accountancy reports, the Form E's. I had marked up in red the areas where the two parties still disagreed. I was aware that it was going to be a combative day in court, and I knew I had to over-prepare. Today, though, it was easy to be distracted.

'I'm meeting David Gilbert in an hour.'

'Is the client coming?'

'No need. Gilbert saw him yesterday,' I said briskly, glad that I had been able to convince my instructing solicitor that an additional pre-hearing pow-wow was not necessary.

'Do you think you'll settle tomorrow?'

'You mean, do I think it will go all the way to court?'

'Think of the lovely fees,' he said, rubbing his hands together.

'I'd rather not.'

Paul took a seat next to me. He drummed his fingers on the walnut surface then laid his hand out flat.

'Are you all right?' he said finally.

'Of course I am. Why do you ask?'

'I don't know. You just seem a bit . . . different.'

'Just busy,' I said, closing my laptop.

'Did you get your silk application in?'

'In the nick of time.' I smiled.

'Nick of time? That's not like you.'

'Like I say, I've been busy.'

Paul nodded, unconvinced.

'I've set you up an appointment with Liz Squires. She heads up JCI consultants. They've coached dozens of wigs through the silk application process.'

'How much is that going to cost me?'

Neither of us spoke. I could only hear silence and I thought how rare that was in a London office in this day and age.

'You do know, if there's a problem you can come and speak to me?'

'I know that. You don't have to worry about me.'

'Don't I?'

'Paul, what's the problem here?'

'I spoke to Justice Herring today. You were supposed to meet him for lunch on Tuesday.'

Malcolm Herring was supposed to be one of the references for my QC application. A well-respected, and connected, high court judge, a glowing report from him would mean you were halfway to silk. But between the hangover and arranging my appointment with Dr Katz, I had forgotten all about it and stood him up.

I squirmed in my chair.

'I was ill and slept for most of the day. I couldn't call to cancel the meeting.'

'You could have got me to.'

'You were already rearranging my work.'

'By the way, Tom took the Brown vs Brown contact order. He got what you wanted.'

'Of course he did.'

Paul rubbed his chin and looked at me with disappointment.

'As I said, if you need me for anything, just say the word.'

'I know,' I said quietly.

His expression hardened, his soft eyes held a hint of warning.

'We're a family in chambers. I will protect you, no matter what. But you have to tell me everything, because I can only help you if I know the truth.'

I smiled and put my hand gratefully over his, and thought how easy it was to lie.

# Chapter 14

Even I was surprised when Donna Joy did not turn up to the Final Dispute Resolution hearing the following morning. The judge was furious, her legal team speechless, and Martin left the room, his face set in granite, when the hearing was adjourned. This was not like a First Directions that could proceed without both parties present. No-show meant no-go at an FDR. The morning was a write-off, and despite Robert Pascale telling David Gilbert that he was worried about Mrs Joy, everyone was understandably irritated, and the lofty high court setting only added to the drama.

Donna's unreliability and selfishness did not shock me one bit. It only made me hate her more. Part of me wondered how it was possible to be so selfish and cavalier, another part couldn't stop hearing Phil Robertson's words: *I bet you those two don't even want to get divorced*. Something told me she was playing games and I was caught up in the crossfire.

Glancing at my watch, I saw that it was not yet eleven o'clock. The hearing would have taken up most of the day, so I now had yawning hours to fill. Martin was nowhere to be seen and I was glad about that. I'd managed to avoid him all week. He'd left a message on the Tuesday suggesting dinner and I'd sent a text back saying I was in court in Birmingham until Thursday, playing deliberate phone-tag until our last-minute conference before the FDR, where a curt professionalism had seemed the order of the day.

'Quick debrief?' said David briskly.

'I'm not sure there's much to discuss,' I said, tightening my lips. 'Besides, Martin's disappeared.'

'I suppose we'll just get a new date then.'

I nodded. 'Why don't you call me later. At least it seems to have shut Pascale up,' I added; the one bright spot had been watching him grovel to his counsel.

I left court and walked back to chambers. My favourite entrance to Temple is a hole in the wall on Fleet Street. Sometimes I think of it as a magic portal, a time machine that whisks you away from twenty-first-century London hustle and bustle into a timeless and magical place. My pace was brisk as I walked along the footpath, past a legal outfitters, a sombre-looking mews house and the Dr Johnson buildings, my anger and frustration evident in every single step. I was at the church now, which never failed to humble me. Its quiet grandeur, its nine-hundred-year history tied up with the adventures of the Knights Templar. I did not consider myself to be a particularly religious person, but I often went inside and I paused for a moment to consider whether I should go in now and feed off its calmness.

As I stopped, I felt a hand on my shoulder. I gasped and spun around.

'Martin,' I said, my heart pounding.

He touched my sleeve and I flinched.

'Why are you avoiding me?' he asked quietly.

'Avoiding you?' I frowned.

'All week. And in court just now.'

'I'm not. What did you expect me to do? Straddle you in front of the judge?'

'Funny,' he said with a half-smile.

It started to rain. I looked up to the heavens to give me a moment to collect my thoughts.

'I looked for you after the adjournment,' I lied.

'I was angry. I went for a walk.'

'It's about to tip it down,' I said, eager to get away.

'Then come under here,' he said, leading me towards the cloisters, where a pile of desks was stacked up against the wall.

It was cool and dark under the arches, as if there had been a sudden eclipse. The distant hum of Fleet Street traffic fell away to nothing, the temperature seemed to dip by several degrees. The air was so still it almost shimmered.

'I can't believe she didn't show,' I said finally.

'I can. She's probably fucked off to Thailand for a detox. I can guarantee that by Wednesday she'll be back in Chelsea, tanned, ten pounds lighter, raving about some seaweed treat-ment – which, by the way, I'll be paying for.'

'She'd do that, in the middle of her divorce proceedings?' I asked, watching a black-suited barrister walk past and cast a discreet, curious glance in our direction.

'I think you've gathered by now that she is completely unpredictable.'

I wedged my handbag defensively by my side.

'When was the last time you heard from her?' I asked, trying to keep my voice steady.

'She called me last week. Sunday, maybe Monday. Warned me not to be an alpha male idiot at the hearing.'

What scared me, what really scared me, was the way he could lie so fluidly.

'So she was intending to be at the FDR?'

'Yes, although we ended up arguing.'

'And that was the last time you heard from her?' I asked, willing my expression not to betray my fear.

'Yes,' he said finally.

*Liar,* said a voice in my head.

He snaked his hand inside my coat and placed it on the curve of my waist.

'Come here,' he whispered.

'No,' I said stepping away until I was backed against the cold brick wall.

'No one's going to see us.'

'Stop, please.'

'Fran, what's wrong?'

'What's wrong is that we shouldn't have got involved. I am your barrister. There are codes of ethics against that.'

'That didn't stop you at Selfridges.'

I turned my head away from him and he cupped his fingers against my chin.

'I'm sorry,' he said, stroking the curve of my jaw. 'The way we met was not ideal. The situation we're in is not ideal . . . but I thought we both felt the same. You make me happy.'

*But you slept with her.*

That's what I wanted to say, but I couldn't. I couldn't admit to having followed them and watching them in the rain, and if I was waiting for a confession from Martin of where he had been on Monday night, deep down I knew it would not come.

His fingers trailed the length of my neck to the thin fabric of my blouse, over my breast, his palms skimming my stiffening nipple. I hated that he could make me like this so quickly, and yet I loved it. As I closed my eyes, heat pulsed between my legs. I wanted this, I wanted him so badly that I felt weak and desperate inside.

'No one's watching,' he whispered in my ear, his warm lips brushing against my earlobe as I screeched to my senses.

'Stop,' I said, grabbing his wrist. 'I don't think we should see each other for a while.'

'Fran, please. It's been frustrating today. No one knows that more than me. No one wants this to be over more than me. I just want her out of my life so I can get on with mine.'

'Really?' I said, as a cold, damp wind skimmed across my cheek.

I didn't wait for his reply. Shaking myself away from him I started walking. He called my name but I carried on without looking back, the heels of my shoes tapping against the paving stones like a Morse code distress signal, which I suppose it might have been.

I spent the rest of the afternoon in the Inner Temple library, not even surfacing for a sandwich or a coffee. I remember very little of that time, except that I got back to chambers shortly before five. I was sitting at my desk, skimming through my diary, wondering how else I could fill my week, how else I could distract myself from Martin Joy, when my office phone rang.

'It's Dave. Dave Gilbert,' said the voice. 'I thought you should know,' he added, and I noticed a troubled inflection in his voice, 'Robert Pascale has just called. He's been trying to locate Donna Joy all day and he's just managed to speak to her sister, who was concerned about her too. No one has seen or heard from Donna for days. She didn't turn up to a dinner party yesterday. Hasn't been seen at her studio since Monday. No one can get in touch with her by phone or email. Robert even sent a trainee to her house, but there was no answer there either. Donna's sister is so worried, she's about to contact the police and report her missing.'

# *Chapter 15*

Most people who disappear turn up within forty-eight hours. I did.

I was eighteen when I ran away from home, a few days after I had finished my A-levels. There had been a party to celebrate finishing sixth form in the college gymnasium, a swansong before we scattered to go our different ways – to apprenticeships, university and junior office jobs.

It had optimistically been advertised as a prom – perhaps someone had watched one too many John Hughes movies – and I'd worn a dress for the occasion, a novelty in those days when I liked to look edgy. I wasn't pretty. Not at all – I had black dyed hair and a nose ring. I wasn't popular either, but that night I'd got lots of attention: smiles, suggestions and heavy-handed flirtation from boys who had previously ignored me. I thought the reason was my green silk Fifties frock or the alcohol that was being surreptitiously passed around the party, but looking back now, it was probably my reputation.

Stuart Masters was one of the few people who had come to our college from the comprehensive school I'd been at before. I'd always liked him, but his longstanding girlfriend

Joanne watched him like a hawk. We'd found ourselves in a corner that night. We'd talked about old times, and during the buffet, we'd sloped off through the fire exit. We laughed, we kissed and before I knew it we were behind the science labs and I was so busy with my lips around his cock that I didn't even notice that someone had seen us.

I can still hear the word *slut* being screamed at me across the makeshift dance floor and it was the first time I had ever been ashamed of my behaviour. The one-night stands and toilet fucks in the clubs of Bolton and Manchester. Twenty-four men, two women whose names I could barely remember.

I had yet to be diagnosed bipolar, yet to be warned about the link between manic depression and hypersexuality. Back then, I didn't think my behaviour was anything out of the ordinary. I was discovering myself, having fun. I did it because I could and I wanted to.

I knew I couldn't go home that night. Not back to the room I shared with my twelve-year-old sister Denise and the distinct possibility that Joanne's mother would have telephoned mine by morning.

On Sunday morning, my mum left the kids with a neighbour and went to the local cop shop to tell them I hadn't come home. They asked her a few questions, requested a recent photograph and told her that this was more common than you would imagine. Angry, emotional teenagers were not generally abducted. They escaped.

But when my friend Jenny Morris got to hear about it, she was concerned. A tenacious little thing with teenage ambitions to be a journalist, she phoned the *Sun*'s news desk and pressed them to assign someone to the story. No story ever ran, and to this day I have no idea if it was because I had turned up in the early hours of Monday morning, or because my disappearance was not as important as I had thought.

I considered myself to be offbeat and original in those days, but recently I read a criminal psychologist report which said that missing girls were more likely to be found inside, while missing boys tended to be found outside. Far from being original, I was true to type.

It was Jenny herself who tracked me down to a bedsit in Fallowfield. A few phone calls was all it took – no wonder she ended up working for the *Daily Mail*. The flat belonged to a musician I had slept with a few weeks earlier. After running away from the prom, I'd taken the bus to South Manchester to go and see him. He was on his way out, already stoned, and let me wait in his tired, shabby room until his return. It was Sunday before he turned up again, but he was a decent bloke and didn't kick me out when I said I had problems at home. And by the time he gave me the bus fare to go and 'face the music', Jenny had already found me.

Mum and her new boyfriend gave me my own bedroom after that. Baby Danny moved back in with them in a cot in the corner of the room, and I had the nursery, covering the teddy-bear wallpaper with pictures from French movies until I packed my stuff up ten weeks later and moved to Birmingham. Life went on. It was just a wobble. I only wanted a bit of attention and to feel loved, and I was sure that was what Donna Joy wanted too.

# *Chapter 16*

Thanks to a dose of Zolpidem, I slept until eleven the next morning. Opening my eyes, I saw my phone pulsing blue on my bedside cabinet. When I reached for it, I saw seven messages and three missed calls from Martin, asking me to get in touch.

It was hard to ignore his instructions, but I did. Instead, I sat up cross-legged and pressed the Google icon, typing in the words *Donna Joy missing*, not knowing what to expect. *Daily Mail* headline news? A BBC story? A Twitter trending feed? But I was almost let down when there was nothing except the same old links and images I had turned up on my previous searches.

I closed my eyes for a moment and let the sense of dread pass, willing to wager, right then, that Donna Joy had 'turned up'. I'd been mulling it over since the phone call from David Gilbert, and the only logical conclusion I could come to was that it was a stunt, a ploy to get Martin back. The thought had given me a moment of gleeful satisfaction at the prospect that perhaps their Monday-night sexual encounter had not been as explosive as I'd first imagined.

Putting the phone down, I got out of bed and went to the

bathroom. I brushed my teeth, flossed them thoroughly and poked around with an interdental brush. Blood dappled my saliva as it hit the sink. I rinsed my mouth with water as the intercom downstairs buzzed insistently.

'It's me. Can I come in?' said his voice through the speaker.

I glanced around the flat, feeling cornered. I didn't want to see him like this, wearing only a T-shirt that barely covered my thighs. The kitchen was steps away. I scurried over to it, found some knickers and jeans in the tumble dryer, put them on and pattered barefoot down the stairs.

I hesitated before I opened the door. I could see the face through the glass, sad, distracted, hopeful.

Slowly I turned the latch and stood in the doorway but didn't let him in.

'Did you get my messages?' he said finally.

'I've just got up.'

He looked down at his shoes and up again.

'Have you heard about Donna?'

I nodded and folded my arms across my chest. 'I heard something. Her sister was worried that no one had seen her all week and has gone to the police.'

'She still hasn't turned up.'

'I'm sorry,' I said, feeling my heartbeat speed up a little.

'The police called me this morning,' he said. 'Asked me some questions.'

'What about?'

'Her state of mind.'

'They're not treating this as suspicious?' I asked incredulously.

'I don't know. I don't think so.'

'So what happens next? About finding her.'

'The police are going round to her house. Her sister Jemma has a key.'

'And then what?'

'Look, I thought we could do something today.'

I frowned at him. 'Martin, you heard what I said yesterday.'

'Please. Just come for a drive. I need to clear my head.'

'Your wife is *missing*,' I said, wondering if I had heard him correctly.

'She's not missing. She'll be somewhere,' he said, and the flash of coldness in his expression surprised me. Did he not see that going for a drive, or enjoying ourselves in any way, would be inappropriate? Then again, Martin knew Donna better than anyone, knew her better than the police, or even her sister. If he wasn't worried, there must be a good reason. I told myself not to take his flippancy as heartlessness.

'Come on, Francine. It'll be a chance to talk.'

'Talk?'

'Please,' he said with passion.

I tried not to think of the ugly, painful image of him disappearing into the Chelsea house with Donna and the lies he'd told me outside Temple Church.

'Wait here,' I said, and went upstairs to get my coat, helpless to do anything else.

His Aston Martin was parked on the street. I climbed into the passenger seat and leant against the window, watching the Saturday traffic. He turned on some music which relieved the pressure to talk.

'Where are we going?' I asked as we travelled through Hackney.

'The coast,' he said, turning and giving me a sideward smile.

A week ago, I would have been ecstatic with that answer. I would have imagined us sitting outside pastel-pink beach huts with cones of chips or eating mussels in some quayside café.

Today it seemed like an awfully long way to go for a drive, an awfully long time to avoid asking the questions that I had been desperate to discuss all week.

We slipped out of London, and ninety minutes later had swung off the main road on to a quieter B road.

The sky had dulled, the sun had gone in, all around were miles of endless grey; clouds, salt-flats and sea that blended into one another like a sheet of creased and faded linen, an empty landscape colour-washed chrome.

I'd seen several road signs over the past few miles, but we were in unfamiliar territory.

'Where are we?' I asked, noticing a dead badger, flattened and bloodied on the side of the road.

'Essex. This causeway leads to the house,' he said, making a sharp right where the road narrowed further, falling away to railings, then water on both sides.

'Bloody hell. Is this an island?'

'Some of the time. At high tide.'

We passed through a quiet village with clapboard houses, a church, a smattering of pubs and on to a coastal boulevard. Another turn and a house appeared at the end of a wide, gravel drive. It was Arts and Crafts in style, with a faded red-tiled roof, high-pitched gables and at least a dozen terracotta chimney pots that stretched into the pewter sky. Scratchy trees, beginning to bud, lined the moss-furred perimeter wall, hardy weeds, knots of tough stems and leaves, curled around the rusty gates. It was obviously neglected – and hauntingly magnificent.

'This is yours, isn't it? This is Dorsea House,' I said, remembering the details of his property holdings.

Martin nodded as the car growled to a stop on the gravel.

'I bought it last summer. It was supposed to be a project. A Babington House that was less than two hours from the city. I had an architect, a design company, ready to start, but I've put it on hold.'

'On hold?'

'The divorce. I don't want to increase its value. Not yet.'

I got out of the car and slammed the door shut. Gulls pinwheeled above us, the wind rustled through the hedges. I took a deep breath of salty sea-air and tried not to be captivated by it all.

'It's big.'

'It used to be a retirement home. It needs a lot of work, but I like its tiredness, its undoneness. Come on. Let me show you around.'

He lingered a moment as if he wanted to take my hand but I pressed on ahead to avoid any embarrassment.

The floorboards creaked as we crossed the threshold. High above us, in the vaulted ceilings, there was a puff of dust and a noise that made me jump – the flapping wings of a dislodged pigeon.

The air was musty; the scent of neglect. Buttoning up my jacket, I stifled a sneeze and moved slowly, almost tiptoeing, towards the back of the house. The rooms, I noted, were furnished, tired leftovers from its previous life. But if Dorsea House was cold and unloved, the views at the rear, over the wide monochromatic expanse of estuary, were of bleak and breathtaking beauty.

The property, and Martin's plans for it, gave us something to talk about. How an old barn would be turned into an oyster bar, serving the Colchester Natives and Mersea Island Rocks the area was famous for. A string of beach huts would become deluxe cottages for stressed-out executives. An outdoor pool would be built leading off from the plantation-style porch at the rear.

A door at the side of the sunroom led on to a deck.

'Let's go outside,' said Martin, looking for a key. When he couldn't find one, I pushed the door hard and it shook on its rotting frame before it opened.

'Clever girl,' he said, not taking his eyes off me.

'You should get that fixed. Before you get squatters,' I said, enjoying my brief moment of triumph.

We took a footpath that hugged the banks of the water. The tide lapped and rasped against the shingle.

I drew a long breath, closing my eyes, and let the smell of iodine and seaweed calm me, like menthol.

'You wanted to talk,' I said finally, opening my eyes and keeping them directed in front of me.

'I lied to you yesterday,' he replied, his voice uncharacteristically unsure.

I kept quiet and steeled myself.

'You asked me about the last time I'd heard from Donna and I said Sunday or Monday. It was Monday,' he said finally. 'I saw her on Monday.'

I didn't look at him. I kept my eyes focused on the pale, watery horizon.

'So why did you lie?'

'She texted me, wanting to meet again. Said we should talk privately before the FDR. We had dinner, went back to the house.'

'And then what?' I goaded.

'We talked, we had a drink . . .'

'And then you had sex,' I said, finishing off his sentence.

'Yes, we did.'

I didn't say anything else for at least a minute.

'Why are you telling me this? I assume there's a reason.'

My voice had morphed into the one I adopted in court when I wanted to make a faintly patronizing point.

'Fran, don't be like this.' He stopped walking. 'It was a mistake and I regret it.'

'It didn't look like that to me.'

Didn't. Doesn't. I hoped he hadn't noticed my slip.

Martin slowed his pace. 'I'd had a drink, she came on strong . . . I didn't tell you yesterday because I know how wrong and weak this looks.'

'Did you enjoy it?' I said, pressing my lips together after I'd spoken.

'Fran, don't make this harder than it has to be.'

The bluish light made Martin look pale, as if all the blood had been leeched from his veins.

'Did she come?' I asked, suddenly wanting to know every intimate detail. He didn't respond.

'I don't think you're over her.' My voice was a whisper, caught on the breeze, but he still heard me.

He stopped and touched my fingers, but I flinched away from him.

'I want to be with you.'

I sank on to a bench and looked out to sea. My stomach was in a tight knot as I forced myself to think straight.

'The other time she wanted to *talk*. Did you fuck her then?'

'No.'

'Tell me the truth, Martin.'

'That is the truth.'

'Then why didn't you answer my calls that night?'

My head was spinning. I wanted answers but wasn't sure if I could bear them.

'My phone died, I swear to you. Look, there's no point me lying about it now. I just want to be totally honest with you because I want to make this work between us.'

'You should have thought about that on Monday.'

'I was an idiot.'

'Yes, you were.'

I picked up a piece of driftwood and threw it into the sea. I watched a wave pick it up and toss it back and forth before I started heading off in the direction of the house.

'Fran, please. Give me another chance. Being with her made me realize how much better it is being with you.'

I turned to face him.

'I can't trust you any more,' I croaked, tears leaking down my cheek. I realized how much I hated feeling like this, like some helpless facsimile of myself that I barely recognized.

He came up close to me and held my face.

'I am in love with you,' he said as I closed my eyes, feeling the caress of his words, and gaining strength from it.

I squeezed my eyes tighter to stop myself from crying. He took another step towards me and rested his chin on my head. I felt powerless to move away as his arms wrapped around me.

'I love you,' he whispered into my hair, and I rested my cheek against the soft wool of his coat, my anger and frustration making way for deep contentment.

We stood there for what seemed like an eternity. His arms dropped to my sides and when he took my hands, it seemed the right thing to do, to clasp my fingers around his.

'Let's get back,' he said, looking out across the reed-studded marshes. Overhead, the clouds grew dark and foreboding. The wind began to whip across the water, forming white, meringue-like peaks and as it came to shore the sea rasped against the beach grass like a rattlesnake.

'There's a storm coming,' he said as we picked up our pace.

We passed through a gate and back into the grounds of Dorsea House. There was a black-painted clapboard shack by the water, festooned with faded orange buoys and blue rope.

'What's this?' I asked as he picked up a brick and retrieved a key.

'An old oyster shed. I like sleeping here where I come to Dorsea.'

'Feel lonely at the main house?' I smiled. 'That's what happens when rich people buy homes that are too big for them.'

'I like listening to the sea and making beach bonfires.'

'A good enough reason.' I smiled as Martin opened the door and beckoned me in.

It was sparse inside. A desk and chair, a wood-burning stove and an iron bed made up like a sofa.

Martin took some kindling and scrunched up copies of the *Financial Times* from a metal bucket and lit the fire. I liked watching him. His feral crouch, his concentration, his masculine hands, smooth and tanned, a cut on his knuckles giving them more ruggedness.

'This place is great,' I whispered, watching the flames take hold. The hut grew warmer, brighter with every crackle of wood.

'Let's stay here tonight,' he said, looking at me.

'I've brought nothing with me,' I laughed, remembering I wasn't even wearing a bra.

Rain started to hammer on the tin roof.

'We might have no choice,' he smiled.

'Is the island going to get cut off?' I asked, thrilled by the idea.

'Perhaps.'

We took off our coats and there was a few moments' silence.

'I'm so sorry.'

'Don't lie to me again,' I whispered, trying not to think of my own deception. That I knew he had met Donna in Chelsea on Monday night, because I had seen them together.

The shed was still icy cold and I could feel my nipples stand to attention under my T-shirt. I watched Martin pull the mattress off the bed and thump it on the floor in front of the fire. He stepped towards me, and then we were kissing. As he pulled my T-shirt over my head, I groaned with longing.

I closed my eyes and listened to the howl of the wind, and the harsh cry of the cormorants overhead. His fingers traced the undulations of my spine. I unzipped my jeans and shook them off, kneeling on the mattress to watch him undress.

He stepped towards me and I took him in my mouth. He held my head, his coarse hair scratching my face, and I breathed him in deeply, the scent of sweat and musk and sex, the taste of him, moist, sour and warm.

'Lie back,' said Martin, as he pulled out of me.

I smiled and lowered myself back as he straddled me.

'Do you want the island to get cut off?'

His voice was low and husky with the anticipation of what was to come.

I nodded my approval, spreading my legs to receive him.

A length of rope lay coiled by the stove. He picked it up, stretched my arms over my head and gripped my wrists tightly. After tying them together, he fastened them to the frame of the bed, and lowered his face closer to mine until I could feel his breath on my lips. I felt bound and captured, as if he possessed me. At that moment, it was the only thing I wanted.

'There's a new moon tonight, so you might be in luck. You might not be able to escape,' he said into my ear as I shivered through cold or sense of danger; I neither knew nor cared.

I was out at sea, out of my depth, the only thing I could think about or cared about was him.

I gave a soft, submissive sigh of pleasure as he traced his mouth over my breasts and abdomen, down and down, until his tongue was inside me, stroking that slick nub until I started to come, my back arching, my trussed fists trying to lift off the floor. I was oblivious to the sharp burning sensation of the rope chafing my skin, oblivious as he kissed me and teased me to a climax of sweet, abandoned desire.

I cried out and the sound merged with the rain and the wind. As he came up from between my thighs, he smiled and began to untie me.

I took small, controlled breaths to calm myself and he lay down in the space beside me.

'I would rather sell the loft than this place,' he said, so quietly that I could barely hear him.

'It won't come to that,' I whispered, feeling cold air seep into the shed through the cracks in the clapboard.

An image of his wife pushed into my thoughts, and as I looked up, watching the shadows of the flames dance on the cracked paintwork of the ceiling, I tried to forget that the last person to see the missing Donna Joy was the man lying next to me.

# Chapter 17

I must have dozed off, lulled by the muffled sound of the wind and rain, but the shrill ring of a mobile phone shook me from my slumber.

I glanced over at Martin, sat upright on the blanket-strewn mattress and immediately I could tell that the call concerned Donna. I watched his brow crease, the muscles in his face tighten; yet again she had the power to fire-blanket my pleasure.

Martin's end of the conversation was short, crisp and professional, which made it hard to work out what the call was about. When it ended, he fell silent and looked thoughtful.

'Everything OK?' I asked, not wanting to intrude but desperate to know what was going on.

'I've got to go,' he said, not meeting my eye.

'What. Now?'

'The police are concerned about Donna,' he said, getting to his feet.

'More worried than they were this morning?' I asked, reaching for my T-shirt. I feared that this was not a conversation we wanted to have naked.

'Apparently. They want to speak to me, so we've got to get back to London.'

'But they've already spoken to you today,' I replied, feeling panic in my belly.

'And now they want to meet me again. Tonight. Someone is coming to Spitalfields at ten.' He picked up his shirt and threaded his arms through the sleeves.

Looking at his bare chest and flaccid cock, I wondered what the police would think if they could see him now. As if he was reading my mind, he grabbed the rest of his clothes and dressed quickly. He rubbed a layer of dust off the window and peered outside.

'Nice night for a drive back to the city,' he muttered. And as he opened the door, an angry swoosh of wind roared into the shack, shaking it to its core. I sensed an ending; with a bleak certainty, I knew that things were going to be unwelcomely different once we stepped out of the cabin.

It was dark outside. Driving rain lashed my face as we ran across the beach and back to the house. I slipped several times, the soles of my shoes skidding on the wet shingle, but each time I scrambled up again, desperate to get to the car.

The house groaned as we ran inside. My hair stuck to my cheeks, and my damp jeans felt claggy against my skin, but there was no time to dry off. Martin locked up Dorsea House and we got into the Aston Martin, my damp coat squelching against the pale leather seats. He switched on the headlights, casting ghostly halos on the front of the building. The corner of my mouth curled upwards, a grim goodbye of regret and wonder. Something told me I would not come back here and I wanted to remember its faded grandeur.

Firing the engine, Martin turned on the wipers. Despite the

power and precision engineering of the vehicle, they struggled to make two clear arches on the windscreen.

'Perhaps we should wait a bit,' I offered as the wheels crunched over the gravel.

'It's been raining this hard for an hour. It could go on all night,' he replied.

Darkness enveloped us as we pulled out of the gates. Pinpricks of light pierced the black hole of night and foul weather, but otherwise it was completely dark.

I strained my eyes and looked for the fishing boats I had seen earlier, hoping that they were all safely moored. Driving conditions were terrible, but things would be far worse at sea.

Martin focused at the wheel, but his speed was steady and I wasn't sure whether this was because of the poor visibility or a recluctance to get back to the city.

In the distance, I could make out the shadowy outline of the mainland. Though less than a mile away, for the past few hours it had seemed blissfully distant, part of another universe. We were nearing the causeway now and already, in the pale beam of the headlights, I could make out a band of brackish, dirty water that ran across the road.

'I don't believe it,' cursed Martin, slowing the car until it had almost stopped. The sound of the seawater sloshing against the tyres was unmistakable.

I knew better than to speak. Martin revved the engine but it growled dangerously, reminding us this was a sports car, not an off-road vehicle.

'There's no way through,' he muttered. I wondered if I would chance it in a £100,000 Aston Martin.

'How long does it last?' I asked as he started to reverse.

'Not sure. An hour, maybe two in the spring tides, but who knows in a flood.'

'Should we go back to Dorsea?'

He shook his head. 'No. There's a pub down the road. We should sit and wait it out. They'll have more of an idea when the road might clear.'

The Anchor was a half-timbered building I had noticed on the way there. Parking right outside, we ran in to find it unsurprisingly empty.

We ordered two coffees from the barman, who suggested making them Irish. From his banter, I wasn't sure if he knew Martin or whether he was just grateful for the custom.

Martin led the way to a banquette table with red flocked seating tucked away in a corner. I glanced across at the only other customers: two old men nursing pints of Guinness. My knee bounced up and down under the table as I waited for Martin to say something.

'So how did you leave it on Monday night?' I asked, pretending to be calm.

'Leave it?' he said, taking his cup of coffee from the waitress.

'How long were you there? At Donna's.'

'Come on, we don't need to talk about that,' he said, taking a sip and avoiding my gaze.

'This isn't about me, Martin,' I whispered pointedly.

I didn't want to interrogate him but I felt myself slipping into professional mode. I wanted him to be prepared for the police, and besides, I wanted to know.

'I left around midnight,' he offered finally.

'Was she awake?'

'She was in bed. She got up as I was leaving.'

'And she didn't give you any idea about what she was doing the next day,' I said, morphing into the person I was in court.

'She didn't mention anything out of the ordinary,' he said with a touch of petulance.

I glanced at the other customers, paranoid that they could hear our conversation.

'I assume you told the police you went round on Monday night.'

He looked uncomfortable but my own panic was building as my thoughts raced ahead of me, looking for angles, clues, solutions. I could see where this was going and it frightened me. The only way I knew how to deal with it was professionally, like a methodical puzzle, although unlike my other cases, I was unable to leave this conundrum in the office.

'I said we met for dinner. To discuss the divorce.'

'And did you tell them you slept with her?'

My bluntness made him frown.

'No,' he said finally.

'Why not?'

'Because it doesn't look good.'

'Too right it doesn't. And it's going to look worse when it looks like you withheld information from them. What about when you left? Where did you go?'

'Back home.'

'How?'

'I walked.'

'You walked? It must be five miles back to the loft.'

'I had a lot of thinking to do.'

Resentment, fear, panic; I could see it all there in his expression.

'Do you think I should speak to a lawyer?'

I saw his Adam's apple bob up and down and I felt a spike of pity for him.

'Not my area of expertise,' I said quietly, randomly reminded of all those friends over the years who'd wanted help with house purchases, speeding tickets and consumer complaints. I was the one-size-fits-all lawyer that everyone thought had the answers to everything.

'A criminal lawyer. You must know someone.'

'But you haven't done anything wrong,' I said carefully, gauging his reaction.

He nodded, the alpha male reminding himself that everything could be resolved if you threw enough resources at it.

'She'll be somewhere,' he said more passionately. 'A friend in the country, overseas.'

'Why don't you call her sister?'

'Right. She's probably been telling the police I'm the big, bad husband who wants to screw Donna over in a divorce. That I'd be better off if Donna just disappeared.'

'She wants to find Donna. Just as we all do.'

He glanced at his watch. He didn't need to tell me the time. The clock behind his head told me it was gone nine o'clock.

'This is going to look great,' he said sarcastically. 'Not turning up for a police interview.'

'You probably shouldn't tell them you were locked in a shed with your divorce lawyer,' I said trying to lighten the tension.

'I thought you said I should tell them the truth, the whole truth and nothing but the truth.'

I felt a flutter of fear. A cold realization that I was now involved. I had joined the cast of a drama I had not auditioned for, and I did not like my part.

Glancing around, I was suddenly nervous of eyes upon me.

'What should I tell them?'

'The truth,' I said firmly. 'You were at your house in Essex and the flood cut off the road to the mainland.'

'I should go and phone Jemma.'

'And maybe I should sit in the car.'

'We've been seen now,' he said, as if reading my thoughts.

He was gone five minutes, although to me, the time seemed to drag on much longer. I prayed he'd come back smiling, but he looked even more unsettled than when he had left the room to make the call.

127

'They searched the house today. They found her handbag and phone,' he said when he'd sat back down.

'I'm sure Donna has more than one bag. One phone even.'

I said it to reassure him, but I was aware that everything I said could sound like a dig at Donna.

'They found her passport too. But not her purse. Landline messages haven't been checked since Monday. She's not been admitted into any of the local hospitals, none of her friends know where she is . . .'

He paused to stir his teaspoon around his cold coffee, splashing dark streaks around the rim of the cup.

'A detective inspector is in charge of it now and the Missing Persons Bureau are involved. There's talk of an appeal being broadcast tomorrow night.'

I'd been to enough family law conferences, attended enough child abduction seminars, to know how this worked. To know that while we had been fucking in the oyster shed, Donna Joy had been passing through cyberspace, her details, her image, the circumstances of her disappearance. To know that someone in authority was taking the fact that she was missing sufficiently seriously. I knew that an appeal meant the media would be involved, stories leaked, information managed. I knew this was not looking good for Martin Joy, and by implication, for me.

'Do they have a theory about what might have happened to her?' I asked after a moment.

'It's always the husband, isn't it,' he said quietly. 'A wife goes missing, and the finger gets pointed at the husband first.'

'I didn't mean that,' I said, putting my hand over his. 'You've done nothing wrong.'

'I should talk to a lawyer. Just to get some advice on how to handle this.'

I noticed a tic pulsing under his left bottom eyelid and

jumped when I felt a hand on my shoulder. I turned quickly and saw the bar manager, who gave us a thin, brown-toothed smile.

'Water on the causeway's thinning out,' he said, clearing up our coffee cups. 'Looks like it's your lucky night, after all.'

I glanced up at Martin, and I could tell from his faraway and troubled expression that neither of us believed him.

# Chapter 18

I was surprised that he was in on a Saturday night and even more surprised that he was alone.

'Coffee or a stiff drink?' asked Tom Briscoe when he opened the door of his Highgate home. It was a terraced cottage overlooking Pond Square, small but with an appropriate air of Georgian grandeur.

'Coffee. Decaf,' I said, already feeling anxious as I stepped inside, not venturing more than a few feet beyond the threshold. The door opened straight on to an open-plan living space. I looked and listened for another person in the property but it was almost as quiet and dark and still as the deserted Highgate square outside.

'I'm so sorry about this,' I said gripping the strap of my handbag tighter. 'I know it's late, but it shouldn't take long.'

'It's fine. Come through,' he said, keeping his distance but directing me towards the sofa with a sweep of his hand.

He disappeared into the kitchen and I looked around the dimly lit space. The dining table was covered in files and legal textbooks, and I could see the soft glow of a laptop screen, a half-eaten sandwich on a plate. I'd always considered Tom to be a bit of a chancer, a privileged public schoolboy who had got where he was through the old boy network, but this scene said something else. A workaholic on a Saturday night, putting in the graft and extra hours.

'Is Hannah not here this weekend?' I asked, taking off my coat. I put it over the back of his club chair, and felt suddenly conscious that I wasn't wearing a bra. I folded my arms in front of me, wondering if I still smelt of sex and the sea. All I wanted now was to get this meeting over with.

'I've told you, it's not that sort of relationship,' he smiled, coming back through and handing me a mug of coffee. It would usually have been my cue to tease him, but the last thing I felt like doing was joking around.

As I curled my fingers around the blue-and-white striped mug, I could feel the steam rise up in front of my face. I sat down on the sofa as he sat in the armchair opposite me.

'So are you going to tell me what's going on?' he said finally, sensing I was in no mood for chit-chat.

I muttered an apology for being so vague when I'd called him on the way back from Essex. As the foul weather had tailed off as we approached London, Martin had become more agitated with every passing mile. It was a side of him that I had never seen before, one I had to admit was not especially attractive.

'You must know a lawyer,' he'd pressed, until in the end I got on the phone and called the one person I knew who might be able to help, even though I felt very uncomfortable doing so.

I was not in the habit of calling Tom Briscoe late on a Saturday night. In fact our paths rarely crossed outside of chambers. But Tom and I went back a long way. We were not close, but we were bound together by history and geography. We had both arrived at Burgess Court to start our pupillage on the same day and had spent every day of our working lives together; if that didn't give me licence to arrive at his house at this time, then I don't know what did. Even so, I didn't like being here. Not when I'd spent the afternoon fucking the client I was here to discuss. I had come here because Martin was desperate and I would do whatever I needed to do to help him.

I took a sip of coffee before I spoke.

'I'm handling a divorce,' I began cautiously. 'And my client's wife has gone missing.'

Tom seemed to perk up a little bit in his chair, whilst I desperately tried to compose myself. I couldn't betray the back-story to what I was about to tell him. I knew how dangerous it would be to do so.

'Missing?' replied Tom.

'She hasn't been seen since Monday, and the police are taking it seriously. There's going to be a TV appeal tomorrow night, unless she turns up.'

I looked at him and noticed that he looked tired, with purple semicircles under his eyes.

'And where do you fit into this?' he said, putting his coffee down on the wooden floor.

'The police are interviewing my client as we speak. I'm the only legal representation he's got right now and he's worried.'

'You mean he's nervous.'

'She'll almost certainly turn up, Tom,' I said, resenting his implication that Martin was feeling guilty.

He didn't say anything and I knew I didn't have long before he would lose patience with me.

'I just need some advice. Martin – my client – is relying on me, and I said you might be able to help.'

Our eyes met, a remembrance of things past, an incident five years ago that neither of us would ever forget. Tom

Briscoe had been a criminal defence barrister back then, the protégé of our former head of chambers, now retired, handling a lot of legal aid work. He did the odd bit of family law on the side, but it was the drama of the criminal bar that he loved – until he was instructed by Nathan Adams, a thug on a GBH charge. Adams was on trial for a vicious attack on his ex-girlfriend, Suzie Willis, which had left her with a fractured spine. It was senior work for one who'd only been at the bar for the length of time Tom had, but his performance in court had been devastating. Cross-examining Suzie on the stand, Tom Briscoe had portrayed her as a habitual drunk, destroying her credibility and had succeeded in persuading the jury that his client was innocent.

Six months later, Suzie was dead – murdered by Adams. He'd hunted her down, taken a knife to her throat and sliced it from ear to ear: her punishment for daring to testify against him.

I'd never had the guts to discuss what happened with Tom directly. How much he had known about Nathan and Suzie's relationship, her long list of suspicious injuries that hadn't been reported to the police, or about Adams' violent history and his links to a West London crime syndicate.

However much he knew, what happened to Suzie Willis made Tom Briscoe jump horses from the criminal bar to family law. The look in his eye told me that he didn't want any reminder of his professional past.

'For a start, do you think he should have a lawyer with him for his interview?' I pressed.

'I thought you said the interview was happening.'

'It is. I think a police officer is visiting him at his house, although he's already spoken to someone earlier in the day.'

Tom stood up and went over to the dining table. He picked up his laptop and brought it across to the sofa.

'I assume they've searched her house already.'

'They found her passport and phone, but they couldn't find her purse. That's obviously a good sign.'

'Not necessarily,' said Tom, looking sceptical. 'I remember a murder trial I observed as a pupil. A woman had gone missing from the family home; the husband said he had no idea where she might be. He was eventually arrested and found guilty of killing her. He'd made it look as if she'd taken off by hiding her personal possessions after he'd disposed of the body.'

I flashed him a look of disapproval.

'What's she called? The wife.'

'Donna Joy.'

I watched him tap away at the keyboard, his fingers rattling over keys. 'There's an appeal online already. A number to contact: Kensington CID.'

My heart was thumping as I peered over his shoulder at the screen. There was a photo of Donna and a description: five feet six inches tall, weight around nine stone, last seen wearing a pink coat and black trousers. She'd gone missing after being escorted home following a night out at the Green Fields restaurant on the King's Road last Monday.

I found myself mentally adding more details to the text as I read it. I could confirm that she had been in the Green Fields for ninety-seven minutes, that she had been drinking, and her hair was at least three shades darker than it seemed in pictures, thanks to a trip to the Josh Wood salon twelve days earlier that she had indiscreetly recorded on Instagram.

The appeal ended by saying that the police were concerned for her welfare, but I doubted that they were nearly as concerned as I was.

'Most people who go missing turn up,' said Tom with a shrug. 'A tiny proportion don't, but out of those, the majority have a history of mental issues or depression that's pushed them into taking their own life.'

'So it's unlikely anything has happened to her,' I said, pleading for reassurance.

'Did she suffer with depression?'

'Not that I know of.'

'Adults have a legal right to disappear, Fran, you know that. And we have no way of knowing what the hell was going on in their relationship. Maybe she's playing games,' he said, as I nodded my approval of his assessment.

'But maybe something has happened to her. A TV appeal means she's been classed as high risk.'

'High risk?' I frowned.

'In danger. In danger of hurting themselves or being hurt. Who was she with on Monday night, any idea?'

'Her husband,' I said flatly.

'Your client.'

'They met for dinner. Apparently they slept together, but he says he didn't spend the night. No one has seen her since. She missed her FDR hearing on Friday and her sister's birthday party the previous night.'

'No wonder they want to talk to him.'

I didn't want to hear that.

'So what's he like?'

'Smart. Very successful.'

'So the press could have a field day with it.'

I'd heard about Missing White Woman Syndrome before and knew that this case came with added drama. Donna Joy wasn't just blonde, white and beautiful. She was estranged from her millionaire hedge-fund banker husband which meant her story came with a ready-made bogeyman.

'He didn't hurt his wife,' I said, hearing protective scorn in my own voice.

'How do you know?'

I thought of us on the Spitalfields roof-tops. *'We just have to hang in there and soon, really soon, it's going to be this. Just us. No Donna, no sneaking around, just me and you.'*

'What do I tell him?' I asked.

'It wouldn't do any harm to talk to a criminal defence solicitor. Matthew Clarkson is very good. He might also want to speak to Robert Kelly. He's a media lawyer, deals with reputation management. If the press start playing silly buggers, he might be worth a call.'

Tom stood up, pulled his phone out of his pocket and scrolled through his address book.

'I suppose your client should start worrying if they make him take part in the appeal,' he muttered as he wrote down two numbers on a piece of paper from his yellow legal notepad.

'Why would that worry him? He wants to do everything he can to help.'

'I'm not sure they'd have the estranged husband there at any press conference, unless they were trying to test his reactions. He might also get a visit from the family liaison officer. Ostensibly they're there to help, but they're also a pair of ears on the ground.'

'My client had nothing to do with her disappearance,' I said, hearing a touch of steel in my voice.

Tom looked at me and for a moment neither of us spoke.

'As you said, I bet she's turned up by morning.'

The mood had shifted. I felt hot and uncomfortable just being here. 'I should go.'

He smiled and glanced at his watch.

'It's late. How did you get here? Did you drive?'

'No,' I replied too quickly, thinking of Martin's car dropping me on the edge of Pond Square. 'I should call a cab.'

'Don't be daft. I'll give you a lift.'

'Honestly, I'll call a cab.'

'Saturday night, at chucking out time? And Uber will be price surging. Come on. I'll grab my keys.'

He ushered me out to a four-by-four parked in front of the house.

'I hope you're charging your client double time for this,' grinned Tom as he deactivated his car alarm, two sharp beeps that pierced the quiet of the night. 'Talk about going above and beyond the call of duty. He's lucky to have you.'

He gave me a look, a knowing half-smile, and a sense of dread made me wonder what, and how much, he had worked out.

# Chapter 19

It was gone midnight by the time I got home.

I hadn't eaten since breakfast – I never did get to eat any fish and chips or mussels with Martin on the beach – and I felt weak and light-headed. There were slim pickings in the fridge: a withered lemon and an opened packet of ham that had darkened and curled, so I made some toast and a Pot Noodle that I found lurking in the cupboard. As I poked the dry noodles with a fork, I checked my phone again for any messages from Martin, but still, there was nothing.

Perching on the sofa I chomped down on my still-hard noodles, unable to wait the required four minutes for them to soften. I debated running a bath, dismissing the idea as soon as it occurred to me on account of our noisy plumbing. After all, it was late and I didn't want to wake Pete downstairs. He was someone I didn't want to remind of my existence.

I ran the time over in my head, trying to work out if Martin would be done with the police yet. I doubted that these sort of interviews lasted very long, if it had even happened at all. Even so, a carousel of images flickered in my mind. Scenes from various movies and cop shows. Suspects being handcuffed and dragged to the police station, interrogations in small dark rooms. I told myself I was being dramatic, but still, I couldn't understand why Martin hadn't got in touch. Not when he had sent me to see Tom Briscoe to discuss his next move. Not when I had sent him a message from Tom's car, asking him to contact me.

Crossing the room, I sat at my desk and turned my computer on.

I checked my emails – all the accounts for which Martin had my email address – and switched my phone off and on to check whether it was working properly.

My next internet pit-stop was the *Daily Mail*. My eyes darted around the home page, looking for any story that might relate to Donna Joy. When I found nothing of interest, I repeated the exercise with every major national media site, then re-checked the Met's police appeal page to see if it had been updated, which it had not.

A voice in my head reassured me that so long as there was no mention of Donna's disappearance in the press, the less we all had to worry about her. But I felt increasingly on edge. My foot was tapping softly on the floor and I was helpless to stop it. I knew that my conversation with Tom Briscoe had not helped matters. In fact, he had angered me with his talk of victims and reputation-management lawyers, his insensitive implication that Martin was somehow involved in his wife's disappearance.

Coffee would help me think, but I knew it was the last thing I needed.

Instead, I went upstairs into my tiny en suite and opened the bathroom cabinet, where a white pot of pills sat next to my dental floss and contraceptives.

When I had gone to see Dr Katz a couple of weeks earlier, he had given me some additional medication. I was loath to take it at the time, but I knew that I needed something to calm me down now. Manic episodes frightened me even more than depressive ones. I was someone who liked to be in control, and I had ordered my life in an effort to keep tight hold of the reins. But over the past couple of days I had felt the gremlins in my head coming to life again.

Tipping back my head, I swallowed the pills then looked at my reflection in the mirror. I was pale and sad-looking. My lips were dry, my tired eyes were rimmed with pink, my skin blotchy in the harsh brightness of the overhead light.

Everything about my appearance screamed nervous exhaustion. I was desperate for sleep, but I knew that was not an option. The only thing that could calm my restlessness was reassurance from Martin.

I moved through to the bedroom and sat on the end of the bed, which only served to make me more anxious. I needed to be out there, fixing things, not eating Pot Noodles and sitting in the dark.

I found myself wishing that I had a car. I didn't have one. Never had. By the time I could afford one, it felt like an unnecessary luxury. But now I felt as if a car, a tiny peppermint Fiat, or some other such girl-about-town vehicle, might give me wings. My mobile phone, in my jeans pocket and pressing into my thigh, reminded me that a solution was only a phone call away.

I called the taxi and didn't hesitate before ringing Martin. It went straight to voicemail and I left a message, willing myself to stay calm. Zig-zagging the room, I took off my T-shirt, found a bra, and picked a white shirt from the wardrobe. Slipping my arms into the crisp sleeves of a clean shirt always empowered me, and tonight was no exception.

I waited in the hallway until the taxi arrived.

London was still buzzing as we slipped through the streets. As I stared out of the window, watching Angel bleed into the fashionable East End, I envied what I saw. Twenty-somethings on carefree nights out, their blithe, intoxicated joy reminding me of my own pleasure just hours earlier that day. But a switch had been flipped, a change in our universe had taken place, and a Greek chorus in my head warned me that I was wrong to be here. In a cab, hurtling towards Spitalfields at one o'clock in the morning, when Martin hadn't even replied to my calls.

It took twenty minutes to arrive at the W.H. Miller warehouse. There was no sign of any police car or 'unmarked vehicle' outside Martin's apartment block, which relieved me. I paid the cabbie and got out of the car. Nerves prickled round my body. Three men with elaborate beards laughed as they came out of a nearby bar, startling me.

The cab trundled off into the distance and the fashionable trio disappeared into the dark, leaving me alone. I walked across the cobblestones towards the warehouse. There was a tree outside I hadn't noticed before; thin, black, spindly. I rested the palm of my hand on its trunk as I looked up to the top floor. There was a faint glow from one of the windows, a sign of life that steeled me to call Martin again.

This time he answered.

'It's me,' I said, trying to tone down the urgency in my voice. 'The police. Have they gone?'

'Yes. Did you speak to your lawyer friend?'

'Yes. He was helpful.' My voice shook, I was shivering so hard from the cold.

'You'd better come up.'

Waiting for the lift, I looked up at the atrium ceiling, noticing that it went all the way up to the roof, as if it had been scooped out of the brickwork and metal. As the lift door opened, sound rattled all the way to the rafters, loud at first, disappearing to a soft echo as it rippled upwards.

Martin was holding a tumbler of Scotch when he opened the door. He tossed it back and barely looked at me.

'I had to come. I'm sorry,' I said, trying to read the expression on his face.

I stopped myself. I didn't know why I was apologizing.

'I should have called,' he said, putting his drink down on the table. 'It was all just a bit stressful. The police were here longer than I expected.'

The room was dark, the only light coming from a floor lamp in the corner.

Martin moved restlessly around the room like a cat, his stockinged feet sliding silently across the parquet.

'She's still not turned up,' he said, wiping his mouth with the back of his hand.

'So what did the police want from you?'

'Details about Monday night. What time I went home. When I got there. Whether anyone could give me an alibi for that.'

'You know a hundred and fifty thousand people go missing each year. That's 0.05 per cent of the population,' I said, trying to make him feel better.

'Been on Google?' he replied. There was a sourness to his tone that I didn't like.

'I'm trying to help,' I said, reminding myself how stressed he must be feeling.

He sank on the sofa and put his head in his hands.

'I'm sorry,' he said, looking up and stretching his hand out for me to take it.

I sat next to him on the sofa. Our thighs touched but I wanted to get closer.

'Our marriage might not have worked, sometimes I don't even think I like Donna any more, but this . . .'

'What did you tell them?' I asked quietly.

'I left at one. Out of the front door. I don't think she locked it behind me because I left her upstairs.'

I found it difficult to concentrate. It didn't seem like the time to ask him, why, if he didn't like Donna, had he fucked her? And there were inconsistencies in his story. He'd told me that he'd left Donna's at midnight, not one o'clock in the morning.

'They even asked me about this bloody cut on my hand.'

The one I had noticed in the oyster shed.

'What did you say?'

'I fell off my bike.'

'Did you?' I challenged.

'Yes,' he replied with irritation.

'So, why are they so worried about her when she has a track record of going away, visiting friends . . . ?'

'No one knows where she is. She has an Instagram account she uses a lot, posting pictures of parties, her artwork, but that hasn't been used since Monday.'

'It's not much to go on,' I said sympathetically.

'Tomorrow they're searching her house again. Specialist officers, apparently. Cadaver dogs.'

'And the police told you all this?'

We looked at each other and we both knew what they would find. His hair in the sink, his semen on the sheets. I looked away and tried not to think about the finer details.

'What about the appeal?'

'We're filming it tomorrow afternoon to go out later that night. The police think I should speak. I should definitely be there. With her family.'

'You should speak to a lawyer before you do anything. You need to tread carefully.'

'What did your colleague say?' he asked after another moment.

'Tom?'

Martin looked at me. 'You were there long enough.'

I heard jealousy in his voice, and I liked it.

'He's recommended a couple of lawyers. You should speak to Matthew Clarkson before you talk to the police again. Robert Kelly keeps things out of the press,' I said, giving him the phone numbers that Tom had written down.

'Keeps what things out of the press?'

'Speculation. The press have to report things very carefully these days, but sometimes insinuation gets through the net.'

I heard him make a soft exhalation of breath.

'This is mad,' he said, shaking his head. 'All I did was go to her house. Our house.'

I nodded, with a sense of shame and disappointment.

I thought about that Monday night when I had followed Donna to the restaurant, and then with Martin to her house. I could picture myself in the pub across the road. But my recollections beyond the first couple of drinks were as clear as they had been when I had woken up on Pete's sofa. At the time, I was embarrassed at the whole sorry episode, ashamed that I had blacked out and woken up with ripped tights and bloody legs, but now I was angry that I had no fragments of memory that could help Martin.

Had I not been so drunk, I might have known the exact time that Martin left Donna's house. I might have seen the front door fly dangerously open; I might have even gone across the road and closed it.

'What do they think has happened to her?'

'I don't know,' replied Martin, his voice barely audible.

'Well, let's think about it,' I said as coolly as I could. 'Perhaps she's OK,' I added after a moment's thought. 'Perhaps she's at a spa or a friend's, or she's in John O'Groats or Land's End and hasn't thought to call, or *has* thought about calling but hasn't bothered because she wants to scare you shitless.'

'And perhaps she's not OK,' said Martin, meeting my gaze and holding it.

'It's a possibility.' I nodded. 'Maybe she got up after you'd left and came after you,' I said, my mind racing through the myriad of options. 'The streets are dark at that time, empty. There are drunk drivers on the road. She could have been knocked down, a hit-and-run, and someone panicked.'

'We can't think like that.'

'We have to,' I said, feeling my eyes widen. 'Donna has been missing for five days and the police are interviewing you. She also could have been hurt in some way. Assaulted.'

Martin let out a sound, a low, guttural moan of the wounded, and when he looked up there was so much pain in his eyes I didn't know where to look.

'I know this is hard, but you're going to have to toughen up, right now.'

He stood up and paced the grey rug slowly as if his mind was in torment. When he looked back at me, it was as if he had come to a decision.

'Look, I'm tired. I need to get some sleep. There's nothing we can do now.'

His body language had become instantly defensive and I knew what he was saying.

'I should go,' I said softly.

'Do you mind?'

I didn't say anything, simply stood up and picked up my bag. I'd been dismissed and I couldn't help feeling piqued.

'With the police coming here, and Donna being missing, I just think . . . I just think we probably shouldn't see each other for a few days.'

I knew what he was saying made sense, but as I looked at him and our eyes locked, for a fleeting moment, I hated him.

# Chapter 20

I slept with my mobile phone under my pillow – although 'slept' would be overstating the facts. Rather I lay there in bed, tense and fretful, going over and over everything, examining every tiny facet until I gave in and scrabbled in my bedside drawer and dry-swallowed a sleeping pill. And even then, I couldn't relax. My mind felt like that moment when the bathwater is swirling around the plughole, faster and faster, forming a silvery whirlpool that sucks everything down, down . . .

But at some point I must have slept because the humming of my iPhone made my eyes snap open. I snatched it up, thumbing the button, pushing the hair from my face.

'Yes?'

'I haven't woken you, have I?'

A voice. Female, light and good humoured. I frowned, trying to reboot my brain.

'Clare?'

A tinkle of laughter. A sound from happier, more carefree times.

'Someone had a late night.'

'You could say that,' I replied, sitting up and pushing the

pill bottle by the bed away with one finger. The label read 'Somnovit', which almost sounded healthy, like a Victorian tonic, but those little tablets filled my head with straw and pushed bamboo slivers under my nerve endings every time. I was prescribed them years ago by my first doctor, who told me that people with bipolar disorder often found it hard to sleep. But sometimes there was no alternative when my mind was humming like the inside of a hive.

Realizing why she was calling, I sat back against the pillow, bracing myself for her words. With a televised media appeal planned for that evening, I didn't doubt that Donna's disappearance would have made the Sunday papers.

'Just checking what time you were planning on getting down here,' said Clare, her voice too perky for what I was expecting.

'Getting down here?' I said slowly.

I'd assumed she was calling about Martin. That she'd read a story about Donna Joy and put two and two together. Worked out that he wasn't just my lover – that he was my client. Worked out that I hadn't been truthful.

'Although at this rate I'm going to have to ask you to bring a paintbrush and overalls,' she continued breezily. 'We were here until midnight last night and it's still not bloody finished. Had to come back at eight to fix coat-hooks in the cloakroom. I am officially now an expert with a Black and Decker power tool.'

There was an almost audible click in my head.

'The launch,' I said with relief. Tonight was the grand opening of the restaurant. It all came back in a rush, all the emails and snatched conversations, the scrabble to find chefs and waitresses and an interior designer who could make Dom's place look like The Ivy on the cheap. It had consumed Clare for months, so much so that she obviously didn't have time to read the weekend papers. But tonight – oh crap, tonight – there was a cocktail party for family and friends and, vitally, the food journalists they had bribed and cajoled into attend-ance.

'Or you can come round to the house for drinks first?' said Clare, an edge creeping into her voice. 'I'm sure I can leave Dom at the restaurant for a while and we can get ready over here together?'

'About tonight . . .' I said slowly.

'Sorry, I forgot,' she teased. 'Martin. Do you want to bring him?'

'No,' I said too quickly. 'I'm just not sure I can come.'

'Not come?'

There was disappointment in her voice, of course. But it was worse than that. It was as if she had been expecting it. Like some people just can't be relied upon.

'Something's come up,' I said, knowing how pathetic it sounded.

'But you've known about tonight for weeks and Dom's had a ham especially imported from Jerez . . .'

I was beginning to get impatient, my attention drifting back to where I had left it before my slumber. The iPad, abandoned on the duvet, demanded to be picked up and I knew there was only one easy way to get my friend off the phone.

'OK, I'll come,' I said, knowing deep down that it was a bad idea. 'I'll just have to move some things around and come straight to the restaurant. That OK?'

The relief in her voice told me just how important it was to her and I felt worse for having tried to back out.

'Thanks, Fran,' she said eagerly. 'See you at seven?'

'OK,' I replied, wondering already what excuse I could give to be gone by eight.

'This it, love?'

I looked up at the taxi driver, slightly startled, and saw a restaurant front with brightly lit windows. Even from here, I could hear the beat of music and the hum of conversation; there were people standing on the pavement outside holding wine glasses and forbidden cigarettes.

'Yes, thank you,' I said, stepping out and straightening my dress as best I could. It was then I saw the sign above the building's propped-open door: *Dominic's*, spelled out in gold script. I'll admit I was momentarily annoyed; it was completely typical that Dom had named it after himself, despite the fact that it had been Clare's hard work and money that had made it happen.

As I stepped inside, I took a breath, my eyes scanning the room, the sea of faces, smiles, laughter. The entire restaurant was full of people who didn't care about anything other than how long the free bar was going to last.

My irritation was undercut by relief then pride as I saw Clare's beaming smile across the room.

'It's a triumph,' I said, going over and hugging her tight. 'I can't believe how many people are here.'

'I know,' Clare laughed. 'We had convinced ourselves that it'd be just us and the waiters. Can you believe Sophie Cole brought the guy from the *Times* along? I thought she was just showing off, but they're here. Dom practically got him into a head-lock as soon as they arrived and he's been feeding him champagne ever since.'

'Sophie Cole is here?'

I didn't know why that made me feel nervous. Sophie had been nothing but warm and welcoming to me, but she was a sharp and shrewd customer, an idea that put me on edge.

Dom looked up from his huddle with the critic and offered me a distracted wave. I felt bad for being so uncharitable about the name – what else was he supposed to call his restaurant? – and waved back.

'So did you get whatever it was sorted?' asked Clare.

I glanced back at my friend, searching her face for clues, wondering what – if anything – she had been discusing with Sophie. Was it innocent chit-chat or a probing question? It was sometimes hard to tell. That was the downside to being friends with a therapist, you could never completely relax. Not when you had something to hide.

'Just some work thing,' I said, grateful for the arrival of a waiter with a tray of wine glasses.

'Big case?'

I realized with a flash of piqued bemusement that she didn't know. She still didn't know about Donna's disappearance. Didn't know about Martin's torment, my torment.

I nodded as I took the first sip of alcohol.

My confession – that my lover Martin wasn't just married, he was also my client – was on the tip of my tongue. And I didn't want it to stop there. I wanted to tell Clare everything: that I had followed Martin and Donna on the night she disappeared. That perhaps I had seen something important, knew something about the disappearance but couldn't quite recall it. Not only was Clare my best friend, I knew this was the sort of thing that she could help me with – after all, she had spent her entire working life dealing with the complexities of the mind. But how could I explain something I didn't understand myself?

But Clare carried on speaking before I could say anything.

'You don't have to work seven days a week you know. Even I've gone old-school and given myself Sundays off.' She smiled as she sipped her champagne.

Something else she didn't know: I wasn't late to her party because I'd been working. I had spent the entire afternoon at the gym, working out feverishly, alternating between trying to forget about the fact that Martin was at that moment filming the police appeal about Donna's disappearance, and obsessing about every detail of it. Where he might be, what he might say, all the while clutching my phone, wondering if it would vibrate in my hand with news from Martin.

'About Martin . . .' I began.

'I'm glad it's just us tonight,' she smiled, cutting me off. 'You know, when you said you weren't coming tonight, I thought you'd blown me off again for sex.'

Her voice was low, playful, but I couldn't ignore the soft rebuke. After all, the last time I'd seen Clare was at the gallery event where I'd invited her along, only to stay an hour before I slipped off.

The realization that those easy, carefree moments were just a handful of days ago made me feel so sad that the air seemed to disappear from my lungs.

'I wouldn't do that . . .'

'You know, I read a piece of research the other day. Apparently, falling in love costs people two close friendships. Not enough hours in the day apparently, something's got to give. So I'd better take whatever scraps you can give me.'

There was a resentful edge to her voice and I knew I had to defuse it.

'We've been busy. Work has been crazy and you've had Dom's restaurant to sort out . . .'

My resolve to tell her about Martin crumbled. It was clear that Clare blamed him for the fact that I had not seen much of her for the past few weeks, so the best course of action was not to talk about him.

Clare shook her head and took a longer swig of champagne. 'No, we haven't stopped for a minute – the paint is still wet,' she said gesturing up to the ceiling with her glass. 'We were still finishing up this afternoon. It's like that old joke about the queen, how she thinks everywhere smells of fresh paint. Must be the same with restaurant critics.'

'You have a bit of Dulux just there,' I said, touching a pale fleck in her hair.

Clare's hand came up to touch mine, her palm covering my fingers.

'Thank you,' she said, her eyes shining. 'It wouldn't have been the same without you here, you know that, don't you?'

Her gaze was so intense, I had to look away, only to see Sophie, coming towards me through the crowds.

She was fixing a shawl over her shoulders looking as if she were about to leave. I froze, caught between wanting to speak to her and wanting to hide.

'Hello, Fran,' she said kissing me on the cheek.

I looked around for Clare, but she had gone.

'Dom's thrilled you came with your friend,' I said, forcing a smile. 'It was so kind of you to sort that out.'

'I told Clare I'd try and I like to stick to my word. Besides, I was hoping to see you.'

'Me?'

She stayed silent for a moment, which was long enough to make me feel uncomfortable.

'I assume you've heard about Donna,' she said lowering her voice. 'What's going on?'

'I can't answer that,' I said honestly. 'No one knows.'

Her eyes watched me and I began to feel like a dormouse under the shadow of a circling hawk.

'How much do you know about her?'

'Donna? Very little,' I replied.

'Really? You're Martin's counsel.'

'What does that mean?' I said, not meaning to sound defensive.

'You're a great lawyer, Fran. I bet you found out everything you could about Donna when you were preparing his case.'

'I have no idea why she's disappeared, Sophie, if that's what you're asking.'

'None whatsoever?'

I could imagine her interviewing prospective employees at the Gassler Partnership, imagine how unsettled she would make them feel. No one would dare tell her a lie, or embellish a CV, because Sophie Cole was the type of person who would catch you out.

I shook my head and she pulled her shawl a little tighter around her body.

'Have you ever met her?' she said, not flinching in her gaze.

I didn't know if there was an accusation in her question but I decided that the best course of action was to avoid it. My fleeting meeting with Donna Joy that day in court was barely anything anyway.

'She's smart. If no one has seen her for a week, there's a reason for that.'

'You think she's trying to manipulate Martin, somehow?'

'Either she's causing trouble, or she's in trouble. As much as I've been worried about the business ever since she filed for divorce, I hope it's not the latter.'

My cheeks had gone hot. I looked up towards the lights, noticing a few patches of ceiling that Dom and Clare had not painted, and when I glanced back at Sophie, she was still watching me.

'You don't look well,' she said. 'Do you need some water?'

I shook my head.

'Well,' she replied. 'I was just leaving.'

I stood rooted to the spot. I didn't dare turn and watch her go out of the restaurant, although a part of me sensed that she was watching me.

I glanced at my watch to check the time, wondering if the televised appeal for Donna's disappearance was the reason Sophie was leaving early too.

Seven forty-five already. I couldn't see Clare anywhere and I was glad about that. I'd shown my face and I could go now, although there was not enough time to get home. Instead, I drifted away from the main room of the restaurant towards the stairs. No one noticed me weave through the crowds and head upstairs. I was vaguely aware of the plans for the first-floor space of the property. Clare had told me that if, when, the restaurant took off, it would be made into a private dining space or even a designer flat they could rent out for a princely sum to help subsidize Dominic's.

But as I looked around the scruffy space, I knew neither of those plans were anywhere near being realized. There were just three rooms up here, all tired and semi-furnished. Clearly, someone – Dominic most likely – had been using one room as an office and living room. There was a desk with a phone, and untidy piles of paper, and a flat-screen television sitting on a box facing an old sofa, with a games console tucked away to one side. My first guess was correct. This was Dom's little hideaway, his man cave where he could while away a few hours on *Call of Duty* while supposedly working on restaurant business.

I felt a little hit of self-righteousness. I'd been right about Dom all along. I had never really liked Clare's husband; at first I had him down as a charming bum, but over the years had been frustrated at the way he had played the handsome dilettante, the restaurant being one of the many glamorous projects that had taken his fancy but had never been fully realized.

First had been the novel that had never hit the bookshelves, indeed it hadn't got beyond a series of long lunches with minor agents, then came the pop-up art space, that seemed designed to allow Dominic to spend his evenings 'networking' at swish Mayfair parties, all of it bankrolled by Clare who worked every hour in order to pay for his endeavours.

But this time I was grateful for his pleasure seeking. He had a television up here and it was exactly what I had come looking for.

I picked up the remote control and clicked it on, scrolling to the news channels, perched on the arm of the sofa. Some unimportant news items first. A scandal involving a politician, some Chinese investment into a steel plant.

'Come on,' I muttered as I followed the red ticker-tape newsfeed across the bottom of the screen.

And then it happened. My heart sped up as the newsreader said the name 'Donna Joy'. A close-up of Martin's wife filled the screen – some beautiful, smiling holiday snap that made my thoughts drift to where she might have been, who she would have been with. Had Martin himself taken that photograph in happier times? At their house in Ibiza perhaps, or on one of their many glamorous holidays in the sun. I didn't want to dwell on it.

The newsreader's voice was more sombre now as she summarized Donna's disappearance over a montage of images: a 'Find Donna Joy' Facebook page, the facade of her Chelsea home and a display of her artwork at the studio which was annoyingly good.

A new face appeared on the screen, one that looked like Donna, but an inferior copy. A woman with the same long hair, but a mousy shade of brown, her skin lacking the expensively tanned radiance of a banker's wife.

A caption explained her identity: *Jemma Banks – Sister*.

'Donna is a beautiful, creative and kind sister,' said Jemma Banks in hard estuary vowels a world away from Donna's honeyed tones. Her voice told me so much more about Donna

Joy than any of my internet searches ever could. It told me about her background, where she was from, and confirmed my suspicions that Donna was a social adventurer, a sharp-elbowed climber, a Becky Sharp, like many other trophy wives I'd met in the past.

By contrast, Donna's sister was an everywoman from an unremarkable suburb, a world away from the prestigious postcodes of her sibling's life. But Jemma's words were real and it was impossible not to be moved by the woman's plea.

'I love her and we all just want her to come home.'

Even though I hated Donna for seducing Martin, for the way she had so casually, so selfishly caused all this trouble, I felt tears well in my eyes as I watched the appeal. Sophie Cole had been right. If Donna had disappeared to a spa or a yoga retreat, she was an absolute minx. But the alternative, that something had happened to her, was too unbearable to think about.

But if I struggled to fill my lungs with air, I almost stopped breathing entirely when a tired and drained-looking Martin Joy came into view.

'. . . so if anyone has seen Donna, please get in touch with the police. Donna, we miss you. If you hear this, let us know as soon as possible.'

'What are you doing?' I said out loud.

I'd suggested he speak to a lawyer but I wasn't sure that they would recommend saying anything at the appeal. It was *obvious* that he shouldn't say anything. He was the husband of a missing woman, and partners were always the first in line if foul play was suspected, especially when they were in the middle of a messy divorce involving a lot of money.

Yet here he was, tired-looking and unshaven – not the sexy, manly stubble I had stroked when he returned from the Swiss Alps, but a five o'clock shadow that made him look furtive, suspicious. Guilty. And as for *we miss you* – it sounded so . . . weak. Not that I wanted him weeping and clutching his chest, but he needed to at least look sincere and committed in his desire to see Donna safe and well.

I felt sick, and it wasn't because I'd been drinking on an empty stomach. Of course I knew the potential for trial by the masses. I'd seen it before: the McCanns, Christopher Jefferies. If the public made up their mind you were guilty – or at least 'suspicious' – it could destroy you. If I had watched that broadcast without knowing Martin, what would I have thought of him?

'Just tell us where you are,' he said to camera. 'Let us know that you're safe.'

'Don't say anything else,' I pleaded, clenching my hand into a fist, imagining the hacks watching this performance, knowing that Martin and Donna were separated and sharpening their nibs for innuendoes of foul play, if not outright accusation. I wanted to climb inside the television and protect him. Hold him. Stop them.

'Don't say anything . . .' I whispered out loud.

I whirled around as I felt a hand on my shoulder.

'Jesus, Fran, what are you doing?'

Dominic was standing behind me, his eyes wide, a deep crease between his brows.

'I needed to check the news,' I stammered.

'The news?' he repeated, looking down at the remote as if I had stolen something from him.

'One of our clients is involved in a story.'

'What have they done?' said Dom, trying to look past me to the screen. 'Killed someone?'

I turned and clicked the off button.

'Nothing so interesting,' I said, carefully placing the remote back where I found it.

'I didn't mean to intrude, I was looking for Clare. Fantastic launch, by the way. The canapés are amazing and the champagne cocktails . . .'

'Well, keep telling Clare that,' he said with a faint smile. 'It's wiped out our savings, so it had better work.'

'Of course it's going to work,' I said, still embarrassed about being caught up here.

Dominic looked at me, his eyes watery, his cheeks flushed and I realized he was drunk.

'I wish you would have said that to Clare six months ago.'

'Said what?' I asked, trying to concentrate on what he was saying.

'You thought a restaurant was just another one of my time-wasting schemes.'

He snorted a playful laugh, but the smile didn't reach his eyes. *Thanks a lot, Clare,* I thought, amazed that she had obviously repeated my misgivings to her husband.

'I never said that,' I said, trying to keep my tone jovial and light.

He raised a questioning brow and I knew I had to pre-empt the direction of our conversation.

'If I ever did say anything, I was just worried you were taking a risk. When Clare said you were about to sign a lease on this place, I thought about that statistic which says two out of every three restaurants close within the first year.'

It was the truth. It felt like the first honest thing I'd said to Clare or Dom in weeks. I *had* warned her that they could lose tens, hundreds, thousands of pounds on a gourmet vanity project. Clare was successful, but she didn't have that sort of cash to lose. When I told her to be cautious, it was with the best intentions.

'Just try not to cause trouble in the future,' he said, taking a casual swig of his wine. He gave me a look, arrogant, belligerent.

'I wasn't causing trouble, Dom. I care about you both.'

I could hear a tremor in my voice. The appeal had already unsettled me and the last thing I needed was a confrontation with Clare's husband.

'Really?'

'Restaurants are high-risk, Dom. I wouldn't be a good friend if I didn't point it out.'

'You didn't want me to open this business, Fran. You did everything you could to put Clare off the idea.'

'When did she say that?'

I was genuinely confused. I had no idea she had actually listened to the caution I had offered.

'She listens to you, Fran. Too much. She listens to you more than she listens to me. But please, just butt out of our marriage, because sometimes I think there are three of us in it. Things never end well, when there are three people in a marriage.'

I thought of me and Martin and Donna Joy and nodded in agreement.

# Chapter 21

It was Monday, early. My office was tidy, a cup of strong coffee already halfway gone, when our head clerk Paul knocked and entered carrying a file under his arm. Usually he'd throw it on my desk, like a knight delivering a head on a plate, but today he waited, holding it close to his chest.

'So have you spoken to Martin Joy this weekend?' he said, putting both hands on my desk.

'Briefly,' I replied, feeling a spidery flush of guilt creep up my neck.

'And?' said Paul, unsatisfied with my answer.

'He told me about the police appeal. I suppose his divorce is the last thing on his mind right now.'

Paul raised his eyebrows; an expression of disapproval. Disapproval of Martin and presumably disapproval of me for being Martin's brief. I very much doubted Paul harboured any concern for the whereabouts or indeed safety of Donna Joy; he was thinking about the firm. Suspicion on Martin put the spotlight on us too and messy tabloid stories were most certainly bad for business, especially when your business was quick, discreet divorces. From Paul's point of view, the Joy case was like the iceberg to his *Titanic*.

'So what's the latest?' he said, his eyebrows still up.

'Mrs Joy is still missing,' I said, aware that I was not quite meeting his eye.

'I am aware of that, I do listen to Radio 4.'

I smiled, but this clearly wasn't a time for levity.

'So what do you think?' I asked. 'Did you see the TV appeal?'

'You mean, do I think he's involved in her disappearance?'

'Yes,' I said more boldly.

I watched him carefully. Paul hesitated and shifted his position, knitting his brows. In the usual run of events, his loyalty to the clients almost surpassed his devotion to the barristers in chambers, but Martin Joy had brought the firm into disrepute, so Paul was conflicted. *Tell me about it,* I thought as I watched him struggle.

'In all my time working in family law, I'm surprised we haven't come across this before,' he said finally.

'Come across what?'

'The conveniently missing wife.'

'*Conveniently* missing?'

'Well, it *is* very convenient, isn't it? What's at stake in this divorce? A hundred million, give or take? Maths is not my strongest point, but I'd guess that a fifty per cent split of a hundred million is a lot of money.'

I made sure that my face didn't give anything away.

'The reason we don't come across it more, Paul, is that, however hard it is for the husband to give up half their net worth, they find the idea of twenty years in Belmarsh even less appealing. Otherwise, we'd be knee-deep in bodies.'

Paul nodded in agreement. 'Still, the police are taking this seriously. They don't do a telly appeal for any Tom, Dick or Harry.'

He glanced at his watch and shifted back into efficiency mode. 'I spoke to Vivienne and Charles last night,' he said, name-checking our two most senior members. 'Vivienne suggested we talk to John Cook at the Beresford Group – a PR outfit. They do reputational management work. I've just called him and he can do a conference call in twenty minutes. I suggest you sit in on the meeting.'

He stood up, still clutching the file, and as I collected my things to go to the conference room, I saw him disappear in the direction of Tom Briscoe's office, no doubt off to give him the work that a few weeks earlier he would have given me.

'There are two ways you can jump,' said the voice of John Cook from the speakerphone in the middle of the table. So far, I had kept absolutely silent throughout the conference call, merely grateful that Vivienne's choice of reputation management expert was not Robert Kelly, whose details I had given Martin. 'You can keep your distance from the police investigation, and close down any enquiries from the media with a short, polite press release that you are simply representing Mr Joy in a family law matter. Or, you could use Mr Joy's unexpected profile to promote your chambers. Donna Joy's disappearance makes this a high-profile case and if she doesn't turn up it could run and run.'

'You mean any publicity is good publicity?' said Paul drinking his coffee.

Charles Napier, our head of chambers, peered at Paul over the top of his glasses with a look of undisguised disapproval.

'Obviously we want to be as supportive as possible to our

client,' said Charles Napier, directing his attention back towards the phone sitting in the middle of the table.

'By the same token, we also need to minimize any potential scandal. That is an absolute imperative.'

'Is there anything I should know about, beyond the usual reputational issues?' asked Cook.

Vivienne shot a look at Charles, who was removing his glasses as if he were emphasizing a particularly delicate point of law.

'We have two barristers up for silk this year, Mr Cook. One of them, Francine here, is representing Martin Joy in his divorce. Whilst one would expect the judicial appointments system to be scrupulously impartial, we can't afford to let any potential criminal investigation into Martin Joy affect the chances of our barristers being appointed Queen's Counsel.'

'In which case we will distance ourselves as much as possible from Donna and Martin Joy,' confirmed Cook. 'Shut down social media references to Burgess Court, draft a press release. I'll get my team on it and call you back this afternoon.'

When Paul and Charles had left the boardroom, I hung back, hoping to talk to Vivienne McKenzie alone.

'What's this really about?' I asked her when she had closed the door behind her.

'"Really about"?' She put her notebook on the table and looked at me quizzically.

'The Beresford Group charge about £500 an hour. Are chambers really prepared to risk that to help me and Tom make silk?'

Vivienne gave me a maternal smile.

'You don't miss anything, do you?'

'Call me a cynic,' I said, realizing my hunch was correct.

Vivienne didn't speak for a few moments.

'You should know that we have been approached by Sussex Court chambers about a possible merger.'

'A merger? Surely this should have been discussed with the tenants.'

'There's nothing concrete to discuss. Yet,' she added pointedly. 'And if such a merger were to go ahead, it could be incredibly beneficial for all of us. Sussex Court are a big, powerful – and, truthfully, more prestigious set than we are. However, we all agree that there are benefits from economies of scale. It's a particularly important step for Burgess Court, as we all know that, moving forward, smaller sets are going to struggle to survive.'

The shock of learning that Burgess Court might be in financial trouble stunned me to silence for a moment.

'What has this got to do with Martin Joy?' I asked cautiously.

'If anything has happened to Donna Joy, and if her husband had anything to do with it, it will attract a lot of unwelcome attention. Sussex Court are conservative. Their head of chambers is positively reactionary. A whiff of scandal might scare them off.'

'But you're talking as if the police have arrested and charged Martin,' I said, hearing my words speed up. 'We have no reason to even believe he is a suspect, no reason to believe that anything awful has happened to Donna Joy.'

'Charles even wondered if you could, if you *should* drop Martin as a client.'

'Drop him?'

She waved a hand. 'He was just being hot-headed. But . . . divorce proceedings obviously can't continue. Even if Mrs Joy turns up overnight, we should encourage Martin Joy to step back from anything litigious. For now, at least.'

'I can't say that to him.'

Vivienne gave the faintest of smiles.

'Yes you can,' she replied, her eyes peering through the thin grey slats of the blinds that covered the picture window to the conference room. 'Because, unless I am very much mistaken, Martin Joy has just turned up in reception.'

# Chapter 22

We were back to where we started. The same room, the same pool of nerves in my belly. It was a different type of anxiety this time though. My heart was thumping, thumping hard with anger and frustration and longing. I hated that Martin had left me hanging for so long, I hated that he had made me seem a liar.

I hadn't missed Paul's look of surprise when he saw me go and meet my controversial client in reception. A look that said, *That's funny. You hardly know Martin Joy. You said you'd hardly even spoken to him. I thought you'd said the last thing on his mind was his divorce.*

Unnerved by his arrival, I hesitated by the blinds, wondering whether to open them completely or close them.

'Leave it,' ordered Martin, as if he had read my thoughts. 'Don't do anything you wouldn't do with any other client.'

'You said we shouldn't see each other,' I said finally.

My voice was almost a whisper. The room was fairly sound-proof, so I knew no one else could hear us, but I could barely breathe, let alone speak.

'I'm on my way to the police station,' said Martin, sitting down at the table. 'We need to talk properly before I go.'

Out of the corner of my eye, I could see Paul still watching us from the other side of the window. I took a seat opposite Martin, opened my notebook and took my pen from my pocket, grateful for the chance to sit down.

'So how was the appeal? I saw it on television,' I said as calmly as I could. 'Were you advised to speak?'

'I've instructed Matthew Clarkson, as you suggested. We met before filming and he suggested I go alone, without legal representation.'

'Were Donna's family there?'

I had only seen Jemma Banks and Martin speak at the appeal, but I knew others could have been edited out.

'Her mum is on a cruise and didn't make it back in time. They filmed it at her sister's house. Jemma and her husband practically ignored me. As you can imagine, it was awkward.'

I could imagine how difficult it must have been for him and appreciated it was a smart move by the police. I imagined myself as a perpetrator, filming an appeal in some anonymous hotel room, a blank canvas, and how much easier it would be for me to lie to the cameras on such an empty stage. Doing the same thing in a relative's house, a personal space, would be a different story, unless you were as cold as ice.

'Did the police say why they wanted you to speak?' I said, feeling guilty for even thinking of Martin as a perpetrator.

'I offered. I've got nothing to hide. Nothing except us,' he said after a moment, his green eyes looking darker.

I shifted in my chair and when I looked up, Martin was still watching me.

'No one can know we've been seeing each other, Fran,' he said. His tone was blunt but his words smarted like a paper cut. I knew right then why he was here. When Vivienne McKenzie had said he was in reception, I had wondered, for one exquisite moment, if Martin had been desperate to see me, desperate for my presence, my wise, reassuring words. But now I knew he was here to clear the decks, get his story in order, and he was doing it all in plain sight.

'This doesn't look good for me either, Martin,' I replied, pulling myself up straight.

He nodded. 'I know. That's why you need to erase every text on your phone from me. Any email that might sound inappropriate.'

'We're protected, Martin. It's legal privilege. Any communication between lawyer and client doesn't have to be disclosed and is inadmissible if it is—'

'I don't want to take any chances,' he replied, cutting me off.

I glanced behind him and saw Paul still standing there. I felt hot under his gaze and my hand was trembling.

'Donna is missing and the spouse is always a suspect. If the police and the press aren't already out to crucify me, they will have plenty of ammunition when they find out I've been seeing my divorce lawyer.'

'Martin, I don't know what you've said to the police already, but you can't lie to them,' I said, feeling a small pulse under my right eye. 'There'll be a hundred things you won't have thought of and if they start digging around your whereabouts over the past week, chances are I'm going to turn up.'

'So you don't mind being open about our relationship?' he challenged me.

I thought about my silk application, about the Burgess Court merger, about my friends in chambers who I had let down.

'Not unless we have to,' I whispered.

'You're my lawyer,' he said, with reassuring authority. 'I'm in the middle of an expensive divorce, so it's only natural that we've spent time together. We went to the coast together, but that was simply so I could show you my assets.'

'You can say that again,' I said, remembering our time in the oyster shed, the taste of his cock in my mouth, and the bristle of his hair against my skin.

He didn't smile at the suggestion of our intimacy.

'You were evaluating the house,' he continued, as if I hadn't even spoken. 'We drove to Essex on a Saturday because you work during the week. We stopped for a drink in the pub because the tide had cut us off.'

'Is that how you remember it?'

I felt his foot touch mine under the table and he didn't take his eyes away from me. It was a small gesture but it was a complicit one, a sign that told me that we were connected, that we were in this together. My relief was palpable.

'I would give every penny I've got for Donna to be OK. But if she's not, if something has happened to her, I want you to know that I had nothing to do with it.'

'I know,' I said, not even having to think about it.

# Chapter 23

Martin didn't stay long. I went back to my office in the eaves of Burgess Court but found it so hard to concentrate I headed out for an early lunch. It was a cold, grey day, the weather failing to launch into anything resembling fresh spring weather, but I wanted to eat outdoors. I put on my coat, grabbed a sandwich from Pret a Manger on Fleet Street and sat on one of the benches by the fountain outside Middle Temple Hall.

My phone chirped and I looked at the incoming text. I winced when I saw it was from Clare.

Can you talk? Just reading about Donna Joy.

No, I didn't want to talk, I thought, realizing she had finally connected all the dots. I certainly didn't want a lecture, and I suspected that would be how the conversation would go if I rang her back.

I stuffed my phone deep into my pocket, and closed my eyes, listening to the tipple-tapple of the water, enjoyed for a few fleeting moments the sensation of the cold flecks of spray that tickled my face. In the distance, I could hear the sound of a piano recital, and for a second, under the shade of the ancient mulberry trees overhead, I felt a sense of calm and comfort that I had not experienced in days.

Heels tapped against the cool flagstone of the court. One set was heavier than the others and as I heard them stop in front of me, I snapped open my eyes.

'Are you all right?' said Tom Briscoe as I looked up to see him standing there. He was dressed in a thick black coat, one hand was pulling his pilot case, the other holding a brown paper bag from our local sandwich shop.

'Just tired,' I replied, embarrassed to be caught by him like this.

'You look like shit,' he said, sitting next to me on the bench.

'Cheers,' I replied, giving the nearest thing to a chuckle I'd managed all week.

He took out a can of Coke and offered it to me.

'Do you want this? You probably need it more than I do.'

I nodded, realizing that I hadn't bought a drink from Pret and a shot of caffeine might be some sort of antidote to a sum total of five hours of weekend sleep. Thanking Tom, I took the can, which felt cold and inviting in my hand, tugged back the ring pull and let the fizzy liquid slide down my throat.

'I owe you one,' I said with a slow, satisfied sigh.

'You're welcome,' he said rummaging through his sandwich bag and pulling out a baguette.

I was glad of the company, and as I watched Tom take a bite out of his lunch, I wondered why we didn't do this more often.

'Was that Martin Joy I saw coming out of chambers?' he asked, casually motioning towards Burgess Court.

I nodded crisply, feeling hurt. I should have known better than to think Tom wanted my company for its own sake. He was here for the gossip. I shifted in my seat and put myself on guard. Tom was nothing if not ambitious. He'd said it himself: we were in a competition, *first one to make silk*. And I had no idea how far he would go to win.

'He's on his way to the police station,' I said.

'I heard he's instructed Matthew Clarkson. He'll sort him out,' he said with a relaxed confidence.

Despite Tom's motives for our impromptu lunch break, despite his obvious curiosity about Martin Joy, I felt reassured by his words. His didn't need to promise that everything would be all right.

'Are you in court today?'

I shook my head.

'Then you should go home.'

'I can't go home,' I said, thinking about the pile of case files on my desk.

Tom shrugged. 'There aren't many benefits to being self-employed. You might as well take advantage of one of them.'

The sceptic in me thought about all the additional work that was being put Tom's way: the file that Paul had been holding that morning, and no doubt countless other applications, injunctions and contact orders that our senior clerk thought I was unable to handle. No wonder he was encouraging me to play truant.

'Just go,' Tom repeated, and as I thought about my empty diary – for the first time in weeks, I hadn't had a scheduled day in court – I threw caution to the wind and decided to have the afternoon in bed.

I honestly intended to go home. I walked down Kingsway to my usual bus stop to take the number 19 north, but when I saw the one that took the southern route I found myself crossing the road to take it.

Nerves jangled throughout my body with the sense that I was setting off on an adventure. Sitting down on the scratchy fabric of the seat, I wanted to be invisible, but on the half-empty bus I felt exposed, as if the whole world was watching me.

The bus went south, almost to its final destination, past the soft sparkle of the Ritz, the patrician grandeur of Knightsbridge, down Sloane Street towards Chelsea. I guessed which stop was nearest to Donna's house and with a tentative finger presssed the bell as we approached the lower reaches of the King's Road.

It was another dark and miserable afternoon, grey clouds and drizzle reminding me of the night that I was last here. I pulled my coat around my waist, so tightly it felt I was corseted, and turned the corner on to Donna's street. Immediately I noticed activity at the house. I crept forward, uncertain steps taking me towards the pub where I had observed her house a week earlier.

I felt too exposed to watch what was going on from the street, so I stepped inside. The warm hop-scented air was like a blanket, swaddling me from the cold damp afternoon. It was almost empty, although that came as no surprise. It was Monday afternoon. I didn't suppose there were too many alcoholics in the Chelsea area and although they served lunch in the pub, that crowd had gone, just some empty glasses and a half-eaten burger on a plate, the only evidence of earlier activity.

I needed a drink. A pretty brunette, washing down the beer-spattered counter with a sponge, stopped what she was doing and asked what I wanted as I approached the bar.

It was a friendly question, the sort she would have asked dozens of times that day, but to me, it felt like an accusation. *What do you want? What are you doing here?* I didn't even know the answer to that one myself.

I asked for a vodka tonic, my hand shaking as I handed over a ten-pound note. There was a bank of tables underneath the window and I crossed the room to take a seat at the one with the clearest view of Donna's house. It was the same table, the same stakeout point as the previous week and as I sat down, I could clearly remember doing the same thing the previous Monday.

I remembered the back of Donna's pink coat going into the house, the dark blot of Martin's arm in the small of her back as he ushered her in.

I could picture a shadow at the window, Donna's slender silhouette closing the shutters, flat lines of golden light illuminating the slim spaces between the slats.

The house had seemed so imposing and still that night, but today as I watched, it looked busy and violated. I could see the scene-of-crime officers in their stark white forensics suits, the cheap-suited detectives, and a gaggle of photographers and reporters. I could see the television vans, the police dog vehicles and the rubberneckers, all being told to keep their distance by an officer barely out of Hendon. I couldn't see any blue-and-white crime scene tape, but it struck me that it was like watching a cop drama with the sound turned off. I'd seen enough of those shows to speculate what was going on inside, SOCO officers on their hands and knees, scouring the floors and carpets for blood, saliva and fibres. There'd be tweezers and evidence bags, areas combed for fingerprints and skin cells as they started to piece together what had happened to Donna Joy. And the scene in front of me told me they didn't think she was missing. They thought she was dead.

I took my phone out of my bag and looked at it. Clicking on the Messages icon, I scrolled through the ones from Martin. Texts about dinner and arrangements to meet. Morning-after texts, intimate texts. Texts that said things we sometimes couldn't say to one another in person.

I want to taste your cunt.

Martin had told me to get rid of them all. But I couldn't.

I didn't want to wipe away our history. I didn't want to pretend we hadn't existed.

I closed my eyes to compose myself, to think methodically, logically, like I did when I pored over my case files. If I got back to my flat at around two in the morning, I was probably in the pub until closing time. I imagined a timeline for what went on inside the house that evening. Did Martin and Donna have sex immediately? Did they close the door and start fucking against the wall, happy, heady and oblivious to anything, everything, especially the fact that I was watching them? More fragments of the evening started coming back to me. There was a delay between their entrance into the house and Donna closing the shutters. That suggested no scenes of passion in the hall – not like the night I had first gone back to Martin's loft, I thought, with a short-lived stab of victory.

No, this would have been a slower, more subtle seduction. I imagined Donna opening a bottle of wine, sitting on the sofa and kicking off her shoes as they talked and laughed about old times and people they had in common.

Perhaps she had got up to refill their glasses and he had followed her. I imagined them in the kitchen, a show-home space with a rack for the claret and a cabinet for her cut-glass stemware. I pictured her choosing the wine, her long artistic fingers stroking the bottles suggestively, at which point Martin would have acted on the impulse they had both been feeling all evening. Perhaps he kissed her on the back of the neck, and pushed up her dress.

The wine would have been forgotten by now. Let's go to bed, she'd have whispered and he'd have picked her up, light as a feather, and carried her to the master bedroom, their room, a place where they'd have made love hundreds of times before. Then and now.

Martin said he left her house at 1 a.m., but I didn't remember any of that. I was probably on my way back to Islington by then. I didn't remember anything beyond the shutters closing and the soft lights taunting me.

I glanced across at the barmaid, wondering whether to ask her if she'd been on duty that night. Did the staff have to kick out a lovelorn dribbling drunk and find her a taxi? Had I been an angry, vocal drunk, or did I sit and seethe silently by the window?

I wanted to know if anyone at the pub remembered me, but suddenly I was too afraid to find out.

My breath was quickening again and I felt helpless to stop it. Anxiety began to suffocate me, emotions were white-water rafting around my body, a thrill ride I was unable to get off.

'Want another one?

The barmaid was standing next to me, clearing my empty glass from the table.

For a moment I couldn't speak and she put a gentle hand on my shoulder.

'Are you all right, love?' she asked and her voice seemed to guide me back to reality.

'Yes. Just feeling a bit dizzy,' I nodded.

'I'll bring some water over,' she replied. 'The kitchen's stopped serving, but we've got crisps behind the bar if you think that'll help. It's probably your sugar levels.'

I watched her fill a jug from a tap behind the bar and she brought it to the table.

'You watching the action out there?' she asked, handing me a clean glass.

'What's going on?' I asked as innocently as I could.

'It's that lady that went missing. We've had the reporters in and out of here all day.'

'The banker's wife? I read about that. She lives on this street?'

The barmaid nodded. 'I used to see her around. Beautiful woman, like a model. I hope she's all right.'

I was grateful for the water but not her observation about the way Donna looked, which made me feel small and unremarkable.

I gulped back the water and when I'd drained the glass, I knew that I'd seen enough, knew that no greater clarity on the events of last Monday night would come to me, and that I should go home.

But as I watched a cadaver dog come out of Donna's house, I also knew that I couldn't just sit there and do nothing. I'd never been a wallflower, always hated playing the victim. Pure grit had taken me from our terraced house in Accrington to Charles Napier and Vivienne McKenzie's upper-middle class, white-collar world, and I couldn't sit back and let those people across the road – the police, the forensics team, the media – turn the screws on Martin. I had to be there for him, I had to help him. Because one glance at Donna's house was enough to tell me that all those people trying to find her were pointing the finger and blaming Martin. I had to help him and I had to start that moment.

I picked up my phone, hoping to see a message from him. Some reassurance that he'd only been asked a few perfunctory questions before being allowed to go home.

But there was nothing, no missed calls or unread texts. So instead of putting my phone away, I sent a message to Phil Robertson, asking him to come and meet me as quickly as possible.

Phil only lived in Battersea, so within twenty minutes I saw him pull up on his bike outside the pub.

'That was quick,' I said, giving him a wave.

'They don't call my neck of the woods Little Chelsea for

nothing,' he grinned as he pulled up a chair. We both knew that Phil's flat was a world away from this pocket of SW3. I'd never been to his house, but I could imagine it. A rented two-bedder, he'd complained on many occasions that he wasn't even the tenant, he was the lodger, the consequence of a messy divorce that had seen his unfaithful wife stay in the family home with their six-year-old daughter, while he was forced to pay £700 a month to a chef called Sean to sublet a double room behind Queenstown Road station.

'I thought we were meeting for coffee, but I'm guessing this is a stakeout,' he said, raising an eyebrow.

'I thought I'd come over to see what's going on,' I told him, feeling suddenly relieved that I had a partner in crime.

Phil got a beer, I asked for pint of lemonade and I told him that I had seen Martin earlier that day and that he was at the police station for further questioning.

Phil just sat and listened and took slow sips of his Stella.

'We need to help him, Phil,' I said feeling fortified by his presence, expecting Phil the divorcee, not just Phil the investigator to jump on board with my idea. But he sat back in his chair unmoved by my appeal.

'I know you're a brilliant lawyer, Fran, but you're Martin Joy's divorce lawyer and this has got to be his criminal team's job now.'

His words were like a personal affront. I couldn't believe he'd be so pedestrian.

'But we have a head start on them,' I said, hearing the panic in my voice. 'I don't know his solicitor Matthew Clarkson at all, but for all we know they might not be even thinking in terms of doing their own investigation. And even if they are, we started a week ago.'

I had a notebook in my bag – Martin's bag – and I put it on the table, opening my ink pen with a satisfying pop.

I liked to write things down. It helped me work things out and clarify my thoughts.

'When we met the other day, you said that you thought Donna Joy was seeing someone. That there'd been mini-breaks, and several nights when she didn't come home. You said you thought she was seeing her husband, but what if it was someone else?'

'Someone other than Martin Joy?'

'It's possible,' I said, forcing myself to remain emotionally unattached. 'She was separated. In her eyes, she was young, free and single. She was an attractive woman . . .' I stopped short of saying beautiful. 'She would have had admirers. Lots of them.'

'It makes sense,' said Phil, nodding.

'You should look into it.'

Phil peered at me over the rim of his glass and frowned. 'Has the client authorized it? Dave Gilbert didn't want me to chase down the mini-breaks . . .'

'That was Martin's divorce. It was just intel-gathering for negotiations on the financial settlement. This is different,' I said, letting my words hang heavily between us.

'So Martin wants us to look into it,' he replied slowly.

'I'll speak to him later, but he wants us to help in any way we can.'

Phil looked as if he was about to shake his head, but finally he shrugged.

'Just make sure you let his criminal solicitor know what we're up to. I don't want to go treading on anyone's toes, all right?'

'Of course,' I replied, standing up to go to the loo.

In the cool, dark bathroom, I felt better already. It was good coming here, I decided. It had been a good idea to meet Phil. Although I couldn't remember any more details about what I saw the night that Donna and Martin met for dinner, I felt as if I had taken a step away from the edge of the chasm. I felt more empowered and finally able to see a way through the darkness.

I placed my hands on either side of the cold enamel sink, then turned on the tap to splash some water on my face. As I looked up into the mirror I could see thin trails of mascara drip from the corners of my eyes, dark and soulful like Pierrot's tears. I wiped it again with the corner of a tissue, reapplied my red lipstick and felt ready to step outside again. I felt back in control, my body surging with emotion and excitement, ideas coming thick and fast about what we could do.

My stomach rumbled and I realized I was hungry. I didn't want to stay in the pub any longer, and wondered if Phil would come for dinner with me somewhere on the King's Road.

I ascended from the basement bathroom, and as I approached our table I noticed that Phil was reading a newspaper, a copy of today's *Evening Standard*.

'Have you seen this?' said Phil, glancing up. His expression was serious and I was immediately on guard.

I sat down and he turned the paper so that I could see it.

'Police have released an e-fit of someone they'd like to talk to,' he said, pointing at the newsprint.

It took a second to register the significance of the picture, but when I did, I felt a wave of panic so strong it almost knocked me off my seat.

'I suppose it's good for Martin,' said Phil, finishing off his beer. 'At least it means they're open-minded, considering that the husband might not be the doer – you know, if anything has happened to Donna Joy.'

I was only half listening, my eyes speed-reading the story that Phil had given me. The news-story that revealed that police would urgently like to speak to a thirty-something woman who was asking about Donna Joy's whereabouts on the evening of her disappearance. A woman with brown hair, wearing a black coat and a green scarf, who had been at Donna's studio around seven o'clock. My eyes flickered to the e-fit – the narrow, distrustful eyes, the almost comically rounded nose, and I was almost offended that it was not a very accurate or flattering likeness of me.

# Chapter 24

'What do you mean, it's *you*?' said Phil, and I took a deep breath and told him as casually as I could that I was the person in the e-fit.

I had to tell him of course. I knew I had to have Phil onside and informed if he was to be able to help me.

'The case was contentious and getting increasingly ugly,' I said, wishing I had another vodka tonic in front of me. 'Donna was still complaining that Martin wasn't disclosing all his assets, and was hinting that she wanted more robust forensic accounting to look into his affairs. I was worried that things weren't going to be resolved at the FDR hearing, so I wanted to chat to her, off the record. See if I could talk some sense into her.'

I was literally making it up as I went along and I knew that from Phil's own personal experience in divorce proceedings he would know it was highly unprofessional of me to try and talk to Donna in this way.

He stared at the newspaper but when he returned his gaze to me, it was with a look of concern.

'Jesus, Fran. You've got to tell the police that,' he said, closing the *Standard*.

For a second I didn't say anything, although I was tempted to tell Phil everything. About my affair with Martin, about the night I sat at this table and watched the house, turning up at my own home, hours later, drunk, bloodied and cut up at the sight and thought of my lover with his wife.

But I also knew Martin needed me out here, fighting his corner, not tied up in the police investigation or being implicated myself. So, for now, I decided to keep those facts to myself.

'I know, I agree,' I said simply, as my heart hammered inside my chest.

The panic was returning. I thought Phil might at least try to make a joke out of it. Tell me that the e-fit looked like a female Morph. That perhaps I should sue the police artists, but he looked worryingly serious.

'Do you want me to come with you?' he said as I grabbed my bag in readiness to leave.

'Don't be daft,' I smiled, knowing that the only coping strategy I could muster right then was some levity. 'I'll pop into the station on the way home. I don't want the police to think they've got a decent lead on something when it's just some workaholic barrister giving her client a little extra help.'

I had to ring Tom Briscoe to get Matthew Clarkson's mobile number. My call went straight to voicemail, but when I contacted his secretary through the firm's switchboard it took me less than a minute to discover that the officers now dealing with Donna Joy's disappearance were based in Pimlico.

The change in location of the team now dealing with her case did not escape me. I spent a few minutes googling the name and number of the officer I had been told to contact and I realized that Donna's case was no longer being handled by Kensington and Chelsea CID, but MIT, one of the murder investigation teams dotted around London. I knew enough about the unit to know that they specialized in murder, manslaughter offences and high-risk missing persons cases. I had no idea why they were taking Donna's disappearance so seriously but I was determined to find out.

DI Doyle, the investigation officer I'd been advised to contact, was based at Belgravia police station on Buckingham Palace Road, and I couldn't help but think how much Donna would have liked that. No squad based in Ealing or Barking for her. Even her disappearance was being dealt with in the most regal SW1 postcode.

The building itself was unremarkable, Brutalist brown-brick Seventies architecture.

I exhaled slowly, wiped my clammy palms on my coat, and announced myself at reception. The seats were all taken and I tried to distract myself by wondering what everyone was here for. The furious-looking suit had probably had his Porsche stolen; the uptight pensioner was reporting a disturbance and I had no idea why the woman with a facial tattoo, simultaneously rocking a buggy and shouting into her mobile was here, but I was not in reception long enough to think of her back-story.

Perhaps Clarkson's office had already phoned ahead, but within a couple of minutes a uniformed policewoman invited me to follow her through a warren of corridors. She said very little, gave no clues about what was to happen next, and I was too busy wondering what to say when I reached my destination to make conversation.

She opened the door to a meeting room, asked if I wanted a cup of tea and disappeared, returning a couple of minutes later with a plastic cup containing an anaemic-looking brew. I watched her leave, and took a grateful sip, feeling hot and on edge as I waited. I stopped myself from checking my phone – I felt as if I were being watched in this sterile, enclosed space and wanted to remain exact and unimpeachable.

It was another few minutes before the door opened again and I welcomed the cool gust of fresher air into the room.

A dark-haired man in a suit, younger than I expected, thirty-something, his bulk straining beneath his jacket, extended a hand.

'Rob Collins,' he said putting his more superior mug of coffee on the table. 'I'm one of the Detective Sergeants working with DI King. Thanks for coming in.'

I wasn't sure if I was relieved or disappointed that I hadn't got the supervising officer, but a voice told me that I just had to get my excuses off my chest and get out of there.

'You're a colleague of Matthew Clarkson,' he said, more of a statement of fact than a question.

'No,' I replied, shaking my head. 'But I am Martin Joy's lawyer. One of them, at least.'

'How many does he need?' said Collins, giving me the slightest smile, a gesture of solidarity that gave me confidence even though I detected an insult directed at the rich banker they had been questioning.

'So. What's this in connection with?' he asked finally, and I knew it was my moment in the spotlight. I'd felt this a thousand times before, the flutter of stage fright, nerves, performance anxiety before I stepped up in court. Every time I stepped up in court, if truth be told. I was not a natural performer; even when I had my knowledge of the law and my conviction in the case on my side, I still felt it, the dread, the doubt, the shiver of naked fear.

My hand was on my knee and even though I was wearing trousers I could feel the dampness of my palm through the material.

'An e-fit that was released to the *Evening Standard* this afternoon,' I said as coolly as I could. 'The police wanted to speak to a woman who had been spotted at Donna Joy's studio last week.'

'That's right,' said Rob Collins, looking more animated.

'It was me,' I replied, trying to strike the right note between casualness and an understanding of the seriousness of the situation.

'You?'

He took another sip of coffee and flipped open the A4 pad he had brought with him.

His face looked more relaxed than it had when he first came in. He'd get a slap on the back for this interview; perhaps tomorrow he'd get a juicier job than interviewing the random people who came forward with 'information'.

'Well, I think it's me,' I added. 'I left work at around six o'clock and went to Mrs Joy's studio. I would have got there at about six forty-five, and I was wearing a black coat and a green scarf, like it says in your appeal. Personally, I don't think the e-fit looks much like me, but I did speak to a lady – grey-haired, in her fifties – who told me that Donna had left for the evening.'

'That would have been Joanna Morrison,' said Collins, writing all this down.

'Who's that?'

'We took a statement off her. She's an artist at the studio. She gave a description to our e-fit artist. Obviously, we thought it was of interest that someone was asking after Donna on the night she disappeared.'

'As I said, it was me.' I drained the remains of my cold tea from the plastic cup.

'What were you there for?' he ventured.

'I have to be careful here,' I continued slowly. 'Client confidentiality. I have an obligation to him to keep certain things private.'

'Tell me what you think you can tell me,' said Collins, his voice hardening a little.

I took a breath and repeated the story I had told Phil Robertson. It was easier to lie this time, so easy it felt like the truth already.

'I've been in this business a long time and I knew things weren't going to settle at the Joy vs Joy FDR. Contentious Final Hearings are never helpful, they are stressful, expensive and I didn't want my client, Mr Joy to go through all that. Mrs Joy's divorce lawyers were being obstructive. I just wanted to see if I could talk to her. Woman to woman.'

I paused for dramatic effect. For a moment I'd forgotten that I was in a stuffy police interview room and not in court. I realized that I was putting on a show and I was impressed with my performance, grateful that I'd had a trial run with Phil Robertson and pre-empted the doubts that Collins might have had.

'And that's why you went to her studio?' he said, trying to look me directly in the eye.

'It's not the textbook way of doing things but, in my opinion, the practical one,' I replied, with the considered, knowledgeable court face I had practised so often in the mirror.

'But you didn't see Mrs Joy at all?'

'As I said, the older lady told me she'd left for the day.'

'So then what did you do?'

I took a discreet deep breath before I said, 'I went home.'

'You went home.'

'Yes,' I repeated in the clearest, most confident voice I could muster.

'And you never saw or spoke to Donna Joy after that.'

'No,' I said, knowing that I had just taken a step down a path I could not turn back from.

# Chapter 25

I rested my head on the cold window of the taxi as I replayed the meeting over and over in my head, wondering if I should have played it differently. I had lied to an officer of the law. A detective sergeant involved in a high-profile missing persons case, a person they most likely thought was dead or certainly in danger. As a lawyer, I knew better than anyone that this constituted perverting the course of justice, a common-law crime, and punishable – in theory – with a maximum sentence of life imprisonment.

For a second I pictured myself dressed in a prison jumpsuit, but forced myself to snap out of it. I had not told Sergeant Collins an out-and-out lie, I tried to convince myself. Just a little white one.

An off-the-record chat with Donna Joy at her studio *could* have been constructive and I did go home that evening. Eventually.

No. What I told Rob Collins was a simplified version of the truth that was better for all parties concerned. Better for the investigation. And my information was useful. Collins said so himself – he had thanked me for coming down to the station and for clarifying the matter of Donna's mystery visitor that night.

I tried to zone out, my eyes not quite focusing on the London buildings and evening lights – smears of red and white in the rain-speckled glass – that sped past. The coloured patterns were hypnotic; after a while, though, they seemed to conspire with the confusion of thoughts in my head to make me feel sick. I was glad when at last the cab stopped outside my flat, my feet connecting gratefully with the pavement, as if I had just dismounted a particularly unpleasant fairground ride.

My building looked dark and lonely. The top-floor flat had been vacant for months and although there had been rumours of a lodger moving in, there had been no signs of life there since Christmas. Pete Carroll's ground-floor apartment was also unlit. When I'd left his flat the week before, he had mentioned he was going away for a few days on a research trip, not specifying for how long. I was glad he wasn't around.

I put my key in the lock and stepped into the hall. I switched on the light but the bulb made a gentle pop and after a brief, bright flash, I was back in the dark. Post was scattered on the doormat. I scooped it up and put it on the hall table next to the two piles of letters, mine and Pete's, that I had sorted on Friday.

My weary body was almost unable to propel me forward up the stairs to my flat and when I stepped inside, I went straight to the living room, collapsing on the sofa and bending my arm so that my forearm covered my eyes.

I desperately wanted to sleep but my mind was so active. I thought about Martin, about what he was doing that very moment, details that Rob Collins, when I had asked, was unable – or unwilling – to tell me. I thought about the forensics team that I had seen in Chelsea and had even given them names – Julia and Tony and Helen. I imagined they had all gone home by now. Taken off their overalls, scrubbed themselves down and returned to their comfortingly ordinary lives, untroubled by victims and criminals. And I thought about Donna. Where was she and what could I do to help find her? The police might believe she was dead, but I didn't want to contemplate it. We would find her, and everything would get back to normal. My work, my life, my relationship with Martin.

I allowed my mind to wander. I allowed myself to imagine myself, one hand on my neat, swollen belly, another holding my lover's fingers. I imagined us walking across a beach, or maybe a meadow as we discussed names for our baby. I imagined us laughing, swimming, drinking, eating, fucking. I just imagined us together. As one.

And then I told myself to calm down. That the emotions surging through me were beginning to feel like mania. When I was younger, before university, before a name had been given to my mood swings, before things had got bad, I liked feeling this way. It was like a drug, a natural high that gave me super-powers. I remember being able to stay awake for hours on end to revise and without it I'm not even sure I'd have got the A-level grades to study law.

I wanted a drink but knew that I should have a herbal tea instead.

Turning on the lights, I went to the kitchen. I opened the cupboard to find the tea bags but the bottle of vodka was where I'd stashed it the day before, hidden behind some tinned soup. I picked it up, put it on the kitchen table and puffed out my cheeks. This was no time for abstinence.

The measure of Smirnoff I poured was a large one and a small bottle of tonic fizzed satisfyingly as I mixed the two.

I knocked back the drink and in an attempt to feel more virtuous went back into the living room to look for my pilot case.

I took out some files, set them on the coffee table and went to change into pyjama trousers. When I returned, I curled up on the sofa and picked up the first file to hand, some pro bono work I'd been handling for the Free Legal Aid centre in Hackney.

Although the centre was well stocked with volunteers, from trainee solicitors to retired silks, I still felt guilty that I hadn't been for several weeks and made a note to go back that week. There was plenty to catch up on, I thought, flicking through a report about the increase in forced marriages in the East End, and a press release about a new centre for victims of domestic abuse, some of whom wanted legal advice on separating from their spouses.

I'd drained my tumbler of vodka when I heard a knock at the door. It startled me and then my heart started pumping with excitement. Martin didn't have a key to my apartment, not yet. But perhaps I hadn't closed the front door properly and he'd taken the liberty of letting himself in.

I put down the file and headed towards the door. There was no time to reapply my make-up but I licked my lips and smoothed down my hair.

I was shocked when I saw Pete Carroll standing there. He looked well, a light sun-tan bringing out a spray of pale freckles on his nose.

'Hi,' he said pushing his hands into his jeans pockets. 'I've been away for a few days. I wanted to see how you were.'

'Where've you been?' I said, not opening the door more than halfway. 'You've got a tan.'

'Rome. A scientific exchange with the university out there.'

We stood in silence and he didn't make a move to leave. I

felt uncomfortable, but after his kindness the week before –
paying for the taxi, letting me crash on his sofa – it felt rude
to leave him standing there.

'Do you want to come in for a minute?' I said. 'I was about
to boil the kettle.'

He followed me into the kitchen, a tiny galley space that
suddenly felt too small when we were both in it. He hovered
by the door while I took two mugs out of the cupboard. The
ritual of making a cafetiere would take too long I decided,
the clock on the wall telling me it was past ten o'clock – so
I got two Starbucks sachets from a canister.

'So what happened in Rome?' I asked as I tipped the coffee
into the cups and turned on the kettle.

'Three doctorate students came over to our place just before
Christmas – so we were invited over there. We were just
observing their work really, sharing ideas.'

'How long before you finish your doctorate, Pete?' I smiled,
trying to be as friendly as possible.

'Another year,' he shrugged. 'Maybe longer.'

He paused and looked at me.

'So how are you? Did you get to the doctor last week?'

'Yes. I'm fine,' I replied with a wave of the hand.

'I googled bipolar. You need to be careful with alcohol.'

He glanced at the vodka bottle and I felt embarrassed.

'I know,' I said, looking away.

'Well, I just wanted to check that everything's all right. I
read the papers on the plane. The banker's wife who disappeared . . .'

He paused before he said it:

'It's not your friend's wife, is it?'

There was a subtle emphasis on the word friend, and with
it came a shift in the atmosphere in the tight, confined space.

Pete didn't give me the chance to deny it.

'I recognized his photo in the newspaper. From the night I saw you by the bus stop,' he said, his words slower, more deliberate. 'You said he had separated from his wife, but that it was complicated.'

For a moment I felt paralysed. I didn't know what to say and welcomed the gurgling sound of the kettle boiling.

I turned away from him to pour the water into the mugs, but I could feel his eyes on me.

'I saw your picture in the paper too.'

His voice was lower now, and it was impossible not to detect the hint of malice. I stirred the coffee with a spoon, watching the swirl of brown liquid go round and round as I felt him take a step towards me.

'You mean, the e-fit?' I said, my voice trying to be steady but still infected with a soft quaver. 'Yes, that was me. I went to her studio to talk to her. To Donna Joy. The police know all about it.'

'So you told the police about you and Martin . . .'

My breath was quickening. The walls of the kitchen seemed to tower up around me like a canyon. Walls that were closing in, closing in, so close I could hardly breathe.

'Told them what?'

'That you're fucking him.'

I gulped hard.

'He's my client,' I said quietly.

'The noises I heard coming from your flat didn't sound very professional,' he said, his thin smile goading me to deny it.

I closed my eyes for a moment, remembering the evening that Martin and I had been to Ottolenghi and seen Pete Carroll on the way home. I was drunk on orange wine, heady on desire. We'd fucked all over the house before we finally made it into the bedroom; on the coffee table, on the stairs, and on the living room floor, when I had climaxed so intensely, I'd gagged my mouth with a cushion. Too late for Pete Carroll in the downstairs flat not to have heard my screams.

I snapped open my eyes and looked at him.

'What's your point, Pete?' I said, feeling every muscle in my body tense.

He took another step towards me and was so close that I could see the wide, hungry dilation of his pupils.

'No point,' he said simply. 'Just a curious observation that the night your lover's wife went missing was the same night you saw them together, followed them. The night you blacked out, and came back here not remembering anything, but still upset, distraught, rambling. How is your leg, by the way? That cut looked nasty.'

'My leg is fine,' I replied.

Pete paused.

'I don't suppose you liked Mrs Joy much. Your relationship with Mr Joy seemed to be going so well. The Ottolenghi dinners, the moonlight walks. And then his wife comes back on the scene . . .'

The heavy suggestion in his words made me shiver.

'What happened that night?' he said more bluntly.

'Nothing happened,' I said, struggling to keep my voice level.

'I'm not sure the police are going to believe that,' he said, staring at me so intensely I couldn't look away. 'In fact, I think it's better if they never get to know, don't you agree?' he said, moving closer. 'Things could get difficult otherwise. Awkward for everyone. Especially you.'

I wanted to challenge him, but I could only nod in agreement.

'Don't worry, I'm your friend. It will be our little secret,' he whispered, as his hand slid around my waist.

He pulled me closer and I could feel his breath on my face,

his hardness through the denim of his jeans. His hand was in the small of my back and his fingers slid down the waistband of my pyjamas.

Closing my eyes, I willed myself to breathe. I wondered desperately how I could get out of the situation, but sometimes I knew it was just better to surrender. At least for now, until I could work out what to do next. Strategic, like sacrificing a pawn.

'You're going to love it,' he moaned, but I doubted it, and his words made my skin crawl. I knew I could push him away, scream, simply yell 'no'. But I didn't. I didn't. And as he bent to kiss my neck, I punished myself with the thought that I had no one else to blame.

# Chapter 26

I woke up slowly, a sliver of dull grey light peering through the crack in the curtain, giving just enough light to hint that night was over. In that moment, it was just the beginning of another dawn, another day that I would greet slowly, lazily with my usual routine; telling myself that I could have five more minutes in bed, taking that time to remember what was my diary, before hauling myself off the mattress to make a cup of coffee. For a sweet and innocent moment, everything felt fine until finally, like falling through a rotten floor, my stomach turned over and I remembered the day before.

Pete's hands on my body.

My lies to the police.

His lips on my skin.

Perverting the course of justice.

The feel of his clammy fingers.

*What have I done?* My muscles tightened, saliva hot in my mouth, by the thought that *he* might still be there in the bed beside me. I froze listening for the soft whisper of another person's breath. When I could hear nothing, I slowly turned my head, cracking my eyelids. The other side of the bed was empty. Pete had gone. I had no idea when. Certainly sometime after I had fallen asleep, although after sex, I was so repulsed with myself, with him, with the situation I had found myself in, that I had been unable to sleep for a long time, even after Pete had rolled over contented and spent, lightly snoring within minutes.

I sat up and observed the indentation in the pillow, a stray, unfamiliar red hair on the sheet – and I felt the sudden violent sensation that I was about to be sick. I covered my mouth and sprinted for the en suite, thumping to my knees in front of the toilet. I heaved over and over like the cold engine of an ancient car, but nothing came except a long string of spittle; it was almost as if my body wouldn't even give me the release of vomiting it out.

I slid back on to the cold tiles, closed my eyes. There was no point wondering if I had made the right decision having sex with Pete Carroll. I hadn't even had time to think it through. It had all happened so quickly; one minute I was listening to his thinly veiled threats, the next, his mouth had been on my lips and it had felt easier to go along with it, than to resist and face the immediate consequences: an angry and vengeful Pete Carroll, who I now knew was entirely capable of bringing my life tumbling down. But right then, that was little consolation. I felt punch-drunk and disconnected from the world around me; edgy and breakable as if I could touch my own skin and it would crumble away to dust.

I hated Pete Carroll, hated him. But most of all I hated myself and all the terrible decisions that had led me down an ever-narrowing alley where I was being squeezed, hemmed in on all sides, no light from above.

*Breathe,* I told myself. *There's always a way out. Think on your feet: it's what you're good at. It's what you do.* I nodded to myself. It came down to this: I could stay here, hunched on the floor. Or I could move, face the world and take action to try and remedy the mess I was in.

Pushing myself up on half-numb legs, I put on a dressing gown to cover my nakedness, trembling fingers tying it tightly around my waist. Then with small, unsteady steps I made my way downstairs to the living room, on red alert for Pete's presence in the flat. Thankfully the place was empty and silent, except for the faint roar of traffic beginning to build up on the street outside.

The vodka was still on the kitchen table from the night before and I was tempted to drink the lot. Instead, I forced myself to drink a glass of water then took a shower, turning up the dial as hot as I could take it, and then as cold as it would go. My skin smarted from the two extremes of temperature but at least I felt cleaner once I'd scrubbed the smell of him into the drain.

I found the oldest and most modest underwear in my drawer, not the strips of expensive lace I'd bought for nights in with Martin, and put them on. I buttoned my white shirt up to the neck and put on my thickest black tights to wear under my sober suit skirt.

I tried not to look at the bed as I dressed but as the stale air overpowered me, I grabbed the duvet and threw it into the corridor, then tore the sheet from the mattress and kicked it down the stairs. I followed it down, grabbed a bin liner from the kitchen and pushed the soiled fabric inside it, fastening it tight in a big black bow.

I washed my trembling hands and opened the kitchen window as wide as it would go, taking big gulps of London air which had never tasted so fresh or so sweet. My hands clutched the cracked white sill, and as I looked down to the tiny backyard below I could see Pete's bike propped against the wall. For a moment I thought of throwing myself out, but then I snapped the window closed.

My little sanctuary suddenly felt alien to me, as if it was no longer mine. At the same time, I was trapped. The man who'd violated me was sitting downstairs, a smug grin on his face, satisfied with a good night's work of blackmail and forced sex, listening to my footsteps, planning his next move. And why not? That was how blackmail worked, wasn't it? Once your victim had succumbed, you could keep coming back again and again, a bottomless well that never ran dry.

I grabbed my bag and coat and ran for the door. If I thought about it, I'd be frozen, hunted prey, a rabbit trapped in her burrow, sniffing the fox on the air. I winced at every step as I went downstairs, eyes fixed on the door at the bottom, my mind picturing Pete's face appearing, leering like Mr Punch, his clawed hands dragging me into his flat. 'You're going to love this,' he'd cackle. '*Love it.*'

But the door stayed closed and I ran out into the street, heels clacking on the pavement, feeling the skin on the back of my neck, expecting his foul touch, his breath, his murmured words. Instead I saw a wink of red ahead of me, the brake lights of the number 19 and I broke into a sprint, jumping on board just as the doors hissed closed.

I found a seat on the lower deck and tried to focus. I had a big case in court that day and knew I needed to pull myself together.

Welcoming the distraction from letting my mind stray back to Pete Carroll, I pulled the file out of my bag, wedged between my legs on the floor, and balanced it on my lap as I flipped through the paperwork, trying to familiarize myself with the case.

My client Holly Khan was trying to stop her ex-husband Yusef taking their ten-year-old son Daniyal to Pakistan for a family wedding, fearing that he might never come back. Yusef Khan, unsurprisingly, was pushing hard against Holly's refusal, and Holly was so afraid that she might lose her child, she wanted a court order to legally stop him. On any other day, I would have relished helping out this vulnerable young woman, but this morning it felt like trying to high-wire walk in a gale. There was no doubt about it – professionally I'd taken my eye off the ball, and my lack of preparation for my cases was yet another source of shame.

I'd barely skim-read the file when we arrived at Holborn. Scooping up my things, I leapt off the bus, feeling my blouse stick to my back as the sweat ran between my shoulder blades.

I grabbed a coffee and hurried down Kingsway.

'Francine!'

As I passed through court security I saw my instructing solicitor Tanya waving vigorously. I quickened my pace and followed her to one of the interview rooms.

It was the first time I'd met the client, which wasn't unusual in family law cases.

'Francine Day, this is Holly Khan.'

My new client was petite and attractive but with a careworn face and eyes that looked on the verge of tears.

'I'm sure Tanya has briefed you well, Holly,' I said, immediately flicking into work-mode. 'There's really nothing to worry about.'

The woman glanced across at Tanya and back to me. I could see how much she wanted to believe what I said.

Strangely, the client's evident nervousness was easing my own anxiety. The familiarity of the work environment, I suppose, the soothing nature of ritual, going over the same old patterns. The law was complicated, but at least it had rules, at least you had some idea what was coming next.

'OK, Holly, here's what's going to happen . . .'

I went over the basics of the case and explained to Holly that the purpose of the hearing was twofold. We were trying to persuade the judge to grant a prohibited steps order, effectively preventing her ex-husband from taking Daniyal out of the country, while his lawyers would be pressing for 'permission for temporary leave to remove'.

'Basically, we're asking the judge to give you legal control of Daniyal's movement, while Yusef is asking for the same thing.'

I peered down at the documents in front of me.

'Why weren't prohibited steps orders put in place at the time of divorce?' I asked, looking up.

The young woman looked startled, like she'd been called in front of the headmaster. 'Sorry,' I said more softly, 'I didn't mean to imply you'd done anything wrong, it's just these are the questions the judge is going to ask in chambers.'

Holly remained frozen.

'We didn't want the divorce proceedings to get ugly,' said Tanya, jumping in. 'We managed to get Holly a good financial settlement through mediation, and at the time we just wanted a clean break. Mr Khan can be a difficult man.'

'But things are different now,' said Holly, her voice small. 'Back then he had a reason to stay in London, but he's lost all his money. Even the money he hid from me in the divorce.'

'Yes,' I said, reading a section of the notes I had underlined in red. 'And I gather you also think Mr Khan might have people after him? We haven't got any statements to support that, I take it?'

Tanya fired back an apologetic grimace. She'd once given me a testimonial for the legal directory: *Francine Day pulls off the impossible time and time again*. And it was clear she wanted me to pull a rabbit out of the hat now.

'Please,' said Holly, looking at us with glistening eyes. 'Can you help me?'

'I will do my best,' I said, trying to project more confidence than I felt. The truth was, I felt nauseous, ill-prepared and jittery, not exactly the best combination for going into court. Some barristers – like Tom – seemed to have a natural ability to busk it on the day, simply arguing the facts as they appeared before them, but I had always been a swotter, only really comfortable when I had all the facts at my fingertips and had prepared for every twist and turn. Today I felt like my safety line was missing. I looked at them both, knowing there were dozens of things I should be saying, but couldn't think of a single one. There was an awkward pause, then Tanya coughed and said, 'Well, we'd better go,' leading us into the court.

I knew Judge Sheldon and Khan's barrister, Neil Bradley, who was professional and competent; rumour had it he, too, was applying for silk this year. We exchanged pleasantries, took our seats and proceedings began; the judge listening to us in turn as we presented the facts of our case.

I'd expected to dislike Yusef Khan, but he was charm itself from the moment we entered judge's chambers. As handsome as a Bollywood actor, he was sharp, convincing, and polite, in contrast to Holly, who was hesitant and glowered at her ex-husband throughout the hearing. This, I knew, was my fault. I should have run through this with her, told her he might be like this, that Neil Bradley – the competent one – would have advised this approach. Wrong-footed, I began explaining Holly's reasons for wanting to stop Yusef taking Daniyal out of the country. I didn't doubt Holly's story that Khan had run into financial trouble. Tanya had told me that his string of restaurants had been subsidized by other interests including brothels and drug-dealing, which he'd pulled the plug on after he'd fallen out with some gangsters. But that sort of thing was hard, almost impossible to prove. We could hardly get statements from either the gangsters or his drug-taking customers, and Khan had recent accounts to show that the restaurants were doing fine. By the time we adjourned for lunch, I knew the other side were leading, but despite Holly's downcast face, I also knew it wasn't the end of the world. A strong closing statement could well be enough to make the judge err on the side of caution. After all, missing a wedding was an inconvenience, but a child being taken from his mother was a serious risk.

'I can't lose him,' said Holly mournfully. 'Yusef is smart. He's so convincing out there. I think the judge believes everything he's saying.'

I went and put my hand over hers.

'I'll be honest, it's difficult for us to prove that Yusef won't return to the UK. But what we *have* proved are the consequences of Daniyal not coming back and being kept in Pakistan by his father. His life would be turned upside down, and a child's welfare is the top priority for any judge.'

She gave me a tight nod and I knew she was trusting me, putting all her eggs in one basket; my basket. And I was in no fit state to live up to that trust.

Tanya came back into the room with tea and drew me to one side out of earshot of Holly.

'So, are you confident?' she asked, looking at me sideways as she blew on her drink. Clearly, she wasn't. I could hardly blame her.

'We still need a fallback position,' I replied briskly. 'The trip to Karachi is supposed to be next week. There might not be enough time for an appeal. So we should put some safeguard provisions in place in case the judge allows them to go to the wedding.'

'Like what?'

'If Yusef doesn't bring Daniyal back home, it's abduction, no question. However, Pakistan is a non-Hague convention country and, as such, negotiating any return can be complex because there are no international agreements to help. But we could ask for Yusef to provide a security bond, or we can get Daniyal's passport left with the British High Commission in Islamabad.'

Tanya snorted. 'Security bond. You might as well get him to say Scout's honour. If he goes to Pakistan, he won't be coming back, you know that.'

'It won't come to that, Tanya,' I said. 'Trust me.'

Tanya raised her eyebrows. 'Well, Holly doesn't really have any other choice, does she?'

A bell rang to say that we were due back in court. I pulled my phone out of my jacket pocket and checked it quickly. Nothing. No message from Martin, nothing from Phil. With quiet resolve, I puffed out my cheeks and went back into chambers.

Immediately it began to go wrong. To give him his due, Neil Bradley was quite brilliant as he summed up Yusef Khan's case for taking his son to Pakistan, pointing out that Holly had previously been in a favour of a trip when they were married, and shooting down our flimsy accusations that his client's business was in trouble. He painted a vivid picture of the wonderful life Yusef had in Britain, including details of a new relationship he had with a woman who lived in Bedford – a crucial piece of evidence we should have known. Everything here was rosy, Bradley argued, so why on earth would Yusef leave all that behind?

'Your honour, I have to reiterate that the consequences of non-return would be life-changing for Daniyal. He is doing well at school, he has just won a much-coveted place at a selective state grammar, he has a wide circle of friends . . .'

Justice Sheldon nodded in agreement as he read through the notes.

Neil was speaking again now. I was trying to concentrate, but my phone was vibrating in my pocket. It wouldn't hurt to have another quick look, I decided, slipping it out on to my lap. I clicked on to Messages to see that there was something from Dave Gilbert.

The words blew off the screen like a hand grenade.

Martin Joy has been arrested.

I re-read the message and my head started to spin. Everything else had faded away so that I could just make out a voice in the background – Neil, or perhaps Justice Sheldon, soft and muffled as if we were underwater.

'Do you have any proposals for safeguards?' the judge's words floated through.

I shuffled my papers ineffectually and tried to speak, but it came out as an incomprehensible stutter. The thought of Martin, arrested, was the only fact my brain could hold, the only thing that seemed to matter. I imagined him in handcuffs being led to a cold, dark cell; imagined him trying to get in touch with me, but not being able to.

My breathing quickened, darts of fierce, frightening energy fired to my fingertips.

Tanya was tapping at my arm but it was as if I had left my body. Floating, drowning, sinking.

There was a hissing in my ear, '*closing remarks*', but I felt as if my brain was shutting down.

'I have to go,' I muttered as I stood up and collected my things.

Tanya stretched out. I felt her hand connect with my gown, but I spun away from her.

'Miss Day?' The judge's voice was confused rather than angry. Perhaps he'd never seen a barrister suddenly jump up and flee the court before.

'Urgent business,' I muttered, and pushed past the tables through the double doors and out into the corridor, my heels tapping against the marble. My white collar felt tight around my neck, the walls pressing, leaning in towards me. I burst through the revolving doors and out into the brightness of the street, gulping at the fresh air, craving oxygen. But I couldn't pause; I had to keep moving, had to get to Martin. The ground seemed to move under my feet as I saw a taxi and dashed for it.

'Where we going, love?' asked the driver, giving me a toothy smile.

I gaped at him: it was only then I realized I didn't know where to go. I was desperate to see Martin, to be close to him. But if he was in custody, I couldn't go there – he needed a criminal lawyer and it would look extremely strange if I showed up now.

'Mayfair,' I said. It was the only place I could think of to go.

# Chapter 27

The offices of the Gassler Partnership were only a stone's throw from Claridges, but at least a century apart; a tall glass building rather than a redbrick townhouse that whispered of Georgian dandies, it had a floor-to-ceiling glass frontage and a huge modernist chandelier hanging over the double-height lobby. I supposed when it came to high-tech finance, sleek and shiny was the way to go. As the taxi pulled to a halt, I tried to phone Sophie Cole one last time; she wasn't as close to Martin as her husband Alex, but at least I had her phone number. When my call went straight to voicemail, I thrust money at the driver and almost fell out on to the pavement.

'Oi! Your wig!' shouted the cabbie with a grin. I turned back and grabbed the silver horsehair mop from the back seat. Stuffing it into my bag, I ran through the stiff revolving doors, almost tripping as I came through, raising a questioning stare from a po-faced concierge manning the front desk.

I glanced behind him, noting that the Gassler Partnership was not the only company in the building. Clearly I would have to get past him before I could speak to Martin's receptionist.

'I'm here to see Alex Cole at Gassler,' I said, suddenly embarrassed at the realization I was still wearing my barrister's robes.

Although I looked a pillar of the establishment at the Inns of Court, he looked at me with suspicion as if I were a drunk or a vagrant.

'Do you have an appointment?'

'If you could just call his office and ask if he'll speak to me, I'd be grateful. Say it's Francine Day. I'm his legal representative,' I said, trying to recover my dignity.

'I think he's still at lunch,' he replied with little enthusiasm.

My fingers drummed against the black marble desk as he picked up the phone and spoke to someone. He seemed to delight in stringing it out before he shook his head and told me that Alex wasn't in the office.

'Could I speak to his PA, then?' I said, leaning forward.

'Do you not have her direct line?' he said with a note of challenge.

'No, I do not have her number,' I said, my voice beginning to crack. 'This is an emergency and I need to speak to Alex Cole now.'

'I can leave a message with reception . . .'

It couldn't wait, not with Martin sitting in a cell.

'Get someone on the phone for me now.'

I could hear myself, loud, aggressive and unconvincing. The concierge stood up and without saying a word, I knew he was about to ask me to leave.

I glanced towards the lift, hearing it ping as the doors prepared to open and began to stride towards it.

The scramble of footsteps behind me fired a thrilling current of energy through my body.

My shoes slipped on the polished concrete. I almost fell, but a pair of hands reached out to steady me.

'Francine?'

The voice was puzzled, a touch annoyed.

I didn't recognize Sophie Cole immediately.

'What are you doing here?'

Her face softened. 'I could say the same about you,' she said.

'Martin, I heard about Martin,' I replied, catching my breath. 'I had to find out what's going on.'

The concierge was standing behind me and I could feel the heat of his disapproval without even looking at him.

'Is everything all right, Mrs Cole?'

'Thank you, Graham. Everything's fine. Francine's with me.'

She stabbed the lift button to stop the steel door from closing.

'Let's go to my office,' she said briskly.

The small space of the lift seemed to contract around us and I knew I had to say something.

'So you've heard about Martin?'

'Of course,' she said, without looking at me.

'I'm sorry but I had to come.'

Sophie glanced at me and then looked straight ahead.

'You could start with taking off your gown.'

Another time, another elevator, I had slipped off my blouse as Martin had pressed my spine against the cold metal door. Those days seemed a very long way away.

I didn't bother to argue with Sophie; I was just grateful for someone else to take control, grateful for her crisp head-girl efficiency.

I bundled the black folds of fabric under my arm and followed her out of the lift. She led the way down a corridor lined with small rooms, each containing someone hunched over a computer screen.

I'd never been to Martin's place of work before, had never really considered what a hedge-fund office would look like, beyond a vague image of red-faced alpha-males staring at Bloomberg screens and shouting 'Buy!' and 'Sell!' into their phones. But there was an unsettling stillness about this place; the only movement the flicker of eyes looking up at me as I walked past open office doors. I wondered what they knew.

I followed Sophie into a corner office that bristled with the trappings of success. A large iMac on the otherwise uncluttered desk, a designer sofa that looked out on to the Mayfair streets below.

'I'm sorry,' I repeated as she closed the door behind us. 'I just had to know what's happened and I thought Alex was the only other person he might have spoken to . . .'

'You can't do this, Fran,' she said, cutting me off. 'I've had to field two calls from the press in the past ten minutes. I was just heading to the lobby to check that there weren't any photographers in the street when I saw you. You can't come pushing your way in here, dressed like Rumpole of the Bailey. This is a *business*, Fran. We could have clients here – we do have clients here. How would it look if you're splashed all over the front pages tomorrow? Think.'

I knew she was right and took a moment to tell her so.

'I know. But when I got the call that Martin had been arrested, I needed to talk to someone.'

Sophie looked at me, then her expression softened.

'If it was Alex, I'd be the same.' She took a bottle of water from the console table and filled two glasses.

'So how much do you know?' she asked, handing me a tumbler.

'Nothing,' I replied feeling another rise of panic. 'Just that he's been arrested.'

'The police went round to the loft shortly before lunch,' she said. 'Thank God he'd taken a few days off work, else they would have turned up here.'

'But they haven't got any evidence . . .'

'The police just want to look as if they're doing something. I should imagine at some point he could take legal action against them.'

'Wrongful arrest,' I said firmly, wanting to believe that he could one day have a claim.

'But right now, we don't want to make things any more complicated than they have to be.'

I looked at her and waited for her to expand. I liked Sophie Cole. Liked her no-nonsense capability, even though it reminded me of the person I used to be. She certainly had more about her than the average wife I met on the high-networth marriage-and-divorce circuit. They were generally attractive but all of them had a touch of steel, a single-mindedness about them. I suppose they needed it. Yet there was a smaller group whose beauty was not the defining quality; the smart wives, the accomplished wives, the women who were as Alpha as their husbands and Sophie Cole certainly fell into this category.

'People want a bad guy, Fran. The press because it sells papers, the police, because they've got a job to do and they want it done. I don't believe that Martin is involved in Donna's disappearance, but if people want a villan, don't give them ammunition. Don't give them the story of his affair with his lawyer. Don't turn up here frantic and panicking and expect people not to ask questions, because they will.'

I felt a wave of shame. She was right, of course – and I

was supposed to be good at this stuff, thinking four moves ahead, anticipating what the opposition was going to say or do. Today I seemed to be frozen, a seized-up machine.

I sat down on the sleek sofa and Sophie joined me.

'They can't charge him,' she said in a quiet, more reassuring voice. 'They've got nothing on him.'

I closed my eyes and nodded. I wasn't just the lover, I was the lawyer. I should have been the one reassuring Sophie that Martin would be released without charge, that his arrest was little more than in a bump in the road until we found Donna. But I wanted to hear someone tell me that everything was going to be all right.

I felt Sophie put a reassuring hand on my forearm and I snapped back into the present.

'Alex is down there with his lawyer. He just texted me. Martin's fine. He's made of pretty strong stuff. If the police think they can spook him into making a confession, they've picked the wrong man.'

'Confession?' I said, flashing her a look.

'False confession.' She replied more deliberately.

'Alex is going to bring him back to our house and we'll put him up there. Martin's been photographed coming in and out of the Spitalfields house for the past few days and I'm worried he'll snap if he's constantly on his own. And we can look after him of course.'

It made perfect sense to hide Martin away from the long lenses and the insinuations, but at the same time I bristled that it was necessary when he was innocent. Most of all, I knew that it would mean there would be a barrier between us. To protect him – to protect us – I had to keep away.

'It won't be forever,' she said. 'Just for now. And you know it's best for Martin.'

*Best for the business,* I thought.

'Best for you,' she added as if she had read my uncharitable thoughts.

'I won't come to the office again,' I said, not looking at her.

'Are you sure you're OK?'

I nodded quickly. 'I was just rattled. Thank you for being the voice of reason.'

Sophie paused before she opened the door.

'I know you love him, but don't let any man ruin your life,' she said with quiet steel. 'You met Martin because he wanted you as his lawyer. And if Martin chose you as his lawyer, that means you're the best. No man is worth risking that reputation.'

I knew she was right before the words had even left her mouth.

# Chapter 28

I wanted to stay in Sophie's ordered, efficient orbit, but that offer wasn't on the table. I was dispatched after another call came through from a journalist, and I could tell that my presence made her jumpy.

The concierge flashed me a suspicious glance as I returned to the lobby, but I ignored him and pushed my way through the revolving doors back on to the street.

I felt naked, floundering, when they deposited me back on the pavement. Gripping the fabric of my gown, I wondered what to do next, inhaling deeply, trying to use the fresh air to clear my thoughts. I knew that I should return to court. My briefcase would still be in chambers, that's if it hadn't suffered the humiliation of being taken to security. But as it was almost four, when most lawyers had left, or were about to leave court for the day, I figured if I could get to the Strand before the courts closed, I could retrieve my possessions without being seen by anyone I knew.

My mobile rang interrupting the planning of my next move.

'What the actual fuck is going on Fran?' boomed Paul into my ear.

I opened my mouth to speak, but it was obvious he hadn't finished his tirade.

'In thirty years of clerking, I have never had to grovel as much as I did this afternoon on your bloody behalf,' he said, his voice shaking with emotion, as if I was someone who had just pranged his brand-new car. 'Tanya Bryan is talking about suing you for malpractice, not to mention the client Vivienne and I had on the phone for something like an hour, demanding we crucify you on Parliament Hill. I mean what the fuck happened?'

He was angry, confused, frustrated, perplexed and I didn't blame him. Until that moment, I had been his model pupil who never put a foot wrong, the safe pair of hands on her way to silk and glory for the practice. Now he'd turned round and discovered I was rotten to the core. I hadn't just been caught smoking behind the bike sheds, I was in free-fall, hurtling towards full-scale delinquency. I didn't say anything for at least five seconds.

'I think I'm having a breakdown,' I said finally.

I hadn't planned the line, or rehearsed the excuse, and although it wasn't strictly medically true, it was how I felt.

It was Paul's turn to fall silent.

'OK,' he said. 'OK,' he repeated more firmly, as if this was finally something that made sense. There was a pause, then: 'Have you seen a doctor?'

A motorbike roared past me, so I slipped into an empty doorway to speak more privately.

'Not yet. But I'm going to.'

'You should. Today.'

I felt like a teenager who had just told her parents that she was pregnant, with Paul as the stricken, disappointed father. I heard him let out a deep breath.

I almost didn't dare ask the next question. I knew what he

was going to say, but I had to hear him say it, despite my hopes that my bizarre behaviour would have prompted the judge to adjourn the case.

'What happened, Paul? With the case, I mean. What happened with Khan vs Khan?'

'The judge granted temporary leave to remove.'

'Any safeguards?'

'No. Apparently you didn't ask for any, so the mother had to hand over the kid's passport.'

'We can appeal . . .' I said, even though I knew there was no way anyone would let me near the case again.

'Fran, leave it. It's done.'

Tears prickled behind my eyeballs, every emotion of the day crystallizing into a knot of panic and pain.

'No. We must, for the child's sake. If you can send someone to pick up my files, I can sort this . . . I'll call Tanya.'

'Please don't.'

I didn't need him to tell me that I was the last brief on earth she'd allow near one of her cases now, let alone this particular fuck-up.

I was only half listening as he continued speaking, though I registered the most salient point of his prophecies: *'We will have to work very hard to avoid a professional negligence claim. I can't imagine her firm will ever instruct anyone from this chambers again . . .'*

But perhaps it was a voice in my head telling me how this would all pan out.

'Fran are you listening?' he asked. 'Where are you?'

'Bond Street.'

'What are you doing there? You need to get home.'

'I know,' I said quietly.

'Do you need me to come round after work?'

It was unexpectedly touching in the midst of a pretty

horrible day. I felt a strong pang of affection for our senior clerk. A strong, embarrassed pang of affection that told me his support and friendship was more than I deserved.

'It's fine,' I replied. 'I just need to take some time out for a couple of days.'

'There's no rush. You left some stuff in court, but I've arranged to bring it back here. I'll reassign your caseload. Vivienne will oversee the Joy case. Obviously there's no legal work there for the moment, but given the way it's blown up in the press, there will be plenty of firefighting.'

I felt sick, my mind immediately turning to the files relating to the case. Vivienne or whoever took over would have to familiarize themselves with those files and I was struggling to remember what I had written in my notes, if there was anything incriminating in there, even if it was only a childish doodle that might expose our relationship.

'Don't do anything yet,' I said carefully. 'Let me speak to a doctor. I think I'm just having a wobble. Maybe some medication will sort me out. Everyone's on something these days, aren't they?' I said, trying to make light of it.

'You know he's been arrested,' he said after a pause.

'Who?' I said, a little too quickly.

'Martin Joy.'

'Where did you hear that?'

'Dave Gilbert emailed me. Didn't he contact you?'

'My phone's been switched off,' I lied.

'If he's charged, it's a PR disaster,' Paul muttered.

'I know,' I said, my fingers gripping the phone a little tighter. Then I rang off.

Paul wasn't to know that I couldn't go home. That my 500-thread-count sheets were now stained with Pete's Carroll's semen, that if I went back and made even the slightest noise, my neighbour might come back and want a repeat performance of what had happened the night before.

Dozens of people scurried past me, the energy of London as overpowering as aftershave, but at that precise moment I'd never felt more alone.

I paused before I sent Clare a message asking if she could meet me. Before Martin, she would always have been my first port of call, my safe harbour and sounding board, but I felt more remote from her than ever, and still hadn't replied to the text she had sent me two days earlier.

I was relieved when she replied almost immediately and we arranged to see each other at her house in Queens Park.

I bought a packet of cigarettes on the walk to Oxford Circus, and stuffed my robe and wig into the five-pence carrier bag I'd asked for when I purchased my nicotine fix.

A stack of *Evening Standard*s were piled high outside the tube station. I reached out to grab my copy, but stopped myself, knowing that reading another Donna Joy story was just torture.

I joined the jostle of commuters streaming into the station and headed for the Bakerloo line. Standing on the edge of the tube platform, I could feel the familiar hum as electricity began to flow through the rails, quickly followed by the rush of warm air as the train sped through the tunnel. I watched the headlights approach, wondering idly how fast an underground train moved as it came into the station, whether you'd feel the shock of the electricity before the speeding carriage smashed into you. Would you be killed instantly? Would you be dragged along, torn limb from limb, just a long red smear some traumatized tube worker or firefighter had to scrub away before the morning rush? But by the time I'd thought all this through, the train was already in the station, a solid wall filling the platform. The doors slid open, and I let the stream of zombie workers and disorientated tourists pass, then stepped inside, numbly sitting on a hard fold-down seat.

I didn't usually take the tube – I preferred the anonymity of the bus where everyone faced away from you, and I liked the fact you could watch London pass by, unobserved. No one ever paid any attention to anyone on a bus. On the tube, people seemed to enjoy peering right into your face, it was almost a sport. Mercifully, the carriage was almost empty, just a smooching couple wrapped up in each other, and an elderly African man, eyes closed, swaying with the motion of the train. I could see my own reflection in the dusty window – eyes sunken, cheeks hollowed out – I averted my gaze.

It was getting dark by the time I got to North London. I lit a cigarette and walked slowly to Clare's house, hestitant to even get there.

I turned into her street and ground the butt into the pavement with my foot. It was cold now too, and I pulled up the collar on my thin black jacket to stop a chill at the back of my neck. For a moment, I allowed myself to slip into self-pity. But then I thought of Martin, at the police station, anxious and afraid, lying on a thin mattress with only rank sweat-stained air to breathe. How I longed to be with him, to stride in there waving my new briefcase, demanding that the duty sergeant release my client or, failing that, lock me up next to him.

Clare lived in a smart terrace, sandwiched in a row of identical houses on a quiet road off Salusbury Road. I knocked on her front door and took a moment to look around her tiny front yard. There was a flower box I had never noticed before on the window ledge, where a clutch of pansies and crocuses were beginning to bud in the soil. A row of empty milk bottles stood in a line on the step, waiting to be collected by the milkman, and the domestic order of the scene made me momentarily forget about my own chaos.

The door opened and a rush of warm air from the hall seemed to suck me in.

I didn't say anything at first and Clare stepped on to her front step, pulling me into a hug.

'Everything's gone wrong,' I said into her shoulder.

'Get yourself inside and we can start with a big mug of tea.'

I followed her into the kitchen, the scene of countless Sunday lunches. The lights had been dimmed, candles lit so that it smelt of figs and flowers; I don't know if this effort had been especially for me, but it did help to soothe my panic.

'Where do you want me to start?' I said, as Clare switched on the kettle.

'Well, I've read the papers. Worked out some of the bits you haven't told me.'

She had every right to be angry with me; Clare was supposed to be my best friend and I'd deliberately kept the details of my relationship from her. An omission, yes, but it might as well have been a fat lie. But there was no disapproval or disappointment in her voice.

'So I assume Martin is your client,' she said, not waiting for me to answer. 'And the Donna Joy in the papers is his wife, correct?'

'Clare, that's why I never said anything at the gallery or the party. It was awkward. And of course, I'm not supposed to be seeing my clients.'

Clare paused and looked embarrassed.

'The *Evening Standard*'s reporting that someone has been arrested.'

'You mean, is it Martin?'

'I don't want to pry . . .' she said.

I nodded and closed my eyes.

'It's a mess, Clare,' I whispered. 'The fact they've arrested

Martin means at the very least they think he's hiding something. I feel so helpless, my head's going round and round . . .'

I sank down on to the kitchen table and put my head in my hands. The kettle had boiled, and Clare made tea. She put the cup in front of me and I wrapped my fingers around the hot mug as she sat opposite me.

'Take it slowly, tell me everything.'

So I told her. I told her how Martin and I had met, and how our relationship had developed after the night we bumped into each other in Selfridges – like lighting the fuse of a fire-cracker. I told her how happy he made me feel, and how desperate and crushed I had felt when Phil had told me that he thought Donna was still in a sexual relationship with her husband. I took a deep breath and told her I had followed Donna and saw her meet Martin at the restaurant, because I had to tell somebody what I had seen.

'You followed Martin and Donna,' she said slowly. 'And that was the last night she was seen alive?'

I knew how it sounded, I could see the concern on her face, but I wanted her to know how I was feeling.

'Clare, I had to find out,' I said, close to tears. 'I had to find out if I could trust him.'

She raised her eyebrows as if to say, Well, you certainly found that out, didn't you?

'So what happened then?' she said. 'After the restaurant? I mean, I read in the papers that Donna Joy just disappeared. Has Martin told you what happened that night?'

I nodded, dreading her next question.

'They went home together,' I replied.

'Did he admit that?'

'I followed them. You'd have done the same,' I said, looking up at Clare, challenging her to deny it, but she didn't react.

'And then?

'I don't know,' I whispered hugging myself. 'The next thing I know, I was at home. I think I blacked out. I don't remember getting there. Pete says I got a cab.'

'Pete? Who's Pete?'

'My downstairs neighbour,' I said quickly, not wanting to discuss him, not wanting to think about him. Instead, I stretched my arm across the table and grabbed her hand.

'Clare, please, I need to know what happened that night I saw Martin and Donna. If I can just remember something, anything, maybe it can help Martin. Maybe I have information locked in here that can help find Donna,' I said, tapping my temple. 'Maybe I saw her leave. I mean, she's unpredictable, selfish. Who knows, maybe I saw someone else go inside or someone come to collect her. A number plate maybe or . . . I don't know.' The words were tumbling out of my mouth and Clare looked at me sceptically.

'Were you drinking?' She was disapproving now.

'I was upset.'

'Francine, you shouldn't drink when you're on your medication, not to mention the condition itself.'

I held up my hands to stop her. 'I know, I know.' We'd had this discussion enough times down the years, I didn't need to hear it again right now.

'How much?' she asked. 'How much did you have to drink?'

'A lot. Look, Clare, you need to help me recover my memory,' I begged. 'Martin needs us to help him.'

'I can't,' she said.

'Because you don't believe he's innocent?' I said incredulously.

'I can't,' she repeated, more firmly.

'What do you mean, *can't*?' I frowned. 'There's got to be a way.'

Clare shook her head sadly.

'Memories lost in an alcohol blackout can't be brought back.'

'What? Why?' I said, hearing the panic in my voice. That wasn't what I wanted to hear. I needed her to help me trawl my memory. She had to help me retrieve some fragment of information that could help Martin.

'Because those memories were never properly imprinted on the brain. The theory is that alcohol saturates the blood and shuts down the hippocampus, the bit of the brain responsible for long-term memories. So those memories aren't lost, Fran, they were never formed in the first place.'

I felt the darkness swirling up around me, like leaves in a sudden wind.

'No, I *have* to help him.'

Clare laid a hand over mine. For a second I thought she was restraining me.

'Look, I know you want to believe that Donna is going to turn up any minute, that Martin's got nothing to do with her going missing. And it might be true. But you've also got to prepare yourself. The police must have strong suspicions if they've actually arrested him. Statistics show that the spouse is by far the most likely suspect in a murder.'

'Murder?' I snapped, cutting her off. 'She's not dead, Clare. She's missing – on holiday. In Hong Kong, at the spa, I don't know. She's somewhere.'

Clare recoiled and I realized I had been too forceful in my reaction. I softened my tone as I spoke again.

'Look, I trust Martin,' I said. 'I know the statistics, I know what everyone is thinking. I've even had those same thoughts myself. But you don't know him like I do. You have to trust me. Please.'

'Shh . . .' she whispered. 'We will work this out.'

I looked at her and nodded. It's what Clare had said when

I was nineteen, when she had found me in the bath, dark ribbons streaming from my wrists. She'd held me while the ambulance came and stayed with me at the hospital, and had been the powerhouse behind getting me the right psychiatric help and support at university. She had seen me at my lowest, at my most vulnerable, Clare had made it OK.

'Do you want to stay here tonight?'

I opened my mouth to tell her about Pete Carroll, but, despite everything, I couldn't. I wasn't even sure yet if it was all real.

'If it's not too much trouble.'

'I'd love you to stay. I hardly see Dom these days. His entire world revolves around the restaurant. I'm not far off ringing the speaking clock for some company.'

'You could call me,' I said finally.

'So could you, you know. I'm always here for you. Always have been, always will be. You only have to send out the bat signal.'

We both smiled at the memory. The 'bat signal' was a code, a pact we had made in the earliest days of my bipolar episodes, an agreement that I'd call Clare and tell her when I was out of control, that I needed urgent help.

'I'm sorry we've not seen that much of each other over the past few weeks,' I said. I was about to tell her that I never want to be that person who disappears when she gets a lover, but under the circumstances it seemed an inappropriate thing to say.

'Come on, I'll ring Dom and get him to send some food over from the restaurant.'

I nodded, grateful beyond words. All I wanted was to curl up, close my eyes and wish everything away.

Everything.

# Chapter 29

As my eyes opened, I felt calm. Nestled under the warm, fresh-smelling sheets, I was, in that moment at least, safe. Then the familiar feeling of dread pushed to the surface, threatening to escalate to panic.

*It's OK, Clare knows everything,* I told myself, fighting the churning in my stomach, *and she's going to help.*

It went some way to reducing my anxiety, but not much. As far as I knew, Martin was still in custody and could well have told them every intimate detail of our relationship, making me an accessory and meaning my career was entirely over. Not that it had much future anyway, I reminded myself, not after my freak-out in court. I'd be lucky if I could get work writing up wills.

I forced myself to take a few deep breaths. Much as I wanted to stay there under the duvet, I swung my legs out and headed downstairs. Both Clare and Dom were gone: no surprise as the kitchen clock told me it was almost noon. It was a shock and I immediately wondered if Clare had put something in my drink the previous night, a sleeping potion from her doctor's black bag, quickly followed by the realization that I wasn't late for

226

work: there was no work for me, at least not until I got my act together.

Clare had left a set of keys on the kitchen table and a note to say that they thought they should leave me sleeping. I don't know why they had left me in bed. I'd mentioned to Clare that I was taking a couple of days off, but that didn't mean I didn't have plenty of things to do.

My first priority was to help Martin, but I also needed to contact Tanya Bryan and Holly Khan. I was ashamed I had run out of court and abandoned my client and I knew that I had to face the music. Hiding under the duvet wouldn't solve anything.

My bag was still on the sofa where I had left it the night before.

A blue flashing light told me I had a message. I skipped a heartbeat, wondering if it was Martin; it turned out to be from Sophie Cole, wondering if I wanted to meet for lunch.

I hesitated for a moment and then replied yes. It would serve no purpose moping around Clare's house. Besides, I wanted to probe Sophie for more information about Martin.

The mobile still in my hand, I gritted my teeth and called Tanya at her office. The gods were smiling, because a receptionist told me she was in court and asked if I'd like to leave a message. I was shocked at how relieved I was to avoid that particular confrontation; my hands were shaking as I put the phone down. There was a solitary foil strip of lithium in my purse and as I took my morning dose, I tried not to think about the fact that I only had a few days' worth of pills in my bag. It wasn't Tanya's anger I feared, but coming face to face with my failings and the very real consequences of letting people down. I was glad to delay hearing about how I'd ruined Holly's life as well as my own, even if the whispers in my head were constantly reminding me.

Apart from my own internal noises, the house was oddly silent. Sunlight streamed through the bay window and I suddenly wanted to feel some warmth on my face so I opened the back door and stepped into Clare's garden, a small square of grass and pea shingle; it was bijou, but it was undeniably a sun trap.

I sat down on one of the bistro chairs, closed my eyes and tipped my head back towards the sky. For one blissful moment I was on holiday, an empty day ahead of me on one of my beloved August trips to Italy. I imagined that the sound of wind through the trees was the sea scraping along the shore and the distinct hum of traffic was the sound of mopeds in a distant piazza.

But only for a moment. Then I was back in London, sitting hunched on a rusting chair, avoiding a long list of things to do.

I went back upstairs and took a shower. I'd heard of travelling light, but even I couldn't resist a snort when I saw my paltry belongings laid out on the bed. A carrier bag containing my wig and gown, and my clothes from yesterday – black skirt, jacket and the stiff-collared white shirt I had worn to court. I slipped on the skirt and bra and took a grey T-shirt from a pile of clean laundry, hoping that Clare wouldn't mind.

I sat on the edge of the bed, rubbing my damp hair with a towel as I browsed the net searching 'Martin Joy arrest', until my phone gave an angry beep, indicating it was almost out of juice. Usually that sound would bring on an irritated sigh, but today I felt something like fear: the idea of being disconnected from news of Martin made me jump up and run to Clare's study, knowing she was scrupulously organized: if anyone had a charger, Clare would.

I rooted through the box labelled 'chargers', throwing mismatched cables aside, dismissing the notion that I shouldn't

be in here, unasked, rummaging through my friend's possessions like it was a jumble sale. I was sweating, shaking, on
edge. I had to find that cable, had to. It was as if my whole
well-being hinged on that one thing. With a whoop of triumph,
I found a wire that fitted and jammed it into the phone,
sinking down into Clare's office chair with relief.

It was too tempting not to hop on Clare's computer to
continue my web search. I tapped the keyboard and it hummed
to life. The screensaver of Clare and Dom on a beach somewhere, arm-in-arm, grinning, a vision of happy togetherness,
didn't help my mood, but I soon lost sight of it when I clicked
on the home page of one of the leading tabloids.

Overnight one of the world's most famous celebrities, an
American reality television star married to a controversial
rapper, had been involved in a violent fracas with a fan. Social
media, along with a shameful amount of the world's supposedly serious news outlets, had gone crazy over it.

On any other occasion I would have rolled my eyes at a
news item about the unfathomably popular, but right then I
was thankful for the insatiable interest the public had for the
primped and pampered as it had knocked Donna Joy from
the headlines.

I scrolled down the page and I saw the story, *Man Held in
Connection with Donna Joy Disappearance.*

I clicked on the piece, my eyes scanning the text as quickly
as they could. With growing relief, I saw that the writer had
carefully avoided using Martin's name or anything that might
identify him as 'the husband'. Press reporting had tightened
up lately, particularly in cases where people had been arrested
but not yet charged, but I suspected this was the work of
Robert Kelly, the media lawyer I had recommended. Bob Kelly
was a master in getting stories squashed or neutered to the
point of opacity. I picked up my charging phone, initially to

call Robert's office for an update – but then decided to go right to the top and call Martin's criminal solicitor. But would he tell me anything? Any lawyer worth his salt would be cheek-by-jowl with Martin in the police interview room right now, and I did not want to disturb that work, no matter how desperate I was to know what was happening.

As I was considering my options, the phone began to vibrate in my hand. I flipped to Messages and saw it was from Martin. My heart thudded as I clicked on it.

Let go. Meet me later. Hotel?

I didn't know which part of the short message excited me more – that he'd been released from custody or that he wanted to meet in a hotel. I touched my face: it was hot and I could feel blood pulsing in my neck. I was light-headed, agitated and uncomfortable. I couldn't sit down, so I got up to pace around the tiny room, clenching and unclenching my hands, shaking off the pins and needles in my muscles. He was free – and he wanted to see me.

I went back to the bedroom and grabbed my purse, then ran back to Clare's desk. I clicked off the news site and jumped on to a hotel booking engine, quickly typing in 'central London hotel'. My hands hovered over the mouse when it asked about the number of guests. I pulled down the list and clicked on 'one'. I knew I had to start thinking ahead, cover our tracks. Sophie had been right yesterday. My relationship with Martin was no one else's business, but exposing it to anyone would not help Martin's cause.

I had to admit I had always enjoyed the illicit nature of my relationship with Martin, and I felt a thrill now as the booking engine threw up hundreds of London hotels. For a moment I imagined us in one of the chicest and most expensive places; crisp white linens, room service bringing us strawberries and champagne. I would run Martin a bath and

He looked up at the ceiling and I could see his Adam's apple rise up and down over his tight throat. I sat down next to him.

'That's pure speculation. Since you and I both know there isn't a body to be found, you don't have anything to worry about, do you?' I offered him a smile. 'Apart from getting caught with me in some seedy hotel room.'

'Yes, that is a much bigger problem,' he said, holding my hand.

I looked up at him.

'I thought you said we shouldn't contact each other.'

I made it sound like I was concerned, that I was making a practical point. Perhaps it isn't wise, should we do the sensible thing and both go home? But that wasn't it at all. I wanted him to confess that whilst he was lying in that tiny cell his thoughts were consumed by me, that I was the one thing that got him through his whole ordeal. I simply wanted to know how much he loved me.

'Right now, you're the only person I feel I can talk to.'

I fought to hide my disappointment. At least it was me he wanted to see; it would do for now.

'How was your lawyer?'

Another practical question. I felt some responsibility here. Matthew Clarkson needed to be good, the best. And although I trusted Tom Briscoe's opinion that he was great, I still felt responsibility.

'Can't say I've had much experience in these matters. But he had my back. Difficult bastard, as a matter of fact. In a good way. I think he was a sound pick.'

'I'm glad,' I replied.

He put his hand into his pocket and pulled out a cheap-looking phone.

'Alex came to the station and gave me this; one of those

disposable things. We should communicate on this number in future. You should get one too.'

'Makes me feel like a spy.'

He gave a soft snort. 'It was hard to see any James Bond glamour in the situation last night, I can tell you.'

He took off his jacket and started rubbing the back of his neck.

'Let me do that,' I said, climbing behind him, placing my hands on his shoulders. 'Sophie said you're going to stay at their house?'

He nodded. 'She's gone into full-on damage limitation mode. Arranged for me to stay with them. I'm not sure how long it's going to shake the press off. Hiding at my business partner's place isn't exactly deep cover, but it's better than going back to the loft.'

He sat forward, head in his hands.

'I can't believe this is happening.'

'Right now, the most important thing is finding Donna. Once she turns up, you have nothing to worry about.'

'And if they find a body?'

'*If,*' I emphasized. 'And if they do, then they'll have evidence. DNA, fingerprints, fibres, things that can help the police track down who has hurt her – and which will prove you had nothing to do with it. Because right now, they are chasing ghosts and ghosts don't leave a trace, which is why they are coming after you.'

I stood up and went to the kettle.

'Now, do you want some tea?'

Finally Martin smiled.

'Thank you,' he said, coming over to me. 'I knew I could rely on you to stay focused.'

*If only you knew,* I thought, as I put tea bags in two cups.

'Given that there's no body and no evidence, did the police say why they had brought you in?'

His shoulders sagged and he looked away.

'They keep saying this is still a missing persons investigation. But I know they think she's dead.'

'Why?'

'She's gone, Fran,' he said, irritation overcoming him. 'She's disappeared – and it's been over a week now. I'm the last one who saw her. By rights, I should hate her. We're getting divorced, she's after half my money – and to most people, that's a *lot* of money. If I was the police, I'd arrest me too. Who else are they going to point the finger at?'

'So what you're saying is, they've got nothing.'

'They have enough, Fran!' he said, his anger flaring. 'I've admitted going back to her place, and there's nothing to back up what time I left. No taxi driver, no CCTV – and even if there was, what would that prove? How long does it take to kill someone?'

He looked at me without blinking, as if he was waiting for me to give some sort of reply.

I knew I had to tell him. I'd been storing it up like a jack-in-the box, but now it was time to pull myself together and help Martin, and that didn't mean keeping everything I knew to myself, no matter how awkward it was to reveal it.

'I think Donna was having an affair,' I said finally.

His eyes opened wide. '*What?*' he snapped.

The kettle was coming to the boil, so I switched it off and busied myself making the tea as a way of avoiding his eyes.

'I hired a private investigator, a guy named Phil Robertson,' I said. 'Any means necessary, remember?' I added, handing him his cup with a challenging look.

'Phil followed Donna and became convinced she was having an affair. In the end he assumed it was with you.'

'Why me?' asked Martin.

'He had two pieces of information. He photographed you and Donna together and noticed that Donna didn't return home on two or three occasions. The most likely conclusion was that she was staying with you.'

'Donna never stayed the night with me.'

I watched his face carefully.

'So if she wasn't at your place, she was somewhere else,' I said slowly. '*With* someone else.' I sat down next to him.

'The way I see it, there are three possibilities. Either Donna is off with this mystery man right now, shacked up in some private cabin blissfully unaware of the hoo-ha it's causing. Or, it's entirely possible that she is aware of what's going on, having read the news online, but is in no hurry to come home.'

'Why on earth would she do that?'

'Spite, mischief . . . She's trying for half your money, remember? It wouldn't help her cause if she was already in a relationship with someone else.'

Martin digested that and I saw a little hope enter his heart.

'What's the other possibility?'

I'd been mulling the theory over and over.

'Perhaps the mystery lover found out about you and Donna, that your physical relationship wasn't entirely over,' I said carefully. 'Maybe it made them jealous.'

'And *they* killed her?'

I nodded slowly, waiting for him to see why this was bad news. It didn't take long.

'But I'd still be the prime suspect,' he said, closing his eyes. 'They find a body, I'm still the one with the motive.'

'And the opportunity.'

He thought for a while, then stopped sipping his tea.

'Any idea who it is?'

'I wondered if you knew.'

'Of course not,' he said, frowning.

'Phil's trying to find out. Did you go to Paris with Donna?'

'Paris?'

'Or Belgium. Or anywhere you'd visit on the Eurostar.'

'No. I always fly to Europe,' he said with some irritation. 'Besides I haven't been anywhere with Donna since last summer. When was this supposed to be?'

'The precise dates are in a file at work. But Phil saw her go through the international terminal at St Pancras. He wasn't booked on to a train so he couldn't follow her.'

'Was she on her own?'

'Yes, but she could have met someone.'

'Where? In Paris? On the train? Why not meet at the station?'

'Because she didn't want to be seen.'

'So Phil, your private investigator – he's looking into this?'

I nodded.

'Is he working alone?'

'He always does. Better that way, when you're dealing with privacy issues.'

'Well, it's not private any more,' said Martin, standing up and pacing around like a cat. 'Get him to put a team together – I don't care how much it costs. If the police are convinced it's me, they're not going to be looking for anyone else. We're going to have to do it ourselves.'

'I need to tell you something else.'

He caught my tone and stopped pacing.

'I saw you go to Donna's house that night.' I paused. I had been dreading telling him this. 'When Phil told me you were still seeing Donna, I was hurt. I wanted to find out if it was true, so I followed her to the restaurant where you met. Then I saw you go back to her place.'

If he thought there was anything strange about that behaviour, he didn't show it.

'And did you see me leave?' he asked.

'I can't remember. I was drunk.'

'You can't remember?' he said with a flash of anger. 'What the hell does that mean?'

'I was drunk. I waited in the pub across the road. Got home somehow. When I woke up the next morning, I couldn't remember a thing.'

He sank to his knees in front of me, taking my shoulders. 'Fran, you have to try and remember,' he pleaded. 'You *have* to.'

'I would if I could,' I said feeling my voice tremble in frustration.

'Then you you've got to think harder,' he said, his voice taking a stronger, more insistent edge.

'I would if I could,' I repeated, my voice barely a whisper. I looked at him and I could see an idea forming in his brain. I knew it was what we were both thinking.

That I could lie for him. That I could tell the police the story I had just told him, except that I could remember seeing him leave.

'I'm sorry I followed you,' I said, before he could ask.

He gave me the faintest of smiles.

'I'm glad you did,' he said, sitting on the edge of the bed.

'Why?'

'Because it means you love me.'

His words made me shiver. As he looked at me, I just wanted to feel him inside me.

'Come here,' he said in a softer voice, reaching a hand out towards me.

'All I wanted to do today was see you.'

'I wanted to see you too.'

'Even though I look like this? I'm in urgent need of some fresh clothes.'

'Not right now, you're not,' I said, feeling bold. I began to unbutton his shirt and pulled him close. Placing my hands on his hair as he buried his head into my skirt, I could hear him breathing me in and I wanted to feel his lips against my skin.

My hands reached behind me and I unzipped my skirt, which fell to the floor with a rustle.

I hadn't had any clean underwear that morning so I wasn't wearing any.

Standing up, Martin loosened his trousers, until he was naked, his body as magnificent as I remembered. Mounting the bed, he turned and propped a pillow under his head, watching me as I finished undressing.

I crawled on the bed towards him, straddling him. For the first time in days I felt vital and powerful. I sat on his thighs and as we kissed, I pushed my breasts against his coarse scrub of chest hair.

He gave a low moan when we came up for air and then grabbed me, flipping me on to my back. He sucked my nipple and then he was astride my body, lowering himself into me.

His head knocked against the headboard, softly, slowly at first then stronger and harder.

I could feel his frustration in every urgent thrust. I held on to him, fingers pressed against his back, feeling his hard, tense muscles under his skin; I had never really noticed how strong he was before, but now his raw power pinned me down. I was unable to do anything but follow his lead. I felt full of him, and as he pushed my thighs apart, it began to hurt.

I groaned, wanting him to be more gentle, but a part of me was enjoying being totally overpowered by him. It was as if he wanted to consume me and I wanted him to possess me too, to go so far inside me that we became one, fused together, forever.

His moans were harder, more feral as he pumped into me. I could feel his anger, his frustration with every urgent thrust.

His hand pushed my legs even further apart in a rough gesture and I felt a sharp overstretch of muscle between my thighs. I tried to cry out but I could barely breathe, let alone ask him to stop.

The slow swell of desire began to fade as I realized I wasn't enjoying this any more.

He grabbed my hair and I could feel my scalp pulling away from my skull. His mouth was pressed against my ear, spittle washing up on my skin as he grunted with each thrust.

I just wanted it to be over and I bucked into him, panting louder and louder as I faked my climax.

The veins on his neck popped and his eyes squeezed shut.

'Donna,' he moaned, and I felt him explode into me.

I didn't want to believe what he had said at first, but I could hear the echo of her name in my head, and had to admit what he had just cried out.

I lay absolutely still, staring at the ceiling as he rolled over. Lying side by side, he reached over and put his hand on my thigh as his breathing began to return to normal, but I didn't want to be near him. Instead, I got up off the bed and walked to the window.

The sky was completely overcast, making the room dark. I folded my arms across my chest and fixed my gaze on a rooftop aerial in the distance.

I stood there until I heard footsteps behind me. I didn't turn to look at him but could feel his breath on my neck.

His arms came around me and I flinched.

'What's wrong?' he said softly.

'You were too rough,' I whispered.

'I'm sorry. I lost control.'

'Don't say anything,' I replied, as he turned me around slowly.

I looked away from him. 'You called me Donna.'

I was stiff and rigid and could feel goosebumps form on my naked skin in the cool of the air conditioning.

'Don't deny it,' I whispered, almost hearing him thinking up an excuse.

'I'm sorry. I didn't mean to.'

Another silence.

'Why? Why did you call me Donna?' I stepped away from him and could feel disgust and bile in my throat.

'Because it's all I can think about. Her name is the only thing I've heard over the past twenty-four hours. I didn't mean it the way you think I meant it.'

'And what way would that be?'

For a second the only thing I could picture was Martin and Donna in bed. The sex raw, unbridled, pure desire. I see him holding her wrists, tight, so tight, her skin is turning purple. I see his eyes flash with longing and pain and fury. I see how easy it would be for him to put a pillow over her face, to muffle her screams and I see him fall away from her lifeless body. I can suddenly picture it all.

'Fran,' he murmured, putting his hand up to my cheek. For a second my breath stopped.

'Fran, please. I wanted to see you today because I love you. Because I need you.'

'I think you should go,' I said.

He nodded, as if he understood and picked up his shirt from the floor.

We both dressed in silence.

'Where will you go?' I asked.

'Alex's house.'

241

I wished I had a drink or cigarette and could barely wait to open the mini-bar.

'Will you call Phil?' he said finally as he hovered at the door.

I nodded, arms still wrapped around my chest and watched him close the door, glad, for the first time ever, to see him go.

# Chapter 30

I decided to stay the night at the hotel. Not because I'd paid for it, although there was a very careful side of me, the side that always made me watch my money, that didn't want to let it go to waste. But after everything that had happened with Pete Carroll and my hour with Martin, I didn't want to look Clare in the eye over the breakfast table or have a prickly encounter with Dom; I just wanted to be on my own.

I made some notes about a potential Khan vs Khan appeal, got an early night, and when I woke up the next morning I called down to reception, extended my stay and then hit the streets, realizing that with not even a toothbrush to my name, it was time to go shopping.

The hotel was a short walk away from the Westfield centre. At ten thirty in the morning, it was already crowded. In my current mindset, it was overwhelming: chatter, muzak and a thousand echoing footfalls congealed into a roar, the endless bodies seeming to bob and weave into my path whichever way I turned. There was however method in my madness, this was a sort of smash-and-grab shopping spree and a gigantic mall was the quickest way to get it done. I bought toiletries from Boots, and some basics from the Gap; underwear, trousers, a couple of fresh T-shirts and a small rucksack to put it all in, and emerged back out into the daylight feeling as if I was about to run away.

I was making my way down Holland Park Avenue when my phone rang. I was surprised to see that it was from Phil Robertson; I'd left him several messages since my conversation with Martin but heard nothing back.

'I was beginning to think you'd skipped the country.'

'Not just yet,' he said. 'Although it's always a possibility. Got a few things to tell you first, though.'

I knew better than to ask him over the phone. Like most investigators who spent their lives easing information from sources and exploiting weaknesses in security systems, he was paranoid as a matter of routine.

'How about we meet in the Japanese garden in the park?'

Open air, but not too open, exactly the sort of spot Phil liked.

'It's a date,' he said.

I killed some time in a local café and was surprised to find him waiting for me on a bench next to the fountain.

'Never knew this was here,' said Phil, sipping a takeaway coffee. 'Never fancied going to Japan but this is nice.'

'How can you not want to go to Japan?'

'Have you been?'

'No.'

'There you go,' he grinned. 'You can't want to go that much either.'

'I do. But I've always wanted to see the cherry blossom in spring or the autumn leaves in October. I tend to be busiest at those times of year so I'm stuck in the office.'

'I didn't know divorce was seasonal,' he said smiling cynically.

I laughed. There didn't seem to be much to smile about in my line of work of late, but I always liked Phil's matter-of-fact approach to life.

'Strangely yes. Lots of people break up after Christmas or the new school year.'

'Fresh starts,' said Pete nodding sagely.

I exhaled softly and tried to soak up the calm of the garden. Weak sun was trying to peer from behind the clouds but it was still empty and I could hear the gurgling sound of the waterfall quite clearly.

'I wanted to speak to you,' I said finally. 'Martin Joy was arrested and he's not convinced the police are looking for anyone else. We need to find out who Donna was having an affair with, to take the heat off him.'

'Which is why I've been avoiding you until I had something to tell you.'

I leaned in to listen to him, nerve endings twitching in hope.

'Without access to Donna's house, her phone, the only way I could find that out was by asking around. I used her social media accounts, society magazine clippings to build up a web of her social circle. I layered that with parties, events I discovered she went to and started speaking to people. Some wouldn't talk. Some had already been questioned by the police. Eventually I found someone. Someone who'd seen her with somebody she shouldn't have been with.'

'*With somebody?*'

'Kissing.'

My eyes widened. 'When was this? Do you know who it was?'

'It was at a party last summer. And it was Alex Cole.'

I was stunned, although when I took a moment to think about it, it wasn't too far-fetched. How many affairs were carried out in plain sight? Co-workers, friends, neighbours

– those were the people you had every reason to trust, which made them the easiest people to fall for.

'It gives Alex Cole a motive,' I said, thinking out loud.

'Do you think so?' replied Phil. 'I'd have said the opposite. The police will think it gives Martin *more* motive to kill Donna.'

'No one's talking about Donna being murdered,' I said sharply.

His face said otherwise. 'Either way, you've got to tell the police.'

I nodded, even though I knew it was a risk.

'They'll want to question Alex.'

Phil sat forward, his face concerned. 'Fran, you do realize this isn't necessarily good news for Martin Joy?'

'It means there's another suspect, Phil.'

'Sure, but you can imagine what the police are going to make of it. They already suspect Martin, and this is only going to confirm it.'

'How?'

'This is how they'll see it,' he said patiently. 'Martin goes back to Donna's house for a bit of kiss and make-up and call-off-the-divorce shagging. Donna tells him about Alex. There's arguing, fighting, Martin loses control. Next thing you know, she's dead. Forget the idea that he got rid of Donna so he could keep his fortune, a simple crime of passion is one of the oldest reasons in the book. From the police's point of view, Martin's now an even more plausible suspect.'

'But if Alex was sleeping with Donna . . .'

He paused as if he were listening to the wind in the trees and then looked at me.

'Were you having a relationship with him, Fran? With Martin?'

I paused for half a beat. There was no point in hiding it from Phil.

'That obvious?'

'Credit me with some powers of deduction,' he smiled ruefully.

'Go to the police, Fran,' Phil said, placing a hand on my knee. 'Before they come to you.'

# Chapter 31

Inspector Michael Doyle, the officer in charge of the Donna Joy case, wanted to meet in Pizza Express in Pimlico at 8 p.m., which seemed a bit irregular, although I was glad of the neutral venue, relieved that I wouldn't have to go back to the Belgravia station interview rooms. I'd already lied to a police officer once this week, and hopefully the informality of a Pizza Express would make things easier. Besides which, I hadn't eaten all day and I was starving.

Doyle was in his forties with dark hair and shrewd eyes, which seemed predictable enough for a senior police officer. That he was eating a salad and sipping tea that smelt herbal was more of a surprise.

'I'm Francine Day,' I said, extending my hand.

'Michael Doyle. Thanks for coming.' He nodded his head in invitation for me to take a seat.

'If this was a cop show we'd be in a greasy spoon eating a fry-up,' I said, trying to get the meeting off on an easy-going note but Michael Doyle looked as if I had offended him.

'My boss just took early retirement. Forty-nine, heart disease and diabetes. The whole department is on a health kick,' he said raising a brow.

I ordered a coffee from the waitress, wondering if I could be out of there before it even came.

'So what did you want to discuss?'

The light was bright overhead and I wished we had a more tucked-away table. When I had called the number that Sergeant Collins had given me, I'd decided that this was the right course of action. My first port of call could have been to tell Martin about Alex, but as he was staying with the Coles, I wasn't sure that was wise, especially as his behaviour at the hotel showed he was unpredictable and on the edge. I could have called Matthew Clarkson, Martin's defence lawyer, but as I didn't know him I wasn't sure if I could get information out of him in return for what I was about to share.

I sat back in my chair and watched Doyle wait for me to say something. I wondered whether training at Hendon involved a psychiatric evaluation of guilt. I had recalled a TV show about a doctor who specialized in deciphering body language and I wondered what Doyle could read from me now.

'I don't know how much you know about the work that I do,' I began.

'As a divorce lawyer?' he said, taking another swig of tea. 'I can guess. I have some experience.'

I smiled back, knowing that I had to tread carefully. Half the coppers I'd ever met were divorced. If his wife had got the house and his kids, then Michael Doyle probably didn't like people like me. Cops in general didn't like lawyers anyway, which put me on the back foot.

'I deal with a lot of high-net-worth individuals and the dissolution of their marriages,' I said carefully. 'That brings an added dimension to my work, we get involved in forensic accounting and other investigative areas that might not be necessary with more regular divorces.'

'And . . .' he said, making a circular motion with his fork.

'Several weeks ago, I asked a colleague to look into Mrs Joy's personal affairs. It's fairly standard practice in high-end divorce settlements when we're trying to work out the fairest financial result for our clients.'

'How the other half lives, eh?'

'My investigator found evidence that Mrs Joy was in a relationship. He discovered that she was involved with Martin Joy's business partner, Alex Cole.'

'I know,' said Doyle, spearing a tomato.

My jaw dropped. 'You know?'

'Lots of Donna's friends have got in touch with information they think might be useful.'

'What have they said?'

Doyle pulled a face but didn't immediately respond.

'Someone witnessed a *romantic episode* between Mrs Joy and Mr Cole,' he said finally.

'Which means what?'

Doyle fixed me with a steely stare which told me he wasn't going to give out any more information there.

'You *are* going to interview Alex Cole, aren't you?' I said, already feeling my heartbeat speed up.

'We already have.' Doyle dabbed the side of his mouth with a napkin.

I gawped at him, feeling blindsided again.

'And what did he say?'

'Miss Day, you are Mr Joy's divorce lawyer and this is a police investigation,' he said, his warning to butt out not even thinly disguised.

'But I'm here, trying to *help* your investigation,' I said, struggling to recover my poise.

Doyle gave a soft sigh. 'Alex Cole was with his wife on Monday evening. They went for dinner and returned home.'

'So he has an alibi.'

His patience clearly wearing thin, Doyle scrutinized the remains of his salad as if it were the slightly preferable option to continuing his meeting with me.

'OK, so can you tell me why my client was arrested when you clearly have no evidence that any crime has been committed?'

Doyle sighed, again.

'Miss Day, I didn't have to see you. I'm sure you can talk to Mr Joy's other legal team if you want to know anything else.'

'If you know I'm going to find out from Mr Joy's criminal solicitor why don't you save my phone bill and just tell me?'

Doyle released a puff of breath as the waitress brought over my coffee.

'What is it you want?' he said finally.

'I need to know what's going on. I need to know why my client was arrested, when there are certainly other people you should be interested in.'

His face remained stony.

'I still don't see what this has got to do with you,' he said. 'Presumably the divorce is on hold given Mrs Joy is not likely to turn up in court?'

He had a point, but I had an answer ready.

'I appreciate you probably couldn't care less about a bunch of lawyers, but this is about my business and we need to know what – and who – we're dealing with. I know any reputational damage to our chambers is none of your concern, but . . .'

He nodded.

'You don't want to carry on defending Martin Joy if he's guilty as hell, right?'

Not exactly what I meant, but if it got me the information I needed, I was prepared to play ball.

'So, is he?' I asked. 'Or rather, can you prove he is?'

Doyle put down his napkin and looked at me.

'Let me put it this way: Donna Joy has been missing for ten days,' he said. 'There's been no activity on her social media accounts that she previously used regularly. Her phone, her bank cards haven't been used. We can't assume she is safe, unless we have evidence to tell us that she is. If anything has happened to Donna Joy we want to find that out as soon as possible as well as who was involved.'

'I think we are all agreed that we want to find out what's happened to her.'

'Then how about you help me out, Miss Day?'

I shrugged non-committally. 'If I can.'

'Donna claimed unreasonable behaviour when she filed for divorce,' continued Doyle. 'Her sister Jemma Banks has been helping with our enquiries. She says that Martin had quite a temper. Were you aware of any episodes of domestic violence in their marriage?'

'Have you never heard of legal privilege?' I said, looking over the top of my coffee cup.

Doyle responded with the whisper of a smile. 'I know you don't have to tell me anything. But I don't need to be having this conversation with you either.'

I let him wait, which also gave me time to think.

'There was nothing of that nature,' I said finally. 'No threats, no violence. It was a marriage gone stale and there were the usual mutual frustrations, but he never laid a finger on her.'

'To your knowledge.'

'I would have heard,' I said plainly.

'Well, we've heard otherwise,' said the policeman.

That stopped me from breathing. I could feel my emotions spiralling, my need to push for more information overcoming my sense to pull back.

'From whom? Her lawyer? Her sister?'

It was Doyle's turn to shrug. He clearly wasn't going to reveal that little detail.

'Quid pro quo, Inspector: why did you arrest him yesterday?'

'Quid what?'

'Come on. I told you something, now it's your turn.'

He remained silent.

'Come on Inspector, you know Mr Joy's legal team will tell me this, it's not a secret.'

He pushed his plate to one side and looked at me.

'Martin Joy had a suspicious-looking cut on his hand when we interviewed him. He said it was a bike accident but officers said the bike looked brand new. Unused.'

'I'm not sure it's possible to tell that . . .'

'Cadaver dogs searched Donna's flat yesterday,' he said after another pause. 'We discovered traces of blood.'

I felt a thickness in my throat and took a breath to compose myself.

'Where?' I asked, trying to keep my voice steady.

'On the bed. In the bathroom.'

'Menstrual?'

Doyle smiled.

'That's what Martin Joy said.'

I felt weak and cold, as if my own blood was slowly draining away.

'We'll find out soon enough,' said Doyle. 'Menstrual blood contains traces of endometrial tissue which we'll discover from forensics. If it's not menstrual blood, then we have to consider the possibility that something happened at the house that night.'

'Can you tell how long it's been there? I mean if it *is* Donna Joy's blood, can it be dated to a specific night?'

Doyle smiled again, sensing my discomfort, presumably interpreting it again as evidence of Martin Joy's divorce lawyer losing faith in her client.

'Clever chaps, these forensic guys,' he said. 'Have to see what comes back from the lab.'

'All right,' I said. 'But you haven't answered the main question: is Martin Joy guilty? Did he kill his wife?'

'You're right, we don't have the evidence right now, but if you're asking for gut feel based on my experience, Miss Day?'

I nodded, feeling dread fill my chest.

'I'd say he was as guilty as sin.'

# Chapter 32

I walked the streets after I left the restaurant, churning my conversation with Doyle over and over in my mind. It was two o'clock in the morning by the time I returned to the hotel, cold and in pain from my shoes that had begun to pinch. But still, I couldn't sleep. It was pointless to even try; I was too angry and frustrated that every move I made turned into a dead end or pointed to a bald truth that Donna Joy was dead.

It was a trick I used with particularly thorny cases, when a killer legal argument seemed elusive: I stopped working, and rebooted. Read or swam, or worked-out at the gym, always thinking, still plotting my next move, but giving my brain some time to breathe. I walked and walked that night and waited until dawn to text Martin on our special number. I kept my message simple. That I wanted to meet him alone. When Martin replied almost instantly, I knew that he wasn't able to sleep either.

Alex and Sophie Cole lived in a big white stucco terrace on a leafy South Kensington streets, the kind you assume have to be owned by oil sheikhs, ancient aristos or flash bankers seeking respectability. All of which made Alex Cole more predictable than Martin Joy with his cobbled Dickensian bolthole, but none of it made me any less nervous as I walked along the neat row of polished black front doors. I was braced for loitering paparazzi or reporters but saw nothing more sinister than a gaggle of Filipino nannies and a tidy blonde in gym kit striding towards her four-by-four. It was an oasis of polished urban calm; no wonder Martin wanted to stay here.

I took the stone steps slowly and pressed the doorbell, wondering who would answer. Martin hadn't wanted to step out in public but had suggested during our sunrise communiqué that we meet at the house in the morning, when Alex was at work and Sophie played tennis. But still, coming here, when I knew what I did – that Alex and Donna had been romantically involved – felt more like poking a hornet's nest with a sharp stick than pressing a bell.

'Hey.'

Martin looked at me nervously through a crack in the door, then opened it wide enough for me to squeeze through.

When I was inside, we awkwardly embraced, the memory of our uncomfortable goodbye at the hotel still hanging between us.

'You're looking much better,' I said. Better than the crumpled, hunted man who had shuffled into that cheap hotel room, at any rate. He'd showered and shaved, dressed in a navy cashmere sweater and dark jeans. Though he looked more like the old Martin, the purple rings under his eyes remained, like a boxer after a hard bout.

'Come in,' he said, leading me through the high entrance hall.

'Wow,' I whistled. 'Nice place.'

In my profession, I sometimes had to visit the homes of the wealthy and they were always impressive, but the Coles' home was something special. There was a soft, almost ghostly calm to the place, as if I'd entered the relaxation room of a very exclusive spa. There were oil paintings on the walls – abstract patterns in shades of white and cream with splashes of colour that gave them a raw dynamic edge – originals, I assumed, although I did not recognize the artist.

'Yeah, Sophie has pretty good taste.'

I nodded, but it was a gross understatement.

I'd spent my working life fighting over properties a lot like this one, arguing over art and furniture, bricks and mortar. It was amazing what people would fight over once they had fallen out of love. I have seen thousands of pounds' worth of legal fees racked up over items of little value – magazine collections, coffee tables, kitchen utensils, things of little financial or senti-mental worth, just so they could point score. Just so they could win. But this house was something else; I understood why someone would want to fight over a place like this.

'I like those paintings,' I said, pointing at three large canvases on the wall.

'Donna did those,' he replied, almost apologetically.

'She's talented,' I said – and it was true.

I tried to ignore how much discomfort it gave me that they were so good. Even when I had seen Martin's ex-wife in the flesh, seen how beautiful she was, I had always managed to dismiss her as a pampered, self-regarding trophy wife, dabbling in art as a way to pass the time between trips to the Harbour Club and Whole Foods. Even when I saw Donna and Martin laughing together in the restaurant on that hazy, rainy night, I had consoled myself with the thought that I was better than Donna Joy: smarter, sharper, more accomplished. Perhaps I had been wrong about that too.

I followed Martin into the living room, which stretched all the way from the front of the house to a wide set of bay windows at the rear. I could hear birds singing outside, but I felt none of their simple joy.

'Coffee?' asked Martin.

'No thanks.'

I waited until I had his full attention.

'I need to tell you something.'

'I sensed this wasn't a social call.'

'I've been to the police,' I said finally and he frowned, not following.

'The police? Why?'

'To talk.'

'What about?'

I knew I had to get the uncomfortable stuff out of the way first. The stuff I'd been desperately trying to push to the back of my mind ever since Michael Doyle had told me.

'Inspector Doyle mentioned domestic violence.'

'*What?*' He sounded astonished. 'You mean between me and Donna?'

I nodded.

'It's utter bullshit. I swear to you, Fran, I have never laid a hand on her. I would never do that.'

'That's what I told Inspector Doyle,' I said, reassured by his bafflement.

Martin pressed a hand against his mouth. I stepped forward and touched his arm reassuringly.

'Look, I went to see Doyle because I finally got hold of Phil – my investigator.'

That sparked his interest and he stepped towards me, but I held up a hand.

'It's not necessarily good news,' I said with a tone of warning. 'Donna was seeing someone. Someone other than you.'

I searched his face for a reaction, but there was only confusion.

'Was this the person she went to Paris with?' he asked.

'We don't know that yet.'

'Then what do you know?'

I paused and tried to inhale in the calmness of the room around me.

'Donna was seeing Alex.' The words seemed to form in the air between us and I looked away, unable to watch the crash of emotions on his face.

'Alex?' he repeated. '*My* Alex?'

I nodded.

'Is this Phil guy sure about this?'

'He hasn't got bodily fluids or video footage, but he's—'

'Then how does he know it's true?' he interrupted, his voice urgent, loud. I could almost see him winding himself up like a spring, ready to pounce.

'I don't believe it,' he said, shaking his head. 'Donna and Alex don't even really get on.'

I noted the genuine disbelief on his face and felt a surge of relief. Phil's words of caution at our meeting in the Japanese garden had been working through my head like a determined earthworm. An affair with Alex gave Martin more of a motive to get rid of Donna. She could have told him, he could have lost his temper. A crime of passion. But unless he had been studying at RADA, Martin hadn't had a clue about Alex and Donna's relationship, however fleeting it might have been. Which made that motive redundant.

I felt guilty for having even considered Phil's theory, but forced myself to recount everything the investigator had told me, while also giving Martin time to let it all sink in.

'And you told the police about this,' said Martin, rubbing his forehead.

'I wanted to tell them as soon as possible.'

He flashed me a look. 'Before me?'

'It's not a competition, Martin. And since your lawyer told you they might re-arrest you, I wanted to make sure the police were aware of any other suspects with plausible motives as soon as possible.'

He considered this and nodded.

'So they're going to bring Alex in for questioning?'

'They've already spoken to him,' I said. This part wasn't going to go well either, I could tell.

'Do you think that's the reason why they let me go? Why they didn't charge me?'

I shook my head sadly.

'They spoke to Alex on Monday.'

The brief look of elation on his face disappeared. He pressed his lips together and I could see him putting the facts together and working out what I had realized hours earlier. Alex had been questioned *before* Martin had been arrested, which meant that they had eliminated Alex from their enquiries.

'Listen,' I said gently, 'this doesn't change anything. The police didn't charge you because there isn't enough evidence – and with the non-existent body, there never will be. If they are speaking to other people, they're still open to other lines of enquiry, which means they aren't convinced you're their man. And you have to be sure before charging someone. Or at least sure that the CPS have a prosecution case with a realistic chance of conviction.'

'But how can the police be certain that Alex wasn't involved in Donna's disappearance?' He muttered the question, as if addressing himself rather than me, and trying to process it all in his head. I noticed a pulse beneath his left eye, beating like a tiny heart. Despite what had happened in the Earls Court hotel room, I wanted to wrap him up in my arms and tell him that it was going to be OK. But I still wasn't sure I believed that myself, not after having spoken to Inspector Michael Doyle. I knew the police weren't going to break their backs helping Martin out of this hole, so someone else had to do it. I had always loved puzzles and cop shows and I liked piecing things together. Wasn't that what I did on a day-to-day basis: look for angles and loopholes, trying to out-think the opposition? And right now Martin didn't need me to be Francine Day the lawyer or even the lover. I had to be the detective.

'The police claim Alex had an alibi for the Monday night, that last night that Donna was seen,' I said, feeling a macabre enjoyment in the situation. 'But for them to discount Alex from the investigation would be to make the assumption that something happened to Donna on that Monday. Why not Tuesday, or Wednesday? Or any day between then and now? What have Alex's movements been since that Monday?'

Martin looked up. 'I'm pretty sure he was at a fin-tech conference on the Tuesday and Wednesday. I can ask around, find out.'

I nodded.

'And here's something else,' he said. 'I've stayed here two nights since Alex was interviewed by the police and he hasn't mentioned it. Don't you think that suggests he's got something to hide?'

I was less convinced than he was. 'I'm not sure the subject of Alex's affair with your wife is something he'd want to bring up over supper.'

He looked at me, then shrugged, conceding the point.

'I look so bloody stupid. Everyone knew about it but me.'

'I'm not sure the police think that Donna's relationship with Alex was serious,' I said.

'Now there's a consolation.'

Neither of us spoke for a few moments.

'How did the police find out anyway?'

'A friend of Donna's had told them. But Inspector Doyle was vague with the details. It was possibly the same person who my investigator interviewed. It's unlikely they'd speak to Phil and not the police, given that Donna is missing and the police have been asking people to come forward with information.'

'And the domestic violence allegations?' He said that more nervously.

'I think that was Donna's sister.'

'Jemma?' he said, raising his voice. 'But she barely speaks to Donna. They're not even remotely close.'

'According to Inspector Doyle, she's helping police with the investigation.'

Martin stood up and walked over to the window.

'When did it start? Did she tell them? When exactly did my business partner start fucking my wife?'

'Yes, I'd like to know the answer to that question myself.'

I spun round, heart jumping at the sound of a voice behind me.

'Sophie,' I breathed. 'I didn't realize you were there.'

'No,' she replied tersely. 'Apparently not.'

She was wearing sports kit, with a gym bag slung over her shoulder. I'm sure that any other day she would have looked like a poster girl for clean living, but now her face looked ashen. The awkwardness shimmered around the room. Martin stood up by the arm of the sofa like a teenager caught taking a fiver out of his mother's purse.

'I thought you were playing tennis.'

'It was called off. Thought I should come back and see you, but clearly I was mistaken.'

There was a faint tremor in her voice and it was hard not to feel sympathy.

'How much of that did you hear?' I said slowly.

'Enough.'

'I'm sorry if you didn't know.'

'I knew,' she said, standing up straighter, as if she were trying to recover her dignity. 'I knew what Alex had been accused of, anyway. As you can imagine, it was something the police brought up when they spoke to me – total fiction, of course.'

Interviewing Sophie wasn't something Inspector Doyle had mentioned in the quid pro quo, but then I supposed that made sense, given that Sophie had apparently given Alex his alibi.

'Not total fiction, Sophie,' I said gently. The door was open and I knew I had to use this opportunity to get as much information out of her as possible. The law made you a predator like that. Spot the fault line and pounce.

'One of my investigation team found out about Alex and Donna when we were evaluating the Joys' financial settlement. I thought Martin deserved to know.'

'Is that what qualifies as family law now?' she demanded, eyes blazing, all the warmth of our previous meetings gone. I could hardly blame her for that.

She turned and looked back at Martin.

'Alex denies it,' she said with absolute conviction. 'It's up to you who to believe.'

I looked at her with a moment's admiration. She was protecting her man, as I had made it my mission to look after Martin.

'But I'm sorry we didn't tell you we'd both spoken to the police,' Sophie told Martin in a more measured voice. 'We weren't trying to deceive you or be dishonest. It's just that we came to the decision we wouldn't make this situation any more difficult than it needed to be.'

Martin rounded on her. '*Difficult?* This isn't some bloody dinner party faux pas, Sophie. The police – the *police* – have said Alex had a relationship with Donna. If anything has happened to her, that gives *him* motive.'

'Bullshit!' she snapped back. 'Alex said they've only ever been friends. And it's not as if you're a paragon of virtue, is it?'

I didn't know what she meant by that. At that precise moment, I didn't want to know.

'Insulting each other isn't helping. Maybe we just need to tell each other what we know about Donna in the week running up to her disappearance. Like how long were you at dinner with Alex on that Monday night?'

'You've got a nerve,' said Sophie, shaking her head. 'You come into my home, accusing my husband of having an affair with one of my best friends, and then you insinuate that he might have had a window in his diary to slip away and kill her.'

I thought I saw a tear glisten in the corner of her eye, but I couldn't be sure.

'I know this is difficult, but we just want to find out what has happened to Donna.'

'It's not Donna you care about,' she said, flashing a look between me and Martin.

She had a point, but I wasn't going to stop now.

'Please, Sophie. Just answer the question. Donna was your friend.'

She put down her bag and sank on to the arm of the sofa. She filled her lungs then let it all out, her shoulders sagging.

'OK,' she said and didn't speak for another few seconds.

'I met Alex after work,' said Sophie. 'Monday is generally our date night. We went for dinner at Locatelli's, came home about elevenish and watched some television.'

'What time did you go to bed?'

'Around midnight. And before you start wondering if Alex somehow slipped out of the house when I fell asleep, I was awake because I left the bedroom to phone my mother. She lives in Chicago, with my step-father. It was her birthday. I hadn't called her and didn't want to miss out speaking to her on the big day. It must have been one thirty by the time I finally got back to bed. Alex was fast asleep when I got there.'

She paused and pressed her lips together. 'As for anything else, any affair: I've never noticed anything strange about the way Donna and Alex have behaved. She's a beautiful woman, obviously, and I'd be a liar if I said I've never been a little bit nervous when she's around. Those summer weeks we've spent in Ibiza, Umbria, afternoons by the pool? Not many wives would feel completely secure lying next to Donna with her little bikinis and her perfect body. But you choose to trust your friends and to trust your husband. There's no alternative, is there?' she said in a cool, composed voice.

She looked at Martin.

'Speaking of which, you should talk to Alex, ASAP, clear things up. We don't want things to be uncomfortable here or at work, do we?'

Martin shook his head, looking down at the floor.

'I should probably go back to my flat,' he said.

Sophie's response was immediate. 'Don't be so childish,' she said, reverting to her crisp efficiency. 'You said yourself the place is swarming with reporters. All right, so you've got to deal with an awkward conversation with Alex, but right now staying here suits all of us.'

I looked at Sophie, not knowing whether to pity or admire her. She was either in complete denial – which I had to doubt, given the woman's almost pathological pragmatism – or she was being magnificently loyal to both of them: Alex, the man who'd almost certainly cheated on her, and Martin, the man who might well have murdered her friend. I watched as she stood, straightening her skirt and raising her chin defiantly. 'Now I think we'd all benefit from a decent cup of tea, don't you?'

# Chapter 33

I left the Coles' house before I was asked to leave. Besides, I couldn't hang around. Vivienne McKenzie had emailed me first thing and requested a meeting at chambers and although I was dreading speaking to her, I knew I had no option but to return to work.

My plan was to slip into Burgess Court, undetected, during lunch. It was a Friday, when most of chambers scattered to local pubs. I figured I could sweep my office, catch up with Paul, speak to Vivienne and be gone before most of my colleagues got back at 3 p.m. The last thing I wanted to do was bat off pitying questions about my meltdown in court, when I had more important things to do.

I was on the bus, gunning towards Piccadilly, when my phone rang.

'Francine?'

I didn't recognize the voice immediately and Alex Cole had to formally introduce himself.

'We need to talk.'

I was no real surprise that he'd called me, although my heart was racing hard. He was calm, but insistent that we

266

should meet. I was annoyed that it interfered with my plan to swoop in and out of chambers, but when he said he could get there within the hour, I reckoned I would still make my two forty-five with Vivienne and leave Middle Temple before the pub crowd returned.

Our designated meeting spot, Riojas, was a wine bar on a Theatreland back street. It looked like a cross between a gentleman's club and an East End boozer: dark wood-panelled interior walls, rickety captain's chairs and marked tables that looked as if they hadn't been replaced since the Krays stalked the streets of Soho.

Alex was already there in a corner table. There was a bottle of red wine in front of him, and a half-full glass of red. I approached him with the sinking feeling I used to get whenever I was sent to see the head teacher for a dressing down.

'Hello, Alex,' I said, sitting down.

He picked up the bottle to offer me some, but I shook my head.

'Don't you drink now?'

He looked at me as if this was both an accusation and a criticism.

'I'm sure it's good but I'm on my way to chambers.'

His lips were stained cherry red, but he didn't look at all relaxed, quite the opposite.

'Sophie said that you'd been round to the house today,' he said finally.

I thought about Mrs Cole's grown-up speech about all pulling in the same direction, but I knew I had been right: her loyalties were to Alex and I couldn't fault her for that, even though I'm not sure I'd have felt the same way.

'Yes, that's right,' I nodded. 'I had some information to give Martin. I assume you know what that was.'

'The same information you gave to the police,' he said tartly.

He downed the rest of his wine, lifting the bottle to pour a refill before he'd even swallowed.

'I could have told the police things too, Fran. About your relationship with Martin. But we didn't.'

'*We?*' I asked, raising a brow.

'Sophie talked me down.'

'I don't suppose that was done entirely altruistically.'

'No, it wasn't,' he said simply. 'We did it for the business.'

A waitress came to take my order, looking uncomfortable, as if she had intruded on a lovers' tiff. I asked for a glass of water and she hurried off to the bar, glancing back until she thought it was safe to return.

'The Gassler Partnership has over a billion pounds under management, were you aware of that?' said Alex, slurring his words slightly. 'Our investors are names you've probably heard of. We have an algorithmic trading method that is the envy of the trade. But above everything else, we have our reputation,' he said, his hand balling into a fist on the table.

'Our reputation as investment managers is tied to the return our investors think we can give back to them. Without that, we're nothing. So what do you think happens when you've got one partner arrested in connection with his wife's disappearance, and another one hauled in to the police station because someone said he was screwing his partner's wife? We're ruined.'

Angry spittle had beaded on his lip and as he wiped it away he tried to compose himself. For a moment I saw the dark side of the alpha male.

'Do you think it's come to that?' I asked calmly. I'd acted for a lot of bankers but I didn't know that much about the financial sector and the fine details of how it worked.

'We have at least two private equity groups interested in acquiring a minority stake,' said Alex, lowering his voice but pointing a finger for emphasis. 'They're still circling. But one investor has already hinted they might pull out their money if there's any more "embarrassment"' – he used hooked fingers to book-end the word – 'and it won't take much to bring the whole house of cards tumbling down. We have to keep everything locked down, Fran. *Everything.*'

He sat forward, peering at me.

'Do nothing without speaking to me or Martin, so we can run it past our crisis-management team. I mean it.'

I shrugged, then nodded, pondering his choice of words. *House of cards.*

'In which case, can I ask you a question?'

He shrugged, his narrow eyes almost disappearing into thin black slits.

'Did you have an affair with Donna?'

'No,' he said finally.

'You're not speaking to your wife now. Or the police.'

He puffed out his cheeks, glanced down at the pink-stained tablecloth and then back at me.

'Look, something happened. Once. A drunken kiss, maybe a year ago. It was at a friend's summer party in the country. I'd had some coke, so had she. It was a warm night, lots of those lanterns hanging everywhere to make it look *romantic.*'

He said the word with disdain and looked into the distance as if he was thinking about that night with equal contempt.

'We didn't sleep together,' he said, looking back at me. 'Frankly, there wasn't time. And there was no relationship once we got back to London. I'm not stupid. Donna is my business partner's wife. And I am also married. Divorce and the dissolution of my business doesn't feel like a good trade for a quick fling. Besides, I love my wife and I love Martin like a brother.'

I let that statement slide.

'So where *is* Donna?' I asked. 'What do you think happened that night?'

I'd had this conversation with myself over and over. I'd talked about it with Clare and Phil, but none of us knew Martin as well as Alex Cole did.

He looked less self-assured now, as if the wine had drained his confidence rather than bolstered it.

'Martin is a brilliant man,' he said, staring at the stem of his glass. 'I knew that the first day I met him at uni. In our group, he just stood out. He had more confidence than the Old Etonians, he was smarter than the postgrad brains. We got taken on by the same bank as part of their trainee scheme. At first I cursed my luck that I was in his intake, that I could never shine when he was among us, but then I decided to ride on his coat-tails.'

He swilled the remains of his wine around the bottom of his glass.

'Martin wanted it more than any of us,' said Alex, his voice quiet. 'That's what always gave him the edge. He was always prepared to work harder than everyone else, go that little bit further.'

'What are you saying, Alex?'

'What I'm saying is that I don't want to think about what happened that night.'

'You believe he could have hurt Donna?'

He snorted softly.

'Speak to some of our business associates. If you told them Donna was after half of his money, they wouldn't be surprised that she has disappeared.'

'What business associates?'

Alex had almost polished off the entire bottle of red wine. He glanced anxiously towards the bar like a junkie after his next hit.

I looked at him, urging him to focus.

'Hedge Funds bet on the market,' he conceded. 'Our fund invests in different ways: bonds, stock, currencies, gold . . . We buy, we sell, we short. Algorithms help – spotting anomalies in the market. But really we're only as good as our information.'

He hesitated.

'Two years ago we were given a tip. Martin had a friend. Richard Chernin. He promised Martin a tip about a billion-dollar merger in exchange for a loan. Martin gave him the money, but the tip didn't come. He must have got cold feet about breaching FSA regulations. But he kept Martin's money.'

He paused for dramatic effect, sinking the last of the wine. I bit my lip and waited.

'Chernin claimed he was being intimidated and threatened to go to the police. A few days later he was the victim of a hit-and-run. He ended up with two broken legs.'

'You're saying Martin was involved?'

Alex continued as if I hadn't spoken: 'Chernin arranged to meet me, in confidence. He was convinced it was Martin who had organized the accident hit, said he'd threatened to kill him if he didn't return the money. With interest.'

I looked at him and found him worryingly convincing.

'If you really believe that about Martin, then why are you letting him stay at your house?'

'What was I supposed to say? No? Besides, we don't know that anything has happened to Donna. She might be fine,' he said, in a tone that suggested he didn't believe it.

'I'm just telling you this because you're his lawyer and I want you to know the full facts. Forewarned is forearmed and all that. If you know what negative information is out there on Martin, you know how you can firefight it. I'd appreciate it if you did me the same favour. If you hear that Martin is going to be charged. I need to know.'

He pulled out his wallet, took out two twenty-pound notes and put them on the table to pay for his wine.

'Love hurts,' he said as he stood up and touched my shoulder. 'Good to see you, Fran.' And he walked out of the bar.

# Chapter 34

Fleet Street was busy as I headed towards Middle Temple. People were already leaving work and I could easily spot the lawyers in their staid suits, pilot cases stuffed with case files for the weekend; their working day not yet over, just changing location from office to home. *That was my life once, not so long ago.* The thought had been casual, but it struck me so hard that I stopped mid-stride, almost colliding with the red-faced businessman coming up behind me.

I mumbled my apology and carried on walking, getting more and more nervous as I approached Burgess Court. Vivienne MacKenzie had asked me to come in to 'discuss the ongoing situation'. At least she saw me as 'ongoing' which was better than 'erased from all records', but still, I wasn't looking forward to our meeting.

It struck me that, however politely Vivienne had framed her email, there was a very real chance of me being asked to leave chambers. It would then be only a matter of time before word got around that I had been kicked out and once that happened, it would be almost impossible to find another set to take me on. Everything I had worked for over the years, every rung of the ladder I had dragged myself up, every mind-numbing Hansard volume I'd crammed would all be a complete and utter waste. I had thrown everything – *everything* – away for a fling with a man I barely knew.

I put one foot in front of the other, tried to ignore the grey sky and the rain in the air, tried not to see them as omens until I got to Burgess Court. The first person I saw as I entered the building was Helen, our receptionist. At least she was a friendly face.

'What are you doing here?' she said, struggling to pull on her coat. 'Paul said you were on holiday. Thought you might be somewhere nice.'

'No, I've just been at home. Here, let me help,' I said, tugging her coat straight.

'A staycation,' grinned Helen, 'I'd love that. Lounging in bed, just watching romcoms and eating pizza – perfect,' she added with a raised eyebrow.

'Something like that,' I said, distracted. I couldn't see Paul in the clerk's room, but he had an unsettling habit of just appearing from nowhere.

'All your messages are on your desk, except for a couple of new ones just here,' she said, grabbing a couple of hot-pink Post-it notes and thrusting them at me.

'Got to go. Supposed to have half a day off today, but time flies. New man's taking me to Brighton this weekend. Meeting him at Victoria in about . . . shit, ten minutes. Enjoy your "break"!'

I smiled and watched her run out of chambers. I put my messages in my pocket, and ran up the stairs to my office in the eaves.

I took a moment to look around the tiny space, my pencils ordered neatly on the desk, a hammered metallic bowl I had found in Amalfi and used for rubber bands and paper clips reminded me of happier times, a neat pile of books, stacked vertically to use every inch of space reminded me of the careful order that my life once had. I sank into my chair, bowing my head and wondered if I would return to that quiet, predictable life ever again.

There was an incoming text from Vivienne who said she was running late.

I was grateful for the extra minutes. I pulled open my drawers, grabbing Phil's file on Donna Joy, shoving it into my bag along with a couple of notebooks and, as an afterthought, the black-and-white grosgrain ribbon that had tied up the box that my designer bag, Martin's gift, had come in.

The lever-arch files containing the Joy vs Joy paperwork were still on the shelves where I kept all my casework. Perhaps there was some detail buried inside that I had missed. I knew I couldn't take them all; the files were too heavy for a start, let alone the questions that would be asked when their absence was noted. I flicked through the fattest one, grabbed the most important statements and made photocopies of them, then replaced the originals. I cased the room one last time, wondering what else I should take, reminding myself that this was my stuff, or at least, most of it.

I sat down at my desk and unscrewed a half-empty bottle of Evian. The water was studded with bubbles. Then again I must have first opened it a week ago. I was losing all track of time.

I put my hand in my pocket and pulled out the Post-it notes that Helen had given me at reception.

The top one was a message to call a solicitor I had promised to take out to lunch. I wasn't sure that anyone would be keen to instruct me, no matter how good the restaurant, once they heard about my court melt-down the other day. I scrunched it up and looked at the next one – and froze.

*2.55 Pete Carroll. Says he will see you at home.*

Helen had drawn a little smiley face underneath the words, a playful code from one woman to another. Finally I understood her hints about staying in bed and eating pizza; I could imagine what she'd been thinking when she'd taken the message. Francine Day finally gets a boyfriend – no wonder she wants the week off.

Suddenly I felt itchy, unclean, as if a toxic spill had infected my workspace, blackening the walls and creeping across the floor, thousands of tiny spider legs tapping towards me.

I shut the door and fled, keeping my eyes on the stairs, fearing to look up at the walls where I knew there was a line of oil paintings: the chambers' founding barristers, swaddled in their black robes and stern forbidding expressions, glaring at me, judging me. *We knew you were weak, Miss Day, we gave you a chance and look what happened. Let us all down – again.*

'Fran, is that you?'

Vivienne was at the bottom of the stairs, as if she had known where I was all along, lying in wait, barring my escape. I had long wondered if Paul had installed secret spy equipment around the building, imagined him, Vivienne and Charles Napier viewing it daily to keep us all in check.

I felt my cheeks flush as I walked closer towards her.

'Let's go into the library,' she said, her manner more brusque and officious than usual.

Vivienne was not really my boss. As barristers, we were all self-employed, but as joint head of chambers, Vivienne was still in charge. Sensing I wasn't going to like what she was about to say, I gripped my bag tighter and sat down at the big walnut table.

'Yusef Khan has taken Daniyal out of the country,' she said without preamble. 'Holly Khan is threatening legal action against you for negligence.'

I stayed quite still as Vivienne looked at me for a response.

'I was wrong to leave court,' I said finally. 'I left before my closing statements but I'm not sure that the judge's decision would have been any different if I had made . . .'

I stopped myself, disgusted that I was even trying to justify my actions. I'd abandoned my client and she had lost her son. She had every right to claim that I had failed her – I had, in the worst way possible, at the most crucial time. Vivienne didn't make a comment.

'Paul has checked your insurance policy,' she said instead. 'Everything is up to date. So if they do successfully sue you, you should be covered. I'm also having a meeting with Tanya Bryan on Monday; she hasn't indicated whether her firm is planning to pay you, but you should be prepared for that too. It might be time to obtain a medical certificate from your doctor, although I'm sure you're aware that any mental health issues could impact on you professionally.'

I could sense it coming. She was going to serve me notice. I was going to be expelled from chambers.

Instead, her expression softened and I felt my breath stutter in my chest.

'I'll take my head of chambers hat off now, shall I?'

She gave me a little smile and I was grateful for it. She had skin in the game on this one; my fall from grace would not reflect well on Burgess Court. Lawyers enjoyed a good gossip as much as the next person and I could imagine how much the industry would relish the scandal of legal proceedings against Martin Joy's counsel.

I had no idea how the merger with Sussex Court Chambers was coming along, but if the negativite publicity surrounding Donna's disappearance hadn't killed it off, then rumours of my reckless professional behaviour might do the job.

'Take a holiday, Fran,' she said more kindly. 'A proper one.

Get out of the city. Go and see your family. I've got a cottage in Devon, which you're welcome to use. It's got a view of the sea, and miles of walks in every direction. Making silk isn't important. Your health is.'

Silk. It had been the last thing on my mind. For so long – nearly fifteen years – it had been my goal, my own personal grail, and now it was like dust slipping through my fingers. But sitting here, opposite Vivienne, a woman, a lawyer I had admired for so long, I suddenly wanted it more than ever.

'QC interviews aren't till September. If I take some time off, publish some papers, then work hard to repair whatever damage I've done to my reputation . . .'

'Corporate burnout is all around us and it's serious,' she said with quiet firmness.

I looked away from her in shame, remembering an Inns of Court story I'd heard as a pupil. How a particularly pompous junior at a nearby chambers used to boast about making High Court judge by forty, but quietly retired by the same age, having been found running naked through Middle Temple one Christmas Eve singing 'Good King Wenseslas'. I didn't want to be a cautionary tale, another egghead who couldn't take the pace of twelve-hour days for fifteen straight years. I hadn't come this far, fought so many prejudices to fail now.

'Do you know why I took a six-week sabbatical last year?'

I wasn't aware that she had. I had a vague recollection of some fabulous holiday involving the Orient Express and a cruise up the Mekong River, but I assumed it was to celebrate a milestone birthday for either Vivienne or her husband.

'I was at breaking point,' she confided. 'I had to get out.'

The most inscrutable face in the business coloured.

'This business isn't easy, Fran. But if we don't accept that we're not perfect, that we're not robots, that we are just people who want a life outside our place of work, if we don't give ourselves a break, then we are going to break.'

'So you're not asking me to leave?'

'Leave?'

'You're not kicking me out of chambers.'

'Of course not. Is that what you thought this was about?'

I nodded back with sinking relief.

'Fran, of all the young barristers that have joined this chambers, out of everyone I've tried to support or mentor, you're the one I'm most proud of.'

'But the merger . . .'

'Take a holiday, Fran. Leave the worrying to someone who has rebooted in the Mekong.'

I walked out of chambers, taking in a lungful of late-afternoon air.

Fountain Square was disappearing into the dusk, although I knew that the longer, warmer nights were just around the corner. There would be a pop-up champagne bar here soon, keeping up the tradition that Middle Temple had once had as a venue for lavish entertaining. Rumour had it that the very first production of *Twelfth Night* was staged in the Tudor hall in the corner of the square. I'd studied the text for A-level and could barely remember anything about the story except that it involved mistaken identity. Strangely, it was the theme I had enjoyed most about the play, that people were not who they seemed. Ironic, I thought, given I'd spent the past few weeks reading people wrongly.

I slung my rucksack over my shoulder when I saw Tom Briscoe stride across the Square.

He waved and we met halfway at the fountain.

'Late lunch?' I smiled.

My mood had lifted after my conversation with Vivienne and I was genuinely glad to see him.

'Something like that,' he replied, pushing back his hair. 'So, you're back,' he said after a moment. 'Good. I was wondering where you'd got to.'

I had no idea if he knew about the Khan vs Khan saga, so I deflected his remark:

'Sounds like you missed me for a moment there, Tom.'

'How can I not miss the daily dose of abuse when I make my morning coffee?'

I pushed my bag further up my shoulder and smiled.

'How are you?' he asked, with a look of genuine concern.

'Not great,' I said honestly. 'But a weekend doing nothing might sort me out.'

'There's a play at Hampstead Theatre, if you fancy it,' he said, not meeting my gaze directly. 'My brother's directing it. I said I'd pop down. You should come.'

'Me?' I said, surprised. 'I don't want to impose. You'll be there with your family . . . Hannah?'

'Actually, no.'

I was certain Tom was just being kind, but I didn't want to complicate things any further by seeing my colleagues socially.

'I'm staying with a friend at the moment. Perhaps another time?' I said, feeling a drop of rain fall on my forehead, feeling grateful for the chance to leave.

'It's about to tip it down. I should go.'

'You're right. I'd better check in with Paul before he sends out a search party to the Devereaux Arms.'

I walked away from him quickly, regretting instantly having turned down the chance to have a normal night out.

'Francine.'

I spun round, hoping that Tom was calling me back. I stopped still when I saw him.

I should have recognized Pete Carroll's voice. Should have known that he might come here.

He stepped towards me, then shifted his feet so that he stood square on the flagstones.

'Who was that man?' he said pushing his hands into the pockets of his puffa jacket.

'Hello, Pete,' I said, ignoring the fat raindrops hitting my shoulders. I wasn't going to give him the satisfaction of letting him see how unsettled I was.

'Did you get my message?' he said with a glassy smile.

The Post-it note. I assumed he'd rung, but he must have come to Burgess Court to see me.

'Just a few minutes ago when I popped into chambers. I've not been working this week.'

'What have you been doing?'

'I've been staying with a friend,' I said, inwardly cursing myself. I knew I shouldn't be giving him information.

'Who? Martin Joy?'

'No, not Martin,' I sighed.

'Then who? That man I just saw you with?'

'He's a colleague from chambers,' I said, stopping myself from using Tom's name.

'He didn't look like a workmate. In fact, I'd say you have a type.'

'Pete, stop it,' I said, irritation overcoming my discomfort. 'What are you doing here anyway?'

'You haven't been home for two nights. I've been worried about you.'

'Well, I'm fine.'

'I was going to cook us dinner on Tuesday but you never showed up. I thought you might be upset because I left without saying goodbye the other day. You looked so peaceful, I didn't want to disturb you.'

'Pete, I have a busy life,' I said, trying to keep my voice cool. 'Work takes me out of town, friends want to see me . . .'

'Good,' he said. 'Because for a moment, it felt like you're avoiding me. Which hurts, seeing as the last time you saw me, I was inside you.'

His words made me shudder but I covered it by pulling my coat tighter around me.

'How is Martin, anyway?' said Pete, oblivious. 'I thought he'd be in custody by now. Then again, perhaps the police are smarter than we think. Perhaps they suspect Martin wasn't the only one at Donna Joy's house that night.'

I didn't say anything. Pete Carroll was unpredictable and I didn't want to provoke him any more than I had to.

'Are you coming home tonight?'

'I don't think so,' I said, starting to shiver. 'Like I told you, I'm staying with a friend . . .'

He leant towards me so that I could feel his sour breath on my face.

'I *will* go to the police, Francine. If you don't come back to the flat this weekend, I'll go and see Inspector Doyle.'

I held my tongue. I wasn't going to bother wasting my breath asking how he knew the detective in charge of Donna's disappearance. Pete Carroll was smart and a world of information was just a few clicks away on the internet.

'So what?' I said, trying to sound defiant. 'I was drunk, I'm not exactly a reliable witness. You really think they will care?'

Pete laughed.

'Oh, I reckon they will. Think about it: you admit to being there the night Donna Joy disappears, never to be seen again. I think they might put two and two together and make five. I know I did.'

I was determined not to let him see he'd got into my head.

The things he was saying were the dark thoughts that I'd been trying to ignore for the past ten days, the thoughts that had been festering in my subconscious, since I'd heard Donna Joy was missing. I still couldn't remember anything about that night, couldn't recall for certain who had gone into the house and when they had left. But what I did know was that *I* had been there. In fact, that was the only thing I was sure of. I had been watching from the pub, then lurking in the shadows. I was the one constant in the scene. But while I couldn't say when Martin and Donna had left, I couldn't account for my movements either, could I?

'It's raining,' I muttered, putting up my collar. 'We should go.'

'Good. I knew you'd see sense. We should get a cab. Hurry back. It's never too soon to start a nice night in.'

I knew how easy it would be to capitulate. To give in to his manipulation to keep him quiet. But I couldn't. Not now. Not now Vivienne MacKenzie had my back and I was making progress, helping Martin. I could hold this together. Make it work.

'Pete,' I said, 'I'm not going home tonight.'

'OK, I get it.' He nodded. 'You're a busy girl. But I'll see you tomorrow, yes?'

His ability to suddenly shift gears disturbed me more than his words: he was twisting the real world to fit his own internal narrative. I flinched as he reached out and took my hand. Although it was clammy and cold, it seared my flesh.

'I know you're a bit worried about the age gap, Fran. But we've got so much in common, you and I,' he said, his voice low. 'I had a peep inside your medicine cabinet when I was at your house. Saw what was in there. I had my own troubles when I was younger, although a spell at the Maudsley sorted me out. We can talk about it tomorrow. I'll cook and I'll tell you all about it.'

'Fine,' I said, pulling my hand free. I didn't want to lie to him, but I had to get away.

'Till then, babe,' he grinned and I turned on my heel, heading towards the street, feeling his eyes on my back, expecting him to grab me at any moment. But when I dared to glance over my shoulder, the bench and the square were deserted. As soon as I turned the corner into a side street, I bent over and vomited in the gutter.

# Chapter 35

I got a taxi back to Clare's, too nervous to take the tube or bus, too paranoid that Pete might follow me. The cabbie was the silent sort, which was just as well because I could barely breathe, let alone speak.

Although I still had a set of Clare's house keys, I rang the doorbell rather than let myself in.

'Fran, I wasn't expecting you,' said Clare, opening the door. 'I thought you'd gone back to your flat.'

She was wearing a pair of slippers and some fleecy pyjama bottoms covered with cartoon characters. I rarely saw her looking anything less than metropolitan and glamorous. Another glimpse into the world of normality and it was the straw that made me crack; I burst into tears.

'Hey, hey,' she said, pulling me in. 'What's the matter?'

'Everything,' I sobbed, my whole body trembling.

She quickly led me through to her living room and turned on the gas fire, filling the cosy space with an orange glow. I perched on the edge of the sofa. I'd sat here dozens of times before, curled into the corner with a glass of wine, my feet under a soft throw. I could barely remember those times now. It was as if the memories belonged to someone else.

'Pete Carroll came to chambers to see me,' I sobbed.

'The bloke who lives downstairs?'

I nodded. 'He's blackmailing me.'

'*What?* What about?'

I looked down at my hands in shame and knew it was time to tell her everything. I took a deep breath and began to speak.

'So he's threatening to go to the police?' Clare cut in.

I nodded and wiped my eyes with the back of my hand. 'He's insinuating that I might have had something to do with Donna's disappearance.' I heard the fear in my voice as I spoke. 'And let's be honest, the police might agree with him.'

'That little shit,' said Clare with venom. 'What does he want? Money?'

I fixed her with a bleak stare.

'Sex.'

Her eyes slowly widened.

'And . . . did you?' she asked.

I nodded. Seeing the revulsion on her face, I tried to justify myself.

'Yes, I had to. He's dangerous, seriously Clare,' I said. 'I'm sure he's had a crush on me for a while, in fact he tried to kiss me on my birthday and I said no. And now it's as if he's intent on revenge. He said that he was treated at the Maudsley. I don't know what for. Maybe he was disturbed. Now I think he might be stalking me . . .'

I took a deep breath to control my hysteria and then put my head in my hands. I wanted to weep, to bawl and sob, but it was as if every muscle in my body was paralysed. Clare came to sit next to me, an arm around my shoulders, but I couldn't look at her.

'Fran, you have to go to the police,' she said gently.

'I think he might beat me to that,' I said bitterly.

'No, he won't,' said Clare. 'And even if he does – so what? He has some half-baked theory about you? Big deal. *He's* the one who's committed a crime. He *raped* you, Fran.'

Somewhere in my head, I knew she was right, but I still shrank away from the word. Rape was something that happened in dark alleys by crazed maniacs, not in your own bedroom by a good-looking neighbour. I knew logically of course that sex by coercion was sex against your will. It wasn't my area of law, but I saw the fall-out in nearby rooms in the advice centres, sandwiched between the bankruptcy proceedings and small-claims court actions, the pale teenage girls, frightened and afraid. Girls who had been threatened that naked photos or porn tapes would be sent viral if they did not acquiesce to more of the same, married women tricked or forced by a brother-in-law or a co-worker. I didn't handle these cases; volunteers with criminal expertise looked after them, and each time, their advice was the same as Clare's. Go to the police. But in truth, the law liked clarity and this situation blurred the edges. It was blurred in my mind.

'The thing that I'm most afraid of is that he might be right,' I said, my voice little more than a whisper.

'That's crazy!' said Clare. 'You had nothing to do with Donna's disappearance.'

'But what if I did?' I said looking at her intently, trying to let her see the guilt I'd been carrying inside me. I had hated Donna Joy – that night more than any other – and in my working life I had seen how destructive the force of hate could be.

'I remember waking up at Pete's, I remember watching Donna's house. But in those four hours in between – nothing. I can't remember what I did, Clare,' I said, desperation creeping into my voice.

'Fran, you cannot seriously think for one moment that you did something to harm Donna Joy.'

'Pete thinks I did.'

'Pete is twisting things in your head to get what he wants.'

'But do you think I'm capable of violence?'

'Fran – this is ridiculous.'

'No, seriously, Clare, I know there's a link between bipolar and violence. There is, isn't there?'

Clare pulled away, shaking her head. 'I have spent half my life trying to remove the stigma between patients with a mental illness and the shit that people connect it with,' she said angrily. 'You've heard what people used to whisper at you: schizo, psycho, loony. None of it is flattering, all of it is wrong and offensive.'

'I know all that,' I said. 'But it's just you and me here, Clare. Please, tell me – is it possible?'

She gave a loud sigh of disapproval.

'If someone is in a severe manic episode, then it's possible, yes. It's possible that someone could be violent.'

'What could they do? If they were out of control, I mean?'

'I've heard of acts of superhuman strength,' she said reluctantly. 'More often, but still uncommon, it's just aggressive behaviour. Sometimes people have to be sectioned when they're having a manic episode and substance abuse can increase the risk of violence and physical assault – but it's still very unlikely.'

She put her hand over mine.

'And I'm talking "could have"s here because you're pushing me – these are extreme instances, Fran. Besides, what you're talking about is something else. This isn't you going batshit and having to be restrained, this is you blacking out for a couple of hours – not the same thing at all.'

She looked at me, the concern turning to irritation, the friend overtaking the psychiatrist.

'Come on Fran, what do you think happened here? You broke down Donna's locked door, delivered a fatal karate chop, then got rid of her body, all before two o'clock in the morning when you arrived back in Islington? Oh, and after hoovering and wiping down every surface with Mr Muscle before you left: I assume forensics have crawled all over Donna's house and found nothing except traces of Donna – and Martin.'

I didn't like her mention of Martin's DNA being collected by the scene-of-crime team, but I had to admit that she was talking sense.

'That still leaves three missing hours from pub closing time. What could I have been doing? If only I could get that time back. If only I could remember.'

Clare stood up and walked over to the window, staring through the glass on to the dark shadows on the street.

'I have a friend who might be able to help,' she said after a moment. 'His name is Gil. He works at the centre, he's a clinical psychiatrist who specializes in trauma.'

I looked at her, a tiny dot of hope growing.

'But I thought you said you couldn't retrieve memories from a blackout?'

'It's not an exact science, and I'm not sure if it can be done in your case. But if there's a way, Gil will know. I think we should see whether it is possible, don't you?'

I jumped up and threw my arms around her. 'Thank you, Clare. You are so wonderful.'

'Hey, it's OK,' she murmured, pulling me close, stroking my hair. For a moment, a memory dislodged. A night at university. The night of the summer ball. It had been such a warm day, the balminess was still in the air and the Sloaney girls on the events committee had done a glorious job transforming the grounds of our halls of residence into a wonderland sprinkled with hurricane lanterns; it was as if the whole place had been dusted with stardust and fireflies, just like the night Alex had described, the night he first kissed Donna. Clare and I had been reckless too. We were drunk and happy, the fairground rides at the far end of the lawns making us even more dizzy and heady. I had felt beautiful that evening in a long vintage dress I'd found in a charity shop. A year earlier, I had been the girl behind the bike shed, the school slut who smoked and slept her way around town, trying to get noticed. But that night I'd felt like a princess in a fairy tale and Clare had been cast in the same spell. I wondered if she ever remembered that night. Those carefree, reckless days of youth – oh, how I missed them.

# Chapter 36

The West London counselling centre looked unremarkable on a wet Saturday morning. The small car park at the front was empty, except for a drizzle-spattered people carrier in a bay marked 'Reserved for doctors'.

'Looks deserted,' I said, suddenly irritated. 'You'd have thought if anywhere needed to be open at the weekend, it'd be a clinic like this. All those people working in stressful jobs all week, why can't they—'

Clare cut me off.

'You're anxious,' she said, tapping the access code into a pad by the door. 'I get it. But bear in mind that Gil might not be able to help. Don't build your hopes up: it's unlikely that anything will happen today. Therapy is a process, not a quick fix. It could take six months of sessions. You do know that, right?'

'Martin will be in prison in six months if I can't help him,' I said, stepping inside and shaking the collar of my raincoat. 'You know *that*, right?'

Clare looked as if she was about to reply, but paused and nodded instead, giving me the slightest of weary smiles as she led me down the white corridors. I knew she was willing to tolerate my loyalty to Martin, but she didn't like it. She was helping me, not Martin.

'This way,' she said, using a swipe card to open a door. 'Gil's on the top floor.'

The stairwell was a glass box, silver ribbons of rainwater running top to bottom, making the outside world look distorted, displaced. I could hear each footstep on every stair, echoing upwards.

Clare seemed nervous too; but I found that reassuring. At the end of a long passage, a single door was open, fanning a wedge of grey light into the corridor.

'Gil?' said Clare, politely tapping on the doorframe.

'Oh, hello, hello.' A tall man jumped up from behind his desk. 'Come in, come in, both of you.'

He was in his late forties, a thin face with a receding hairline, but he was surprisingly fashionably dressed, like a trendy sixth-form teacher. The most striking feature, though, were his eyes: coal-dark and mischievous. I liked Gil Moore on sight.

'You must be Fran,' he said, shaking my hand. I wondered how much Clare had told him, then immediately wondered how much *I* should tell him.

'Excuse the room,' said Gil, scooping up a half-eaten sandwich and dropping it into a wastepaper basket. 'Crappiest space in the building, but I'm only here two days a week.'

'Don't worry,' I said. 'My office is no better. Where are you usually based?'

'At Baverstock Hospital,' he said, distractedly rearranging his desk like a housewife surprised by visitors. 'I mainly do trauma work: patients with post-traumatic stress disorder – a lot of ex-military, as you might imagine.'

There were some framed certificates on the wall next to a pile of CD cases on a shelf. Tilting my head, I could see The Smiths, Jesus Jones, Royal Blood. I don't know what I had been expecting – someone old and fusty in a black turtleneck, gentle classical music playing in the background, perhaps.

'I should leave you to it,' said Clare, who hadn't moved from the doorway. 'My desk could do with a tidy too.'

'Says the most anally retentive person in the building,' smiled Gil.

Clare looked down, colouring a little. 'You know me too well,' she mumbled, then with raised eyebrows towards me, disappeared. *Interesting,* I thought, feeling a pang of regret. Partly due to the realization that here was a corner of my best friend's life I knew nothing about, and partly disappointment that Clare hadn't ended up with someone like this smart, compassionate man. Instead she had chosen Dom; or let herself be chosen.

Gil took my dripping coat and hung it on a rack by the door. He waved me to a grey fabric sofa – Habitat, once upon a time, I thought – and slid his office chair into position opposite me.

'So you're Clare's best friend?'

'I suppose so,' I said, perching awkwardly on the sofa. 'I'm surprised we haven't met before.'

'I've only been here six months, hence the smallest room in the building,' Gil explained. 'I was in America for a long time before that.'

He shifted, leaning on the armrest.

'Clare tells me you had a blackout?'

So we were straight into the session. Efficient, direct: my kind of guy. Clare had chosen well.

'I need to remember what happened,' I said, watching him for a reaction – disapproval, perhaps, or hesitation – but he simply nodded. Clare's friend or not, I suppose I was just a patient, another problem to be solved.

'Good, well why don't you tell me what you do remember?'

Haltingly, I gave Gil a brief outline of how I had arrived at my neighbour's flat at two in the morning, stressed and agitated, with very few memories of what had gone before. I thought my bipolar might be relevant, so I filled him in on that too.

'Do you have a history of blackouts?' he asked.

'Not really. Not since university. I was a binge drinker in my first year – nothing too unusual there, I suppose, but I'd go to a Wine Society meeting and wake up the next day fully clothed, not remembering a thing. For a while I assumed it was the booze, but I was lucky enough to run into a GP at the college practice who paid attention, especially aften an episode of self-harming. Eventually, I was diagnosed with bipolar.'

Gil nodded, making a note on a pad on his lap.

'I take it you gave up Wine Soc?' he smiled.

'Switched to badminton,' I said. I liked how easy it was to talk to him, but there was also something that had been weighing on my mind.

'Clare said if I was drunk I won't ever be able to remember. Is that true?'

Gil let out a breath and sat back, lacing his hands behind his head.

'The real answer to that question is, it depends. The trouble with therapy is that the brain is infinitely complex. If you're a heart surgeon, you're basically working with a few pipes. Fit them all together in the right way, and you can reasonably expect everything to work once you've sewn the patient back up. Not the same with the mind, I'm afraid.'

He must have sensed my distress, because he smiled re-assuringly.

'That's not to say we haven't worked out a *few* things over the years,' he went on. 'Yes, Clare's right in saying that sometimes memories lost in a blackout can't be brought back, but that's assuming the blackout was related to your alcohol consumption.'

'So there are other possibilities?'

'Lots of them. For example, I hear a lot of anecdotal evidence of minor memory lapses in bipolar patients. Psychosis, fugue states, any sort of dissociation – which is my field of expertise, happily.'

He gave me an ironic smile. 'Or not so happily, depending on your point of view. Heart surgeons don't often have crying patients to treat.'

'That's because they're usually asleep,' I said.

'Good point,' he grinned. 'Should pay more attention with a barrister, shouldn't I? All right, tell me about the night you can't remember.'

I nodded, looking down at my clasped hands, surprised at how nervous I felt. I had wanted so badly to remember that night, but now the moment was here, I was frightened. Frightened that I wouldn't remember and frightened that I would. More than anything, I wanted to help prove Martin's innocence, but did I really want to relive seeing my boyfriend with his wife? Did I want it confirmed that he thought so little of me that they had slept together? And of course, there was the accusation Pete Carroll had added to the mix: that I had been involved in Donna's disappearance. I certainly wasn't sure I wanted to relive that, if it was true.

'Relax,' said Gil, his voice deep, smooth. 'Just the broad strokes of what happened that night for now. So I can get an idea.'

I had no option but to tell him. I described how I'd followed my boyfriend to his ex-wife's house, watching from the pub opposite. How my next memory was waking up in a neighbour's flat, apparently having been helped inside, my memory all but wiped, like a book with missing pages.

'How much did you drink that night?'

'That's the point: I can't remember. Nothing beyond the first drink anyway.'

'And I assume you were upset that your boyfriend was going to his wife's house for sex?'

My eyes met his, but there was no judgement there, just curiosity and shrewdness. That unnerved me, and again I wondered how much I was prepared to reveal to this stranger.

'Have you heard of this term "dissociation"?' he asked.

I shook my head.

'It's the separation of reality,' said Gil, putting his pen down. 'It can be as mild as daydreaming or as extreme as alternative identities. I see it a lot with combat and abuse victims – they block out those disturbing memories. It's the brain's way of protecting itself from uncomfortable feelings – it simply pretends it never happened.'

'And you think that's what my amnesia is? Dissociation?'

Gil nodded. 'It's what we call a dissociation fugue – a one-off event. Generally it's caused by trauma, but it can be brought on by drugs or alcohol. The patient has memories but the mind has essentially closed them off. The brain is in denial.'

'So in those cases, it's possible to retrieve the memories. How?' I asked, eager to get started.

'By kicking the doors in,' he said, standing up. He moved across to the corner of his office and with a quiet grunt, picked up a piece of equipment and began setting it up. It looked like a portable projector screen, only more high-tech. 'The problem with the subconscious is in the name,' said Gil as he worked, folding out the apparatus. 'It's *sub*-conscious, below our consciousness. All this interesting stuff is going on in there, but we can't get to it. So we need to find a way to trick the brain into opening up.'

'There, I think that'll do it.' He stood back to admire his handiwork: a long thin box sitting on top of a tripod, wires trailing from the back.

'What we're doing here today is a version of that,' said Gil, crossing to the window and pulling the blinds. 'It's called EMDR: eye movement desensitization and reprocessing, which is just a fancy title for this.' He clicked a hand-held controller and blue lights pulsed across the front of the box from left to right, accompanied by a low-level 'zip' noise with each pulse. Another click and it stopped.

'That's it?'

'Looks daft, but it's very effective, I assure you. What's happening is that we're mimicking the movements of the eye during REM sleep – the part of sleep where you're dreaming, when the brain is shuffling things around and trying to make sense of what you saw and did during the day. Once we can access that state, we tend to find the memories just come tumbling out.'

I looked at the box, then back to Gil, my stomach tightening.

'You're anxious,' said Gil, sitting down. 'Don't be. The beauty of EMDR is that we're asking the brain to look at these memories in a detached way. It's as if you're viewing it on a movie screen, without the attendant trauma. We use this for combat veterans and rape victims: it wouldn't be very productive to make them go through all that again, you'd just be re-traumatizing them, compounding the terror. But EMDR can still be dramatic; I've had abuse victims turn back into children, even their speech patterns change to kiddy-speak.'

He held up a finger. 'Note I said *dram*atic, not *traum*atic. When it works, it's usually quite liberating.'

I nodded, telling myself I could do this.

'All right, sit back,' he said. 'Get as comfortable as you can and tell me about Martin.'

His voice was soft and deep, calming. And yet I was nervous, hands clammy, fighting the urge to wipe them on my skirt. I closed my eyes and tried to get used to the dark. I was disorientated – as if I had lost time and been plunged back into night.

'Martin's my boyfriend,' I began slowly. 'Well, sort of. He's a client of mine. We shouldn't really be seeing one another.'

'Presumably that was a source of anxiety. A relationship that was out of bounds.'

'Yes. I'm also applying for silk – that's a big promotion for me. You have to be good, responsible. Affairs with clients, clients that are still officially married, don't really go with the job description.' I tried for a smile, but it didn't quite fit.

'Are you in love?' asked Gil simply.

I gave a nervous laugh, but suddenly wanted to admit the force of my feelings to someone.

'Yes, I am. I love him so much that it scares me. I've never felt like this before, it's as if I have woken up and just experienced all these emotions for the first time.'

'Do your emotions feel out of control sometimes?'

'Yes.' It was almost a whisper, but in the dark, in that intimate room, it felt like a shout. My voice shook as I continued:

'Most of the time I feel like a car with no brakes. When I'm with him, it's like I'm freewheeling and I've got the wind in my hair and I'm so happy. But I'm never really calm.'

'And that's why you were feeling stressed that night?'

'I was stressed because I thought he was still sleeping with his wife. That's why I followed them.'

'OK, describe what happened. As much as you can remember. What were you wearing?'

I opened my eyes and looked at him.

'What was I wearing?' I frowned, surprised to discover that I couldn't remember. I could recall Donna's pink coat, but me? Nothing.

'I don't know.'

'OK,' said Gil, and clicked his remote. The blue lights flashed across the screen. Zip . . . zip . . . zip.

I laughed. It all seemed so stupid, like some Sixties spy

movie where a camp megalomaniac was trying to brainwash the hero.

'Just go with it,' said Gil. I nodded, taking a deep breath. I had to do this. For Martin, if nothing else. I watched the blue lights bumping across the box. It was kind of restful, like fairy lights on a Christmas tree. Zip . . . zip . . . zip.

'OK,' said Gil, clicking his remote to shut off the lights. 'Now tell me what you were wearing.'

'A black coat.'

*Obviously* I was wearing my black coat. I always wore my black coat.

'Don't worry,' said Gil, clicking the lights back on. 'No rush, just relax and watch the lights.'

I sank back as they skidded past, zip . . . zip . . . zip. They weren't bright, a soft azure blue, like the sea on a poster advertising Greece or Italy. Santorini, I thought suddenly. I'd been there in my twenties, the beaches were amazing . . .

'Black coat, a green scarf . . .' I said, unsure if these were details I had gleaned from the *Evening Standard* e-fit, or whether I was beginning to remember. As I concentrated harder, more came into focus. I could almost see myself walking down the street. 'I was wearing what I usually wear for work. A white shirt, dark skirt.'

Gil clicked off the lights.

'Now describe the weather.'

I frowned, straining. I could almost feel it, but it wasn't quite there.

'No, I . . . I can't quite . . .'

'Fine,' said Gil, switching on the box. 'Go with the lights again.'

Zip . . . zip. It was soothing now, watching them move, like water over rocks.

'It was horrible – the weather, I mean,' I blurted, the words forming without thought. 'It was raining, cold, so cold I put my hat on. I remember thinking the rain would wash my make-up away.'

Gil clicked the lights off.

'You're doing really well. So what did you see first?'

I narrowed my eyes, peering into the gloom.

'I saw Donna. I followed her from work and I saw her meet him in a restaurant. They were laughing, drinking wine. They went back to her house. I went to the pub. I got a drink and sat by the window.'

'And then what?'

'I can't remember,' I said feeling distressed.

'It's just pictures, Fran. Nothing can hurt you here,' said Gil, his voice rich in the darkness.

The lights came again. Zip . . . zip. Blue and soft, blue, blue, green, seeing new tints here and there.

'I remember his hand touching the small of her back,' I said haltingly. 'I saw this, this easy familiarity between them, something I didn't have.'

*Oh God, he was so relaxed with her.* Zip . . . zip. Then Gil's voice again, reassuring, strong.

'And how did that make you feel?'

'It made me realize that everything Martin had told me had been a lie.'

'What else? What else, Fran?'

'I didn't blame him. Why not have sex with two women, if you could get away with it?'

I opened my eyes, looked at my new confidant, defiant, challenging him to react, but his face was impassive.

'What do you remember about the pub?'

Gil seemed to be turning the lights on and off at random now, or perhaps I wasn't following the sequence any more. Somehow I felt I was in both places at once; in the clinic, safe and relaxed, and back in the pub, staring across the street.

'It was busy. Busier than a normal Monday night. I think there was a party or a quiz night in the room upstairs. When I went to the bar, someone asked me if I knew the answer to a question. I like quizzes. And I knew the answer, but I had to get back to my seat to watch the house.'

The memories were coming, but I could feel myself getting more and more stressed. Or rather, I was feeling the distress from that night, feeling the tightness in my stomach as I watched Martin touch her, felt the fluttering pulse – zip, zip, zip – but at the same time it wasn't me there, it was someone else.

'Why do you think Martin lied to you?' asked Gil.

'He screwed his wife,' I said bitterly, my words a little slurred. God, I needed a drink.

'How do you know? Maybe they weren't having sex.'

'They were,' I said flatly. 'I remember the way she looked up at him when they got to the house. I remember the way he touched her shoulder, urging her inside. A light was on.'

A blue light, flashing on and off. On and off.

'What else, Fran? Just go with it.'

'A light went on,' I said. 'In the upstairs window. Her bedroom.'

'Why do you think that means they were having sex?'

I knew the tactics he was using and it was working, but I still couldn't give myself over to it completely. Gil had said people could relive the trauma, feel those same feelings and that was true. I could feel bile rising in my throat, feel the burn of the vodka, the pain in my chest as the implications sank in. I felt it all, as if I was sitting there in the pub, staring across the street, but at the same time it didn't feel real. The upset was there, the anger and the betrayal, but it was more like I was noting it, observing it.

'I *know* what they were doing,' I said, my voice low but strong. My head was swimming and my T-shirt felt tight around my throat, but I still felt good, it was like the picture was coming into focus. I could see them in the house, just as I had seen them that night, seen every act of pleasure I had ever enjoyed with Martin, except instead of my face, my naked body in the slideshow, it was Donna's body writhing beneath his. But Gil was right. I *hadn't* seen it, hadn't seen any of that. All I had seen was a light. A *light*.

'That's what I saw,' I said, jumping up.

'Fran, wait – please.'

'No, I can't,' I said, suddenly feeling strong, unburdened. 'Gil, I know what happened.'

Gil stood up and opened the blinds, flooding the room with daylight, his figure backlit – like Martin. And then I remembered it all. Not just fragments, but the whole thing, joined up, a memory I could grasp.

'I remember.'

I remembered it being dark and cold. I remembered Donna and Martin going into the house. I remembered the pub, the vodka tonic, the seat in the window. I remembered the quiz question: 'Name Queen's bass player.' I remembered the upstairs light going on and all the assumptions I had made. And then I remembered the front door of Donna's townhouse opening, that overhead porch light illuminating Martin from behind as he ran down the steps and disappeared into the darkness.

'He left, Martin left,' I said.

And I remembered looking back up at the tall, white building, and seeing someone open the thin slats of the shutters. The cloud of hair and delicate features of Donna watching Martin go. Donna Joy was at the window. She was still alive when Martin left the house. Which meant, almost certainly, that he didn't kill her.

It meant he was innocent.

# Chapter 37

I said goodbye to Gil and stood in the reception of the West London counselling centre, nursing a cup of water as I listened to a car door slam and Gil's car drive away.

As I started sipping the cool drink, I realized my earlier anxiety had been replaced by something more determined. A desire to get this situation fixed, because now I knew I had the key.

Clare appeared on the stairs. She must have seen Gil leave from her office window.

'How was it?' she asked when we came face to face.

'Extreme.'

'Are you OK?'

'I feel drunk.'

'*Drunk?*' she said with alarm.

'I don't suppose you've got any mints in your bag?'

'Maybe we should go for a walk. Get some fresh air,' she said, bemused.

I nodded, turned towards the exit.

'What happened?' she asked after another moment.

'He blew the bloody doors off,' I said throwing my cup into the bin.

Clare shook her head, not able to understand why I was quoting *The Italian Job*.

'Look, I need to speak to Martin,' I said, my eyes scanning the room and settling on the reception desk. 'Do you mind if I use the centre's phone?'

'Of course not. Fran, what's going on? Did Gil help? Have you been drinking?'

I was already sitting in the receptionist's empty chair, using the main switchboard to dial the number of Martin's disposal phone, which I had written on a piece of card.

I grabbed a red biro from the pen pot and started doodling as my heart raced, anxious for him to pick up the phone.

'Hello.'

'It's me.'

'Is everything OK?

'Oh yes,' I replied, starting to laugh. 'Things are definitely beginning to look up.'

'We should meet.'

'Meet me now,' I said, my voice an urgent whisper. 'Don't say anything to anyone, but let's meet as soon as you can. Somewhere we can talk privately. Just you and me and no one else.'

Part of me was beginning to feel like a spy. My instinct to use the centre's phone rather than my own mobile, my suggestion to meet on Hampstead Heath, it all had a touch of the George Smiley about it. I considered, for a moment, that it might be worth an application to the secret services if my legal career went down the drain. Then again, I felt sure that MI5 would be just as discerning as the Bar.

Clare dropped me off at the car park near Kenwood Park. I felt giddy as I walked across the meadows, excited to see Martin again, excited about the news I had to tell him about my session with Gil.

I didn't know the heath particularly well. I was sure you could come every day for years and not discover all its nooks and crannies.

There was a short spell a couple of years ago when I had decided to leave behind the treadmill at the gym and escape into the great outdoors. I had a vague notion that I was going to enter a ten-kilometre race. My career seemed to have stalled and I was on the hunt for a new challenge. So every Sunday I would catch the bus through Holloway, Archway and up the hill towards the Heath, and then I'd run and run.

It was during that time I got to know about Wood Pond. The clue was in its name – a stretch of water surrounded on the south by meadow and woodland. It was less famous than the celebrated swimming ponds, and although it got busy in the summer, I doubted there would be many people there on a grey and gloomy Saturday.

'Are you sure you don't want me to come with you?' said Clare as I got out of the car.

'Don't be daft,' I said, buttoning up the coat that she had lent me the day before.

'I can wait for you here,' she pressed.

For a moment I wondered why she was mollycoddling me, and then I realized that she didn't want me alone with Martin in a remote and lonely place. Despite the memory that Gil had dislodged, the memory that I had told Clare about on the journey to Hampstead, I knew that my friend didn't trust him.

I pushed my hands in my pockets and walked down the hill away from Kenwood House, over the glades, towards the trees. I found a bench by the pond and sat and waited until I saw a figure coming towards me, no more than a dark silhouette at first, until I could make out his face.

He was wearing jeans, a baseball hat and a navy overcoat I didn't recognize. He looked ordinary somehow, like a local taking his dog out for a walk. I guessed that was the plan.

Grinning, I resisted the urge to run towards him, arms open.

'You beat me,' he said, as he sat down next to me on the mossy bench. 'How did you get here?'

'Clare gave me a lift.'

'I'm going to have to get you a car,' he said casually. I supposed in Martin's world, that was the sort of thing men did. They bought women cars.

'The only thing a man ever got me from a garage is a bunch of half-dead flowers.'

Martin looked at me, one eyebrow raised.

'Do men really do that?'

'Someone buys those carnations.' I shrugged. 'And the Ferrero Rocher.'

'That's never been my style,' he said, gazing out over the pond.

Two women with Nordic walking poles in each hand stopped close by to admire the view, leaning on their sticks and blowing out their cheeks as if they had just ascended Everest.

'Let's walk,' I said, taking his hand and leading him away from the pond. I closed my eyes, enjoying the sensation of our fingers entwining.

'I remembered something,' I said when we were in the trees. It was cooler here, the light dimmer, more intimate. 'I remembered you leaving Donna's house. And I saw Donna up at the window, watching you leave.'

Martin stopped in his tracks and took me by the arms, his dark green eyes wide.

'You're kidding. I thought you said you couldn't remember a thing?'

'I went to see a therapist this morning.' I could feel a smile filling my face. 'He had some techniques that helped me remember.'

He looked at me as if I was the only thing that existed in the world, then pulled me into a tight hug. Then he stepped back and looked at me again, the delight on his face plain.

'You're my alibi,' he said, gripping my fingers.

I wanted to join in with his excitement but knew I needed to inject some reality.

'I'm not exactly a reliable witness, remember? I was drunk.'

'That's for the experts to decide.'

We carried on walking, deeper and deeper into the woods. I just missed stepping on a used condom, a reminder how the heath was used by others for secret assignations. The wind brushed through the leaves and I could hear a raven caw in the branches above.

'Thank you for not doubting me,' he said.

'I did,' I said honestly. 'I considered it anyway. Because you lied.'

'I haven't lied about anything,' he said, frowning.

'You said you fell off your bike. That's how you got the cut on your hand. Doyle doesn't believe you because the tyres looked clean.'

'I didn't fall off my bike,' he said, fixing his gaze on a line through the trees.

'Then why did you say you did?'

He glanced towards me.

'Because I can't remember how I cut myself. But it sounded so lame, I just thought of something plausible to say. I thought that would be better than just admitting that I didn't know.'

'You didn't have to lie to me about it.'

'I know and I'm sorry. I think I just convinced myself it was true. But the cut had nothing to do with Donna. I know that much.'

He gripped my hand. The day was cold but his hands were warm. He laced his fingers through mine and led me deeper into the woods.

'Alex called me after I saw you yesterday,' I said, as the trees became thicker and the air seemed to cool. 'Sophie had obviously told him I'd been to the police, so I met up with him.'

'What did he have to say?'

I shrugged.

'Stuff,' I said. 'Nothing that important. I don't trust him.'

Martin shook his head.

'I don't trust him either.'

I turned to face him. 'Have you had a look around the Coles' house?'

'What am I supposed to look for? An ice-pick?' He'd attempted a joke but there was no humour in his voice.

'Did you check if he went to that conference on the Tuesday and Wednesday?'

'He was there both days and met clients for dinner in the evening. A couple of people at the tech conference said he was acting a bit strangely on the Tuesday. One of them asked him if everything was OK, but he dismissed it. Said he was just hung-over.'

I wasn't sure if the information was significant, but I could tell that Martin was trying to sift through the pieces in his own head too.

'Anyway, regarding the trust issue, you should know I had my partnership agreement couriered over to me from the company lawyer,' said Martin, his expression grave. 'I knew there was a morality clause in there, but I didn't remember how stringent it was.'

'This is an agreement between you and Alex?'

Martin nodded.

'If either partner brings the company into disrepute, it's grounds to terminate the agreement and the partner in breach has to offer up his shares to the other person.'

'*Disrepute?* It's a woolly word.'

'Thanks for the legal tip.'

'What do you think it means in practical terms?'

'It means that if I continue to be implicated in Donna's disappearance, I could be ousted from the Gassler Partnership.'

'What, even if you're not charged with anything Alex gets to keep your shares?'

'He can buy them, but there's all sorts of ways to manipulate that price down, not least if Alex encourages some investors to remove their cash.'

'He can be dangerous. He knows stuff about you.'

Martin frowned.

'We all have our dark corners and Alex probably knows yours better than anyone,' I said without stopping. 'If he's got incentive to discredit you, he might well use that information.'

'What dark corners?'

'Some guy named Richard Chernin?' I said after hesitating. 'Apparently Alex thinks you had him "fixed" to get a deal.'

I looked at him, hoping he would deny everything, but Martin put his hands into his pockets and stared straight ahead.

'Making money can be a dirty business, Fran,' he said. 'Sometimes you have to negotiate hard. Have I done things I regret? I'm afraid so.' His voice trailed off.

'Like what? What do you regret?'

I needed to know everything he was capable of.

Martin shook his head and looked away from me.

'I want to know,' I pressed.

'What do you want to know, Fran?' he snapped, his face colouring. 'That I've screwed prostitutes because I didn't want to offend a client? That I've paid for information so I can short a trade, colluded with other bankers, done business deals with African despots and tyrants on their private jets? Deals I know were paid for in blood money? Yes, I've done it. No, I'm not proud of it. But it happens. Greed is what makes the world spin.'

'So now I know,' I said. 'I know your dark corners too.'

I waited for my moral compass to forbid me to be in love with this flawed man, but all I felt was the same fierce longing I had always felt when I was with him.

'So what do you think we should do?' he said after a pause. 'If you tell the police you saw me leave Donna's house at one o'clock in the morning, they're going to ask why you were there. I don't want to drag you into this, Fran. I don't want them treating you like they've been treating me. Like a criminal.'

'I'm sure they've already got their doubts about me,' I said, and I told him about the e-fit and about my meeting with Sergeant Collins and the lies I told him. Martin swore under his breath and ran a hand through his hair. 'Christ, I bet you wish you'd never met me,' he muttered.

'Not for one moment,' I replied, reaching for his hand. He fell quiet as if he was thinking.

'Since we can't tell the police about what you saw, we need to do this another way,' he said, with more resolution in his voice. 'We need to find Donna and we need to make sure the police are considering other people as suspects. Because I had nothing to do with it.'

'Neither did I,' I whispered.

'I never thought you did,' he said, turning to face me. My back was against the broad trunk of a sycamore tree. I leant back against its wrinkled bark and felt his soft lips on mine, his thumb and forefinger stroking my earlobe tenderly.

'I love you,' he whispered.

'I want you.' I replied softly, feeling the soft swell of arousal.

He wrapped his coat around me and as soon as I was hidden between its woollen folds, I unzipped his jeans. When he sprang free I took him in my hand, moving him up and down as he moaned in desire. I fumbled around with my own clothes, hitching up my skirt, guiding him inside me. I stretched my neck so I could see a tangle of branches and a glimpse of grey sky overhead and I didn't care about anything, not Alex or Donna or the police. The only thing that mattered was him and our togetherness.

We collapsed on the moss and leaves when we had finished. He put his arm across my shoulder and for a time that seemed like forever, we sat there quite still.

Afterwards, we walked around the entire circumference of the heath, hand in hand like two young lovers, past the swimming ponds and the bandstand at its most southerly tip, then west, towards the pretty pergola, up towards the Spaniards Inn, where we sat outside by the road, with two pints of craft beer, revelling in the stories on the back of the menu; the pub's mention in Dickens' *Pickwick Papers*, and its links to high-wayman Dick Turpin. If we both appreciated the folly of being seen out together in a public place, we didn't mention it. Not that anyone seemed to give us a second glance, let alone point out that the man in the baseball cap had been all over the newspapers in connection with his missing estranged wife.

It was almost seven o'clock by the time we got back to Kenwood House. I followed Martin to a sleek black Audi in the car park.

'Is this yours?' I asked, as he pip-pipped the alarm.

'It's Sophie's. The police have taken mine. I suppose they're hoping to find a boot full of blood.'

'That's not funny.'

He shrugged and we climbed in.

'Where should I drop you?' he asked.

I realized I didn't have anywhere to go. No work, no home, didn't much relish the thought of Clare's disapproving looks.

'Do you think Sophie will mind if we go for a drive?' I asked him.

'Where did you have in mind?'

'Chelsea?' I said. It seemed fitting for such a vehicle, with cream leather seats and a smooth walnut dash. In the corner of the windscreen was a parking sticker for one of London's most exclusive gyms. I wanted one of these cars too, I wanted that sort of gym membership. For so many years I had derided bankers' wives and the choices they made: giving up their lives and not using their brains, allowing themselves to be nothing more than someone's chattel. And yet, for all my hard work and professional success, I worked out at the crappy local gym and I travelled by bus. I wanted Sophie's life. I wanted Donna's life. I wanted the Coles' gorgeous house with its calm tones and made-to-measure drapes, I wanted Donna's wardrobe and bags and effortless, gliding beauty. I wanted to be Martin's wife.

'Whereabouts in Chelsea?' asked Martin, breaking my reverie, gunning the engine.

'Donna's,' I said, looking across at him.

'Fran, come on, that's not helpful.'

'Trust me,' I said.

He looked at me for a moment, then nodded and turned the car south. Saturday-night traffic snarled the city, a constant drizzle turning the tarmac oily. It took over an hour to get to the King's Road. Martin parked just down the road from the pub where I had sheltered the night of Donna's disappearance. We had an indirect view of her house and I noticed that the forensic vans had gone.

He switched off the engine and we sat quietly.

'We bought the house because of those gas lights,' he said, pointing up at the distinctive streetlamps overhead.

'They have those in Spitalfields too. You obviously have a type.'

Out of the corner of my eye I saw him smile.

I focused on what I had come here to do.

'So you think you left Donna's at about midnight?' I said. 'Pete says I arrived back in Islington at two.'

'Who's Pete?' he said crisply.

I couldn't believe I'd been caught out so easily. I was beginning to forget what I had said to whom.

'My neighbour. We met him at the bus stop on our first date,' I said, trying to quickly move on. 'I'd had so much to drink after I saw you walk into Donna's house that night I couldn't even find my house key. The taxi driver had to bang on the door and woke Pete up.'

'Does Pete have a key to your house?' he asked, his disapproval prickling across the space between us.

'No. He let me sleep on his sofa.'

I was glad it was dark. I didn't want anything, not the colour in my cheek, or the dryness of my lips, to give away that I was not telling him the whole truth. We'd had such a good afternoon together and shared so much. We hadn't just talked about the dark side of his business dealings, the things he'd had to do to be successful, which he had offloaded with the embarrassed relief of one discussing his past with a priest. We'd talked about our pasts, our happy memories, our school days, when we were both smart, geeky kids craving attention.

'You slept at Pete's house that night?' he repeated.

'I didn't have much choice. I was too pissed to find my keys and he couldn't exactly leave me on the street.'

'Could he not have helped you find your keys and let you into your own apartment?'

'Well, he didn't,' I said firmly, wanting to cut the line of conservation dead. 'Maybe that's a bit creepy, but I was so out of it, I couldn't object.'

That seemed to keep him quiet for the moment. I didn't want to tell him anything else. I remembered what Alex had told me about Richard Chernin and I hated to think what Martin might do if he knew that Pete Carroll was blackmailing me. If he knew that we'd had sex in my bed, I thought that he might kill him.

'I want to nip outside for a moment, see if I can jog loose any memories of where I went when the pub closed.'

I exhaled deeply as I stepped out into the cold air. I didn't turn to look back at the car. I knew without looking that Martin was watching me.

It took me a moment to get my bearings. The pub was on the corner and Donna's house was to the right.

Some of the houses on the opposite side of the street had pocket gardens at the front. Some had a low wall, others had a hedge, others still had thin black railings. I tried to remember my flashback in Gil's office, working out my position so that I could replicate my view of Donna. I saw a house that looked empty with it dark, filmy windows. It had both a low hedge and some steps that led down to a basement flat.

I positioned myself at the entrance and crouched down on the cold stone looking up at Donna's house. If she'd been standing at the window, I'd have had exactly the same view as the image I remembered. I must have come here to watch the house after I'd left the pub. I took a moment to see what else I could recall.

Nothing came immediately. I looked left, where I could see a flow of traffic at the end of the street and then right, where a metal bar across the road prevented vehicles from continuing to the adjoining street.

After a few minutes, I stood up, with nothing to show for my experience except numb buttocks.

I walked back to the car and got in.

'Do you remember anything else?' asked Martin with more enthusiasm.

'No. But I found where I must have hidden to watch the house.'

We sat in silence, punctuated only by the sound of our own breathing and the faint rumble of traffic in the distance.

'Tell me why you went back to Donna's,' I said after a moment.

'Fran, please.'

'When did you start fucking? Straight away, or was there a bit of seduction?'

Martin stayed quiet.

'Did it turn you both on? Playing hard to get with your spouse.'

'Don't do this. Don't torture yourself,' he said, putting his hand across the gear stick.

'That's what I am doing,' I whispered without looking at him. 'It's what I did with Gil this morning. It helps you dislodge your memories.'

Martin looked at me intently and nodded.

'We arranged to meet to discuss the FDR,' he said finally. 'We met for dinner. A place we both used to like. We had a bottle of nice wine. She was funny, flirty. It was a relief after all the sniping there'd been between us. So I went back to her place.'

'You must have been enjoying yourself.'

'Donna was always very good at making you feel special.'

315

'Is that what you liked about her when you first met?'

'The first time we met, I just thought she was beautiful. Sexy too. Vulnerable but knowing, as if she was pretending. She intrigued me. We were engaged after six weeks. Married within three months.'

'Where did you meet?'

'In a bar near the store where she worked. She asked me to buy her a drink. Then she told me to take her home.'

I wanted to ask him why men fell for that, but perhaps it was obvious. Men liked obvious.

'Was she good in bed?'

He looked at me, questioning whether I really wanted to know.

'Was she?' I repeated.

'She could fuck for England,' he said quietly. 'She had edges. She liked doing things that others didn't. She liked risk. Games. She could talk dirty better than anyone. She made me feel like a king.'

I thought of the messages he'd sent me over the weeks. The ones that made me want to touch myself. I remembered my shy responses and realized, right then, what he had been goading me to do. He wanted me to talk dirty back. Martin wanted me to be Donna. And I'd failed him.

I could feel my breathing become more shallow as my heart raced.

'Is that why you went back to Donna's that night? Did I not satisfy you?' I said, convinced that he found our sex life too vanilla.

'No,' he said passionately. 'It was one night that spiralled out of control.'

'Tell me about it,' I said coolly. 'Tell me about that night. Did you decide over dinner that you were going to fuck her?'

'I don't know. I didn't meet her with that intention.'

'What happened when you got back to her house?'

Martin exhaled softly as if he were trying to remember it step by step.

'We had a drink. She went upstairs. When she didn't come back down, I went to see where she was. She was on the bed in some sexy stuff.'

'Like what?'

'Underwear, heels,' he said.

'Then what happened?'

'I joined her on the bed. We started kissing. It went from there.'

'How did you do it?'

'Fran, please, stop this.'

'No. I want to know,' I said, feeling the pressure build. I felt on fire with envy and rage and longing. I was on the edge, like a ten-pence piece in one of those amusement arcade machines I used to love as a child. The ones you fed with your coins until they spilled over, over, exploding with a satisfying rippling sound of money against money.

'We did it every way, Fran. And then we did it again and enjoyed it even more than the first time.'

'So why did you leave? If you were enjoying it so much, why didn't you stay in her bed all night?'

'It wasn't a good idea.'

'Did she ask you to go or did you leave first?'

'It doesn't matter . . .'

'Tell me. Who suggested it?'

'She did,' he said finally, another slap across the face.

We didn't speak for at least a minute. I closed my eyes and tried to imagine them in that top room. I gripped the car door and there was a flash of memory, tantalizingly close, like a forgotten word on the tip of your tongue. But my mind wouldn't take me there. When I opened my eyes Martin was staring straight ahead.

'I read a quote once,' he said finally. 'A quote from a famous CEO describing his ideal woman. He said, "She's someone who could get me out of a Third World prison."'

I didn't reply. His earlier words still stung.

'I think he meant his ideal woman would have heart and grit and smarts. That's what I thought the first time I ever saw you. That's what I loved about you. Not just the fact that you are beautiful.'

He turned to look at me. 'When this is over, do you want to move into the loft?'

He said it so hesitantly, I felt my resistance soften.

'You don't have to feel sorry for me just because I have a creepy neighbour,' I said, putting my guard up.

'A creep with a crush on you lives downstairs, so yes, I'd rather you didn't go on living in that flat on your own a minute longer than you have to. But that's not why I want you to move into the loft.'

He paused before he spoke again.

'I want you to move in because I think it might be nice to try living with me and *not* be married to me. We can be not married for a little while and then see how things go from there.'

My heart started to beat fast. I wasn't sure if he was making a practical suggestion because he didn't like Pete Carroll and was lonely and afraid and needed someone on his side, by his side. Or whether he was actually proposing to me.

Mrs Martin Joy. It felt so right.

# Chapter 38

It was past ten o'clock by the time we drove into Queens Park. I still felt wired, manic; the day had been too weird, too emotional, and I wanted a cigarette to calm me down. I hardly smoked any more and certainly didn't want Martin to see me, but there was a small Juliet balcony in Clare's spare bedroom, and I imagined opening the door, lighting up and watching the orange glow in the dark.

'I need a few things from the shop,' I said, as the Audi turned down Salusbury Road. 'You can drop me off here.'

'I'm not dumping you out in the dark. Which shop do you want to go to at this time?'

'I think there's a little supermarket near the train station. Park in one of the side streets and I can run in.'

The supermarket was surprisingly busy. People coming out of pubs and piling out of the tube station all with the same idea: cigarettes and alcohol, for those impromptu parties or quiet, mournful midnights.

I enjoyed walking up and down the aisles under the fluorescent lights, feeling a normal person for once, living a normal life. Close enough, anyway. I bought a packet of Marlboro

Lights which I stuffed in my bag and a can of Coke and a packet of wine gums to cover my tracks. *Master criminal, me.*

As I stepped back into the street, I could see Dom's restaurant across the road and I stopped to look. The windows were all lit up, the tables inside looked rammed. Perhaps Clare's investment in Dom's latest vanity project might actually pay off. I watched two couples leave arm in arm, laughing and talking. And behind them was another figure, pulling on his coat and flipping up the collar. My heart sank when I recognized Dom: I'd hoped to slide into Clare's place unnoticed, then relax with my illicit nicotine hit. Now Dom would get back before me and be sitting in the living room or kitchen: I wouldn't be able to avoid him or his baleful stare. But Dom didn't turn left, towards the house. He went the opposite way and then disappeared down the quiet residential street where Martin had parked. Odd.

I waited until he vanished into the darkness and then ran across the road, dodging the traffic, back to the Audi.

'Got everything you need?' said Martin, as he fired the engine.

'Turn around and go that way,' I said, twisting in my seat.
'What?'

'I've seen something – someone. I want to see where he's going.'

Shrugging, Martin did as he was asked. As his headlights lit the way, I scanned the street for Dom but couldn't see him. Either he'd gone into one of the houses, or he'd got into one of the parked cars.

'Go slow,' I whispered, and the Audi slowed to a crawl. Ahead on the right was a silver hatchback with the interior light on, two people in the front.

'What's the matter?' asked Martin, but I was too distracted to answer. The street was dark, which meant I could see into the car as we passed. A couple kissing but as we were moving I couldn't see more.

'Turn the car around,' I said, as Martin reached the end of the road. 'Go back, go back.'

With a soft sigh, Martin did a three-point turn and proceeded back the way we had just come. The silver hatchback was coming towards us.

'Pull in to let them pass,' I ordered, and the Audi nipped into a space.

The hatchback growled past and I didn't need the light from an overhead streetlamp to see that it was Dom in the passenger seat. The driver was a woman: blonde, young. Pretty.

'Are you going to tell me what that was all about?'

For a moment, I couldn't speak, I was too angry, thinking of Clare, so loyal, so gullible, funding Dom's many ego-boosting schemes and waiting patiently at home.

'That was Dom,' I said quietly. 'Clare's husband. He was kissing that blonde in the car.'

'And that blonde wasn't Clare, I take it?'

'I didn't get a good look at her. But it wasn't Clare, I know that much.'

'Wow,' said Martin, looking across. 'Well, do you still want me to drop you off at her house?'

I paused for a moment, then nodded. Clare had always been there for me and now she needed my support, whether she knew it or not.


Martin kissed me goodbye and I put my key in the lock with a sense of dread. Clare's house was still and quiet. All the lights were off except for a lamp in the living room. A mug and a paperback thriller had been left on the coffee table, otherwise there were no signs of anyone downstairs. I crept up to the first floor. The door to the master bedroom was slightly ajar and I could see Clare's form under the duvet, fast asleep. It was barely ten thirty; still early for a Saturday night, and I felt guilty that I hadn't been there to keep her company.

I went to the spare bedroom at the back of the house, no longer in the mood for a cigarette. Though I climbed into bed and closed my eyes, my mind was too active to sleep. I had just nodded off when I was awoken by the sound of voices. I was groggy, but I could make out they were Dom's and Clare's. I thought I could hear her crying. I stayed as still as I could be until the noise died down. Although my eyes were closed, I could feel a presence at the door. Had they been open I would have seen Dom's face peering through the crack, watching me.

# Chapter 39

When I woke up, I was clear-headed enough to know that I couldn't hang around the house all morning. Clare and Dom had definitely argued the night before, and I could only imagine how awkward it would be, seeing the two of them over breakfast.

I climbed out of bed, smoothed down the duvet and tipped the contents of my rucksack on to it. I couldn't believe it had come to this. Living out of a back-pack, with only two pairs of clean knickers to my name. More worrying, I only had enough lithium tablets to last me another couple of days. If I had to leave Clare's house and get anything, I knew I should really head back to my flat to reload even if I had to risk bumping into Pete.

Peering round the door, I wondered if anyone was up yet. I was embarrassed to see either of my hosts but knew I couldn't stay in the bedroom forever.

I nipped across the hall with my washbag and went into the bathroom to brush my teeth. I was desperate for a shower but I didn't want to wake anyone with the noise of the jets.

At least a mint-flavoured mouthwash and quick wash made me feel better, ready to face the day.

Whatever that might bring, I told myself, looking in the mirror.

I pulled on some clothes and went downstairs, expecting to be alone, but Clare was sitting at the breakfast bar, still in her shorty pyjamas, hair tied up in a messy topknot and her face bare. I wasn't sure if she looked tired, upset, or whether I just wasn't used to seeing her without make-up.

'God, you scared me,' I said, clutching my chest. 'I didn't think anyone was up.'

'Paperboy was up before anyone,' she said, sliding a Sunday tabloid across the breakfast bar. 'You'd better read it. I think it's what you'd call a hatchet job.'

I turned the paper the right way up and scanned the page she'd left open. It was the picture I saw first. A big colour photograph of Donna laughing in a field. The image was slightly pixelated, as if the photograph was old or had been blown up too big. I suspected it had been taken some years before, as Donna looked very young and happy. Her hair tied back in a ponytail, her smile wide and goofy. She didn't look like a banker's wife; there was none of that 'look but don't touch' *froideur*. If you were looking for a perfect positive PR shot, it was pretty damn close, all it needed was a puppy in the shot to be pitch perfect. The headline was simple . . . *Where* is *Missing Donna?* But the text was more complicated.

At first glance, it was a rehash of events leading up to and since Donna's disappearance. But the juxtaposition of the supplementary photographs – Martin at a high-society £10,000-a-plate dinner, Martin looking shifty and dishevelled as he left his Spitalfields loft apartment – portrayed the Joys' marriage as a case of 'Beauty and the Beast'.

The divorce proceedings got a mention, but thankfully there were no references to chambers or myself. From Martin's point of view, though, Clare was right: it was a hatchet job. A hatchet job that had been carefully vetted by a lawyer, but a hatchet job all the same. It stopped short of accusing Martin of any wrongdoing directly, instead it painted a picture of a beautiful bohemian wife and her ruthless, financier husband, reminding the reader on at least three occasions that fat-cat bankers were responsible for the global economic downturn and pretty much every social problem thereafter. That was the story here: evil Martin Joy The Banker, versus his lovely caring wife Donna. There was half a page on her work with children and animals, work I hadn't previously heard about, not to mention her fundraising and general goodness.

'There's something in *The Times*, as well,' said Clare apologetically. 'Doesn't really mention Martin, but more of the same about Donna, implying her disappearance is highly suspicious.'

I went to the sink and ran myself a glass of water, aware that Clare was watching me closely.

'Have you spoken to the police yet about what you remembered?' she asked.

I shook my head, although I knew the clock was ticking for Martin. This media attention would put the police under pressure to make another arrest or at least give some signal that there were developments in the case.

God, what a mess. This wasn't at all how I'd expected the day to pan out and it was barely eight o'clock. I looked back towards the stairs.

'Where's Dom?' I said.

'Out. Running, I guess.'

'Everyone's started running,' I said with a weak smile.

'I doubt Dom is actually running,' she said, her voice brittle.

She looked up and I saw something in her face before she turned to switch on the kettle.

'Is everything OK? With you and Dom, I mean?'

'We had a bit of a ding-dong last night. Sorry if it woke you.'

'What was it about?'

'It was nothing,' she said with a wave of the hand. 'Frayed tempers, that's all. No one said opening a restaurant was easy.'

I took a step towards her. 'Clare, come on,' I said gently. 'You can talk to me you know.'

'You've got enough on your plate,' she said, waving me away.

'Clare, I'm your friend.'

She shook her head, unwilling to show her weakness.

'I was just annoyed he came home late. I know it was a Saturday night and he had to work, but I called the restaurant at ten thirty and the waitress I spoke to told me he'd left about half an hour before. I just wanted to know where the hell he'd been.'

'What did he say?' I asked, curious to know how much he'd deceived her.

'He said he'd been in the upstairs flat, doing the paperwork. Accused me of being tired and grouchy.' She gave a thin smile.

I paused before I said anything else. I was sick of the lies and hated seeing my friend like this. And I could tell she knew Dom's story was bullshit.

'Clare, I saw Dom in a car last night. With a woman. Some blonde I didn't recognize.'

She narrowed her eyes at me. 'When was this?'

'A little after ten o'clock. Martin gave me a lift home. I stopped at the Sainsbury's on Salusbury Road. I saw Dom leave the restaurant. He got in a car on one of the side streets.'

'How do you know?'

'I followed him.'

'That's becoming a habit, isn't it?' she said tartly.

'Clare, I'm just telling you what I saw.'

'Oh, and that's pretty reliable these days, isn't it?'

Her words upset me, but I forced myself to remain calm. I wouldn't want to hear it either, if I was in her shoes.

'So what then?' she asked, her arms folded. 'Did they drive off?'

'Eventually.'

'Eventually?'

I took a deep breath. I didn't want to hurt Clare but I didn't want Dom to get away with treating my friend so badly, the way she had allowed him to do for years and years.

'I saw them kissing in the car,' I said finally.

'He was kissing this blonde?'

She put her hand up to her throat, moving her fingers in circles as if she was trying to manually force air into her lungs.

'Are you certain?'

'It was dark, but yes, I could see inside the car.'

'Even though it was dark?' I knew she was challenging me, so I paused, thinking. I wanted to make sure I told her exactly what I had seen.

'You're not sure, are you?' said Clare, a laugh in her voice. 'You're not sure it was Dom. This could all be crap.'

'There's a chance I was mistaken, but I don't think so,' I replied. 'I didn't see the woman clearly, but it was definitely Dom.'

Her hand curled into a ball and she hammered it down on the breakfast bar.

'Don't say these things unless you are sure,' she said, her voice harsh. 'Just because you're not happy and have made the wrong choices, don't point the finger at other people's relationship's.'

'I told you because I care about you,' I said softly. 'You work so hard, Clare. You've supported Dom through every business and you think that you're helping him, but the truth is, he resents you. Sometimes you don't want to see what's in front of your eyes and you need someone else to tell you the truth.'

'The truth?' she barked. 'You should take a look at your own bloody life, Fran!' She grabbed one of the papers and shook it at me. 'Read what the headlines are saying about your dreamy new boyfriend.'

'Please, Clare, I'm only trying to help. If you don't want me to—'

'What? You'll walk out again? You're good at that, aren't you? Only coming crawling back here when you're falling apart.'

I gaped at her, unable to believe what she was saying.

'Why don't you fuck off to your fancy new friends?' she sneered. 'They seem to have plenty of time for you – at least when it suits them.'

'Clare, please . . .' The ferocity of her words frightened me.

'Just go,' she hissed, wiping her eyes.

I nodded. I'd known her long enough to know that she had a sting in her tail. That although she would calm down, for the time being, the best thing would be to leave her alone.

'Fine,' I said. 'But at least think about what I've told you. Ask the staff at the restaurant, ask Dom. Ask yourself if you've got the marriage you want,' I said.

She folded her arms in front of her chest, her defiant eyes glistening with unshed tears.

'Some of us don't have any choice,' she said.

'There's always a choice,' I said.

'Not for me,' said Clare, shaking her head. 'I'm pregnant.'

'Oh, Clare.' I stepped forward to embrace her, but she brushed me away.

'No!' she shouted, backing off, her hands up in front of her. 'Just leave me alone, can't you? Piss off to Martin and Sophie, and leave us to live our own lives without bloody judging us.'

'Clare, I didn't mean—'

'Please,' she said, pointing towards the front door. 'Just go.'

So I did what she had clearly always expected me to. I walked out the door.

# Chapter 40

I started walking south, not really knowing where I was going. I wanted to feel angry, betrayed, but in truth I could understand Clare's reaction. Why should she trust me? Why would she turn to me when things went wrong? She was right, I hadn't treated her like a friend, I'd treated her like some distant relative, only appearing on her doorstep when all my other options had run out. Clare had always helped me, cared for me, and I had rewarded her loyalty by pretty much ignoring her whenever things were going well.

So I was wounded, but not entirely surprised that Clare hadn't told me about her pregnancy. Since Martin, there had been secrets between us – I had certainly kept things from her. Years ago, we had always shared confidences and excitement. I remember the morning after she had first met Dom, in a bar in Islington watching a World Cup match on the big screen. She'd told me how they'd kissed when England had scored and been glued at the hip for the rest of the night, finding themselves in an underground jazz bar in Camden, winding back through North London until they ended up at his Kentish Town house-share at dawn. God, she'd looked happy, I could still see the sparkle in her eyes as we'd plotted her next move; should she call, wait for him, or engineer another meeting? As it happened, Dom did call and they had been together ever since. Not a happy ever after, perhaps, but there had been a time when they had both been head over heels. We didn't laugh as much these days and certainly didn't dissect and over-analyze our relationships as we once had: but then who did?

But still. It hurt that we'd drifted so far apart, right at the moment Clare finally needed me. Not that I was any kind of expert in this field.

I'd made my mind up years ago that I wasn't going to have kids – or rather, my bipolar made my mind up for me. It wasn't recommended to try for a baby when you were on lithium, and I didn't want to ever risk coming off it. Clare, of course, had shared my decision – or at least she had sat there and held my hand as I'd wept and talked it out. I guess that alone would have made discussing her own pregnancy difficult for her, even if I hadn't become distant. But friendship was a two-way street and I cursed myself that I had never even asked.

I came to a sudden halt in the middle of the street as a thought struck me. Now I was moving in with Martin, the subject of children was something we might have to discuss.

Panic filled my belly. Not because I was worried my reticence to procreate might put him off, but the exact opposite. Suddenly, powerfully, I knew I wanted to have children with this man. I felt giddy, delirious, too many thoughts crowding my head to process. Finding a replacement drug for my lithium . . . finding another flat because the loft would never be suitable for a child . . . choosing a name for him or her . . . which of us would the baby look like?

Our future was exciting. All we had to do now was fix the problem of Donna Joy.

I glanced up and noticed that I'd arrived in Notting Hill, on Portobello Road, near a café Clare had mentioned that sold rose lattes. Picking up a paper from the newsagent, the same Sunday tabloid that Clare had shown me, I went into the café and over a pastel-pink coffee, I read the story again from start to finish, feeling my temper flare once more. It was gutter press at its lowest. How any journalist could write this and still have a clear conscience was beyond me. And I knew exactly who to ask for more details: Jenny Morris, my old friend from school, my friend who had helped find me when I had run away from home in the summer before university.

Jenny had come up – or down – a similar route as myself, both beginning at the same ordinary Northern sixth-form college, then taking opposite forks in the road when we'd felt the inevitable pull of the capital, Jenny into journalism, myself into the law.

I hadn't seen her for years, but the last I remembered she was working on the daily version of the same tabloid that I was holding in my hands.

When I tapped her name into Google, her LinkedIn profile came up. She was still working at the paper, although her current position was listed as deputy features editor – a step up from the last role she'd told me about. Jenny being relatively senior at the tabloid was good and bad. Good in that she would have her finger on the pulse of everything that was happening, bad in that she wouldn't give up that information for free, however fondly she remembered me. I smiled, remembering an exposé she had written for the student news-sheet on exam-fixing. It was explosive, well researched and backed by a solid investigation in the course of which Jenny had bought a stolen exam paper in a dimly lit car park. Unfortunately, the embarrassed college principal had taken his revenge by arguing that Jenny's illicit purchase meant she was breaking exam rules herself and so he'd expelled her. Jenny had simply rung the *Manchester Evening News* and got herself a commission to write a piece on the failure of Britain's corrupt education system to support free speech.

I found her number in my contacts and wondered if it would still work. I hadn't used it for years. We'd met a handful of times when she first moved to London, having transferred to one of the nationals. She was, of course, always full of the latest gossip on everyone and everything, usually some lurid 'real story' behind the one the papers had dared to print, but we'd both found it harder to find the time to meet up and, if truth be told, found it harder to ignore the fact that our professions were incompatible. How could I tell Jenny some amusing anecdote about a divorcing couple when it could – let's be honest, *would* – appear in the following morning's paper? Nothing in that situation had changed – if anything, recent events had only intensified the conflict of interests. But I badly needed to hear the story from another perspective. I hadn't seen Jenny's name on any of the 'Missing Donna' reports, but she would have heard every detail in their daily conferences and, most importantly, would have a good feel for which way the police were leaning. I just needed to avoid any more surprises and Jenny could give me that. What her price would be, I could only guess. I pressed 'call'.

Jenny arrived at the café within the hour. Her voice on the phone had sounded so familiar, it wasn't until I sat down to wait that I realized I had no idea what she'd had to rearrange to come over to Notting Hill on Sunday morning. Cancelling a brunch date with a partner? Watching a son play soccer from the sidelines? I didn't even know where she lived. But my instincts had been correct; as a journalist she could not pass up on a meeting with someone involved in the most high-profile missing persons case in years. And then there she was, striding confidently through the tables, arms wide.

'Hello, stranger,' she grinned, giving me a big hug as I stood up to greet her. She was heavier than I remembered, and her face rounder, but that only made her smile more dazzling and warm. Charisma, that's what had got Jenny where she was. People instantly liked her and wanted to tell her things – then forgave her when she repeated them in print. I knew I needed to keep that in the forefront of my mind.

'I'm good. And glad to have an excuse to get back in touch,' I said; and it was true. I was surprised at how much I'd missed her.

Perhaps it was simply reassuring, seeing someone from your youth, a link to more simple times, or maybe it was because she knew me when we both had everything to prove and nothing to lose.

'I'm sorry I dragged you out like this,' I said as she sat down and signalled to the waitress for coffee.

'I only live in Kilburn,' said Jenny. 'Besides, the editor is obsessed with Donna Joy. Actually, we all are, as you might have noticed,' she laughed, tapping the paper on the table in front of me. 'Nothing like a missing persons case to sell papers, especially when the missing girl is gorgeous and married to the current version of the panto villain.'

I smiled, hiding the fact she was describing the man I wanted to be the father of my children.

'So you're his lawyer,' she said as her coffee was delivered.

'Divorce lawyer, yes.'

'I must be slipping,' said Jenny. 'If I'd known that I would have given you a ring when the police told us they were arresting Martin Joy.'

'Would you?'

She smiled back. We both knew the answer was yes, but

only if it worked for the paper and the story. It wouldn't have been a courtesy call; at best she would have called for a reaction quote, just as the paper was about to go to print, giving their 'victim' little time to get an injunction.

'So I have to ask, do you think Martin Joy would be up for doing an interview?'

I allowed myself another smile and looked at my watch.

'Two minutes. I wondered how long it would take you to ask.'

Jenny cracked up laughing and I couldn't help joining in. She was shameless, but at least you knew where you stood with her, and that wasn't something you could say about most of the people I was involved with at the moment.

'Come on, what do you think?' she urged. 'I've been deputy features editor forever. I'm not on the editor's Oxbridge social scene, so I need to deliver something juicy to bag a promotion.'

I looked at her, knowing that these situations were about give and take, information traded like goods at a medieval market.

'I'm not sure he wants to talk,' I said, as if it had only just occurred to me. 'But I can certainly ask. He had nothing to do with Donna's disappearance and he might be keen to set the record straight after the hatchet job your paper did on him this morning.'

'Sunday edition,' Jenny pointed out. 'Same name and same owner, but we're a whole different team. And I can tell you my editor is not happy about the Sunday edition running the Martin Joy story first.'

'Well, perhaps he'll cheer up when I persuade Martin to talk to you instead.'

Unlike Inspector Doyle, Jenny certainly knew the meaning of quid pro quo – she understood it was her turn to offer something.

'So why did you want to meet?' she asked, her eyes shrewd.

'Simple question, really: where is she?' I asked. 'What happened to Donna Joy? Nothing's going to help my client – and my practice – better than finding Donna Joy and absolving her husband once and for all.'

'I get that,' said Jenny, 'but I'm features, not news. Why are you asking me?'

'Because you're the best,' I said honestly. 'You found me in a Fallowfield bedsit when no one else had a clue where I was – and, as you say, it sounds like your editor needs reminding of how good you are.'

'Flattery will get you everywhere,' she smiled.

'Seriously, Jens, I'm sure you know what the police are saying. You've always had your ear to the ground. Even at college you knew which teachers were having affairs.'

'As I said, the editor is pissed off about the Sunday edition running the story. We've got something better cooking, but it's something the legal team needed to pick over with a fine-tooth comb. The Sunday paper went with a softer story – as you probably saw, it's all insinuation, no facts – but still it's taken the wind out of our sails when it comes to running anything else this week.'

'So what's this better story?' I pressed.

Jenny shook her head slowly.

'Fran, I'm not stupid. You're his lawyer. I say anything, your team will be serving us an injunction by tomorrow morning.'

'Jen, this is important to me. As a friend, tell me.'

'Can you get me an interview with Martin Joy?' This was Jen the hack playing hardball, not my old school friend, but I couldn't blame her for that.

'He'll do whatever I say.'

'Really,' she said, raising a speculative eyebrow. 'In other circumstances, I might be quite envious of you there. Martin Joy is pretty hot.'

I nodded impatiently. 'What's your story?'

Jenny dropped a sugar cube into her coffee and stirred it slowly.

'The police aren't officially saying that Martin Joy killed his wife, but that's what they believe. They've got tons of stuff on this guy. And so have we.'

I felt a thickness in my throat.

'Like what?'

'Our guys on the City desk say he's a ruthless operator, completely devoid of empathy. He's a tyrant in the office too. One secretary who used to work at the place said he'd grabbed her by the throat. All she'd done was cut someone off when she was trying to transfer a call. Another employee was bullied so much by him she had a miscarriage. Or so she says.'

I was feeling sick, but couldn't show it. I waved a dismissive hand, trying not to let her see that I was shaking.

'It's all hearsay, Jenny. Not much better than the groundless rumours the Sunday edition ran. Anyway, it doesn't mean Martin Joy had anything to do with his wife's disappearance.'

'Maybe,' she said, conceding the point. 'But the police have also found Donna's diaries. She was scared, Fran, in the weeks leading up to the divorce. Martin was threatening her, warning her not to pursue a claim in the business. He said he would make life very difficult for her if she did.'

Again I did my best to look sceptical. 'Sounds like the standard toxic back-and-forth couples have when they separate. I've heard that stuff a hundred times.'

I was aware that I was beginning to sound defensive. Jenny was smart, intuitive. I didn't want her to suspect my relationship with Martin was anything more than professional.

'But if Donna died before any financial settlement was put

in place, Martin Joy keeps his entire stake in the business, right? All his money, assets, everything. You're a lawyer, you know that. He's a ruthless man and his business is everything to him. Plus, as well as motive, he had opportunity. Joy said he left his wife's house at midnight. CCTV cameras have finally picked him up walking across London at 2 a.m. But what was he doing from the time he arrived at her house? Even if he didn't kill her and dispose of the body himself, he's a wealthy guy with criminal connections. We've heard rumours that one of his business acquaintances ended up in hospital over an insider-trading deal gone wrong.'

I kept my face neutral. 'But if Donna was so scared, why did she agree to have dinner with him the night she went missing?'

Jenny shrugged.

'Joy's charming, isn't he? Most psychopaths are.'

I should have been unsettled by this deluge of anti-Martin propaganda, but I found myself switching into professional mode, taking in all the information, looking at every angle, creating a picture. And even though I was clearly biased towards Martin's innocence, I still wasn't convinced, not by this flimsy evidence and not by the idea that Martin Joy was a psycho. I'd seen the way that Donna had looked at him that night at the restaurant. Hers was the seducer's smile, not his. I knew Jenny was watching me, waiting for a reaction.

'Sounds like a load of crap,' I said, and Jenny began to laugh.

'Why didn't we stay in touch, Fran? I miss you.'

'I don't know,' I replied. 'I guess we let work get in the way.'

'Two Northern girls who climbed London's greasy pole and ended up meeting for the first time in years to talk about our lives in crime.'

I looked at her cynically.

'You saying we should have stayed in Accrington and got a job at the bank?'

'I'm saying for my next job I might try and be *Country Life*'s afternoon tea correspondent,' smiled Jenny over her coffee glass.

'The simple life,' I nodded distractedly.

My phone started ringing. It was an unknown number so I excused myself from the table to answer it.

I didn't recognize the voice until Inspector Michael Doyle introduced himself.

'Sorry for the intrusion on a Sunday, Miss Day, but can we arrange a suitable time to come round and speak to you?'

'Can't we discuss it over the phone?' I said.

'I think it's better if we meet face to face,' he said, his tone much firmer than on our previous meeting.

'I'm not at home at the moment,' I said, my lips beginning to feel dry. 'Can I ask what this is about?'

'Just come down to the station then,' he said, and I knew right there and then that things were starting to unravel.

# Chapter 41

Inspector Doyle looked as if he didn't want to be in the station on a Sunday lunchtime either.

'So, Pete Carroll, your downstairs neighbour, came to see us this morning,' he said, sipping from a plastic cup of coffee that looked grey and cold.

'He said that on the night Donna Joy was last seen, you arrived home in the early hours, upset, with blood on you, saying that Martin Joy, your boyfriend, had been with his wife and that it had upset you.'

Pete Carroll. My stomach twisted in hatred at the thought of him. I'd known how vile and manipulative he was, but hadn't appreciated he would deliver on his threats so soon. Emotion clogged my throat as I replayed my meeting with him over and over. I'd made it perfectly clear that I was not interested in him romantically but had tried not to agitate him too much. I thought it had been the best way to play it, but I had obviously been wrong.

Doyle looked back at me as if waiting for me to say something, but I chose to keep silent. Within two minutes of me sitting in front of the detective inspector I knew what sort of conversation this was going to be. I knew enough about criminal law to know that anything I said could be seized upon.

'You're also aware that Mr Joy has a property on Dorsea Island in Essex. I believe that you've been.'

Again I didn't respond.

'We interviewed the manager of the Anchor Pub on the island and he says you were in there together, five days after Donna was last seen.'

He threw his empty coffee cup in the bin and looked at me.

'We'd like to take some fingerprints, and a few other samples, if that's all right with you.'

'Fingerprints. What for?' I replied, feeling the earth begin to spin. 'I don't want to give you any fingerprints.'

'Then we're going to have to arrest you,' he said matter-of-factly.

The only person I wanted to speak to was Tom Briscoe. I didn't care about our rivalries any more. He was simply the one person that I trusted.

He came within forty minutes – I had no idea how he'd got down from Highgate so fast and even allowed myself the mischievous thought that he'd come direct from the bedroom of some Belgravia-based girlfriend. Perhaps the person he'd taken to see his brother's play.

'Thought you might need that,' he said, handing me a Starbucks outside the station.

I'd hardly ever seen him out of a suit. Today he was wearing jeans, a polo shirt and a beige Harrington jacket. He reminded me of a college professor – or at least how one would look in a Hollywood movie.

'What's that?' I asked, tasting the sickly liquid.

'Girl's drink.'

He grinned at me and momentarily I felt buoyed.

'The inspector in charge let me out to make a call, but he's treating me like a criminal.'

I felt tight pains begin to gather in my chest and raised my hand to rub my breastbone.

'You're only here to answer some questions,' he said with a friendly pat on the shoulder. 'You're free to come and go as you please.'

'But if I answer the questions truthfully it's not going to look good for me.'

I knew I had to tell him everything. The whole unvarnished truth – or what I could remember of that truth – about my affair with Martin, the night of Donna's disappearance, our trip to Dorsea Island and my subsequent lies to the police. I knew I had to tell him everything.

'Should we go inside and find a meeting room?' he said more efficiently.

I shook my head, paranoid that the police station might be bugged.

'Can we just stay here?' I asked, perching on a wall and gripping my fingers around the cup.

I glanced around, looking for CCTV cameras or eavesdroppers but the street had a Sunday stillness to it. My foot started tapping on the pavement as I opened my mouth to speak.

'Have you seen Martin since his arrest?'

'Yes.'

'Are you still involved with him?'

I nodded, then avoided his gaze, wondering what my colleague must think of me.

'Tom, I followed them to Donna's house. I remember seeing Martin leave, and Donna watching him from the window, but I can't remember anything else. Pete's evidence that I turned up at my flat dazed and confused incriminates me. This is going to destroy me, my career.'

'Fran, don't get ahead of yourself,' he said reassuringly. 'There's still no body. Without a body it's going to be nearly impossible to get a conviction. And right now, the Met need a successful conviction.'

'Of course they do. They want to do their job.'

'Remember the Rachel Miles case last year? A string of men were arrested after her body was found in Leas Wood. In the end it was her boss – someone they'd barely interviewed. They got their man, but there was so much bad publicity and two civil suits for wrongful arrest . . . The Met won't want to make that mistake again.'

'So you don't think I'll be arrested?' My first sliver of hope on a depressing day.

'On some nutjob's testimony that you ripped your tights in a cab? Not likely.'

I nodded, wanting to believe him, but finding it hard.

'We'll sort this, Fran, trust me. I won't let anything happen to a friend or a client of mine.'


'So let me get this right?' said Doyle, resuming our meeting in the confines of the interview room. The office carpet was tacky under my feet. 'You are the barrister instructed to work on Mr Joy's divorce. You began an affair with Mr Joy, and on the night that Donna Joy was last seen, you followed her from her art studio to a restaurant where she met her husband. You then followed them to her house and eventually arrived back at your own address at two o'clock in the morning, where you were let in by Pete Carroll, who reports that you were bruised and bleeding.'

'I was not bruised and bleeding,' I said, determined to hold my ground. 'I must have fallen over and ripped my tights. There was a bit of a cut, but that was about it.'

Doyle didn't look convinced.

'Were you jealous that Mr and Mrs Joy had resumed their relationship?'

'I wouldn't say they'd resumed their relationship. I found it strange, yes, that Martin went to her house, but it hardly suggested that their divorce was off.'

'A barmaid at the Walton Arms says she remembers someone sitting by the window all night. On their own. We think that person was you.'

'I was there for a while, yes. I was waiting to see what time Martin left.'

'But you don't remember him leaving.'

All his questions sounded like blunt statements of my guilt.

'Yes, I do. It was late. I don't remember the exact time, but it was after the pub had closed. I remember looking over at the house, watching Martin leave, and then seeing Donna at the window.'

'Neither of them saw you.'

'No.'

'Martin Joy said he left the Chelsea house at around midnight. Pete Carroll says you got home at about two o'clock in the morning. That's two clear hours. What were you doing?'

'I was a bit drunk, so I don't really remember. Obviously it takes a while to get from Chelsea to Islington.'

'Did you go and see Donna Joy?'

'No.'

Doyle gave a small, disapproving sigh.

'Miss Day, it's difficult to know what to believe. We have a statement taken from you by my colleague Rob Collins six days ago in which you claimed you went to Mrs Joy's Studio, but when she wasn't there, you went home.'

'I was embarrassed. I was protecting myself.'

'What from?' he asked.

'From looking guilty of something.'

'So you didn't want to look guilty.'

I couldn't believe I'd been caught out so easily.

Tom Briscoe rolled up his sleeves and looked at Doyle.

'Francine is here to answer any questions you've got and she's been honest and cooperative. We can leave at any moment, but we want to help as much as we can.'

'Then we'd like to have a look around your apartment,' said Doyle, fixing me with a look.

'Why?' I said, unable to disguise the panic I felt.

'I'm afraid we must call an end to this interview,' said Tom, standing up. 'You're on very precarious ground here, Inspector Doyle. There's nothing to suggest Miss Day has committed any offence. Nor have you produced any evidence that Donna Joy's disappearance is anything more than an unhappy woman who wants to escape the gilded cage and the shame of divorce and has gone on a temporary walkabout.'

He paused as if he was standing at the Old Bailey about to make his closing remarks. 'It's not for me to tell you how to do your job, Inspector, but we all know that you've already had one person in custody and had to release them without charge. You are going to appear trigger-happy if you do it again. Besides, the real story here is that Pete Carroll is exploiting the fact that he opened the door to Miss Day that night, and has subsequently been blackmailing her, demanding sex and threatening to use the information he had on her if she refused to comply. I need to discuss with my client whether we are going to report that sexual assault. I think, under the circumstances, she needs to be treated with tact and respect, not this barrage of damaging innuendo.'

My hand clenched. I wanted to shout out *Go on, search my apartment. I have nothing to hide.* But Doyle glanced from Tom to me and simply nodded.

'We'll be in touch tomorrow,' he said, closing his notebook and switching off his tape recorder. 'Stay local, Miss Day,' he said. 'Stay local.'

It was after six o'clock by the time we stepped back out on to Buckingham Palace Road. I took big gulps of air as soon as I was outside. I was someone who needed control in their life but I felt helpless. Right now, Tom Briscoe felt like my only safety net, so I reached out and grabbed his hand, squeezing it as tightly as I could.

'It's OK,' he said, not flinching at my touch.

I let go quickly and turned to face him.

'I should have told them to go ahead and search my flat,' I said, letting go of his hand and shaking my head with frustration.

'That wouldn't have improved your position,' he replied carefully.

'Then what will?'

'We're working on it,' he said, bumping his shoulder against mine as we walked.

In other words, neither of us knew the answer to that question.

'Fancy getting something to eat?' he asked.

'Lost my appetite.'

'Police stations do that to you.'

'Do you miss it?' I asked. 'Criminal work.'

'You're not a criminal,' he replied.

'You were good back there.'

He gave a soft smile and I thought he was going to make a joke of it, but he didn't. 'I do miss it. It's what I always wanted to do. Every Saturday at school I used to go to the bookshop in Windsor and buy a detective novel. I read everything from Sherlock Holmes to Ian Rankin. It was my weekly puzzle ration. My parents were against me joining the police. So I became a lawyer.'

'Why defence work?' I asked, imagining a young Tom Briscoe in his Eton tails, his nose in an old paperback in some shady spot by the Thames.

'Because in the books, the villains were always the most interesting.' He smiled, then added: 'And because sometimes, the accused isn't the villain.'

'You shouldn't have let the Nathan Adams case put you off something you loved doing.'

'No,' he said quietly.

'I mean it, Tom.'

He looked straight out in front of him, into the gloaming.

'I did love it. Even though I was always asked, how can you do it? How can you work for the defence? I always gave the same answer. To my family, curious friends or people I met at parties. I did it because I believed in our justice system. Because it's not up to me to make up my mind that someone is guilty or not.'

He hesitated before he continued.

'But I'll never forget Suzie Willis coming up to me outside court after Adams was found not guilty. After I'd got him off. Her eyes were red from crying. She was shaking. Not from anger or frustration or injustice. But out of fear. She was with her lawyer who turned to me and said, 'We'll just have to wait until next time.' And she was right. Adams was found guilty eventually, but the next time he was violent against his girlfriend, he murdered her. And I felt that was on me.'

His voice cracked with emotion and it was my turn to put a reassuring hand on his arm, but he put his hand in his pocket to discreetly shake me off.

'Do you want a lift somewhere?' he said brusquely. I realized we'd stopped by his car.

I didn't reply at first, not knowing where home was any more, where I felt safe and wanted.

'I've got a spare room, if you don't want to go back to your flat. You'll have to share it with my squash kit, but I've just bought a new Heston Blumenthal coffee machine and you can road-test my macchiatos.'

I had to admit, the thought was not an unappealing one.

I'd long believed that the course of our lives was decided by choices, not fate, and at that moment, I wondered if I should have made better ones. Perhaps if I had chosen Tom Briscoe, I wouldn't be standing outside a police station on a Sunday afternoon, being threatened with arrest in connection with the disappearance of my lover's wife.

No. A life with Tom Briscoe, or someone like Tom Briscoe, might have had a reassuring rhythm; no intense excitement but a shared appreciation of each other's skills and talents and a contented day-to-day life.

Not that Tom had ever shown any romantic interest me, a voice in my head reminded me.

'Tempting, especially the posh coffee, but it's fine,' I said, shaking myself out of my thoughts. 'I've put you out far too much already.'

'It's not a problem.'

'I should go home. I've seen the police. Pete Carroll can't blackmail me any more.'

Tom shook his head. 'You should have told me about Carroll. I could have done something.'

I raised a brow. 'Like what? Jumped him at the bus stop? We both know there's nothing we can do. I can't injunct him or get a restraining order. I'm not his girlfriend and he's not been convicted or even arrested for anything.'

'There are things we can do, Fran. You know that.'

I shook my head to strengthen my resolve.

'I should go home. Pete Carroll isn't the most important thing I need to deal with right now.'

I got in the passenger seat and Tom drove across London, distracting me with gossip from chambers. The potential merger with Sussex Court was out in the open now. Tom thought it was a sound business move. If he had any thoughts about my discredited reputation threatening the merger, he didn't say anything.

When my stomach rumbled above the soft music of the stereo system, he stopped at a kebab shop near my apartment and went inside, returning with a couple of chicken burgers and cans of Coke.

He stopped the car in a side street and I opened the polystyrene box that was on my lap, licking my fingers to avoid grease and breadcrumbs getting on the upholstery.

'We're a class act, aren't we,' I said, grinning as I felt ketchup slide down my chin.

'I like to think so,' said Tom, opening his can with a hiss.

'This is good,' I sighed, realizing how hungry I was. 'When you're a QC, promise me you won't be above going to the local kebab shop.'

'When we make silk, I'll take you to Kebab Kid in Parson's Green to celebrate. Best chicken shawarmas in London.'

I didn't reply. We let the silence hang in the air, not wanting to say out loud what we were both thinking: that I'd be lucky to avoid a jail sentence, let alone make silk.

'Thank you for being a good friend.'

'To think you never used to like me,' he chided.

'I've never not liked you.'

'Come on, I know you thought I was a pompous tosser.'

'Not true.'

'So true,' he smiled. 'It's why I avoided you for almost our entire first year in chambers.'

'You avoided me because you thought I was weird.'

'Not weird. Cool. Too cool, actually. I remember turning up that first day at Burgess Court. I had my new suit, new haircut, new robe. I thought I was the dog's bollocks. And then I met you. And I realized I was just this public school geek with no street smarts whatsoever. If I ever avoided you it was because you were so hip and smart I was a little bit intimidated by you.'

'People never stop surprising you.' I smiled under my breath.

'It's why I stopped being judgemental a long time ago.'

He drove me to the flat and I instructed him to park the car on a nearby street, not wanting anyone to see me get out.

'Are you sure you're all right?' said Tom.

I felt another flutter of panic, wondering if Pete Carroll could see me.

'You don't mind seeing me into the house, do you?'

Tom nodded as if he understood.

It felt strange being back. Already it had a faint, stale unlived-in smell. As I turned on the light I saw the bin with my duvet in it. I turned back to the door and double-locked it.

'Come on, why don't you pack up some things and come stay at my house?' said Tom, noticing how on edge I was.

I knew how easy it would be to grab some more lithium pills, and a suitcase of clothes, and go to Tom's, but I was tired, so tired. I just wanted to stop running.

'I hate the idea of Pete Carroll being downstairs. Hate it,' I whispered. 'But I've been moving around since Tuesday, Tom. I can't keep on like this. Besides, Pete doesn't have anything on me anymore.'

'I think you need to make an official report to the police,' he said finally.

I didn't reply.

'It's not too late, Fran. Although there are things you should do. Don't wash your sheets. Keep any evidence you think you might have.'

I looked at the bin liner again and felt sick. I wanted Pete Carroll to be punished, but I wasn't sure I was strong enough to go through the trauma of reporting sexual assault.

'Can I just not think about anything for a little while?' I said, gripping my hands and pressing my fingers together.

'I'll make you some coffee,' he said.

As Tom headed into my tiny galley kitchen and pulled two Cornish striped mugs out of the cupboard, I felt enormously sad that we hadn't been to see the Hampstead play together. There were some people who were decent. Some people you could trust.

# Chapter 42

In my dream I am drowning. The water is coming up to my mouth and then it slips down my throat. Slowly at first, until the water gets too deep and even though I am tipping my head back I can't quite catch enough air. Once the liquid starts filling my lungs, my vision begins to cloud. All I can see are bubbles, just out of reach, fluttering to some halo of light above me. I stretch my arms out and try to swim, but I am so weak I can barely move. And as I start to sink, my eyes close and my arms rise and my last thought is that it is all over.

The bleep of an incoming text woke me up.

I blinked hard, disorientated at first, but when I realized it was only a nightmare, that the bleep hadn't come from a set of electronic pearly gates preparing to open, I stretched out to pick up my phone.

I hesitated before I clicked on the envelope icon, wondering who it might be from, but it was only Jenny Morris, apparently just out of morning conference, where she had mentioned the chance of a Martin Joy interview to her editor, who was apparently 'very keen'.

A knock at my bedroom door made me jump a second time. It took me a few seconds to remember that Tom Briscoe had slept on my sofa, another moment for it to sink in that I was too embarrassed for him to see inside my room, and how I had slept, in an old sleeping bag on top of a towel.

'Just wait, I'm coming,' I said as I wiggled out from under the folds of camouflage nylon.

Tom had his shoes and jacket on by the time I got downstairs.

'I should go,' he said. 'Can't exactly turn up for chambers like this.'

'I don't know,' I said with a half-smile. 'People have been talking about getting rid of formal court dress for years.'

'Not sure I want to be the first one to lower the tone,' said Tom.

'Thanks for staying . . .' It seemed inadequate, but I couldn't find the words.

'Are you taking some time off work?'

I shrugged. 'Vivienne suggested that I go away for a few weeks. On Friday, that sounded tempting. But I guess things are different now. I'm not sure Inspector Doyle would think Thailand qualifies as local.'

'You should keep your phone on,' said Tom, back in lawyer mode. 'Doyle might want to see you again this week. I expect he'll contact you through me, now. Just be ready.'

'You are going to make a great QC,' I said as I unlocked the door. I genuinely meant it. On impulse I kissed him on the cheek and for a long minute, his cool, confident face looked self-conscious.

I'd been wary about coming home, but there was comfort in being back on familiar territory. I rifled through my cupboards, looking for breakfast, and was forced to settle for some Christmas leftovers – a half-eaten box of Matchmakers and a tub of Heroes I'd been given by my cleaner. It was hardly avocado on toast, but a mindless chocolate binge was just what I needed.

I went back upstairs and undressed while I let the shower run hot. Too restless to stay under the jets longer than a couple of minutes, I jumped out, towelled myself down and went to get dressed: jeans, T-shirt, jumper and boots that I laced up tightly. I lit all the candles, opened the windows, and put a fresh sheet and pillow cases on the bed.

After I'd tidied and cleaned and scrubbed, I stopped to make myself a drink, and sat down at the dining table. I was desperate for another session with Gil, but he'd told me at the counselling centre that he was going on holiday in a couple of days and I figured he was probably at the airport, desperate to forget about clients like me. Meanwhile it was another lively Monday morning for the likes of Inspector Doyle and his team. I had no doubt that my name would be brought up in their start-of-the-week meetings, where officers, bright-eyed and eager, fuelled by coffee and talk of 'new leads' would present their evidence against me and Martin Joy.

My eyes fluttered to my neat shelves stuffed with box files and books. In the gaps were mementoes like the small silver cup I had won at university for mooting, and a beautiful David Linley box given to me by a grateful client. Reminders that, once upon a time, I had been considered good.

Sliding my mug to one side, I stretched across to a pile of yellow legal notepads and pulled one on to the dining table.

Fight back, I muttered to myself. It was something my grandfather had said to me the summer I'd left sixth form. After the shame of the school prom and running away, he'd taken me for a long walk over the hills. We could almost see Pendle Hill in the distance and he told me about his time in the war, stories of Spitfires and secret missions to Normandy towns where he'd been trapped behind enemy lines, but had never given up and finally he made it home where he'd forgotten what he'd done and simply started again.

Fight back, he'd said, and even though I was never sure if his stories were true – I'd never seen any medals or heard anything about his heroics mentioned in our family, but it was the conversation that made me get my act together.

The conversation that stopped me feeling sorry for myself and playing the victim.

I lost my nose-ring and found a part-time job. Swapped my history degree for the department of law when a string of A grades in my A-levels told me I was good enough to do whatever I wanted to do.

Fight back.

There was a black fineliner on the table next to my reading glasses, which I'd had for months but couldn't yet admit I needed. I looked at the blank page, and then started writing. I wrote a list of motives for both Martin and Alex, and suggestions for what might have happened to Donna if she hadn't been killed or abducted. I wrote down what I could remember from my conversations with Inspector Doyle, Phil Robertson and Jenny Morris: the blood in Donna's bed, Martin's ruthless reputation, Donna's trip to Paris and her affair with Alex Cole. And I wrote down what I had seen with my own eyes: that Martin had left the Chelsea house more or less when he said he did and Donna had watched him go.

I looked down at the page, but it was just a jumble of names and words, a series of shapes, black on yellow, like hazard tape. I moved my pen across the paper, scribbling arrows and lines as if I were trying to connect the dots, but I didn't have enough information.

For a moment, I was tempted to have another conversation with Sophie Cole. With the exception of Martin, she seemed to know Donna better than anyone. It was possible she knew something of significance, even if its relevance hadn't so far occurred to her. But after the confrontation we'd had over Alex and Donna's possible affair, calling Sophie wasn't an appealing option.

Looking for inspiration, I grabbed my rucksack that was hooked on the back of the chair, pulled out the Sunday tabloid I'd bought the day before, and re-read the story about Donna:

> Beautician Jemma Banks, 42, told police that her sister's disappearance was completely out of character. 'Donna was looking forward to my birthday party in our home town. It wasn't like her to miss it.'

I frowned as I re-read the paragraph. Martin had maintained that Donna and her sister weren't close, but she certainly seemed central to helping the police in their enquiries. And if Donna was going to Jemma's birthday party, that suggested the two sisters were closer than he thought.

It was surprisingly easy to track Jemma Banks down. The electoral roll, company house records, Facebook – there were a number places where you could find out an alarming amount of details with just a few seconds and a few pounds.

Stuffing a mini Bounty into my mouth, I grabbed my coat and rucksack, pulling out the old clothes that I been storing in there since Thursday and throwing my pants and T-shirts into the laundry bin when my phone chirped.

It had been on my mind all morning that I ought to phone Clare. I felt bad, the way we'd left things yesterday, and although she'd made it clear that I wasn't welcome to stay another night, I still hadn't got back in touch to say so.

I'm sorry.

I read the text again, but there was no name of sender and I didn't recognize the number.

Who is this? I typed back, eager to get out of the flat.

Pete

I forced myself to breathe. I had no idea how he'd got my number and I suddenly felt as if he was watching me.

I looked down at the phone without moving and then shook my head, I needed to fight back, to get back control. Not willing to take it for another second, I went downstairs and knocked hard on his door.

I felt possessed, consumed with rage. Last night every noise from downstairs had made me jump, but now all I wanted was to punch his weaselly face.

He opened the door and must have detected my fury.

'How did you get hold of my number, Pete?' I said, not waiting for him to speak.

'The girl on reception at your work, gave it to me.'

'Well she had no right to,' I hissed pointing my finger in his face.

'Calm down, Fran. I only wanted to apologize.'

'Oh, so you didn't mean to go to the police and accuse me of murder?'

'I'm helping their investigation. Everybody wants Donna Joy found. Don't you?'

He paused and studied me intently. And I matched his stare. There was a red spot on the side of his nose and a white pustule above his eyebrow.

'Now you're here, you can tell me: who was that man this morning, the one leaving your apartment at eight o'clock?'

'That's none of your business, Pete.'

He shrugged. 'We've got to keep our eyes open for strangers wandering around the building. It's only sensible. The other day, my friend found a vagrant urinating in his communal hall.'

He leant against the doorframe, more casual now, more cock-sure than when he had first answered the door.

'I believe it's the same man I saw on Friday,' he said. 'Your colleague. Have we moved on to an office romance now?'

'Yes, he's a lawyer. Because, yes, I'm taking legal advice. We were discussing my situation. He stayed over because, frankly, my neighbour has been behaving unpredictably.'

'That wouldn't be me, would it, Franny?'

'Fuck off, Pete.'

It wasn't my best line, but I was sick of him.

'Don't say that, Fran. I care about you.'

I turned away, bracing myself for him to call out my name, but I was relieved when I heard the door shut. I took the steps two at a time and ran on to the street, not stopping until I reached the car-hire place near my favourite deli in Highbury Fields.

Martin had been right about needing a car. Jemma Banks lived in Colchester, which wasn't too difficult to get to from Islington – it was only a short hop to Liverpool Street station and then an overground train to Essex, but I felt vulnerable enough as it was and didn't want to have to rely on anyone for anything.

ZipCars rented vehicles by the hour, but I put down my credit card and asked for a week. I felt a surge of power and urgency as the young assistant pushed a set of keys to a Fiat Panda in front of me and I clutched them in my hand.

The only time I ever drove was on my annual vacation to Italy, so it felt strange sitting on the right-hand side of the car. I took a few moments to familiarize myself with the vehicle, pushing the gear stick from side to side, and revving the clutch pedal slowly with the sole of my boot. The engine gunned to life. I typed Colchester into Google Maps on my phone and as the synthetic voice told me to turn left, I did as I was told and tried to work out my next move.

I'd worked out from my web search that Jemma Banks owned a beauty salon called Tans and Talons on the outskirts of town, on a strip of shops that included a pet store, an off licence and a Chinese takeaway.

When Google Maps told me that I had arrived at my destination, I slowed the car almost to a stop, but when I noticed that the salon looked busy I went back into the town centre, parked the car and went for lunch at Prezzo on the high street.

I checked my messages and emails as I ate. There wasn't much – just some work-related correspondence and a text from Tom Briscoe checking that I was OK. When there was nothing from Clare, I called her as I waited for the bill but was relieved when it went to voicemail.

It was almost four o'clock by the time I got back to Jemma's shop. As I'd hoped, Tans and Talons was now empty. Through the plate-glass window I could see a solitary figure sweeping up and rearranging magazines in a wall rack. A gust of wind picked up an empty Coke can on the pavement and it rattled along the flagstones as I opened the door of the salon.

'Sorry, darling, I'm about to close,' said the woman. Propping up her broom up in the corner, she walked across to the reception desk. 'We can make an appointment for another day, if you like,' she said, her acrylic nail skimming across the book on the counter. 'Got some availability for tomorrow in fact.'

'I wasn't after anything like that,' I said watching her. When she'd appeared on TV for the appeal I had noted the similarities between the two sisters. Jemma's face had been pale and washed out on that occasion which emphasized the differences between the women but in the flesh they were less obvious. Jemma's eyes were a more ordinary shade of green, and her floral blouse was the sort you'd find in a supermarket, not in an expensive designer store. Jemma lacked gloss and the subtle boost that came with expensive grooming; but otherwise they could have been twins.

'Another journalist?' said Jemma closing the book, her tone not hard but one of weary recognition.

'No. Martin Joy's lawyer,' I said, trying to inject a note of sympathy into my voice.

Jemma looked at me with suspicion. 'I've spoken to someone from your office already.'

'His divorce laywer. We haven't met.'

'So how can I help?' she said, without much enthusiasm.

'I just need a few minutes of your time.'

Jemma glanced at her watch and looked doubtful.

'I've got to get home. That's why I'm closing early. My daughter's been on a school trip for the past week and she's due back anytime. I wanted to be home before she is.'

'I can come with you. We can talk on the way.'

Jemma raised her brow.

'I should have known Martin would have got himself a terrier. Crufts variety.'

I wasn't sure if there was a compliment in there somewhere. Either way I wasn't going to dispute what she had said. I wanted her onside.

I stayed rooted to the spot until she went to a back room and returned with her coat and bag.

She turned off the lights and walked out on to the street, waiting for me to follow her, then locked the glass door behind us.

'It feels wrong to be working at the moment,' she said as she locked the front door and put the keys in her handbag. 'But working helps. Takes your mind off things. Don't you find that?'

Without waiting for a response to her first question, she asked, 'You come from London then?'

'Yes. My car's just here if you want a lift.'

Jemma shook her head as she zipped up her parka. 'We're only round the corner. Easier to walk.'

I quickened my pace to follow her to a Thirties estate tucked away behind the parade.

Jemma nodded towards a red-brick terrace not unlike the one I had grown up in.

'We used to live there with Mum and Dad. Donna lives in another world now, but I only moved a hundred yards down the road. People are like that, don't you think? Get as far away as they can from where they grew up, or stay tight to where they grew up. It's split right down the middle – stick or twist. Which one are you? Your accent's not Southern.'

'I grew up in Lancashire. I moved down to London for work.'

'No lawyers in Manchester?' she chided.

She had me down as a Donna. A type-A Icarus who thought she was too good for her hometown.

'There was a lot of coverage in the newspapers this weekend. You were quoted a lot.'

'Misquoted, more like,' said Jemma, stuffing her hands in her pockets.

I looked at her in surprise. 'You mean they made up quotes?'

'I think the expression is "sexed it up",' she said. 'I had a lot to say to that journalist, but I didn't think it was the time or the place. I've never thought trial by media was particularly helpful, and I was worried it might muck up our case. That can happen, can't it?'

She looked at me for an answer this time, and I could tell that she actually wanted my advice. Since I wanted something from her, I thought it wise to play ball.

'You're right, it's not helpful for any hatchet jobs or witch hunts to appear in the press. Besides, Martin has only been arrested, not charged. And he was released after twenty-four hours. Insinuations in the media can backfire. A feeding frenzy could end up with the papers being prosecuted for contempt of court.'

'This is us,' she said, pointing to a small semi-detached. There was an old Corsa in the drive and a rusted barbecue left hopefully for the refuse collection.

She opened the front door and I went inside, taking a minute to look around.

'How many children have you got?' I asked, waiting to be invited through.

'Two. Ella's fifteen, Josh started uni in Bournemouth last September.'

The room was dim. She switched on a lamp and I went into the living room and sat on the sofa.

'Tea?'

I nodded and she disappeared into the kitchen. I took a moment to look around the room. It seemed a happy place. An old piano festooned with photos of the kids: on a trampoline, at school sports day. Framed pictures of her children on the wall – all freckles and gap-toothed smiles.

I'd not been inside Donna Joy's multimillion-pound townhouse, but I knew it would be a world away from this cosy, lived-in space.

'Why do you want to speak to me?' she asked once she'd poured the tea and sat down on a chair under the window.

I had my story prepared. The same one I had told Jenny.

'Martin is my client. By extension, he's a client of the place where I work. They're worried about possible damage to the firm's reputation.'

Jemma looked teary.

'I've always wondered when Donna's social aspirations would get her into trouble. She always had big dreams. This life wasn't big enough for her,' she said, looking around. 'She wanted more, and to get more she started hanging around with people who had more. She moved to Chelmsford when she was seventeen, inching her way towards London even then. She got in with the rich Essex lot. Her first proper boyfriend, Charlie, he was a gangster's son. I tried to tell her why rich people were rich. How you have to be hard, ambitious, ruthless to become wealthy in the first place. But she didn't listen. She didn't even seem surprised when Charlie ended up in jail for fraud.'

She paused to sip her tea.

'Donna always joked that she was Martin's project.'

'You don't like Martin?' I ventured.

Jemma shrugged. 'I did at first. I thought he was different. You know he's not from money? Lost his parents when he was young, was brought up by his grandparents. Worked his way through college, made his millions in the city . . . He seemed generous to his friends, did a lot for charity. It was hard not to respect him.'

'What happened?'

'I didn't see Donna much,' she said, shaking her head. 'Not for the longest time. I'm not daft. I know she doesn't like being reminded of where she came from, even if it means not seeing her big sister. But over the past year, I started to see her a bit more. I think she needed someone to talk to, someone not in her world. It was just a couple of lunches at first, but more so lately. Then a few weeks ago, we were supposed to meet for afternoon tea, but she cancelled. I phoned her up

– thought a chat was better than nothing, and she asked me to come round to her place in Chelsea. We were supposed to be meeting in London anyway, so that was fine with me. Besides, I was worried about her. I thought the stress of the divorce was getting her down. When I got to her house, she had a bruise around her eye.'

She let out a long breath and continued.

'I knew he'd hit her, even before she told me. Apparently they'd met to discuss the court case. They'd argued and he'd lashed out and thrown his phone at her. She said it had happened before. After she'd been on a shopping trip to New York.

'She told me she'd had to get away because Martin was being so vile; he was taking a lot of coke, drinking a lot, business was stressful and he took it all out on her. He was furious when she got back and hit her. She said she'd been scared for her life and that's why she filed for divorce.'

I took a few seconds to process it. I knew Martin liked a drink, but I'd never seen him take drugs. I knew how much cocaine fuelled the City. But drugs, violence . . . ? I tried to work out when this phone-throwing episode had happened. He'd admitted that they'd met up to 'talk' in the days following our meal at Ottolenghi's. We'd barely discussed what had been said – I'd found it too painful to go there – but he had given no indication that their meeting had gone badly.

As for the anecdote about the New York shopping trip – that was very different to the one he'd told me.

'None of this came up in the divorce proceedings, Jemma. Domestic abuse was never mentioned. Donna never applied for a restraining order, there was nothing to suggest she was scared of Martin.'

Jemma was shaking her head.

'Donna liked creating this illusion of the perfect life. She was embarrassed about the bruise. She'd never have let me see it unless she wanted to talk through what he had done and get my advice on what she should do about it.'

'And what did you say?'

She paused and looked at me.

'I told her she should report it to the police, but I'm not surprised she didn't. Donna would want to distance herself from domestic violence. Pretend it never happened, dress it up as something else, because things like that get out in those sort of social circles. Image, reputation was everything to my sister.'

I let her words sink in. I'd always wondered what Martin and Donna really had in common, and now I knew. It was their outward appearance to the world that mattered, absolutely, to both of them.

'Why did you report Donna missing?' I asked quietly. 'What made you think something was wrong?'

Jemma gave a sad shrug.

'A few days after I went to her house in Chelsea she came back to Colchester for the afternoon. I closed the salon and we came back here. We dug out old photographs, talked about old times. It was like old times. She liked it so much, she said she wanted to see everyone again. I decided to throw a birthday party and invite all the old crowd. She was looking forward to it so much. But when she didn't turn up, when she didn't call me on my birthday, when I couldn't get in touch with her, I knew something was off.'

'Even though she goes away so often?'

'If you're asking me if my sister is unreliable, I think we both know the answer to that one. But she wanted to come to my party. She promised.'

I bought some time before I spoke again, sipping my tea even though it had lost its heat.

'Did she tell you she was having an affair with Martin's business partner?'

'An affair?' she repeated, frowning.

'Did she mention him?'

'No. Never. I don't believe that she was having an affair.' She looked at me with those cat-like eyes, so like her sister's.

'How do you know?'

'I just got the impression she was a bit sick of men.'

'You were hardly close, Jemma, and it's a very personal thing to discuss.'

'We were close enough,' she said defensively. 'Our lives were very different but we are still sisters. We shared a bedroom for six years when we were growing up, laughed, cried, worried about boys. We used to lie in our twin beds at night, not able to quite get to sleep, talking for hours. I just think I'd have known if she was involved with someone else, happy about being with someone else.'

'But something did happen with Martin's business partner. He admitted it.'

She looked at me, her expression harder this time.

'We don't know what's happened to Donna, but don't go putting the blame on my sister,' she said coldly.

'I'm not blaming her—'

'You're dealing with a charming, brilliant and manipulative man, Miss Day. A man who will stop at nothing to keep his money.'

She was interrupted by a knock at the door. Jemma pulled back the curtain behind her and peered outside.

'My daughter's home. I think I've said enough,' she said, standing up. She waited for me to stand up, to indicate that my audience with her was now over.

And as I stepped back out on to the unfamiliar provincial street, I wondered if it was a good idea even going there.

# Chapter 43

'Is that Fran? It's Jenny.'

'I'm just driving,' I said, stretching the truth a little. I'd put the key in the ignition, but I was still parked outside Jemma's shop checking Instagram, scrolling through Donna's feed, seeing if I could find evidence of a bruise.

'Can you pull over a minute? We need to talk.'

I sat back in my seat, knowing I couldn't avoid her forever.

'I'm sorry I've not got back to you about the interview yet. I haven't even spoken to Martin. As you can imagine, things are a bit difficult for him at the moment. I'm only his divorce lawyer, so I'm not high on his list of priorities.'

'Whatever happened to "he'll do whatever I say"?' replied Jenny, and I deserved the remark.

'I'll definitely push for it, Jen. I will, although I have to warn you, this isn't America. You know, fugitives doing Barbara Walters.'

'Fran, the news team want to run a story on you,' she said.

For a moment I was almost flattered.

'Why?'

'They think you're involved with Martin Joy. Romantically.'

'That's ridiculous.'

I hope she didn't know me so well she'd notice the quaver in my voice.

'You've been spotted together. By a pub landlord in Essex, by a neighbour of Martin's . . .'

'I'm his lawyer,' I said, feigning indignation. 'We've had to see each other. On many occasions.'

'It's just a heads-up, Fran.'

'That's nonsense. Absolute nonsense,' I said, feeling myself go red in the face.

'You are involved with him, aren't you?' she said more quietly. 'That's why you care so much.'

I realized she didn't have to help me like this.

'It's complicated,' I said finally.

'It always is.'

The sky was turning dark. There were flat black clouds ahead, coming in from the North Sea.

'Can you hold them off?' I said, my turn to ask for the favour.

Jenny hesitated.

'I'm the deputy features editor, Fran. I commission interviews with the cast of *TOWIE*, I don't have any sway over the news team. I'm only telling you what I've heard. But if you give me something with Martin, some sort of exclusive, then maybe the editor will be prepared to do you a trade.'

'I'll call you tonight,' I said, ending the call, then gunning the engine, venting my frustration on the accelerator.

The rain started within minutes, so hard that it covered the windscreen in sheets of water.

I sat forward, and peered through the glass like an old lady reading a book. I could hardly see anything and had no idea where I was. I regretted not taking the satnav option at the rental-car place. With my phone battery on 25 per cent, I didn't want to drain it any more just to find my way out of Essex.

My trip to Colchester hadn't really got me anywhere. I'd heard the domestic violence rumours from Doyle, and although they sounded more authentic coming from Jemma's mouth, I tried not to take them as gospel. I just couldn't. And now, with the newspaper on my back on top of everything else, I felt as if time was slipping through my fingers and I had no way to stop it.

I forced myself to think. The police had nothing concrete on Martin, nothing on me, so long as there wasn't a body. On the mind-map that I had drawn that morning, that was the glaring hole, the missing piece, where was Donna? I had suspects and motives, but I had absolutely no idea what happened in those hours after Martin Joy had left Donna's house.

Had he doubled back after I had seen him leave? Did someone else call on her? Did I, came the niggling voice? And where did you hide a body in Chelsea without anybody noticing?

I wiped the steam away from the window and looked up at a signpost ahead.

I was obviously going the wrong way for London, and was prepared to signal to turn around when I saw the word *Dorsea*.

I had no idea that Colchester and Dorsea were so close, but when I stared hard at the horizon, I could make out a line of charcoal sea ahead.

I knew immediately where someone might take a body. To a lonely house, by the sea, a mile from the nearest village, a house with the soundtrack of the sea, where the waves crashed and scraped on the shore and no one could hear you scream.

The causeway was clear when I got to the island a little over ten minutes later. I had no idea when the tide was due to come in, whether I would find myself cut off. I passed Dorsea's strip of shops, the tiny fire station and the pub where Martin and I had sheltered from the storm. I felt a stab of annoyance at the bar manager who had reported us to the police, and kept on driving.

Dorsea House loomed on a thin ridge of bluff after just a few minutes. It looked magnificent, framed by a darkening violet sky. There was a line of yellow police tape across the gates at the entrance to the drive. The police had been here. Of course they had. If you had a missing person and a husband who was the prime suspect in her disappearance, of course you would search his remote, empty house by the sea, where it would be so easy to hide someone, so easy to kill someone. Why hadn't I thought of it before?

There was no one here now and I couldn't help but think that was a bit shoddy. If I was in charge of the investigation, I would have combed the place from top to bottom. Instead they had the forensic team and the cadaver dogs at Donna's Chelsea home.

I snaked around the building to the conservatory, remembering the door that was sticky but unlocked and as I pushed against the splintered frame, it opened with a rattle.

The house had definitely been searched. There were rings of dust where vases and plant pots had been moved, books had been pulled off shelves.

I moved around the house, eyes scanning every corner, not really knowing what I was looking for, but trying to think like Martin if he had brought Donna here.

Would she have been alive or dead?

Was I looking for signs of a body being dragged across the parquet, or blood splattered on the wall? If Martin had brought her back here, how and when had it happened? I didn't know the answers to any of those questions.

I went upstairs, hearing the stairs groan as I ascended. There was a gentle breeze coming into the house from a crack around a skylight window overhead. A voice in my head, the sensible side of me, told me to go back to London. It was gone six o'clock, dusk had fallen and it was almost dark. What would it achieve, me being here, other than landing me in further trouble with the police, who had obviously been here, searched the place and found nothing of interest.

The stairs led to a wide-open landing with rooms going off in every direction. I looked in one, and then the other. Most were empty except for threadbare carpet, but two or three were partially furnished with stuff from its days as a nursing home, the old, half-broken things the previous owners hadn't been able to sell off and hadn't wanted to take with them. Humming with nervous energy, I poked around an armoire, opened a chest of drawers, then stopped, almost laughing at the ridiculousness of my actions – as if I was going to find Donna Joy's dead body behind a couple of cushions.

I pushed the conservatory door open and walked towards the shore, inhaling deep breaths of salty sea air to calm me. Part of me wanted to keep walking into the sea until the water came over the top of my head and I too disappeared.

I stopped at the oyster shed and thought of happier times. Back when I thought that Donna was still at a spa or on a shopping break, and that her going missing was just a cry for attention. I'd been annoyed with Martin at the start of that day. Angry that he'd met his ex-wife for dinner that week and lied to me about it. I wondered how many other lies he'd told me.

I bent down and picked up the brick where I knew the key was hidden. I opened the shed and went inside.

My energy levels sagged as I entered the tiny space. This was where it all began – the turning point in our relationship, when it went from one fraught with the usual frustrations and suspicions to something more sinister. The phone call that woke us up, the call for Martin to go back to London. The police were on to him even then. Our normality over.

I looked at the wood fire and saw there were still embers in the grille, no doubt from the night that we were there, the blanket left as I had folded it on that Saturday night. I reached out and touched the iron bed on which we had made love.

I knew that everything pointed to Martin having had something to do with Donna's disappearance, but I didn't want to believe it. The police didn't know Martin like I did. But still . . . It was hard not to think about Donna's beautiful face, hard not to think about what Jemma Banks had said. I knew that he'd hit her . . . Exhaustion crystallized into anger. My hands, still touching the mattress, clenched into a fist, grasping the folds of white. I thought of Martin and Donna and Pete Carroll, and cried out in frustration, dragging the fabric off the bed in one violent swipe, and then fell to the floor, sobs choking in my throat.

For a moment, I couldn't even hear myself breathe. It was as if the whole world had fallen still. I opened my eyes, seeing and hearing everything come back into focus, and there, on the floor, was a wink of gold I hadn't noticed before. It must have been dislodged from its hiding place when I had tugged at the sheet. I leant forward and picked it up. It was a necklace – a twist of metal on a delicate chain. I put it in the palm of my hand, examining it like a fossil hunter inspecting a stone.

It was intricate and expensive-looking. I turned it over with my fingertips and against the pink of my skin, I could see that the curve of thin gold was shaped into the letter D. I knew then that it was not the first time that I had seen this necklace. There had been another time. That day in court. The day when this necklace had been hanging around Donna Joy's slender neck.

# Chapter 44

He told me she'd never been here. He'd told me that himself. Martin Joy was a liar. I couldn't remember exactly what Donna's necklace was like from those few minutes I had spoken to her at the High Court, but I distinctly remembered the initial sitting at the base of her throat like a shell settled on the sand, and I knew it would be unlikely for her to have two such similar pieces of jewellery. They had to be the same.

And now Donna was missing, gone without a trace. There was no trail of breadcrumbs, nothing to help anyone find her – until now.

For her necklace to be here, in the oyster shed, meant that she must have come here sometime between the moment I saw her in court and the day she disappeared.

An image flashed into my mind in a shutter of light, Martin and Donna, naked on the day bed, hands grasping, fingers in mouths, hands in hair, frenzied, desperate as they approached climax, just as I had been. It would have been so easy for a delicate necklace to snap and slither off her sweat-soaked body and get lost in the folds of the bedclothes.

It was strange that I wanted it to be true, because I couldn't think about the alternative. A struggle, right here in the shed. Where we'd made love and slept.

I sat on the edge of the bed, holding my head in my hands as if I could keep it from splitting. I had been here before, of course, I recognized the darkness, the black thoughts creeping in from the corners – and I knew what came next. I could feel a blade slicing through my skin, see the beads of red rise to the surface, feel the release, like a pressure valve hissing, squealing, screaming to take back control.

I opened my eyes and tried to steady myself. I was desperate to give Martin a chance. Another one. I needed to know if he could lie to me again.

Was I so worthless, useless, unlovable that he could treat me like this.

*Although he treated Donna worse.*

I had to know. Pulling out my phone, I dialled his number. My heart was pounding as I listened to the ringtone, waiting for him to answer.

'Thank God you called. I've just spoken to Matthew Clarkson. He said you were interviewed by Inspector Doyle last night.'

'Did Donna ever come to Dorsea House?' I asked, willing my voice to stay calm.

'What's this about, Fran? Was everything OK at the police station?'

'Answer the question, Martin. Did Donna ever come to Dorsea?'

'No,' he said after a second. 'Never. Her sister doesn't live too far away, but she's never shown any interest in going. Not while it's still a wreck.'

I forced myself to think. I forced myself to be brave.

'So you're sure she's never come?'

'Why? Where are you? What's all this about?'

'I'm in Essex. I'm at Dorsea.'

'What the hell are you doing there?'

I could hear the worry in his voice. The wind was whipping around the shed so it was hard to hear, but the quaver of panic was unmistakable.

'Fran are you all right? Why the hell have you gone to Dorsea? Are the police still there?'

'No, it's empty. I came back to the oyster shed. I've found Donna's necklace.'

'Donna's necklace?'

'A golden D on a chain.'

'How do you know its Donna's?'

There was a longer pause now. I could see him frowning, thinking even though he was dozens of miles away.

'I saw her once. In court. The day we thought she'd missed the First Appointment hearing. She came late and I met her. Only briefly. She didn't know who I was. But I knew her. I remember her pink coat and a chain with a D on it – identical to the one I've just found in the oyster shed. Did you take her to Dorsea House, Martin?'

'Never. I swear to you. She never went. Fran, we need to talk about this. Come back to London and let's meet. Not at Alex and Sophie's. Somewhere private.'

'I don't want to see you, Martin.'

'Fran, please. Be sensible. Will you just come back? How did you get to Essex? I can send a car for you if it's too late to get the train.'

'Why is her necklace in the oyster shed?'

'I don't know. Perhaps someone put it there,' he said.

He paused.

'Fran, this is important. You need to bring me the necklace.'

'So you can get rid of it?'

'You have to believe me: Donna has never been to Dorsea

House. Yes, it might be her necklace, but I can't think of any reason why it would be there, unless someone put it there. Someone like Alex?'

I tried to catch up with his train of thought.

'Alex might have seen Donna wearing the necklace,' he said, with more panic. 'He might even have bought it for her. But if he had anything to do with her disappearance, if he wanted to frame me for it, because he wants my shares in the company, he could easily have bought another one and planted it in Dorsea. You have to believe me,' he said, now sounding distressed.

I didn't know what to believe. He was either a desperate man fearfully trying to prove his innocence or a slick and convincing liar. Was I being a fool?

'Please, don't go to the police, Fran?' his voice was soft and pleading.

'Give me one good reason why I shouldn't,' I replied.

'I don't have one.'

It felt like the first honest thing he had said to me in the entire conversation.

'I am being set up by Alex, Fran. I know it. He wants the company. All of it. If you only believe one thing I say, trust me on this. Help me prove I'm innocent.'

'I don't know, Martin. I don't know.'

I ended the call with a simple touch of a button. I put my phone back in my pocket and looked at the necklace, curled up in the palm of my other hand.

I took a moment to look at it and then struggling slightly with the clasp, I put it on and somehow I felt bolder as if it wasn't a necklace, but a shield.

I returned to the car and drove back into town. At this time, it would still be a ninety minute drive back to London and I needed some food and the bathroom before I even thought about it.

As I approached the café on the high street I noticed that it was shut. There were two pubs on either side of the road. One of them had been where I had stopped for a drink with Martin when we were waiting for the storm to pass, but I had no desire to go back in there. The other pub was more modern looking with a chalkboard sign on the pavement that said there was a restaurant and vacant rooms, both of which sounded appealing.

I pulled into the car park and went inside.

I hovered by the bar and looked around. There were a few couples eating and the steaming piles of sausages and mash that were being brought out of the kitchen looked and smelt good.

I picked up a menu from the bar.

'That's just for bar snacks,' said a girl pulling a pint she looked barely old enough to drink. 'If you want food, grab a table and we'll be with you in a minute.'

'How much are the rooms?'

'Seventy-five pounds a night.'

Another member of staff, a boy a little older than the barmaid, came up to her and made a quip. The girl laughed and flirted with him before handing him the pint.

'I'll take one,' I said, trying to catch her eye.

She wiped her hands on her jeans and looked ruffled.

'OK. I'll go and get you a key.'

'And could you send some food upstairs?'

My room was in the eaves and had painted black beams that I suspected were fake but designed to make the place look olde worlde. There was no minibar, but there was a small sugar bowl filled with Lotus biscuits next to the kettle.

I grabbed all three packets, sat cross-legged on the bed and ate the lot, not caring if it might spoil my appetite for the burger I had ordered from room service.

Laying back on the pillow, I stared up at the ceiling, at those fake black beams, stark lines against the white paintwork. For a moment I was back in Gil's office, letting the ribbons of light help me remember the night that Donna disappeared. No further memories had dislodged; I wasn't sure I wanted them to any more.

Had I really seen Martin leave the house, or had that memory been jumbled up with something else? I thought I had seen Martin and Donna; Martin in the street, Donna in her upstairs bedroom, but perhaps they had left together. Was it possible that Martin had somehow lured her out to Essex? I had no idea how he would have managed that after midnight, but I decided to let my mind run with the idea to see where it would take me.

*You're dealing with a charming, brilliant and manipulative man who will stop at nothing to keep his money.*

It was impossible to shake Jemma's words from my head. I felt a thickness in my throat as I wondered if she was right, and I had been so wrong to trust Martin Joy and let him into my life?

Of course there had been warning signs, glimpses of his dark corners, and I had ignored them, mistaking them for passion and intensity.

My mobile phone was still in my hand and I lifted it closer to my face, tapping the words *charming* and *manipulative* into a web search. Was it my lawyer's brain kicking in?

The entire first pages were stories about psychopaths and sociopaths and I remembered something Clare had joked about at the art gallery. How out of all careers, bankers and CEOs tend to demonstrate the highest psychopathic personality traits.

I was led to a feature about psychopaths in the workplace, another about sociopaths being great in bed.

Psychopathy, I discovered, was a psychological condition based on diagnostic evaluations. They appeared to be intelligent and sincere, powerful, charming and often manipulative to the extent that not even those closest to them ever suspected their true nature. Common traits included a tendency to display violent behaviour and difficulty in forming emotional attachments. They showed a readiness to take risks, displayed a lack of empathy and remorse, and low tolerance of others. A raft of psychologists had suggested that the recent financial crisis was a direct result of corporate psychopathy and the prevalence of psychopaths on Wall Street. Journalists, police officers and psychiatrists also had some of the highest proportions of psychopaths comparative to the population. So too did lawyers, a thought I didn't want to dwell on much more.

The more I read about the workplace psychopath the more I thought that Martin fitted the stereotype. Charming at work. Charming in life. Charming in love. I had been seduced from the very beginning. The smile that always held something back, a something that made me want to please him more. There were the grand gestures – the handbag after our first meeting, the casual 'I'll buy you a car' . . . I couldn't deny that I had been flattered and drawn in by that extravagance.

I felt sure that was what had happened to Donna too. So socially ambitious that she had seduced him, and overlooked all the faults in her marriage until a battering put her over the edge.

A knock on the door disturbed me from my thoughts. I went to answer it and took a room service tray from the barmaid I had met twenty minutes earlier. She peered over my shoulder, no doubt wondering what had brought me to Dorsea Island, all alone on a Monday night. It struck me that perhaps I was the subject of local gossip. Dorsea Island felt like the end of the earth, but its residents would be as plugged in to the news as someone in Canary Wharf. Martin Joy owned the biggest house on the island; that would have got him talked about even before the disappearance of his wife. The manager of the neighbouring pub had told the police that he had seen Martin with me, and I didn't doubt he'd told friends and neighbours the same story, embellished and dramatized every time.

I went to sit down at the small desk by the window, and put my food tray in front of me. I took the silver cloche off the plate to reveal a slightly soggy burger. Relish fell off a fold of lettuce on to the plate as I pressed my hand on the damp bun. It was too big to fit into my mouth, so I cut it with the steak knife that was glistening on the tray.

When my phone rang, I was tempted to leave it, but part of me hoped that it was Martin, calling back with an explanation about the necklace, calling back to explain everything away.

'It's Tom. I've been looking for you, where are you?'

Not who I was expecting, although I was still happy to hear from him.

'Have you read the *Post* online?'

It took me a minute to realize he was talking about the digital edition of Jenny's paper.

'No, why?' I said, not wanting to admit I had just been on the internet but had been researching sociopaths.

'The *Post* has run a story on you, Fran.'

'Oh God,' I whispered, feeling the panic rising inside.

'They're not quite accusing you of a relationship with Martin Joy, but it's running close.'

*Shit.*

'Have you spoken to Vivienne or Paul?' I asked him.

'I've only read it this minute. Looks like the story was posted a few minutes ago, so maybe you can speak to them about it before they have a chance to call you.'

If I had a paper bag I would have started breathing into it.

'Also . . .'

*Don't tell me,* I wanted to scream. I wasn't sure that I could handle anything else.

'Inspector Doyle wants to see you tomorrow.'

'What does he want?'

'I don't know exactly. But he mentioned that Pete Carroll contacted him again. Apparently, you threatened him at the flat this morning.'

'Threatened him? I might have sworn at him, but that was about it.'

'Fran, we need to report what he did to you last week. Officially. We can go down to the station tonight. There's a great team at Islington.'

'I can't,' I croaked.

'I've dealt with members of their Sapphire Unit before – they're incredibly supportive.'

'I meant I can't make it tonight.'

'Why not?'

'Because I'm in Essex.'

'What the hell are you doing there?'

'I went to Martin's house.'

'You're kidding me.'

'Don't worry. He's not here.'

'But you were supposed to stay local. Fran, you can't put a foot wrong right now—'

'What time should we meet tomorrow?' I replied.

'Fran, you've got to come back to London.'

'What time should I see you?'

He sighed with resignation.

'We're meeting him at eleven.'

'Then I'll see you at ten thirty,' I said, and rang off.

I bit into my burger but I wasn't hungry any more. I pushed the plate away and drew a knee up to my chest, perching my heel on the edge of the chair.

Tom was right. What was I doing here? Entire police forces hadn't been able to solve some of the most famous missing persons cases of our time so what hope did I have over Inspector Doyle and his team?

There was 10 per cent battery left on my phone but I had to check out the *Post* story.

## LAWYER GETS CLOSE TO MARTIN JOY
### Story by Jenny Morris

I knew what had happened immediately. Knew that I had been stitched up.

The news item was thin, to say the least. If Jenny was after her Watergate scandal, then this was hardly it.

Ms Day wouldn't comment on the exact nature of her relationship with the husband of missing beauty Donna Joy, but did admit 'it's complicated'.

As I continued reading, I was struck by the fact that I wasn't even disappointed by Jenny's betrayal. Deep down, I had expected it.

She'd known that getting exclusive access to Martin Joy was unlikely and she had just wanted to save her own skin. That's what it was about for everyone these days, wasn't it?

Scrambling up the ladder, striving, achieving, possessing, getting on, no matter what the cost.

I nibbled at a chip, wondering if I should put in a call to Vivienne. I owed her that much. On its own, having a relationship with a client was probably not enough to get me expelled from chambers, but when you put it alongside everything else – admitting to being at Donna's house that night, harassing Pete Carroll – I knew I was finished.

Unless Donna turned up. Or unless her body was found and the suspect was someone other than me or Martin.

I knew right then that I had two choices. I could either turn the necklace over to Inspector Doyle and rely on him to clear my name. Or I could believe Martin and try to prove the link between Alex Cole and Donna's disappearance.

Martin had pleaded with me to trust him. Was now the moment I took that chance?

I forced myself to think but it was hard, anxiety and fear clogging every cog and wheel in my brain.

My thoughts circled past Martin and Donna, and back to Tom.

Something my friend had said about a previous case, made my thoughts stop.

When Tom had defended Nathan Adams, he had argued that even though his client had a reputation as a thug, it didn't necessarily mean that he'd harmed his wife. But it remained a source of deep shame for Tom Briscoe that he had been successful in that line of defence and Suzie was subsequently murdered.

Tom's words resonated hard.

*'Suzie's lawyer was devastated. She told me, 'We'll just have to wait until next time.'*

I thought about the significance of what Suzie's lawyer had

said. Everyone had known that Nathan Adams was an abusive psychopath but Tom's brilliance in court and a lack of concrete evidence, had meant he had avoided conviction.

But Nathan Adams was now in jail, serving a life sentence for murder. The police and the CPS had eventually got him because Adams had been violent a *second* time.

I felt giddy with the beginnings of an idea and let it collect speed. I picked up the steak knife from my plate and wiped it with the napkin. Slowly, I changed my grip, so that I was not holding it like cutlery, but like a weapon.

And then, without thinking any more about the danger of the plan that my mind was suggesting, I put on my coat, put the knife in my coat pocket, picked up my phone and started walking back to Dorsea House.

# Chapter 45

I knew I had to make the call as soon as I left the pub otherwise I might never make it.

I hesitated as I scrolled through my contacts list and puffed out my cheeks.

He answered almost immediately.

'I wasn't sure you'd ever speak to me again,' he said in a voice that suggested he was surprised to hear from me. 'Where are you? It sounds as if you're in a wind tunnel.'

'I'm just walking,' I said, pressing the phone closer to my face so that he could hear me.

'I need to tell you something,' I said. 'I need to tell you everything.'

There was a long pause – a pause that gave me time to reconsider and back out of what I had decided to do.

'Go on,' said Alex Cole.

I wished I had a cigarette. I needed nicotine or alcohol and had neither to calm my nerves. Instead I put my index finger to my mouth and nibbled at my nail until I spoke again.

'I know we're all still hoping that Donna is safe and well somewhere. And I'll be honest, part of that is because I don't think that Martin had anything to do with her disappearance.'

'I think we all agree with you there,' said Alex in an encouraging tone.

'As you know, I had a private investigator look into Donna's affairs. That's how I found out about your relationship.'

'Jesus, Fran. How many times do I have to tell you? It wasn't a relationship—'

I cut in, not letting him finish.

'My researcher also told me that Donna and Martin were still having sex. I knew they were meeting the night of her disappearance, and I followed them. They went to Donna's house, but I saw Martin leave some time later.'

'Have you told the police this?' He sounded incredulous.

'Yes, but I'm not sure they believe me. In fact, I'm certain they don't. Yesterday, they almost arrested me.'

'Arrested you? Shit.'

'As you can imagine, it doesn't look good for me, being involved with Martin, sneaking around, following him and Donna. If you were the police, you'd think I was an obsessive mistress. Dangerous even.'

'Why are you telling me this?'

I swallowed hard. I had to do this.

'Because I've got evidence against Martin. And because I don't know what to do with it.'

'What evidence?'

I told him about the necklace and Martin's insistence that Donna had never been to Dorsea.

'If I wanted to get rid of someone, that's where I'd take them,' Alex muttered. 'My lonely old house by the sea.'

'The police have obviously searched the place, but they didn't find the necklace.'

'Or a body, presumably.'

'I doubt they found anything significant, otherwise the forensics team would still be there,' I replied.

I paused before I told him the rest of my plan. Although it was cold, I was lightly sweating. My palm was damp against the back of my phone, my breath was unsure and ragged in my chest.

'I'm staying at Dorsea House tonight. Tomorrow I'm going to take the necklace to Inspector Doyle.'

'Does Martin know all this?'

'No,' I said quickly. 'And don't tell him. I'm only telling you because you deserve to be prepared. If Martin's arrested, if he's charged this time, you'll probably need time to deal with the fall-out from the story.'

'Thank you. I appreciate everything you've done for us.'

My hands were shaking as the connection cut off. Now, I just had to wait.

I paced around for a few moments before I picked up the phone again.

'It's Fran.'

'Thank God,' said Martin, sounding relieved.

'When you cut me off earlier, I started to panic.'

I steadied myself. 'Can we meet tomorrow morning?'

'Of course,' said Martin, hopefully.

'I've got an appointment with Inspector Doyle at eleven. Perhaps we can meet at nine thirty in Pimlico. If I'm late, wait for me. I'm staying at Dorsea this evening and the rush-hour traffic back into London might be bad.'

'Can't you come home tonight? We could get a hotel like last time.'

'I'm here now. Besides, the weather's so bad, I think I should stay put. You don't mind if I stay at the house, do you? It might be too cold in the shed, but I noticed there were some beds on the first floor.'

'Have you still got the necklace?'

'I'm wearing it,' I said, touching my throat.

'Have you decided what you're going to do with it?'

'I don't know, Martin. We'll talk about it tomorrow.' Holding the necklace tightly it felt as though it could strangle me. 'We just need to find Donna, that's the only thing that can help us now.'

'Tom, it's me.'

'Tell me you're driving back to London.'

'Not tonight,' I said, not allowing myself to be swayed.

'I've just spoken to Doyle. He didn't want to give much away about tomorrow's meeting, but I think we have to prepare ourselves. They've found the mini-cab driver who brought you home. Apparently he picked you up on the King's Road at one thirty and drove you back to Islington. The staff at the Walton Arms have confirmed that everyone had left the pub by eleven twenty. Doyle's going to want to know what you were doing for two hours in Chelsea.'

'You know I don't have the answer to that, Tom.'

'I've also spoken to Matthew Clarkson.'

I could tell by the pause that I wasn't going to like what I would hear next.

'The blood found in Donna's bed. It wasn't menstrual.'

I tried not to picture it. Maroon clouds on white Frette like alkali on litmus paper.

'Forensics think that Donna bled in her room that night. They're working on blood-splatter analysis to theorize what might have happened.'

How did Martin smash his knuckles? How did I gash my leg? How did Donna bleed? Why did she bleed? So many questions were throbbing in my head, I thought they might burst out.

'Fran, please. Come back to London. If the police find out

you've flouted their orders, if they find out you're at Martin's house, there is every possibility that they'll arrest you.'

'I'm going to have to take my chances.'

'I think we need to start gathering a legal team.'

'We don't need that. Not yet. But I do need you to do something for me. I need you to come to me. It's a big ask, but it might be the one thing that will put an end to all this.'

# Chapter 46

My grandfather liked to take me fishing. After my parents got divorced, my mum liked to get me out of the house. There wasn't much to do around our town when you were fourteen. The bar staff at the pub were always asking for ID and we used to get busted by the local vicar whenever we took our cider and cigarettes to the park.

Fishing was never going to be the ideal sport for a teenage girl and I wasn't particularly patient, could never sit around for longer than an hour as I waited for something to bite. But I loved my grandfather's box of bait feathers, those tiny plumes of red, turquoise and green he would attach to his hook with his tough, nicotine-stained fingers. They were little bursts of colour in my otherwise drab world.

I hadn't thought about those afternoons by the river for a very long time, but suddenly they were all I could think of. Safe memories, ones I could trust . . .

I grabbed my coat, and closed the door of my room behind me. I took a tides timetable as I left the pub, throwing a pound coin into the honesty box as I went. Out on the high street, I zipped up my coat and let the salty, iodine smell of the sea lead me to the coastal path. There was a parade of fishermen's huts to my right, and a strip of shale beach peppered with moored boats to my left as I walked quickly away from the pub, letting the sounds of nature soothe me. The scraping of the sea against the pebbles and the wind through the coarse grass that lined the tarmac path. My eyes drifted out to sea and I watched the dots of light move slowly across the water; container ships taking their loads to Europe, Africa and beyond.

I stuffed my hands in my pockets and decided that I would look into taking a cruise when all this was over. I imagined myself dressing for dinner, and drinking Martinis in a walnut-panelled Art Deco-inspired bar. I'd talk to interesting retired couples, and play shuffleball on the deck like a heroine in an Agatha Christie novel.

I'd never been on a cruise before and suddenly I was desperate to do it, along with all the other things I had wanted to try but never got round to because work had got in the way. Cookery courses in Tuscany, horse-rides in the Andalusian mountains and long train journeys from St Petersburg to Siberia or a road trip from New York to LA. Pottery classes and playwriting courses, learning Italian and taking up the saxophone. All of them were on my wish-list, all of them I resolved to do if I could make it through the week.

Dorsea House loomed ahead, imprinted black against the navy-and-mauve-striped sky. The clouds holding the earlier rain had cleared and stars were beginning to twinkle, like sugar sprinkles on blue velvet, the full moon a dandelion clock suspended in the heavens.

I followed the string of lights along the coastal path all the way back to the house and went in through the unlocked door of the conservatory.

It was dark and silent inside, except for the soft coo of the pigeons I knew had made their nest somewhere in the rafters. I used the light of my phone to look for a light switch, even though I had no idea if power was still connected. When I located one by the door of the conservatory, I sighed with relief when an overhead bulb flickered on.

I moved from room to room, turning on lamps and light switches until the place felt more inviting. I pulled dust sheets off furniture, coughing as powdery grey clouds mushroomed off the fabric.

I felt possessed. The wheels were in motion now, and although I knew I could stop them by returning to London, I also realized that playing it safe would not help my position.

I'd made many poor decisions over the past couple of months. I might be arrested or expelled from chambers. I had no chance of making silk and had two men proclaiming to be in love with me. On the face of it, that was one bright spot, considering I had been single for so long, but when you considered that one was a potential murderer and the other a rapist, you could safely say that things could be better.

Not returning to London, telling Alex Cole and Martin Joy where I was – alone in an old house by the sea – also seemed one of my most stupid ideas. Being here alone made me vulnerable. Disposable. But that was precisely the point. On the edge, I was back in control and fighting back.

I reminded myself of a recent divorce case I'd handled, hoping it would help me rationalize what I was doing. The law had always been my comfort blanket, my safety net, and I needed it to help me now. My client had been a well-known footballer, and although I didn't know very much about soccer, I knew enough to know that he was considered one of our greatest-ever players – as it turned out, both on and off the pitch. His wife Candace had filed for divorce when the news of her husband's affair with his physiotherapist had made week-long headlines in the *Sun*. Things turned ugly, with accusations of infidelity flying from both sides and my client unwilling to let go of fifty per cent of his fortune to someone he now claimed was a gold-digger.

It was not my job to judge who deserved what. I was under instructions from my client to salvage as much of his fortune as I could, and so when our case came to court, I devoted ninety per cent of our energy to trying to prove that my client was a genius. That his talent was so unique, so special that it accounted for a special contribution to the marriage, so he deserved more of the marital assets than she did.

Even my client's solicitor didn't agree with my strategy; and as fees racked up, neither did the client. It was too high a risk, too few men had convinced a judge of their exceptional ability to overturn the usual ruling of an equitable financial split.

But the gamble paid off. As I explained to my jubilant client outside court, if you wanted the big win, you had to take the bigger risk.

Despite being inside, I shivered in the cold. Or maybe it was fear. If either Alex or Martin came to the house tonight, it would undoubtedly be with the purpose of silencing me. I had no idea how far they were prepared to go.

I sat in an armchair under the soft glow of a reading lamp and tried to decipher the tide tables. According to the chart, the high tide at 1.25 a.m. would bring waters of 4.94 metres. From what Martin had told me during our last visit, that was on the cusp of what was needed to flood the causeway. I reminded myself that it was only a prediction, and that it was entirely possible that no one would cross to Dorsea tonight. I was using myself as bait, but perhaps there were no fish in the river. Perhaps neither Alex nor Martin had anything to do with Donna's disappearance. Perhaps, perhaps . . .

Sitting alone in the dark, I found my thoughts drifting back to that night. What else had I seen? What had I been doing in those two hours between seeing Martin leave the house and getting in the taxi? I still didn't know.

I checked my phone. The battery level was down to 8 per cent. I dimmed the stark-blue brightness of my screen to save power, but before I put the phone back in my pocket, I texted Clare.

I'm sorry about yesterday. I miss you. I'm in Essex tonight but let's please speak tomorrow.

As I pressed send, somehow it felt like a goodbye.

I was getting sleepy. That would never do.

There was no coffee or even a kettle in the kitchen, so I had to make do with splashing cold water that glugged out of the tap on to my face.

There was a small library at the house that I guessed had been used as an activities room when the property had been a care home. Board games were still stacked up on the bookshelves: backgammon, draughts and Scrabble, the boxes bleached from age and the sun. There were piles of magazines too: *The Field*, *Boating* and *Country Life*, with cover dates that stretched back almost a decade.

I picked up a couple of issues and went upstairs. I chose a bedroom at the back of the house. It had a window seat and a huge bay window that overlooked the darkness of the sea.

It was also one of the few rooms that still contained a bed, which was made up with blankets and a pillow. I patted it down and brushed the dust off the bed-linen, then I hung my coat on a peg behind the door.

Ten o'clock. Ten thirty. Waiting, watching.

Phone battery 6 per cent.

I squeezed out some internet access. There was a fire station on the island and the police were based in Colchester, a few miles down the road. Even with an emergency call, the police might take fifteen minutes to get to Dorsea, but the fire services could be here within minutes.

'Come on, Tom, where are you?' I muttered out loud. I thought Tom might be the first to come. He was coming from North London, so by rights, he was the closest. But what was taking so long? It had been ninety minutes since I called him, surely he should be here soon.

The air smelt damp and musty. I opened a window to let in the breeze and I could hear the distant foghorn of one of the ships I had seen earlier disappearing into the darkness.

I sat on the bed and listened to the quiet, straining my ears for the thrum of a car engine growling up the drive.

I widened my eyes to stay alert. My plan depended on me staying awake. It could be disastrous if I fell asleep. I flicked through one magazine and then another, learning all about boxing the compass, and salmon fishing seasons. I tried to absorb every word of text, every picture, hoping it would distract me from the hammering of my heart.

When my phone rang, I scrambled to answer it.

I fumbled with the screen when it told me it was Tom. 'Fran, you have to leave the house.'

'Why?'

'I've got a bloody flat tyre.'

Ice-cold energy fired to my fingertips.

'I'm only in Chelmsford, so it shouldn't take too long to fix it and reach Dorsea, but I don't want to take any chances. Get out of the house. You shouldn't be there alone. Find somewhere to stay. There are two pubs on the island. Both of them have rooms. Just go there and I'll come and get you.'

'OK,' was all I managed to say back.

I hesitated as I took my coat off the hook. Stick or twist. Stay or leave.

It felt as if I had come too far to turn back now, but Tom was right, it would be safer at the pub.

I touched Donna's necklace around my neck, willing her to help me, woman to woman.

The weather was fierce outside now and I could hear the rush of water streaming down the broken gutters. But then I heard it, a noise through the rhythmic beats of the rain.

I went out on to the dark landing and could hear it more clearly out there. The low growl of a car engine, then pale pinpricks of light coming towards the house. I was glad the drive was long and the car was moving slowly in the weather.

There was no time to get out, but I knew I had to think quickly. It was impossible for Tom to have got here from Chelmsford so quickly, so it was someone else approaching the house.

The phone was shaking in my hand. I clicked on to contacts but I was trembling so much I could barely make the call.

I didn't have Inspector Doyle's direct number but I did have one for Sergeant Collins.

I connected to his number and waited for the ringing sound to kick in. But Sergeant Collins didn't pick up. Instead it went straight to voicemail.

I forced out my words. I hadn't anticipated feeling so helpless, so paralysed.

'Mr Collins. Sergeant. This is Francine Day. This is an urgent call in connection with the disappearance of Donna Joy. I am at Dorsea House on Dorsea Island in Essex. Repeat, Dorsea House on Dorsea Island. It belongs to my client, Martin Joy. I've told him I've got evidence against him and he's come to find me. Please call me back. I am frightened. I have reason to believe he might hurt me.'

I knew I sounded a nutter. I couldn't help thinking it as the words tumbled out of my mouth. The words of a paranoid woman. I had no idea if Sergeant Collins would believe me. Speaking to a messaging machine did not fill me with any confidence that anyone would be able to help me.

I tried Belgravia police station but another machine informed me that 24/7 front-desk counters were available at alternative locations.

My heart was hammering so hard I thought it would fall out of my chest on to the floor.

Who else – 999? Fire or police or ambulance?

I just wanted to see someone. Anyone. Whoever could get here the quickest.

I dialled emergency services and a calm voice asked me what service I required. I tried to picture Dorsea Island's high street and its pocket-sized fire station.

'Fire,' I replied, knowing it was my only chance.

'I'm at Dorsea House on Dorsea Island and there's smoke. I need someone to come as quickly as possible.'

The calm voice asked me to talk through what had happened.

'I'm upstairs in the bedroom. I can smell burning.'

'Can you see fire?'

'Yes,' I lied. 'I can see flames downstairs from my bedroom window. I am in a dangerous situation. Please come quickly.'

I peered out into the gloom and made out the shape of the sports car. A black Audi.

Sadness swamped me. Martin had come. I'd been so wrong, so wrong about everything.

I'd wanted to trust that he would never do anything to hurt me. That's what had really brought me to Dorsea Island. It was a test. A test to see whether he loved me, and he'd failed. I'd failed.

I found some strength from somewhere and texted Clare and Phil Robertson.

Martin Joy killed Donna Joy. I am at Dorsea House on Dorsea Island. I have evidence and he has come to find me.

I watched the dial spin round and round indicating that the texts had not yet sent. 'Come on,' I moaned in frustration.

I heard a car door slam. I ran back into the bedroom and shut the door, leaning against it as I tried to regulate my breath.

I knew I could hide or I could confront him and tell him that it was useless to try and silence me. I had told everybody about the necklace: Doyle, Collins, Tom Briscoe, Phil Robertson. Donna Joy had been here. I knew it and so did everyone else.

Or I could fight. The knife from the pub was still in my coat pocket. I fished it out and squeezed my fingers around the black wooden handle.

Climbing into bed, I pulled the blankets up to my chin, my fist still closed around the knife, ready to strike.

I heard the stairs creak and then footsteps pause outside the door.

The moon disappeared behind a cloud and the room became even darker, my eyes straining to see anything except a series of shadows.

The door opened with a groan. I expected him to at least call out my name, but instead there was a silence that felt as if the world had stopped turning.

I closed my eyes, pretending to be asleep. The knife was sweaty in my trembling palm. I didn't believe that he would hurt me. I couldn't believe it.

I could feel his presence in the room now. I opened my eyes and looked at the shape at the bottom of the bed.

'Martin, don't,' I said softly.

The figure came towards me. Through the darkness I noticed that he was wearing clothes as dark as the night sky and a black ski-mask that covered almost all his face.

'Martin, please,' I said, feeling a tear run down my cold cheek. 'I knew you would come. I've called the police. And the emergency services. Someone will be here any minute—'

His hand went over my face and I started to struggle. He was strong.

I gulped for air but the palm pressed over my nose and mouth meant I could take nothing in. Images flashed in front of my eyes. The hotel room. Martin kissing me, holding my wrists, pinning me down. The pub in Chelsea, the noise of the quiz upstairs, loud, loud like a football match. Everyone leaving, people laughing. Alone on the street. Watching, waiting. An unlocked gate to a basement flat. Black spikes. Cold step. Sitting down, waiting, watching.

The hand was pressing down. I still couldn't breathe and my whole body was screaming out for oxygen. An open door. Martin on the street. Donna at the window. Foggy, sleepy. Too much to drink. Head spinning. Donna on the street. A dark saloon car. A blonde cap of hair. Exhaust fumes. A taxi. Searing pain. Blood on my tights. It was all coming back to me in a torrent.

I willed myself to stay strong but I was fading fast. 'Francine.'

Someone shouted my name. The pressure eased from my face and body as I registered that the intruder was being hauled away from me. I scrambled to a sitting position, the knife ready in my fist, and I could see two people locked in combat, hands grappling and taking violent swings at each other.

It took a second for me to recognize Martin, a further moment for my brain to connect the dots, to realize that he was fighting the intruder, which meant the man in the ski-mask was someone else.

My heart pumped furiously as my sweaty palm gripped the knife.

'Alex, stop!' I screamed, my mind already piecing it together. I knew I had to help Martin but what would happen if the blade sliced through the wrong limb? My eyes glanced right to an old vase on the bedside table. I dropped the knife and slid off the bed, lifting the vase with uncertain hands. Everything seemed to blur. Noise, motion, shadow. Martin grabbed at his attacker's ski-mask, pulling it off as I prepared to swing. There was a shattering of glass, a cry and scream, and then I could see Martin framed at the broken window. He turned around and took me in his arms. I could smell sweat and fear but I stayed still there for a few moments, just grateful to be alive, before turning back to the window. And then I peered through the broken shards of glass down on to the patio below and I could see nothing but Sophie Cole's white face staring up at the sky.

The fire services came first and then the paramedics, who had to come from Colchester.

I could barely speak to any of them and let Martin take control, not even wanting to watch or listen. Instead I found a quiet corner of the house and hugged my knees close to my chest, the sound of the sirens and their blue lights melting away into the darkness, as Sophie was taken off to hospital and the fire team realized that they had nothing left to do.

A voice on the breeze reached me, yelling that the causeway was flooded and it would be another hour before traffic could get through, although Inspector Doyle from Belgravia police station had been notified and was already on his way.

'How are you doing, love?' A female police officer came into the room and put a blanket over my shoulders. 'Is there a kettle anywhere?'

'No. You won't find one here,' I said.

She looked at me, as if she was wondering what sort of life I lived here in Dorsea House. No doubt she imagined me as a mad Miss Havisham, and certainly I felt a mental fragility in common with one of Dickens's most famous characters.

'By the way, I think a friend of yours is here to see you.' When I looked up, Tom was hovering in the doorframe.

I struggled to my feet and let him wrap his arms around me.

'You made it,' I said into his shoulder.

'Just made it over the causeway. Better late than never.'

'Well, you missed all the action.'

He didn't find it funny.

'I'm so sorry, Fran.'

'I didn't need you,' I replied.

'No, you never did.'

He meant it as a compliment, and I allowed myself to smile back gratefully.

'I heard people talking,' he said. 'Apparently Sophie Cole is alive. They're amazed she survived the fall.'

I nodded, not sure I would ever be able to forget the sight of her lying on the concrete, like a puppet with its strings cut.

'Sophie is one of life's survivors. She's fit, strong. I'm sure she'll live.'

'I should go. I think Martin wants to talk to you.'

'Just stay for a bit longer,' I said, not sure how I felt about being alone with Martin.

'I was wrong about him,' said Tom after a second. 'I was sure he was the one who killed Donna. I apologize. I should have trusted your judgement.'

'No, I was wrong about him too,' I said, more to myself than to my friend.

'Tell him I'll meet him outside,' I said after a moment.

I was ignored by everyone as I shuffled on to the drive, the blanket around my shoulders trailing along the gravel. I knew that someone would want to interview me eventually, but I was a bit-part player now. There was a bench on the front lawn under a beech tree and I perched on its edge as I watched Martin follow me outside.

'Thank you,' I said as he sat down beside me. 'Thank you for being there.'

He didn't reply, just reached out a hand and squeezed my shoulder.

'How did you know to follow Sophie?' I asked. I was trying to piece it together, but my head felt too foggy.

'Because I know how smart you are. When you called me and told me that you were at Dorsea and you had the necklace, I knew that you were testing me, goading me to come to the house. But I thought, I hoped, you'd have done it to Alex too. And I was right. My only surprise was that it was Sophie who left the house to come and find you, not Alex.'

'So they were in this together?' I said slowly.

Martin put his cold hand over mine. 'I don't know. I'm sure we'll find out soon enough.'

He paused before he spoke again.

'I can't believe Sophie would do this. You think you know people . . .' he said quietly.

I looked up and saw that he was crying.

'Don't, it's over,' I said softly.

'I just wonder what they did with her. What they did to Donna,' he said, blinking away his tears.

I slipped my arm through his awkwardly.

I felt as if I was sitting next to a stranger, but I didn't want to see him like this.

'We need to find her body,' said Martin, composing himself.

'She'd like a big funeral. Donna loved people. We'll get everybody there. She'd like that.'

I felt tears well in my own eyes. So much so that it was difficult to focus on what was in front of me. I wiped my face with the back of my hand as I heard the sound of feet crunching across the pea-shingle. I looked up and saw a uniformed policeman, one with an air of command about him.

'Mr Joy?' he said, looking unsure.

Martin nodded.

'Inspector Bannister, Colchester force. Inspector Doyle from the Met is on the way, but I thought you should know this before he comes . . . One of my colleagues is with Sophie Cole at the hospital. They've managed to have a short conversation with her . . . Obviously, we've not been able to confirm this yet, but she's telling us that your wife, Donna Joy, is still alive.'

# Chapter 47

I woke up alone in the oyster shed to the sound of a gull cawing and wheeling overhead. The stars had dissolved and the night sky had paled. The sun was beginning to rise across the estuary, its pinkish rays making long metallic ribbons across the water, the bleak beauty of the landscape replaced by something almost pretty.

It was a moment before I realized that it had been the sound of knocking that had actually woken me up.

Inspector Doyle stood at the door of the shed. 'Someone said you'd come out here to get some sleep.'

'I was almost delirious. I just needed a rest.'

'How are you feeling?' he asked, coming inside and sitting on a rickety chair.

'Felt better,' I replied, noticing my dry throat.

'Where's Martin?'

'Still at the house.'

I looked at him expectantly. 'Have you spoken to Sophie Cole yet?'

'My colleagues have. From what I can gather, she's got a broken back, legs, ribs. We're waiting on a full evaluation but she'll probably have to stay in hospital for a few days before being transferred somewhere else.'

'Has she been charged?'

He nodded. 'Intent to commit grievous bodily harm. And for perversion of the course of justice.'

I was disappointed. I knew that Sophie had wanted to kill me. The charge didn't seem to fit the crime.

'What about Donna?' I said, sitting up. 'Have you found her yet?'

Doyle paused before he spoke.

'Apparently she's in France. Sophie Cole has given us an address. A couple of my officers are on their way to check it out.'

'*France?* What's she doing there?'

Fragments of memory came back to me. Phil watching Donna go through international departures at the Eurostar terminal, Martin buying his grandparents a farmhouse in the Loire.

'Hiding out,' said Doyle simply.

I shook my head to indicate that Doyle was going to have to explain further.

'Donna Joy staged her own disappearance. Donna and Sophie. They were in it together.'

I paused to take it in. Imagined what was going on behind the scenes. Was Sophie Cole already trying to plea bargain, pushing blame onto her missing friend?

'She wasn't abducted?'

Doyle shook his head.

'We're not sure why they did it, yet. Hazarding a guess, I'd say they wanted to frame Martin to make some fraudulent claim on the business.'

I nodded. 'That was what Martin thought. There's a clause in his partnership agreement that if Martin brings the business into disrepute, Alex Cole can acquire his shareholding.'

I sat up higher against the day-bed but immediately felt dizzy and brought a palm to my forehead.

'Are you all right?' said Doyle with a look of concern.

'I think so.'

'You should go and get yourself checked out at the hospital. I obviously need to take a statement from you, but that shouldn't take long. Then I can give you a lift into Colchester. I have to go back to the hospital too.'

He hesitated.

'I'm sorry you had to go through this, Fran. You should have left it to us. What you did was bloody dangerous.'

'I know,' I said, still feeling shaken. 'But when you're desperate, you'll do anything to try and put things right.'

'I assume that's why you lied to us.'

I tried to read his tone but couldn't tell if his remark was support or criticism.

'I knew how bad it looked, following Martin and Donna that night. That's why I told Sergeant Collins that I went straight home after I went to Donna's studio. I was wrong, but I was scared.'

My heart was beating fast. I knew where all this could end; being charged with an attempt to pervert the course of justice, disbarment from my profession.

'Just don't get into any more trouble,' he said with the comforting ghost of a smile, and I felt my whole body relax.

# Chapter 48

Martin came with me to the hospital but I didn't want him to be there. Donna was alive but my relationship with her husband felt dead.

He waited with me in A&E. I was a priority case, apparently, speeded through on a nod from the police, but still it took two hours to be seen and treated. I was given a chest X-ray and some paracetamol for my headache.

'Let's get back to London,' said Martin, settling an arm across my shoulder. 'Finally we can go back to the loft.'

'I think I should go home,' I said carefully.

'We've had some resolution tonight, Fran. But it doesn't change the fact that Pete Carroll is dangerous. For a minute I thought he might have had something to do with Donna's disappearance. I thought he might be so in love with you, he was willing to kill Donna and frame me to get me out of the picture.'

'If you ever get bored of finance, you should consider a career in writing fiction,' I smiled, wanting to shake him off.

He looked at me and put both hands on my shoulders. 'Move into the loft. Maybe not now, this week, this month. Perhaps we should wait until all this is over and we can get on with our lives and start afresh. But I can't wait to live with you.'

I couldn't deny that he was beautiful. That his green eyes were the most extraordinary colour, that he had the most muscular and tanned forearms that were the very definition of manliness. Living in a multimillion-pound warehouse conversion with Martin Joy, having incredible sex on tap, and a lifestyle that was straight out of a movie would be a dream for thousands of women. But not me, not any more.

His eyes narrowed, as if he'd felt my rejection.

'You don't believe any of those rumours, do you? That I hit Donna.'

I didn't say anything.

'Fran, it's bullshit. Donna set me up. The whole thing was lies.'

'I believe that,' I said quietly, although I still couldn't shake the thought of his bullying in the workplace. He had never denied that.

I pulled away and put my hand on his shirt.

'I need the bathroom. Then I want to find a coffee. Do you want one?'

'Sure,' he said distractedly. 'I'll wait here.'

I walked down the corridor until I came to the coloured, annotated map on one of the walls, directing people towards cardiology, outpatients and the eye clinic; every department, every ward was listed as I looked to see where I was going.

I'd heard Inspector Doyle on the phone, heard where he had to go to see Sophie Cole, and I followed the map to get there.

At some point, I affected a limp – I always said I had potential as an undercover spy – and no one stopped me as I made my way towards the private room where Sophie was recovering.

I didn't need to see two plain-clothes policemen talking at the door to know which room Sophie Cole was in. I hung back and watched as one cop glanced at his watch and disappeared down the corridor to speak to a nurse. When the second cop took a call, walking towards the window to get a better signal, I knew it was my chance.

She looked like a ghost lying on the thin bed.

Her back and both legs had been broken. She was attached to a drip. One arm was in a cast, both legs were cased in pins and rods, but Martin had already told me that the doctors were not sure if she would ever walk again.

Her bed was slightly raised so that she could look around the room. She moved her neck slowly. I wondered if it hurt her.

'What are you doing here?' she asked in a small voice.

'I wanted to see you.'

She looked as if she was about to point out that I shouldn't be here, but as if it was too exhausting to bring it up, she looked away.

'Why did you do it, Sophie?'

I waited for a reply but she remained silent.

'You have to tell me. You owe me that. You and Alex have everything. Was it not enough?'

'Alex had nothing to do with this.' It was said with an almost undetectable note of regret.

'Then why?' I whispered, taking a step closer to the bed.

The silence almost swallowed the room.

'The value of the Gassler Partnership is its algorithmic model,' she said finally, a dribble of saliva sliding down her chin. 'All their technology was built around a system I created. It was my idea.'

'You weren't a computer scientist.'

'No. But I pulled all the strings. I found them the best

quants, the best computer and data scientists, I set it up. But my name wasn't above the door or on the letterhead. There were no shares in my name, no credit from the industry. No credit from Martin or Alex. They'd pushed me out.'

I watched her eyes trail out of the smoked-glass window as if she were collecting her thoughts, no doubt wondering how she would do things differently if she had her time all over again.

'Have you any idea what it's like being married to men like Martin and Alex?' she said, looking me in the eye now. 'Men obsessed with money and status, men consumed with ego and their own sense of self-importance. Right now, you're only seeing the good stuff,' she said, trying to smile like a benevolent old sage. Instead her expression looked pained and cracked.

'You're impressed with their confidence, their easy charm, the baubles they bring you, the clothes and the handbags. They use those things to reel you in. Then they trap you and control you.'

I knew she was struggling to breathe but I was desperate to hear it all.

'You make excuses for them for a long time, and then you can't stand it any more, but they bring in the clever lawyers – people like yourself – to screw you.'

'So this was about money,' I said slowly. 'Donna would have got an eight-figure settlement. Was it not enough? It would have been more money than she could have spent in a lifetime.'

'It was easy to persuade Donna it wasn't enough,' she said, with a whisper of triumph.

Her voice was getting weaker. I moved as close to the bed as I could. Close enough to see her bloodshot eyes and hear her shallow breaths.

'Alex was having an affair. Not with Donna. With some bimbo at work. He's so stupid, he had no idea that I knew,' she said, not looking me in the eye.

'I could see how it was all going to pan out,' she continued. 'The algorithm was being constantly upgraded by the team I had put in place. It was getting better all the time. But I knew that the more profitable and valuable the business became, the more I would get slowly squeezed out of my marriage, replaced by some tart who contributed nothing but flattery and sex. So I decided to do something about it.'

She gazed out of the window as if she were remembering how it all happened.

'Donna had wanted to leave Martin for years. She never really loved him but she loved the lifestyle, which was why she stayed with him for so long. I never thought Martin would have the balls to file for divorce but when he said their marriage was over after Donna's New York trip, I knew it was time to put the wheels in motion. I told Donna to file for divorce first. Found her a great divorce lawyer. 'The Piranha'. But I knew Martin would find a great lawyer too. I knew he wouldn't give up half of everything he'd worked for without a fight. And when it started to look like Donna might not get 50 per cent, I reminded her how unjust that was. I told her there was another way.'

She was fading fast, too weak to talk. I helped her fill in the gaps, speaking out loud as I tried to work out her plan.

'So you staged her disappearance. You knew that Martin would be the only suspect, you knew how to take advantage of the morality clause in the partnership agreement.'

'Donna did her bit, composed some diary entries about Martin's nasty temper and started buttering her sister up. Told her a few stories about domestic violence – that wasn't difficult to believe. She went to her sister's house – took her passport. Poor cow never went anywhere, obviously never noticed it had gone.'

Sophie paused to catch another breath. 'The week of the FDR she invited Martin to her house. He still couldn't resist her. They had sex. She asked him to leave.'

'And you picked her up.'

'I'd arranged to go out with Alex that night. I had to sort *his* alibi out, just in case. We got home. I put a Zopiclone in his drink, and picked a fight with the intention of sleeping in the guest room. When Alex was out cold, I collected Donna and drove out of London. I'd arranged for someone to get her on a ferry to France, under the radar. Jemma's passport was too risky to use at this point. By the next morning she was in France. She was to stay just outside Paris until I could get her somewhere further out. She wanted to go to Bali. She liked it there. It wasn't hard to sell her the idea of a couple of years in the sun.'

'And then what?' I said, not believing the audaciousness of the two women.

'Once Alex got full control of the company, the plan was to help him build it. Gassler delivers such a great return, people would soon forget about Martin Joy and his involvement in the company. And I've got investors lining up. Befriending rich wives is a powerful strategy,' she said.

'Then I was going to divorce him. Unlike Donna, my claim to a 50 per cent split was much stronger.'

'What was in this for Donna?'

'Do the maths. Thirty per cent of Martin's assets or split a much bigger pie with me. Donna was greedy. She was easy to persuade.'

'Was it all worth it?' I said, so quietly I wasn't sure that she heard me.

'It wasn't about the money. It was about the principle,' she hissed as if she had found energy from some deep well of fury.

'You cared so much about that principle, you were prepared to kill me?'

'It wasn't supposed to pan out like that.'

She met my gaze and at that moment, I believed her.

'I just wanted Martin out of the company,' she said slowly, deliberately. 'I wanted him disgraced, and gone. We just needed enough suspicion to force him out. That's all. That's why Donna left the house as she did. She didn't ransack it, or broadcast *violent struggle*. We were subtle, suggestive.'

'What about the blood in the bed?'

'Simple. A finger-prick blood test. Surprising what you can get from fleshy fingertips. As I said, we didn't want *The Texas Chainsaw Massacre*. Just a hint of trouble.'

Sophie gave a weak sniff of irritation.

'But then Alex told me you'd followed Martin that night. Followed him back to Donna's like some lovesick puppy. You were Martin's alibi and so you spoiled everything, by being as pathetic as the other women who hanker after men like Martin Joy.'

All I could do was shake my head. She was pale, broken in her bed. It took a few seconds before she continued her story.

'But I'd started something, Francine. So I had to finish it. I suggested that Martin come and stay with us after his arrest. I wanted to keep an eye on him. I had a heart-to-heart with him one evening and asked about his relationship with you. He told me he loved you but was worried you were mentally fragile. He didn't need to tell me that, though. I'd already seen the razor scars.'

'You thought I'd be easy to get rid of. The unstable lover who'd already tried to kill herself.'

'Alex said you rang him last night. Said you were paranoid. Delusional. But he also said you'd found Donna's necklace that I'd planted at Dorsea. That was meant for the police. I couldn't believe they didn't find it. Sloppy.'

'So I was too troublesome to have around.'

'Donna was the same,' she muttered.

I noticed that she'd said it again. Donna *was*.

'Why do you keep referring to Donna in the past tense, Sophie?'

'Past tense?'

'I noticed it when we met at the Gassler office.'

'Does it matter?'

I felt the cold prickle of goosepimples as I began to understand.

'She's dead, isn't she? You've told the police that she's in France. But she's not, is she?'

Sophie didn't reply.

'Donna is dead, isn't she, Sophie?' I said, taking another step towards the bed. 'She could have just come home at any time when you were worried that Martin had an alibi. But she didn't. Because she couldn't.'

'She was as stupid as you are,' Sophie whispered. 'A reckless coward. I didn't trust her to stick to the plan. I knew she would have slipped up, bought a phone, left footprints on social media. Or had a wobble and decided she just couldn't go through with it.'

'You didn't want to split the money with her, did you?'

I heard the door open behind me. I turned and saw Doyle holding a coffee cup, looking at me with disappointment but not complete surprise.

'You should leave,' he said firmly. I knew better than to argue.

'I didn't want to hurt you, but you got in the way,' said Sophie and I walked out of the room and didn't look back.

# Chapter 49

*Two months later*

The Summerhouse restaurant in Little Venice seemed the perfect place to meet Clare for lunch. It was near the counselling centre and its location, right next to the canal, was perfect for early summer afternoons.

'I can't believe it's gone for fifty grand over the asking price,' said Clare, spearing an olive as I told her about the sealed-bids frenzy on my flat.

'For a minute I was tempted to keep hold of it,' I confided, sipping my apple juice. 'I thought the heat had gone out of the London property market, but clearly not.'

'No, you did the right thing,' said Clare sagely, resting a hand on her belly.

I nodded, knowing that she was right. Pete Carroll moved out within a week of everything that happened at Dorsea. Whether he was ashamed, or afraid that I would report him to the police, I would never find out. I didn't know where he'd gone. Even his post petered out quickly. I sometimes wondered if he'd ever even existed.

Even now, I wondered if I had made the right decision not

to press charges against Pete in those days after Sophie's arrest. He had taken advantage of my vulnerability. He had abused me and deserved to be convicted and punished. But after everything that had happened, I simply didn't need the additional stress of formally reporting what he had done, despite Michael Doyle and Tom Briscoe's encouragement. My sanity was the most important thing to me, not revenge or even justice. Was that right? Was it selfish? I don't know what other people would have done under the same circumstances, but for me it was the right choice, at least at that moment in time. I needed to regroup and get stronger. Getting rid of the flat was part of the process of moving on from everything that had happened. But at some point, I liked to think I would find Pete Carroll, and report him, because I wasn't sure if I would ever properly heal if I didn't. I owed it to myself and I owed it to others who have been in my position.

'How did your meeting go with Dave Gilbert?' I asked as the waitress brought over a salad, bursting with heritage tomatoes the colour of newly minted pennies.

'I liked him.'

'Best divorce solicitor I know. And how's Dom behaving?'

'Moved the waitress into the upstairs flat with him. I'm sure she imagined it would be quite glamorous, hooking up with the boss. Just wait until she finds out how cramped it is with all his man-crap.'

My friend gave a rueful smile. She was putting on a brave face, but I knew that she wasn't finding the separation easy. As it turned out, everyone who worked at Dom's had known he was having an affair with his Polish waitress. It had been going on from the moment he had recruited her, and they'd been slipping away for a quickie, either upstairs or back to her house, even before the restaurant had opened.

At least Clare and I had our cruise to look forward to.

We were going to sail around the Adriatic and Aegean seas the following month and I couldn't wait to walk around the fruit markets of Venice, the whitewashed back-streets of Mykonos, and see the terracotta rooftops of Dubrovnik. I had bought a dozen sundresses for our trip, quite unlike anything else in my wardrobe, strappy, flirty things in a kaleidoscope of colours and patterns. Clare, meanwhile, was calling it her baby-moon and had already invited me to be her birth-partner.

'So come on. How was your date with Gil last night?' I asked, when we had finished our food.

'It wasn't a date,' she said indignantly.

'I thought you went for a meal,' I chided.

'We went for a burger in a pub where a Smiths tribute band were playing. It was all about the music.'

'Right,' I smiled.

'So what time are you seeing him?'

'Two-thirty,' I said, glancing at my watch. 'It's only a ten-minute walk from here, isn't it?'

Clare nodded. 'I'll come back with you.'

She looked at me more intently. 'Are you ready for this?'

I nodded. It had taken me a while to come round to the idea of counselling to process everything that had happened. I'd had enough therapy and medication in my life for my bipolar, but the flashbacks and nightmares wouldn't go away. I still found it difficult to go to isolated places, even the changing rooms at the gym sometimes unnerved me when no one else was around.

But I trusted Gil Moore, and agreed that I needed to work through the various issues that I had probably always had, but which had been inflamed by everything that had happened with Martin and Donna Joy and Sophie Cole.

It had taken several weeks before I'd been willing to talk

about it with anyone, even though I had read every column-inch of news, every feature that had been penned on the case that seemed to have picked up the nickname, 'the First Wives' Revenge'. Sophie had become notorious, but she had also managed to collect some heat as an ultra-feminist icon, a symbol of empowerment for waging war on controlling capitalist husbands. I wondered if the people who lauded her knew how terrifying it had been for me on Dorsea Island. Or that she'd killed Donna Joy in the pursuit of her plan.

The police never did find Donna in France, or anywhere else for that matter. She is still missing – Chelsea's very own Lord Lucan, although there have been 'sightings' in such far-flung locations as Paraguay and Papua New Guinea.

Sophie Cole denies having had any conversation with me about having harmed Donna. It's true – she didn't admit it to me outright, but I saw the look in her eye and I *knew*. I knew what she had done to her. How that will stand up in court, I don't know. That day will come. Inspector Doyle is building his case against Sophie, trying to pin her down for something more than breaking into Dorsea House and attacking me, scouring CCTV footage to see her leaving London with Donna, to find out where they went. I will help in whatever way I can, although deep down, I know that if interest in the case wanes, if Donna's body is never recovered, if there is no evidence to suggest that Donna has done anything other than abscond, then Sophie will get away with murder.

Better than anyone, I know that there is no room for speculation and conjecture in the witness box, but whenever I am still and alone, I think about what might have happened to Donna Joy in those hours after her disappearance.

I think about what I would say, what I would hypothesize,

what story I would weave as the prosecuting barrister, not as a civilian giving evidence.

I think about Donna Joy getting into Sophie's car that night, after she had asked Martin to leave her bed, and Sophie, anxious but prepared at the wheel of a car she had bought for cash, waiting for her. I think about them driving out of London, a gleeful Thelma and Louise, high on friendship, freedom and adrenalin, and their arrival at an out-of-season rental or an off-the-radar outbuilding, somewhere remote and undetected.

I think that Donna didn't leave for France immediately. In fact, I think she didn't go to France at all, even though she had taken her sister's passport and done a dummy run on the Eurostar – that mysterious mini-break that Phil Robertson had witnessed all those weeks before. I believe that Donna Joy stayed in her lonely hideaway, waiting impatiently for Sophie's next command. But I believe that she had got cold feet about the entire plan, and wanted to back out before she had even been reported missing. And when Sophie came to see Donna, to persuade her to remain committed to their idea, that was when she killed her, when she hid her body in a shallow grave or a sceptic tank. Or maybe Donna met some other desolate ending that she'd never imagined for herself.

I know how easily Sophie Cole's defence barrister could destroy my story. I have a notebook at home, hidden away in my gym-clothes drawer, with the lines of arguments I would use in court, if I was representing Sophie.

I know how I would fight to make any grainy CCTV footage and recognition evidence of Sophie and Donna inadmissible. How I would hunt down answers about Martin's obsessive girlfriend. The woman who watched Donna's house the night she disappeared. The unreliable mistress who had reason to want Donna dead.

But those thoughts stay in my notebook, because I don't want to think about them any more than I have to.

We walked to the West London Counselling Centre in near silence. I liked watching the sunlight glint off the canal and the swans glide across the water. Clare had recommended that I start looking for the good in everything, reminding me that simple pleasures were all around us. And she was right, there were plenty of things to smile about in my life. My flat had sold quickly and for a healthy profit. I remained with Burgess Court chambers – our merger with Sussex Court would happen any day now – and Tom Briscoe had become a close friend. He'd tried to persuade me not to withdraw my Queen's Counsel application, but as I'd told him half a dozen times, I wasn't sure I could handle the rejection this time round. Besides, there would be other opportunities to apply.

Daniyal Khan came back to the UK after a two-week holiday in Pakistan, just as his father had promised. Perhaps Yusef Khan's relationship with his new girlfriend in Bedford was more serious than we'd imagined. Perhaps Yusef wasn't quite the villain we'd thought, certainly not where his son was concerned. Love conquers all.

As for my own love life, I had decided that I was better off alone. At least for now. Martin Joy still rings me sporadically. We are still linked by Donna Joy – now as witnesses for the prosecution against Sophie Cole. At some point we will no doubt see each other in court.

But my feelings for him dissolved as quickly as they had ignited.

I just wanted to forget that entire period of my life and it was as if my emotions understood that too.

I said goodbye to Clare as she collected her messages from

reception. I was instructed to go to the first floor, which was a departure from my earlier visit.

'Nice room,' I said to Gil, looking around the bright space of his new office.

'Someone left. I was prepared to pay more, but I like to tell myself it's a promotion,' he smiled.

'So no blue lights today.'

I wasn't sure they'd be helpful. Whenever I closed my eyes at night, I could still see the flashing sirens closing in on Dorsea House. I knew Gil wanted to get me to talk about that night, but I wanted it to be as stress-free as possible.

'No lights. Just conversation,' he said.

I sat in an old club chair and rubbed my palms nervously on my lap.

Gil came and sat down opposite me. I wondered if there had been any spark between him and Clare at the pub in Putney. Whether it was just two friends on a night out, just as Tom Briscoe had invited me to a comedy club the following Friday. Or whether there was more to it? As they were co-workers, I wondered whether it was sensible for Clare and Gil to get involved. But then, how else were people supposed to meet a partner? I had tried to remind myself of that on the many times I had cursed myself for getting involved with my client. It wasn't wrong. It was normal. No one is perfect. We follow our leads and cues, taking opportunities where they present themselves, mixing with people with whom we have things in common. Perhaps that was why I had bought a new dress for my night out with Tom. Perhaps why I had started to feel butterflies when we made mugs of tea together in the tiny kitchen at chambers.

Gil and I made small talk. He asked me a few questions, writing my responses down in his notebook.

'So today we're going to talk about that night at Dorsea Island. Are you ready for that?'

'Be gentle,' I said with a soft, nervous snort.

Gil crossed his legs and put his hand on his lap.

'I know it's difficult to remember that night, Fran, but without it, Sophie Cole might never have been caught. If you think about the positive things that came out of that evening, it will help to heal the negative emotions you associate with it.'

'Where do you want me to start?' I asked haltingly.

'Why don't you tell it to me like a story. I find that helps. Creates an initial distance before we work through your feelings in more depth.'

I nodded at his suggestion. I was the little girl who loved books. The teenager who wanted to write a novel. As an adult, stories sounded like a good way of working through everything that happened.

I took a deep breath and steadied myself. I was strong and ready to move forward. I closed my eyes and allowed the silence to transport me back to Dorsea Island as I began to speak.

'It's funny how the mind can block out the memories it no longer wants to store, you must know that. But if I close my eyes, I can still hear the sounds of that night in May. The howl of an unseasonably cold wind, the rattle of the bedroom window, the rasp of the sea against shingle in the distance . . .'

# Acknowledgements

Thank you to my agent Eugenie Furniss, Liane-Louise Smith, Rachel Mills and Lucy Steeds at Furniss Lawton. Also to Drew Reed, Marcy Drogin and Toby Jaffe at Original Films.

Kimberley Young, Eloisa Clegg, Felicity Denham, Claire Ward and all the team at HarperCollins haven't just helped bring the book to life but have made the publishing process such fun that I've been known to pop in for a marketing meeting and still be found lurking in the offices three hours later. Thanks also to Katherine Nintzel and the fantastic team at William Morrow.

Lots of people generously gave me their time and expertise to help out with the plot. Brilliant family lawyers Michael B and Fiona S walked me through up-to-date developments in family law, divorce proceedings and financial remedy. Any mistakes are mine. Suzanne P was my early reader, sounding board and eagle eyes. We started our legal career together and are still great friends, even though I left working in law a long time ago. We can talk books and law over rhubarb cocktails any time. Dr Jim gave terrific insight into the fascinating and complicated subject of blackouts and memory

*J.L. Butler*

retrieval. Thanks also to Goat, Scarlett Taor and Benny Harvey.

*Mine* was just a word document called 'Thriller' sitting on my desktop for a very long time. Thanks to all my family for their support, especially my son Fin, who cheerfully wandered the streets of Chelsea with me, plotting Francine's moves, and my husband, John, who championed it from the start and never seemed to mind when I wanted to talk about plot points when he wanted to watch *Game of Thrones*. This one's for you.